D1270078

# THE MODERN LIBRARY
### of the World's Best Books

# LEO TOLSTOY

### Short Stories

*The publisher will be pleased to send, upon request,*
*an illustrated folder listing each volume*

## THE MODERN LIBRARY

# LEO
# TOLSTOY
## *Short Stories*

❦❦❦❦

SELECTED *and* INTRODUCED *by*

# ERNEST J. SIMMONS

*The Modern Library*
*New York*

ACKNOWLEDGMENTS  For permission to reprint the following stories, the editor wishes to thank:

The World's Classics for "The Raid," "The Wood-Felling," "Sevastopol in December 1854," "Sevastopol in May 1855," "Sevastopol in August 1855," and "Meeting a Moscow Acquaintance in the Detachment" from *Tales of Army Life*; for "A Billiard-Marker's Notes," "The Snow Storm," "Lucerne," "Albert," "Three Deaths," and "Strider" from *Nine Stories,* translated by Louise and Aylmer Maude; and for "The Porcelain Doll," translated by Aylmer Maude, from *The Kreutzer Sonata and Other Tales.* Published by Oxford University Press.

*The Russian Review* for "A History of Yesterday," translated by George L. Kline.

*Library of Congress Catalog Card Number: 64-11997*

THE MODERN LIBRARY

is published by

RANDOM HOUSE, INC.

BENNETT CERF  •  DONALD S. KLOPFER

Manufactured in the United States of America

# CONTENTS

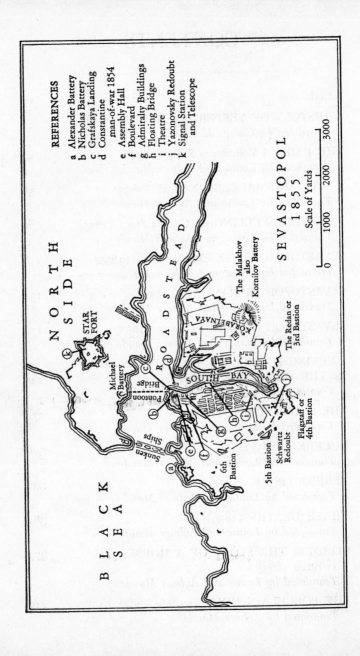

REFERENCES

a Alexander Battery
b Nicholas Battery
c Grafskaya Landing
d Constantine
  man-of-war 1854
e Assembly Hall
f Boulevard
g Admiralty Buildings
h Floating Bridge
i Theatre
j Yazonovsky Redoubt
k Signal Station
  and Telescope

SEVASTOPOL
1855

Scale of Yards

0    1000    2000    3000

NORTH SIDE

STAR FORT

BLACK SEA

Michael Battery

ROADSTEAD

Pontoon Bridge

Sunken Ships

SOUTH BAY

6th Bastion

5th Bastion

Schwartz Redoubt

Flagstaff or 4th Bastion

The Redan or 3rd Bastion

The Malakhov also Kornilov Battery

KORABELNAYA

# INTRODUCTION

## I

The purpose of the present collection is to bring together in one volume all of Tolstoy's completed short stories before he embarked on his first full-length novel, *War and Peace*. They were written between the ages of twenty-two to thirty-four, that is, from 1851 to 1863—his first literary period. In such an undertaking one is immediately confronted with the ancient quibble: how long is a short story? For during these years Tolstoy also published eight other pieces of fiction (*Childhood, Boyhood, Youth, A Landlord's Morning, Two Hussars, Family Happiness, Polikushka,* and *The Cossacks*) that may be described as short novels or novelettes. None of these has been included here because they are not short stories and also because they have often been published separately and collectively in accessible inexpensive editions. In length, theme, and manner of narration, all the tales in the present collection—with the exception of 'Sevastopol in August,' which it seemed inadvisable to separate from its companion pieces—fulfill the textbook definition of the short story, though this form is often distorted nowadays by some practitioners of the genre who, like television advertisers of headache nostrums, find a special virtue in escalating the ingredients. To be sure, several of the pieces require defense as short stories, but this will be offered in due course.

All four of Russia's most celebrated novelists began their literary careers with the short story and each has contributed one or more tales that would find honored places in any comprehensive anthology of the country's best examples of the genre. Tolstoy continued to write short stories throughout his whole long life, but this collection of his earliest efforts, which contains several of his finest tales, is particularly important, not only for the intrinsic worth and charm of these stories, but also for an understanding of the inception and development of a narrative art which found its fullest expression in the great novels. Here we observe the youthful Tolstoy eager for literary fame, agonizing over the fear of failure and then boyishly jubilant over success, yet always boldly experimenting with form and content.

Tolstoy started scribbling as a boy, and in his early diary, which he began at the age of eighteen and continued, with interruptions, throughout the remainder of his life, we may observe him serving an unconscious apprenticeship to the novelist's art of selection and analysis. In numerous entries dealing with his inner experiences as a youth, he reveals an intense interest in the suppressed motives of behavior. And his fondness for classifying all manner of human attributes in the diary suggests his later talent for conquering the subconscious by an application of penetrating understanding.

Certainly the transition from this kind of analysis in his youthful diary to that in his first piece of fiction, 'A History of Yesterday' (1851), was a natural and easy one to make. The beginning of the narrative concerns an evening spent with distant relatives. Then, on his way home, the hero animadverts amusingly on drivers and carriages. And finally, as he drops off to sleep, he speculates on the problem of dreams. All this Tolstoy apparently intended to subordinate to the design of a larger work. It was an unusual performance for a beginner and it is unlike anything in Russian literature up to that time. Though it is a fragment, it is entirely self-contained and may readily be regarded as a completed short story. To the technique of delving into motivation in his diary, he has added the spice of Laurence Sterne's analytical method in the *Sentimental Journey*, which Tolstoy had been reading and part of which he later translated as an exercise in style. Sterne's influence is obvious in Tolstoy's concentration on peculiar details, in the posturings and digressions, in the analysis of conscious and subconscious thoughts and feelings of characters reacting to particular situations, and in the transformation of all the confused associations of thought that enter the hero's head as he falls asleep. The twenty-two-year-old Tolstoy reveled in his newly discovered powers of analysis and it was a pity that he failed to go on with the work, but he never returned to this exuberant abandon in his fiction.

Perhaps one reason why Tolstoy did not continue with 'A History of Yesterday' is that shortly after starting it he set out on a long journey to the Caucasus with his brother Nikolai, who was an army officer there. He had become dissatisfied with what he considered an idle and even debauched life on his estate at Yasnaya Polyana and in Moscow and Petersburg, and he believed that a radical change was essential. He remained in the Caucasus for more than two years, serving first as a volunteer, then as a cadet, in an artillery battery, and he distinguished himself in fighting bravely against the fierce hill tribes.

Along with his rugged army existence and the usual soldierly carousing, Tolstoy also led a life of the mind and literature. He read much, thought hard about various deep subjects as his diary testifies, and wrote a great deal. In fact, much of his initial literary period is closely associated with the Caucasus, for it was there that he finished his first published work, the autobiographical short novel *Childhood* (1852), began its sequel, *Boyhood*, wrote the short story 'The Raid' (1852) and later three others which were based on his Caucasian experiences, and started several more tales and articles.

Sure instinct rather than the trial and error of experience seemed to guide Tolstoy's early encounter with the exacting demands of art. As he labored over the manuscript of *Childhood* we find repeated entries in his diary to the effect that the writing went badly, the rewriting worse. 'Without regret,' he reminded himself, 'I must destroy all unclear places, prolix, irrelevant, in a word, all things that are unsatisfactory even though they may be fine in themselves.' And without compunction he adhered to his rule that no additions, however talented, could improve a work as much as a deletion. Indeed, before he finished the fairly lengthy manuscript of *Childhood* to his satisfaction, he had accumulated four separate drafts. Yet so doubtful was he of favorable critical reaction that he refused to append his full name to the published work, signing it simply with the initials of his given name and patronymic.

However, the praise of public and critics was high, and

among the most enthusiastic readers of *Childhood* were Turgenev and Dostoevsky in his far-off exile in Siberia. Young Tolstoy was enormously grateful to read in one review: 'If this is the first production of L.N., then one ought to congratulate Russian literature on the appearance of a new and remarkable talent.' Though he was not yet certain that he wished to settle on the career of writing, this initial success encouraged him to seek new material for his pen. He found plenty of it in his present surroundings and absorbing army life, and not a few of the officers and soldiers he got to know well became the heroes and villains of his Caucasian tales. In addition there were spectacular scenery, beautiful native girls, and the inimitable Cossack settlers in the village where his battery was stationed. Tolstoy now set out to treat realistically the themes of war and Caucasian life, which only some twenty to thirty years before had been so romantically written about in exotic tales in verse and prose by his predecessors Pushkin, Marlinsky, and Lermontov. Here, in 1852, he began his brilliant short novel *The Cossacks*, which was not finished until ten years later, and he wrote his short story 'The Raid.'

Without reflecting adversely on Tolstoy's powers of imagination and invention, which were considerable, it must be said that the autobiographical element in his fiction is extraordinarily prevalent. That is, his own life of recorded experience, rendered effective by subtle choice of detail and penetrating psychological analysis, is the life that he transposes into art, a fact that may help to account for the amazing 'truthfulness to life' in his fiction so often commented on by critics. Nearly every tale in this collection is an outgrowth of some personal experience of Tolstoy's. For example, the Caucasian group ('The Raid,' 'The Wood-Felling' and 'Meeting a Moscow Acquaintance in the Detachment') belongs to this category. So does 'A Billiard-Marker's Notes,' which, despite its setting, also properly falls into the Caucasian group in the sense that it was inspired by a disastrous gambling experience Tolstoy had with a billiard-marker in Tiflis, where he had gone in 1851 to take an army examination. It is an excellent illustration, however, of how Tolstoy can turn a rather attenuated autobiographical experience into an independent, powerful, and poignant study of moral degeneration. It is also possible that some of his own spiritual distress over loose living at this time entered into the story.

Within the limitation of the short-story form, the principal characterizations of the military figures in these Caucasian tales are studies in some depth, and the significant action is nearly always narrated with a realism quite fresh for that time. In this military environment it was almost inevitable that the youthful Tolstoy, with his restless questing mind, should reveal an interest in such abstract questions as: What constitutes bravery? ('The Raid'), or: Into what categories should soldiers be classified? ('The Wood-Felling'). Yet these concerns are never allowed to obtrude on the essential unity of the stories. And the subject that was to dominate so much of his thinking in later years—the rightness or wrongness of war—is also touched upon. In fact, in 'The Raid,' and to a certain extent in 'The Wood-Felling,' there is more than a suggestion of his later ruthless analysis of conventional thinking about military glory. But he was not yet blind to the heroism of the simple plain soldier or officer, and his accounts of incidents in this connection in 'The Raid' provide the main charm of the tale.

After more than two years in the Caucasus, Tolstoy grew weary of his life there and eventually managed to obtain a transfer to an artillery brigade in active service on the Danube, where the Russians were fighting the Turks (he had by now obtained a commission in the army). Not long before he left, perhaps in one of those periods of disillusion not infrequent in his youth, he wrote in his diary: 'Literature is rubbish and I should like to set down here rules and a plan of estate-management.' Contemporary literature was declining, he decided, because authors were producing too many light books for the sake of commercial gain. But a bit later he also noted in his diary: 'Literary success that satisfies one's own self is obtained only by working at every aspect of a subject. But the subject must be a lofty one if the labor is always to be pleasant."

The trip home in January 1854 to Yasnaya Polyana where he spent his furlough was uneventful save for a fierce blizzard that inspired his memorable story 'The Snow Storm,' which he wrote the following year. The sole theme is the storm, but it is so vividly realized that it takes on the human attributes of an intensely imagined character. Like Chekhov's celebrated story 'The Steppe,' which also features a storm, the tale is really a tone poem of the elements. The repeated motifs of snow and wind have almost the quality of the incremental repetition of a folk ballad. So acute is the sensuous perception of bitter cold that the reader imaginatively experiences the sensation. The striking contrast of freezing weather and the traveler's dream of a hot summer day, drawn from Tolstoy's childhood, is a most effective device.

## II

Not long after Tolstoy joined the active army on the Danube in March 1854, England and France came in on the side of the Turks and the struggle turned into the Crimean War. A wave of patriotism swept over Russia when the allies besieged Sevastopol, the first invasion of the country since the time of Napoleon. Nor was Tolstoy immune to this feeling, whatever doubts may have occurred to him about the futility of war during his Caucasian experiences. And as in the Caucasus, the muse once again vied with Mars for his devotion. He had already sent off the manuscript of *Boyhood* to the publisher and now he continued to peck away at *The Cossacks, The Novel of a Russian Landowner,* and *Youth,* the sequel to *Boyhood*. We get a characteristic picture of the young lieutenant sitting during his off-duty hours in a bomb-proof shelter of the dangerously exposed Fourth Bastion of the besieged city's defenses, writing away at his first Sevastopol piece. Shells burst outside, bullets whistled over the parapet, and Tolstoy would occasionally look up from his writing to catch the macabre front-line humor of soldiers playing 'Noses,' or as they entered or left the shelter.

Purists might well reject Tolstoy's three Sevastopol

'sketches,' as they are sometimes erroneously called, as fiction. On the other hand, one could hardly regard them as articles of a super war correspondent. For whatever else they may be, they are art of the highest quality, in the same sense that Dostoevsky's *House of the Dead* is art and not simply a reporter's write-up of his life in a Siberian prison. If these pieces are mostly accounts of what Tolstoy observed and experienced at Sevastopol, he renders them immeasurably effective by employing artistic devices of fiction—setting, careful selection of precise detail in description, dialogue, development of characters through analysis of human motivation and feelings, and in the third narrative—possibly also in the second—there is as much plot as one finds in most of his indubitable short stories.

'Sevastopol in December 1854' skillfully recaptures the spirit of the early days of the siege in a series of brilliant genre pictures of the city and swiftly limned portraits of its typical inhabitants and defenders. The chief characteristic of the strength of the Russians, Tolstoy points out in his description of the fighting men at the Fourth Bastion, is his simplicity and obstinacy. This moving but realistically frank account of the self-sacrificing heroism of the defenders and their unswerving determination to repulse the invaders raised the flagging hopes of a nation sick with the carnage and suffering of Sevastopol. A new dimension had been added to the young Tolstoy's literary popularity in Russia. A month after the publication of the piece he entered in his diary: 'Have now reached a period of real temptation through vanity. I could gain much in life if I wished to write without conviction.'

'Sevastopol in May 1855,' however, is emphatic proof of the firm manner in which Tolstoy turned his back on this temptation. For as the bloody siege wore on he began to understand more clearly not only the horrible futility of it, but also the base human motives and practices of men who created war and then battened on such human folly. His altered attitude is clearly reflected in this second Sevastopol piece in ironic passages, satirical touches, and in forthright criticism of those officers whose 'patriotism' is translated into terms of per-

xiv ))                                          Introduction

sonal gain. Purely literary effects are not neglected, however, especially in the wonderful description of the night action. Nevertheless, Tolstoy plainly wished it to be known, as though somewhat ashamed of idealizing some aspects of war in the first Sevastopol account, that he would no longer compromise with truth, and he announced the fact in ringing terms in a famous sentence at the end of 'Sevastopol in May,' which may be regarded as his credo for the rest of his long life as a writer and thinker: 'The hero of my tale—whom I love with all the power of my soul, whom I have tried to portray in all his beauty, who has been, is, and will be beautiful—is Truth.'

In a letter to N. A. Nekrasov, editor of the *Contemporary,* which accompanied the manuscript of the second Sevastopol piece, Tolstoy wrote: 'Although I'm convinced that it is incomparably better than the first, I'm certain that it will not be liked.'

This was an understatement. The angry President of the Censor's Commission denounced the manuscript because of its 'ridicule of our brave officers, the brave defenders of Sevastopol.' He agreed to its printing only after he had entirely altered the tone of the narrative by changes and deletions. Then, when the editor refused to publish it, the censor insisted, for he realized that he had virtually transformed the piece into a propaganda document for the government. The editor, however, would not place Tolstoy's name on 'Sevastopol in May' when it appeared in print.

The chagrined Nekrasov wrote Tolstoy of his indignation over what had happened: 'Your work, of course, will not be lost . . . it will always remain as proof of a strength that was able to speak such profound and sober truth in circumstances amid which few men would have retained it. . . . You are right to value that side of your gifts most of all. Truth—in the form you have introduced it into our literature—is something entirely new among us. I do not know another writer of today who so compels the reader to love him and sympathize heartily with him as he to whom I now write. And I only fear lest time, the nastiness of life, and the deafness and dumbness that surround us, should do to you what it has done to most of us, and kill the energy without which there can be no writer—none at least such as Russia needs.'

Sevastopol was abandoned by the Russians in August 1855, and Tolstoy was happy to be sent as a courier to Petersburg in November. It was there, in the course of the next month, that he wrote 'Sevastopol in August 1855.' Now, in this third narrative, on the fall of the besieged city, he is very much the storyteller. Well-developed characters, especially the Kozeltsov brothers, add an increment of unity to a loosely constructed plot. In the studied objectivity, and particularly in the leisurely, panoramic method of narration and in the manner in which plot is sacrificed to accumlating detail, one may detect the influence of Thackeray, whom the young Tolstoy had been eagerly reading and admiring over this period. Though the lyric passages of the first Sevastopol piece are not duplicated, some of the didacticism of the second is present in the arraignment of peculation in commissary matters, a practice that deeply troubled Tolstoy and one which, when he refused to subscribe to it, got him into serious difficulties with his fellow officers. But the whole narrative is suffused with a tragic note of despair over the abandonment of the city where so many thousands had perished and which heroic soldiers were still ready to defend. The treatment of war and the characterizations of military figures in the three Sevastopol pieces anticipate Tolstoy's artistic achievements in these respects in *War and Peace*.

## III

Back in Petersburg, Tolstoy, now sick of war, sent in his resignation from the army. While waiting for an official acceptance, he enjoyed the social life of the capital and his reputation as a literary hero established by the popularity of the Sevastopol pieces. Under the eager sponsorship of the older Turgenev, Peterburg's literary leader at that time, the twenty-seven-year-old Tolstoy was soon presented to many important authors, and publishers and magazine editors competed for his writings. The liberal wing of the progressive *Contemporary,* which he had previously favored, sought his support against the emerging radical group connected with this important magazine. But Tolstoy preferred to do his own thinking and was a bit contemptuous of principles or opinions which he himself had not advanced. Turgenev's letter to P. A. Annenkov hits off the curious prickly charm of the young literary hero: 'Imagine, for more than two weeks now Tolstoy has been living with me, and what I would not give to see you both together! You cannot picture to yourself what a dear and remarkable man he is, although I have nicknamed him the "troglodyte," because of his savage ardor and buffalo-like obstinacy.' Tolstoy disliked the radicals of the *Contemporary* and condemned the liberals for what he thought was the insincerity of men who failed to practice what they preached. He soon quarreled with Turgenev and ended by offending the leadership of the *Contemporary,* whose growing emphasis upon social significance in literature disturbed him.

During 1856 Tolstoy continued his literary efforts, publishing two short stories already mentioned, 'Meeting a Moscow Acquaintance in the Detachment' and 'The Snow Storm,' a large fragment of a novel, *A Landlord's Morning,* and the fine novelette, *Two Hussars.* He also made much progress on longer works, especially *Youth,* which was published the next year, and in 1856 his first collection, *Army Tales,* appeared, and *Childhood* and *Boyhood* in a single edition. Now for the first time, however, critical reaction to his fiction was cool, even hostile, perhaps a reflection of the changing attitude of liberal Petersburg critics whom he had annoyed and who found in these tales no political or social significance that would respond to the progressive spirit of the age. Meanwhile Tolstoy was expressing a desire to strike out on new literary paths far removed from this popular demand. He jotted down in his diary: 'How I long to have done with magazines in order to write in the way I'm now beginning to think about art: awfully lofty and pure.'

At the end of 1856 Tolstoy at last received his discharge from the army and in January of the next year he set out on his first trip to Western Europe, a journey that he had long been anticipating. All the excitement of touring in strange countries absorbed his intense nature and left little time for developing his thoughts about the new direction which his literary art must take. Then occurred the incident of the little itinerant singer before the fashionable hotel at Lucerne, whose songs the wealthy tourists appreciated but absent-mindedly neglected to reward. In a very short time the outraged Tolstoy dashed off that powerful homily in fiction—'Lucerne.' It is hardly an example of the new art he was thinking about, but it does mark a significant shift of focus from the objective realism of his war tales to what might be described as the subjective realism of a moralistic emphasis. Here he deliberately employs his art to illuminate and condemn the materialistic civilization of the West by comparing the shallowness and human insensitivity of its sophisticated members with the natural man represented by the little street singer. In this fictionalized moralistic tract the voice of Rousseau rings loud and clear in Tolstoy's opposing nature, morality, and art to political laws and organized government. 'Lucerne' is a signpost pointing the direction of much of his future thought.

Although 'Albert,' which was also written abroad, may have been an effort along the lines of the 'awfully lofty and pure' art which Tolstoy had mentioned in his diary, it is infected, in a negative sense, with the moralizing of 'Lucerne.' In any event, he was concerned with the question of art, which he firmly believed must be based upon moral truths that went deeper than the 'convictions' of the politically and socially minded authors of the *Contemporary*, and 'Albert' was intended to convey this belief. For the story, which may have been connected with Tolstoy's experiences with a talented but drunken violinist whom he had befriended, is essentially a protest against society's inability to understand and protect real art. The trouble is that the morally sick musician seems more in need of a doctor than the encouragement of a heedless public incapable of appreciating virtuoso performances on the violin. The tale is saved, however, by the wonderful lyrical description of the effect of superb music on a listener, a scene obviously inspired by Tolstoy's own powerful reactions to fine music.

In the case of the brief story, 'Three Deaths,' there can be no doubt that Tolstoy wrote it to exemplify the moral truth of pure art. Without questioning the very concept of pure art, critics have differed on the effectiveness of its realization in this tale. In any event, the moral truth brought out in the contrast between harmony with creation in the death of the old peasant and the tree and disharmony in the death of the querulous invalid lady is altogether too pat and artistically unadorned to carry conviction.

When Tolstoy returned to Russia from abroad in the middle of 1857, he was chagrined to discover that his literary reputation had vanished. 'Lucerne' and 'Albert' puzzled both public and critics and the later 'Three Deaths' did not help the situation. It was whispered about that Tolstoy had lost his grip, that the great literary promise of his early fiction had come to nought. And in the light of the social tendentiousness that now gripped literature, it was not surprising that in his next considerable effort, *Family Happiness* (1859), a short novel inspired by an early love affair, he should once again disappoint readers and critics.

Perhaps a feeling that he was out of tune with contemporary demands in literature, in addition to an urge he had experienced abroad to find new outlets for his incredible energies, prompted Tolstoy to give up creative writing at this time and plunge into the exciting field of educational theory and practice. Over the next three years he ran his fascinating school for peasant children at Yasnaya Polyana and wrote extensively on educational matters.

The first period of Tolstoy's literary development had about ended. During these years he had written a very considerable amount of fiction in which many of the characteristic qualities of his mature art are apparent. In these early stories, whether he is treating war, family happiness, or exemplifying moral truths, both in subject matter and in his method of conquering reality by a fresh, uninhibited analysis of human thought and action, Tolstoy moved artistically in the direction of the great novels to come. It seems that the customary initial period of imitation and immature attempts was avoided in his artistic development. With little faltering and few false moves, he mounted at the first try the immortal steed of great art.

Marriage in 1862 brought to an end Tolstoy's educational experiments and reawakened in him the urge to resume his creative writing. He completed a brilliant novelette of peasant life, *Polikushka,* and *The Cossacks,* an outstanding short novel, both of which were published in 1863. And that same year he wrote a short tale, 'Strider: The Story of a Horse,' which did not appear in print until years later. The idea for it may have been suggested by an incident that took place in 1856, when Tolstoy visited Turgenev's estate. On one of their walks together the two writers passed before an old broken-down horse, and Tolstoy, patting it affectionately, began to describe what he imagined the horse was thinking and feeling at that moment. The account was so vivid that the astonished and delighted host declared that Tolstoy must at one time have been a horse. In any event, his equine hero is modeled on a real horse, Kholstomer, quite celebrated in Russia for his enormous stride and speed. Tolstoy may have refused to publish the story at this time because it could easily have been construed as a contribution to the literature of social significance which he so much deplored. For the tale is really a satire, from the point of view of a horse, against the evils of modern society, especially the institution of property. The uncanny manner in which Tolstoy humanizes the horse by projecting himself into the consciousness of the poor old piebald gelding is remarkable and an artistic *tour de force.* In the end, after the sustained realism of the animal's horrible death, the horse emerges as a more useful and dignified creature than its human owners.

The curious little story 'The Porcelain Doll,' with which this collection ends, was Tolstoy's share of a joint letter which he and his pregnant wife wrote to her sister in 1863. On the surface it appears to be a slight thing intended merely to amuse both his wife and sister-in-law, but throughout this deftly turned miniature tale runs the ancient tragedy of the bedroom. Tolstoy, a tremendously active and passionate man, deeply resented the frigidity of his young wife, particularly accentuated during her first pregnancy. She noted in her diary at this time: 'The role of the physical side of love plays a great part in him. And that is awful. For me, on the contrary, it means nothing.' The porcelain doll of the story is a symbol of his intense emotional frustration. However, his naïve wife seems to have missed the point, for at the end of the letter she comments to her sister: 'He has invented this that I am porcelain, such a rascal! But what does it mean—God knows.'

This revival of interest in creative writing at the time of his marriage supports the conviction that Tolstoy could no more give up literature than he could cease his search for truth; one was the essential medium for the expression of the other. At the low point of the chilly reaction of critics to his fictional efforts in 1859, Tolstoy delivered an unusual address to the Moscow Society of Lovers of Russian Literature. He deplored the fact that the public and critics had begun to think that the problem of all literature consists only in the denunciation of evil, in the debate and correction of it, in short, in the growth of a civic feeling in society. On the contrary, he concluded his remarks: 'There is another literature, reflecting eternal and universal human interests, the most precious, sincere consciousness of the people, a literature accessible to every people and to all times, a literature without which no single people, gifted with strength and richness, has ever developed.'

Tolstoy's early fiction had been an important step toward the creation of such a literature in Russia. Now, in 1863, he began the long hard task that was to lead to his greatest contribution to it—*War and Peace.*\*

ERNEST J. SIMMONS

\* All the numbered footnotes in the text not signed L. T. (Tolstoy) are contributed by the translator Aylmer Maude. The few footnotes designated by an asterisk are by Ernest J. Simmons. The footnotes in 'A History of Yesterday' are by the translator, George L. Kline.

# LEO TOLSTOY

*Short Stories*

# A HISTORY OF YESTERDAY*

I am writing a history of yesterday not because yesterday was extraordinary in any way, for it might rather be called ordinary, but because I have long wished to trace the intimate side of life through an entire day. Only God knows how many diverse and diverting impressions, together with the thoughts awakened by them, occur in a single day. Obscure and confused they may be, but they are nevertheless comprehensible to our minds. If it were possible for me to recount them all so that I myself could read the tale with ease and so that others might read it as I do, a most instructive and amusing book would result; nor would there be ink enough in the world to write it, or typesetters to put it in print. But to get on with the story.

I arose late yesterday—at a quarter to ten—because I had retired after twelve. (I have long since made a rule never to retire after twelve, yet this happens to me at least three times a week.) But there are circumstances in which I consider this rather a fault than a crime. These circumstances are of various kinds; yesterday they were as follows:

Here I must apologize for going back to the day before yesterday. But then, novelists write whole stories about their heroes' forebears.

---

* The first known piece of Tolstoy's fiction, written in 1851 when he was only twenty-two. It was not published until after his death, and the present translation is the first in English. The opening section of the narrative, the beginning of a longer work which Tolstoy planned, was inspired by an evening he spent at the home of distant relatives, Prince A. A. Volkonsky and his wife, who later served as the model for the 'little princess,' wife of Prince Andrei Bolkonsky, in *War and Peace*.

I was playing cards; not at all from a passion for the game, as it might seem; no more, indeed, from a passion for the game than one who dances the polka does so from a passion for promenading. Rousseau, among other things which he proposed and no one has accepted, suggested the playing of cup-and-ball in society in order to keep the hands occupied. But that is scarcely enough; in society the head too should be occupied, or at the very least should be so employed as to allow silence equally with conversation. Such an employment has been invented: cards. People of the older generation complain that 'nowadays there is no conversation.' I do not know how people were in the old days (it seems to me that people have always been the same), but conversation there can never be. As an employment conversation is the stupidest of inventions.—It is not from a deficiency of intelligence but from egotism that conversation fails. Everyone wishes to talk about himself or about that which interests him; however, if one speaks and another listens, the result is not a conversation but a lecture. And if two people come together who are interested in the same thing, then a third person is enough to spoil the whole business: he interferes, you must try to give him a share too—and your conversation has gone to the devil.

There are also conversations between people who are interested in the same thing, and where no one disturbs them, but such cases are even worse. Each speaks of the same thing from his own viewpoint, transposing everything to his own key, and measuring everything with his own yardstick. The longer the conversation continues, the farther apart they draw, until at last each one sees that he is no longer conversing, but is preaching with a freedom which he permits only to himself; that he is making a spectacle of himself, and that the other is not listening to him, but is doing the same thing. Have you ever rolled eggs during Holy Week? You start off two identical eggs with the same stick, but with their little ends on opposite sides. At first they roll in the same direction, but then each one begins to roll away in the direction of its little end. In conversation as in egg-rolling, there are little sloops that roll along noisily and not very far; there are sharp-ended ones that wander off heaven knows where. But, with the exception of the little sloops, there are no two eggs that would roll in the same direction. Each has its little end.

I am not speaking now of those conversations which are carried on simply because it would be improper not to say something, just as it would be improper to appear without a necktie. One person thinks, 'You know quite well that I have no real interest in what I am saying, but it is necessary'; and the other, 'Talk away, talk away, poor soul—I know it is necessary.' This is not conversation, but the same thing as a swallowtail coat, a calling card, and gloves—a matter of decorum.

And that is why I say that cards are an excellent invention. In the course of the game one may chat, gratify one's ego, and make witty remarks; furthermore, one is not obliged to keep to the same subject, as one is in that society where there is only conversation.

One must reserve the last intellectual cartridge for the final round, when one is taking his leave: then is the time to explode your whole supply, like a race horse approaching the finish line. Otherwise one appears pale and insipid; and I have noticed that people who are not only clever but capable of sparkling in society have lost out in the end because they lacked this sense of timing. If you have spoken heatedly and then, because of weariness and boredom, you cannot muster a reply, the last impression lingers and people say, 'How dull he is. . . .' But when people play cards this does not happen. One may remain silent without incurring censure.

Besides, women—young ones—play cards, and what could be better than to sit beside a young lady for two or three hours? And if it is *the* young lady, nothing more can be desired.

And so I played cards. We took seats on the right, on the left, opposite—and everything was cozy.

This diversion continued until a quarter to twelve. We finished three rubbers. Why does this woman love (how I should like to finish this sentence here with 'me'!) to embarrass me? —For even if she didn't I would not be myself in her presence. It seems to me either that my hands are very dirty, or

that I am sitting awkwardly, or else a pimple on my cheek—
the one facing her—torments me. Yet she is in no way to
blame for this: I am always ill at ease with people whom I
either do not like or like very much. Why is this? Because I
wish to convey to the former that I do not like them, and to
the latter that I do, and to convey what you wish is very difficult. With me it always works out in reverse. I wish to be
cool, but then this coolness seems overdone and I become too
affable. With people whom you love honorably, the thought
that they may think you love them dishonorably unnerves you
and you become short and brusque.

She is the woman for me because she has all those endear-
ing qualities which compel one to love them, or rather, to love
her—for I do love her. But not in order to possess her. That
thought never entered my head.

She has the bad habit of billing and cooing with her husband in front of others, but this does not bother me; it would
mean no more to me if she should kiss the stove or the table.
She plays with her husband as a swallow plays with a blossom, because she is warmhearted and this makes her happy.

She is a coquette; no, not a coquette, but she loves to
please, even to turn heads. I won't say coquette, because
either the word or the idea associated with it is bad. To call
showing the naked body and deceiving in love coquetry!—
That is not coquetry but brazen impudence and baseness. But
to wish to please and to turn heads is fine and does no one any
harm, since there are no Werthers, and it provides innocent
pleasure for oneself and others. Thus, for example, I am quite
content that she should please me; I desire nothing more. Furthermore, there is clever coquetry and stupid coquetry: clever
coquetry is inconspicuous and you do not catch the culprit in
the act; stupid coquetry, on the contrary, hides nothing. It
speaks thus: 'I am not so good-looking, but what legs I have!
Look! Do you see? What do you say? Nice?'—Perhaps your
legs are nice, but I did not notice, because you showed them.
—Clever coquetry says: 'It is all the same to me whether you
look or not. I was hot, so I took off my hat.' I saw everything.

'And what does it matter to me?' *Her* coquetry is both innocent and clever.

I looked at my watch and got up. It is astonishing: except
when I am speaking to her, I never see her looking at me, and
yet she sees all my movements.—'Oh, what a pink watch he
has!' I am very much offended when people find my Bréguet
watch pink; it would be equally offensive if they told me that
my vest is pink. I suppose I was visibly embarrassed, because
when I said that on the contrary it was an excellent watch,
she became embarrassed in her turn. I dare say she was sorry
that she had said something which put me in an awkward
position. We both sensed the humor of the situation, and
smiled. Being embarrassed together and smiling together was
very pleasant to me. A silly thing, to be sure, but together.—
I love these secret, inexplicable relationships, expressed by an
imperceptible smile or by the eyes. It is not that one person
understands the other, but that each understands that the
other understands that he understands him, etc.

Whether she wished to end this conversation which I found
so sweet, or to see how I would refuse, or if I would refuse, or
whether she simply wished to continue playing, she looked at
the figures which were written on the table, drew the chalk
over the table—making a figure that could be classified neither
as mathematical nor pictorial—looked at her husband, then
between him and me, and said: 'Let's play three more rubbers.' I was so absorbed in the contemplation not of her movements alone, but of everything that is called *charme*—which
it is impossible to describe—that my imagination was very far
away, and I did not have time to clothe my words in a felici-
tous form. I simply said: 'No, I can't.'

Before I had finished saying this I began to regret it,—that
is, not all of me, but one part of me. There is no action which
is not condemned by some part of the mind. On the other
hand, there is a part that speaks in behalf of any action: what
is so bad about going to bed after twelve, and when do you
suppose you will spend another such delightful evening?—I
dare say this part spoke very eloquently and persuasively (al-

though I cannot convey what is said), for I became alarmed and began to cast about for arguments.—In the first place, I said to myself, there is no great pleasure in it, you do not like her at all, and you're in an awkward position; besides, you've already said that you can't stay, and you would fall in her estimation. . . .

'Comme il est aimable, ce jeune homme.'

This sentence, which followed immediately after mine, interrupted my reflections.—I began to make excuses, to say I couldn't stay, but since one does not have to think to make excuses, I continued reasoning with myself.

. . . How I love to have her speak of me in the third person. In German this is rude, but I would love it even in German. Why doesn't she find a decent name for me? It is clearly awkward for her to call me either by my given name or by my surname and title. Can this be because I . . .

'Stay for supper,' said her husband.—As I was busy with my reflections on the formula of the third person, I did not notice that my body, while very properly making its excuses that it could not stay, was putting down its hat again and sitting down quite coolly in an easy chair. It was clear that my mind was taking no part in this absurdity. I became highly vexed and was about to begin roundly reproaching myself, when a pleasant circumstance diverted me. She very carefully drew something which I could not see, lifted the chalk a little higher than was necessary, and placed it on the table. Then she put her hands on the divan on which she was sitting and, wiggling from side to side, pushed herself to the back of it and raised her head—her little head, with the fine rounded contours of her face, the dark, half-closed, but energetic eyes, the narrow, sharp little nose and the mouth that was one with the eyes and always expressed something new. At this moment who could say what it expressed? There was pensiveness and mockery, and pain, and a desire to keep from laughing, dignity, and capriciousness, and intelligence, and stupidity, and passion, and apathy, and much more. After waiting for a moment, her husband went out—I suppose to order the supper.

To be left alone with her is always frightening and oppressive to me. As I follow with my eyes whoever is leaving, it is as painful to me as the fifth figure of the quadrille: I see my partner going over to the other side and I must remain alone. I am sure it was not so painful for Napoleon to see the Saxons crossing over to the enemy at Waterloo as it was for me in my early youth to watch this cruel maneuver. The stratagem that I employ in the quadrille I employed also in this case: I acted as though I did not notice that I was alone. And now even the conversation which had begun before his exit came to an end; I repeated the last words that I had said, adding only, 'And that's how it is.' She repeated hers, adding, 'Yes.' But at the same time another, inaudible, conversation began.

*She:* 'I know why you repeat what you have already said. It is awkward for you to be alone and you see that it is awkward for me,—so in order to seem occupied you begin to talk. I thank you very much for this attention, but perhaps one could say something a little bit more intelligent.'

*I:* 'That is true, your observation is correct, but I don't know why *you* feel awkward. Is it possible that you think that when you are alone I will begin to say things that will be distasteful to you? To prove that I am ready to sacrifice my own pleasures for your sake, however agreeable our present conversation is to me, I am going to speak aloud. Or else you begin.'

*She:* 'Well, go on!'

I was just opening my mouth to say something that would allow me to think of one thing while saying something else, when she began a conversation aloud which apparently could continue for a long while. In such a situation the most interesting questions are neglected because *the* conversation continues. Having each said a sentence, we fell silent, tried once more to speak, and again fell silent.

*The* conversation—*I:* 'No, it is impossible to talk. Since I see that this is awkward for you, it would be better if your husband were to return.'

*She:* (Aloud) 'Well, where is Ivan Ivanovich? Ask him to

come in here.' . . . If anyone does not believe that there are
such secret conversations, that should convince him.

'I am very glad that we are now alone,' I continued, speaking silently, 'I have already mentioned to you that you often
offend me by your lack of confidence. If my foot accidentally
touches yours, you immediately hasten to apologize and do
not give me time to do so, while I, having realized that it was
actually your foot, was just about to apologize myself. I cannot keep up with you, and you think me indelicate.'

Her husband came in. We sat for a while, had supper, and
chatted. At about twelve-thirty I went home.

## In the Sledge

It was spring, the twenty-fifth of March. The night was clear
and still; a young moon was visible from behind the red roof
of a large white house opposite; most of the snow was already
gone.

Only my night sledge was at the entrance, and even without the footman's shout of 'Let's go, there!' Dmitri knew quite
well that I was leaving. A smacking sound was audible, as
though he were kissing someone in the dark, which, I conjec-
tured, was intended to urge the little mare and the sledge
away from the pavement stones on which the runners grated
and screeched unpleasantly. Finally the sledge drew up. The
solicitous footman took me under the elbow and assisted me
to my seat. If he had not held me I should simply have
jumped into the sledge, but as it was, in order not to offend
him, I walked slowly, and broke through the thin ice which
covered the puddle—getting my feet wet. 'Thank you, my
friend.' 'Dmitri, is there a frost?'—'Of course, sir; we have a
bit of a frost every night now.'—

—How stupid! Why did I ask that?—No, there is nothing
stupid about it. You wanted to talk, to enter into communication with someone, because you are in high spirits. And why
am I in high spirits? Half an hour ago if I had gotten into my

ink you're going?'—When this cry is ad-
hole vehicle, the passenger involuntarily tries
ious, or gay, or unconcerned expression—in a
t he did not have before. It is evident that he
ased if the situation were reversed. I have no-
ntlemen with moustaches are especially sensitive
s sustained by their vehicles.

goes there?'

hout came from a policeman who had in my presence
ry much offended by a driver this same morning. At
rance across from his sentry-box a carriage was stand-
a splendid figure of a driver with a red beard, having
ed the reins under him, and resting his elbows on his
es, was warming his back in the sun—with evident pleas-
e, for his eyes were almost completely closed. Opposite him
he policeman walked up and down on the platform in front
of his sentry-box and, using the end of his halberd, adjusted
the plank which was laid across the puddles near his balcony.
—Suddenly he seemed to resent the fact that the carriage was
standing there, or else he began to envy the driver who was
warming himself with such pleasure, or perhaps he merely
wished to start a conversation. He walked the length of his
little balcony, peered into the side street, and then thumped
with his halberd on the plank: 'Hey you, where are you
stopping? You're blocking the road.' The driver unscrewed
his left eye a little, glanced at the policeman, and closed it
again.

—'Get a move on! I'm talking to you!' No attention.—'Are
you deaf? Eh? Move along, I said!' The policeman, seeing that
there was no response, walked the length of his little balcony,
peered into the side street once more, and evidently was getting ready to say something devastating. At this point the
driver raised himself a little, adjusted the reins under him,
and turning with sleepy eyes to the policeman, said, 'What
are you gaping at? They wouldn't even give you a gun, you
simpleton, and still you go around yelling at people!'

'Get out of here!'

The driver roused himself and got out of there.

sledge, I wouldn't have started to talk.—Because you spoke
elegantly when taking your leave, because her husband saw
you to the door and said, 'When will we see you again?'—
Because as soon as the footman caught sight of you he
jumped up, and despite the fact that he reeked of parsley, he
took pleasure in serving you.—I gave him a fifty-kopek piece
a few days ago.—In all our recollections the middle falls away
and the first and last impressions remain, especially the last.
For this reason there exists the splendid custom of the master
of the house accompanying his guest to the door, where,
twining one leg about the other, as a rule, the host must say
something kind to his guest. Despite any intimacy of relations,
this rule should not be disregarded. Thus, for example, 'When
will we see you again?' means nothing, but from vanity the
guest involuntarily translates it as follows: *When* means,
'please make it soon;' *we* means 'not only myself but my wife,
who is also pleased to see you'; *see you* means, 'give us the
pleasure another time;' *again* means, 'we have just spent the
evening together, but with you it is impossible to be bored.'
And the guest carries away a pleasant impression.

It is also necessary to give money to the servants, especially
in homes that are not well regulated and where not all the
footmen are courteous—in particular the doorman (who is the
most important personage because of the first and last impression). They will greet you and see you off as if you were a
member of the family, and you translate their complaisance—
whose source is your fifty-kopek piece—as follows: 'Everyone
here loves you and honors you, therefore we try, in pleasing
the masters, to please you.' Perhaps it is only the footman who
loves and honors you, but all the same it is pleasant. What's
the harm if you are mistaken? If there were no mistakes, there
would be no . . .

'Are you crazy! . . . What the devil!'

Dmitri and I were very quietly and modestly driving down
one of the boulevards, keeping to the ice on the right-hand
side, when suddenly some 'chowderhead' (Dmitri gave him
this name afterwards) in a carriage and pair ran into us. We

separated, and only after we had gone on about ten paces did Dmitri say, 'Look at that, the chowderhead, he doesn't know his right hand from his left!'

Don't think that Dmitri was a timid man or slow to answer. No, on the contrary, although he was of small stature, clean shaven—but with a moustache—he was deeply conscious of his own dignity and strictly fulfilled his duties. His weakness in this case was attributable to two circumstances: 1) Dmitri was accustomed to driving vehicles which inspired respect, but now we were driving in a small sledge with very long shafts, pulled by a very small horse, which he could hardly reach even with a whip; what is more, the horse dragged its hind feet pitifully—and all this could easily evoke the derision of by-standers. Consequently this circumstance was all the more difficult for Dmitri and could quite destroy his feeling of [self-confidence?].[1] 2) Probably my question, 'Is there a frost?' had reminded him of similar questions that I had asked him in the autumn on starting out to hunt. A hunter has something to daydream about, and he forgets to hurl a well-timed curse at the driver who does not keep to the right-hand side. With coachmen, as with everyone else, the one who shouts first and with the greatest assurance is right. There are certain exceptions. For example, a droshki-driver cannot shout at a carriage; a singleton—even an elegant one—can hardly shout at a four-in-hand; but then, everything depends on the nature of the individual circumstances and, most important, on the personality of the driver and the direction in which he is going. I once saw in Tula a striking example of the influence that one man can have on others through sheer audacity.

Everyone was driving to the carnival: sleighs with pairs, four-in-hands, carriages, trotters, silk cloaks—all drawn out in a line on the Kiev highway—and there were swarms of pedestrians. Suddenly there was a shout from a side street: 'Hold back, hold back your horses! Out of the way there!' in a self-assured voice. Involuntarily the pedestrians made way, the pairs and four-in-hands were reined in. And what do you

---

[1] This word is illegible in Tolstoy's manuscript.

think? A ragged cabby, brand... his head, standing on a brok... jade, tore through with a... one realized what was... out laughing.

Although Dmitri is a... has a kind heart and spare... not as an incentive but as a c... his horse on with the whip: this... nity of a city driver. But if the trotte... entrance, he will 'give him one.' I had oc... presently: crossing from one street to anoth... was hardly able to drag us along, and I noticed... perate movements of Dmitri's back and hands an... clucking that he was having difficulties. Would he... whip? That was not his custom. But what if the... stopped? That he would not tolerate, even though her... didn't need to fear the wag who would say, 'Feeding tim... eh?' . . . Here was proof that Dmitri acted more from a consciousness of his duty than from vanity.

I thought much more about the many and varied relations of drivers among themselves, of their intelligence, resourcefulness, and pride. I suppose that at large gatherings those who have been involved in collisions recognize one another and pass from hostile to peaceable relations. Everything in the world is interesting, especially the relationships which exist in classes other than our own.

If the vehicles are going in the same direction the disputes last longer. The one who was to blame attempts to drive the other away or to leave him behind, and the latter sometimes succeeds in proving to him the wrongness of his action, and gains the upper hand; however, when they are driving on the same side the odds are in favor of the one whose horses are more mettlesome.

All of these relationships correspond very closely to the general relationships in life. The relationships of gentlemen among themselves and with their drivers in the case of such collisions are also interesting.—'Hey there, you scoundrel,

I looked at the policeman. He muttered something and looked angrily at me; apparently he was embarrassed that I had overheard and was looking at him. I know of nothing that can offend a man more deeply than to give him to understand that you have noticed something but do not wish to mention it. As a result I became embarrassed myself; I felt sorry for the policeman and went away.

I love Dmitri's ability to give people names on the spur of the moment; it amuses me. 'Get along, little cap! Get along, monkey suit! Get along, whiskers! Get along, washerwoman! Get along, horse-doctor! Get along, bigwig! Get along, M'sieu!' The Russian has an amazing ability to find the incisive epithet for a person he has never seen before, and not only for an individual, but for a whole social class. A member of the lower middle class is a 'catdealer,' because, it is said, they trade in catskins; a footman is a 'lapper,' a 'lickspittle'; a peasant is 'Rurick'—why, I don't know; a driver is a 'waggon-eater,' etc., —it is impossible to list them all. If a Russian quarrels with someone whom he has just met, he immediately christens him with a name which goes straight to the most sensitive point: 'crooked nose,' 'crosseyed devil,' 'thick-lipped scoundrel,' 'snub-nose.' One must experience this himself to realize how accurately such epithets always hit the sorest spot. I shall never forget the insult which I once received behind my back. A Russian said of me, 'Oh, he's a snaggle-toothed one!' It should be known that my teeth are extremely bad, decayed, and sparse.

## At Home

I arrived at home. Dmitri hurried to climb down and open the gate, and I did the same so as to pass through the gate before him. It always happens this way: I hurry to go in because I am accustomed to do so; he hurries to drive me up to the porch because he is accustomed to that.—For a long time I couldn't rouse anyone with my ringing. The tallow candle had burned very low and Prov, my old footman, was asleep.

While I rang I was thinking as follows: Why is it always repugnant to me to come home, no matter where or how I live —repugnant to see the same Prov in the same place, the same candle, the same spots on the wallpaper, the same pictures? The whole thing is positively dismal.

I am particularly tired of the wallpaper and the pictures because they have pretensions to variety, and after looking at them for two days in a row they are worse than a blank wall. This unpleasant sensation upon coming home is due, I suppose, to the fact that man is not meant to lead a bachelor's life at the age of twenty-two.

It would be quite different if I could ask Prov as he opens the door (he has jumped up and is clumping with his boots to show that he has been listening for a long time and is wide awake): 'Is the mistress asleep?'

—'No sir, not at all, she's reading in a book'—That would be something: I should put both my hands behind her head, hold her at arm's length before me, look at her, kiss her—another look, and another kiss; and I would not feel lonely on returning home.

Now the only question that I can ask Prov—to show him that I have noticed that he never sleeps when I am not at home—is: 'Did anyone call?'—'No one.'—Every time I ask this question Prov answers in a pathetic voice, and I always want to say to him, 'Why do you speak in such a pathetic voice? I am very glad that no one called.' But I restrain myself; Prov might be offended and he is a man of dignity.

In the evening I usually write in my diary, my Franklin journal, and my daily accounts.

Today I didn't spend anything because I haven't even a half-kopek piece left, so there is nothing to write in the account book.—The diary and the journal are another matter. I ought to write in them, but it is late; I'll put it off until tomorrow.—

I have often heard the words, 'He's a frivolous person; he lives without a goal.' I myself have often said this, and I say it not because I repeat other people's words but because I feel in my heart that this is bad and that one should have a goal in life.

But how is one to do this—to be a 'complete person and have a goal in life'? To set up a goal for oneself is impossible. —I have tried this many times and it does not work. One should not invent a goal, but find such a one as harmonizes with man's inclinations, which existed previously, but of which one has just become aware. It seems to me I have found such a goal: a well-rounded education and the cultivation of all my talents. One of the principal accepted means for its attainment is the diary and Franklin journal. Every day I confess in my diary everything that I have done badly. I have my weaknesses written out in columns in the journal—laziness, mendacity, gluttony, indecision, the desire to show off, sensuality, lack of *fierté*, etc.,—all such petty addictions. I post my transgressions from the diary to the journal by placing little crosses in the columns.

As I began to undress I thought: 'Where in all this is your well-rounded education and the cultivation of your talents, of your virtue? Will you ever attain to virtue by this path? Where is this journal leading you?—It serves you only as an indication of your weaknesses, which have no end, and which increase every day. Even if you overcame these weaknesses you would not attain to virtue.—You are only deceiving yourself and playing with this like a child with a toy.—Surely it is not sufficient for an artist to know what things should not be done in order to become an artist. Surely one cannot accomplish anything worthwhile merely by negatively refraining from doing harm. It is not enough for the farmer to weed his field, he must till and sow. Set up rules of virtue and follow them.—It was the part of my mind which is occupied with criticism that said this.

I became thoughtful. Surely it is not enough to destroy the cause of evil in order to bring about the good. Good is positive and not negative. And it is sufficient that good is positive and evil negative for the very reason that evil can be destroyed but good cannot. Good is always in our soul and the

soul is good; but evil is implanted. If there were no evil the
good would develop freely. The comparison with the farmer
is not valid; he has to sow and plow, but in the soul the good
is already sown. The artist must practice and he will master
his art, if he does not conform to negative rules, but he must
[be free] [1] from arbitrariness. Practice is not necessary for the
exercise of virtue—the practice is life itself.

Cold is the absence of heat. Darkness is the absence of
light, evil the absence of good.—Why does man love heat,
light, and good? Because they are natural. There is a cause of
heat, light, and good—the sun, God; but there is no cold or
dark sun, no evil God. We see light and rays of light, we seek
the cause and say that there is a sun. Light and heat and the
law of gravitation prove this to us. This is in the physical
world. In the moral world we see good, we see its rays, we see
that there is a law of gravitation of the good towards something higher, and that its source is God.—

Remove the coarse crust from a diamond and it will spar-
kle; throw off the envelope of weaknesses and you will find
virtue. But is it possible that it is only these trifles, these little
weaknesses which you write down in the journal that prevent
you from being good? Are there not greater passions? And
why is such a large number added every day: *it is either self-
deception or faintheartedness*, or something of the kind. There
is no lasting improvement. In many respects there is no progress at all.—Again the part occupied with criticism made this
observation.

It is true that all the weaknesses that I have written down
may be reduced to three classes, but since each has many degrees they may be combined in infinite ways. 1) Pride, 2)
weakness of will, 3) deficiency of intelligence.—But it is not
possible to relate all weaknesses individually to a given class,
for they result from a combination. The first two classes have
decreased; the last, as an independent one, can make progress
only with time. For example, I lied recently, and clearly without cause. I was asked to dinner. I refused and then said that

[1] This word is illegible in Tolstoy's manuscript.

I could not come because I had a lesson.—What kind?—An English lesson, I said, when I actually had gymnastics. The reasons: 1) lack of intelligence, that I failed to observe at once that it was stupid to lie, 2) lack of resolution, that I did not say why, 3) stupid pride, assuming that an English lesson is a better excuse than gymnastics.—

Surely virtue does not consist of correcting the weaknesses which harm you in life. It would seem in such a case that virtue is self-denial.—But that is not true. Virtue brings happiness because happiness brings virtue.—Whenever I write candidly in my diary I do not experience the least vexation toward myself for my weaknesses; it seems to me that when I avow them, they have already ceased to exist.

This is pleasant. I said my prayers and lay down to sleep. In the evening I pray better than in the morning; I understand better what I am saying and feeling. In the evening I do not fear myself, in the morning I do—there is much before me.

Sleep in all its phases is a wonderful thing: the preparation, falling asleep, and sleep itself.—As soon as I lay down I thought, 'What a delight to wrap oneself up warmly and immediately forget oneself in sleep.' But as soon as I began to fall asleep I remembered that it is pleasant to fall asleep, and I woke up. All the pleasures of the body are destroyed by consciousness. One should not be conscious; but I was conscious that I was conscious, and I continued to be conscious, and I couldn't go to sleep. How annoying! Why did God give us consciousness when it only interferes with life?—Because moral pleasures on the contrary are felt more deeply when they are conscious.

Reflecting thus, I turned over onto the other side and in so doing uncovered myself. What a disagreeable sensation to uncover yourself in the dark. It always seems as if some one or something is clutching me or something cold or hot is touching my bare leg. I covered myself up quickly, tucked the blanket in under me on all sides, hid my head and began to go to sleep; it seemed to me that under this blanket no one and nothing could reach me.—My thoughts ran as follows:

'Morpheus, enfold me in your embrace.' This is a Divinity whose priest I would willingly become. And do you remember how the young lady was insulted when they said to her: 'Quand je suis passé chez vous, vous étiez encore dan les bras de Morphée.' She thought Morphée was a name like André or Malaphée. What a comical name! . . . A charming expression, *dans les bras;* I picture to myself so clearly and elegantly the condition *dans les bras,*—and especially clearly the *bras* themselves—dimpled arms, bare to the shoulder, with little folds of skin, and a white chemise indiscreetly open.—How wonderful arms are in general, especially if they have a little dimple!—I stretched. Do you remember, Saint Thomas forbade stretching. He is like Didrikhs. They rode with him on horseback. The baiting was fine. Gelke rode beside the district police officer hallooing to the hounds, and Nalyot was doing his best, even on the frozen mud. How vexed Seryozha[2] was! He's at sister's.—How lovely Masha[3] is—if only I could find such a wife! Morpheus would be good on a hunt, only the naked one must ride, or else you might find a wife.—Bah, how Saint Thomas rolls—and the lady has already set off to overtake them all; she stretches out in vain, but then that wonderful *dans les bras.*—Here I suppose I went to sleep completely.—I dreamed that I wanted to overtake the young lady, suddenly there was a mountain, I pushed it with my hands, pushed it again—it collapsed; (I threw down the pillow) and I came home to eat. Not ready yet. Why not?— Vasili was swaggering loudly (it was the mistress of the house asking from behind the partition what the noise was, and the chambermaid answering her; I heard this, that is why I dreamed it). Vasili came in just as everyone wanted to ask him why it wasn't ready. They saw that Vasili was in his undershirt and that there was a ribbon across his chest; I became frightened, I fell on my knees, cried and kissed his hand; it was as pleasant to me as though I were kissing her hands,—even more so. Vasili took no notice of me and asked,

---

[2] Tolstoy's brother, Sergei Nikolaevich.
[3] Tolstoy's sister, Maria Nikolaevna.

'Have you loaded?' The Tula pastry-cook Didrikhs said,
'Ready!'—'Well, fire!'—They discharged a volley. (The shut-
ter banged.)—Vasili and I started to dance the polonnaise,
but it was no longer Vasili, it was she. Suddenly, oh horror! I
notice that my trousers were so short that my bare knees were
showing. It is impossible to describe how I suffered (my legs
became uncovered; for a long time I wasn't able to cover
them up in my sleep, but finally I did). We continued dancing the polonnaise and the Queen of Württemberg was there;
suddenly I started to dance a Russian dance. Why?—I couldn't
restrain myself. Finally they brought me an overcoat and
boots; but even worse: no trousers at all. It cannot be that I
am awake; surely I am asleep. I woke up.—I went to sleep
again.—I thought, then I could no longer think; I began to
imagine things, but I imagined them connectedly and pic-
torially; then my imagination went to sleep; dark images remained. Then my body went to sleep too.—A dream is made
up of the first and last impressions.

Sleep is a condition in which man completely loses consciousness; but since a man goes to sleep by degrees, he also
loses consciousness by degrees. Consciousness is what is called
the soul; but the soul is regarded as something simple, while
there are as many consciousnesses as there are separate parts
of a human being. It seems to me that there are three such
parts: 1) mind, 2) feeling, 3) body.—1) The first is the highest and this consciousness is an attribute of intelligent people
only; animals and animal-like men do not have it. It goes to
sleep first. 2) The consciousness of feeling is also an attribute
of men only; it goes to sleep next. 3) The consciousness of the
body goes to sleep last and seldom completely.—Animals do
not have this gradation of consciousness, nor do people when
they are in such a state that they lose all consciousness—after
a strong shock or when intoxicated.—The consciousness of being asleep awakens one immediately.

The recollection of the time which we spend asleep does
not proceed from the same source as do the recollections of
real life—i.e. from memory, the ability to reproduce our impressions—but from the ability to group impressions. In the

moment of awakening we unite all the impressions which we received while going to sleep and while asleep (man almost never sleeps completely) under the influence of the impression which caused us to awaken. This process is the same as falling asleep: it proceeds by degrees, starting with the lowest faculty and ending with the highest. This takes place so rapidly that it is impossible to detect it, and being accustomed to consistency and to the form of time in which life manifests itself, we accept this aggregate of impressions as a recollection of time passed in sleep. In this way you may explain the fact that you have a long dream which ends with the circumstance which awakened you.—You dream that you are going hunting, you load your gun, flush the game, take aim, fire—and the noise which you take for the shot is the water bottle which you knocked onto the floor in your sleep. Or you come to see your friend N., you wait for him, and finally a servant comes in and reports that N. has arrived; this is actually being said to you by your own servant to wake you up.

If you wish to check the accuracy of this explanation, you should not in any case believe the dreams which are told you by people who always dream something significant and interesting. These people are accustomed to draw conclusions from dreams according to the principles of fortune-telling; they have set up a certain form to which everything is reduced. They supply what is lacking from their imagination and omit everything that does not fit into this form. For example, a mother will tell you that she dreamed that her daughter flew up into the sky and said: 'Farewell, mother dear, I shall pray for you!' And what she really dreamed was that her daughter climbed up onto the roof and said nothing, and after she had climbed up the daughter suddenly became the cook Ivan and said, 'Don't you climb up here.'

Perhaps what they tell is made up by their imaginations from mere force of habit; if so, this is a further proof of my theory of dreams. . . .

If you wish to verify what you yourself experience, recall your thoughts and images at the time of going to sleep and of waking up, and if anyone watched you while you were sleep-

ing and can tell you all the circumstances which could have
produced an effect on you, you will understand why you
dreamed what you did and not something else. These circumstances are so numerous, depending on your constitution, on
your digestion, and on physical causes, that it is impossible to
enumerate them all. But it is said that when we dream that
we are flying or swimming this means that we are growing.
Notice why you swim one day and fly another; recollect
everything, and you can explain it very easily.

If one of those persons who are in the habit of interpreting
dreams had dreamed my dream, here is how it would be told.
'I saw Saint Thomas running and running for a long time, and
I said to him: "Why are you running?" and he said to me: "I
am seeking the bride."—So you see, he will either get married
or there will be a letter from him. . . .'

Note also that there is no chronological order to your recollections. If you will recall your dreams, you will realize that
at some time in the past you actually saw what you dreamed
later.—During the night you wake up several times (almost
always), but only the two lower degrees of consciousness—
body and feeling—are awakened. After this, feeling and body
go to sleep again—and the impressions which were received
at the time of this awakening join the general impression of
the dream without any order or consistency. If the third,
higher consciousness of understanding awoke also and afterwards went to sleep again, the dream would be divided into
two parts.

## Another Day [On the Volga]

I took it into my head to travel from Saratov to Astrakhan
by way of the Volga. In the first place, I thought, it is better
in case of bad weather to travel a longer distance rather than
jolt over bad roads for seven hundred versts; besides, the picturesque banks of the Volga, the dreams, the danger—all this
is pleasant and may have a beneficial effect. I fancied myself
a poet, I called to mind my favorite characters and heroes,

putting myself in their places.—In a word, I thought, as I always think when I undertake anything new, 'Only now real life is beginning; until now it has been merely a preface which was hardly worth bothering about.' I know that this is nonsense. I have observed many times that I always remain the same and that I am no more a poet on the Volga than on the Voronka,[1] but I still believe, I still seek, I still wait for something. It always seems to me when I am in doubt whether to do something that a voice says: you won't really do that, you won't go there, and yet it was there that happiness was waiting for you; now you have let it escape for ever.—It always seems to me that something is about to start without me.—Although this is silly, it is the reason why I travelled by way of the Volga to Astrakhan. I used to be afraid and ashamed to act on such silly grounds, but no matter how much I examine my past life, I find that for the most part I have acted on grounds that were no less silly. I don't know how it is with others, but I am used to this, and for me the words 'trivial' and 'ludicrous' have become words without meaning. Where are the 'large' and 'serious' grounds?

I set off for the Moscow ferry and began to saunter about among the boats and rafts. 'Are these boats taken? Is there a free one?' I asked a group of barge-haulers who were standing on the shore. 'And what does your worship require?' an old man with a long beard in a gray peasant's coat and lamb's-wool hat asked me.—'A boat to Astrakhan.' 'Well, that can be managed, sir!'—

---

[1] A stream on the grounds at Yasnaya Polyana.

# THE RAID

## *A Volunteer's Story**

❖❖❖❖❖❖❖

*The portions of this story enclosed in square brackets are those the Censor suppressed, and are now published in English for the first time.*

---

## *CHAPTER I*

War always interested me: not war in the sense of manœuvres devised by great generals—my imagination refused to follow such immense movements, I did not understand them—but the reality of war, the actual killing. I was more interested to know in what way and under the influence of what feeling one soldier kills another than to know how the armies were arranged at Austerlitz and Borodinó.

I had long passed the time when, pacing the room alone and waving my arms, I imagined myself a hero instantane-

---

* Written in 1852, *The Raid* was the first of several works based directly on Tolstoy's youthful experiences in the Caucasus. As a volunteer in the army he took part in the critical incident described in the tale, and several of the leading figures are modeled on officers he knew well. Passages deleted by the Russian censor and reintroduced in this translation indicate that even this early Tolstoy had begun to think in terms of opposition to war, which eventually resulted in his utter condemnation of it.

ously slaughtering an immense number of men and receiving
a generalship as well as imperishable glory for so doing. The
question now occupying me was different: under the influence
of what feeling does a man, with no apparent advantage to
himself, decide to subject himself to danger and, what is more
surprising still, to kill his fellow men? I always wished to think
that this is done under the influence of anger, but we cannot
suppose that all those who fight are angry all the time, and I
had to postulate feelings of self-preservation and duty.

What is courage—that quality respected in all ages and
among all nations? Why is this good quality—contrary to all
others—sometimes met with in vicious men? Can it be that to
endure danger calmly is merely a physical capacity and that
people respect it in the same way that they do a man's tall
stature or robust frame? Can a horse be called brave, which
fearing the whip throws itself down a steep place where it
will be smashed to pieces; or a child who fearing to be punished runs into a forest where it will lose itself; or a woman
who for fear of shame kills her baby and has to endure penal
prosecution; or a man who from vanity resolves to kill a fellow
creature and exposes himself to the danger of being killed?

In every danger there is a choice. Does it not depend on
whether the choice is prompted by a noble feeling or a base
one whether it should be called courage or cowardice? These
were the questions and the doubts that occupied my mind
and to decide which I intended to avail myself of the first opportunity to go into action.

In the summer of 184– I was living in the Caucasus at the
small fortified post of N——.]

On the twelfth of July Captain Khlópov entered the low
door of my earth-hut. He was wearing epaulettes and carrying
a sword, which I had never before seen him do since I had
reached the Caucasus.

'I come straight from the colonel's,' he said in answer to my
questioning look. 'To-morrow our battalion is to march.'

'Where to?' I asked.

'To M. The forces are to assemble there.'

'And from there I suppose they will go into action?'

'I expect so.'

'In what direction? What do you think?'

'What is there to think about? I am telling you what I know. A Tartar galloped here last night and brought orders from the general for the battalion to march with two days' rations of rusks. But where to, why, and for how long, we do not ask, my friend. We are told to go—and that's enough.'

'But if you are to take only two days' rations of rusks it proves that the troops won't be out longer than that.'

'It proves nothing at all!'

'How is that?' I asked with surprise.

'Because it is so. We went to Dargo and took one week's rations of rusks, but we stayed there nearly a month.'

'Can I go with you?' I asked after a pause.

'You could, no doubt, but my advice is, don't. Why run risks?'

'Oh, but you must allow me not to take your advice. I have been here a whole month solely on the chance of seeing an action, and you wish me to miss it!'

'Well, you must please yourself. But really you had better stay behind. You could wait for us here and might go hunting —and we would go our way, and it would be splendid,' he said with such conviction that for a moment it really seemed to me too that it would be 'splendid.' However, I told him decidedly that nothing would induce me to stay behind.

'But what is there for you to see?' the captain went on, still trying to dissuade me. 'Do you want to know what battles are like? Read Mikháylovski Danílevski's *Description of War*. It's a fine book, it gives a detailed account of everything. It gives the position of every corps and describes how battles are fought.'

'All that does not interest me,' I replied.

'What is it then? Do you simply wish to see how people are killed?—In 1832 we had a fellow here, also a civilian, a Spaniard I think he was. He took part with us in two campaigns, wearing some kind of blue mantle. Well, they did for the fine fellow. You won't astonish anyone here, friend!'

Humiliating though it was that the captain so misjudged my motives, I did not try to disabuse him.

'Was he brave?' I asked.

'Heaven only knows: he always used to ride in front, and where there was firing there he always was.'

'Then he must have been brave,' said I.

'No. Pushing oneself in where one is not needed does not prove one to be brave.'

'Then what do you call brave?'

'Brave? . . . Brave?' repeated the captain with the air of one to whom such a question presents itself for the first time. 'He who does what he ought to do is brave,' he said after thinking awhile.

I remembered that Plato defines courage as 'The knowledge of what should and what should not be feared', and despite the looseness and vagueness of the captain's definition I thought that the fundamental ideas of the two were not so different as they might appear, and that the captain's definition was even more correct than that of the Greek philosopher. For if the captain had been able to express himself like Plato he would no doubt have said that, 'He is brave who fears only what should be feared and not what should not be feared'.

I wished to explain my idea to the captain.

'Yes,' said I, 'it seems to me that in every danger there is a choice, and a choice made under the influence of a sense of duty is courage, but a choice made under the influence of a base motive is cowardice. Therefore a man who risks his life from vanity, curiosity, or greed, cannot be called brave; while on the other hand he who avoids a danger from honest consideration for his family, or simply from conviction, cannot be called a coward.'

The captain looked at me with a curious expression while I was speaking.

'Well, that I cannot prove to you,' he said, filling his pipe, 'but we have a cadet here who is fond of philosophizing. You should have a talk with him. He also writes verses.'

I had known of the captain before I left Russia, but I had only made his acquaintance in the Caucasus. His mother,

Mary Ivánovna Khlópova, a small and poor landowner, lives within two miles of my estate. Before I left for the Caucasus I had called on her. The old lady was very glad to hear that I should see her 'Páshenka', by which pet name she called the grey-haired elderly captain, and that I, 'a living letter', could tell him all about her and take him a small parcel from her. Having treated me to excellent pie and smoked goose, Mary Ivánovna went into her bedroom and returned with a black bag to which a black silk ribbon was attached.

'Here, this is the icon of our Mother Mediatress of the Burning Bush,' said she, crossing herself and kissing the icon of the Virgin and placing it in my hands. 'Please let him have it. You see, when he went to the Caucasus I had a Mass said for him and promised, if he remained alive and safe, to order this icon of the Mother of God for him. And now for eighteen years the Mediatress and the Holy Saints have had mercy on him, he has not been wounded once, and yet in what battles has he not taken part? . . . What Michael who went with him told me was enough, believe me, to make one's hair stand on end. You see, what I know about him is only from others. He, my pet, never writes me about his campaigns for fear of frightening me.'

(After I reached the Caucasus I learnt, and then not from the captain himself, that he had been severely wounded four times and of course never wrote to his mother either about his wounds or his campaigns.)

'So let him now wear this holy image,' she continued. 'I give it him with my blessing. May the Most Holy Mediatress guard him. Especially when going into battle let him wear it. Tell him so, dear friend. Say "Your mother wishes it." '

I promised to carry out her instructions carefully.

'I know you will grow fond of my Páshenka,' continued the old lady. 'He is such a splendid fellow. Will you believe it, he never lets a year pass without sending me some money, and he also helps my daughter Ánnushka a good deal, and all out of his pay! I thank God for having given me such a child,' she continued with tears in her eyes.

'Does he often write to you?' I asked.

'Seldom, my dear: perhaps once a year. Only when he sends the money, not otherwise. He says, "If I don't write to you, mother, that means I am alive and well. Should anything befall me, which God forbid, they'll tell you without me."'

When I handed his mother's present to the captain (it was in my own quarters) he asked for a bit of paper, carefully wrapped it up, and then put it away. I told him many things about his mother's life. He remained silent, and when I had finished speaking he went to a corner of the room and busied himself for what seemed a long time, filling his pipe.

'Yes, she's a splendid old woman!' he said from there in a rather muffled voice. 'Will God ever let me see her again?'

These simple words expressed much love and sadness.

'Why do you serve here?' I asked.

'One has to serve,' he answered with conviction.

['You should transfer to Russia. You would then be nearer to her.'

'To Russia? To Russia?' repeated the captain, dubiously swaying his head and smiling mournfully. 'Here I am still of some use, but there I should be the least of the officers. And besides, the double pay we get here also means something to a poor man.'

'Can it be, Pável Ivánovich, that living as you do the ordinary pay would not suffice?'

'And does the double pay suffice?' interjected the captain. 'Look at our officers! Have any of them a brass farthing? They all go on tick at the sutler's, and are all up to their ears in debt. You say "living as I do". . . . Do you really think that living as I do I have anything over out of my salary? Not a farthing! You don't yet know what prices are like here; everything is three times dearer. . . .']

The captain lived economically, did not play cards, rarely went carousing, and smoked the cheapest tobacco (which for some reason he called home-grown tobacco). I had liked him before—he had one of those simple, calm, Russian faces which are easy and pleasant to look straight in the eyes—and after this talk I felt a sincere regard for him.

## CHAPTER II

Next morning at four o'clock the captain came for me. He wore an old threadbare coat without epaulettes, wide Caucasian trousers, a white sheepskin cap the wool of which had grown yellow and limp, and had a shabby Asiatic sword strapped round his shoulder. The small white horse he rode ambled along with short strides, hanging its head down and swinging its thin tail. Although the worthy captain's figure was not very martial or even good-looking, it expressed such equanimity towards everything around him that it involuntarily inspired respect.

I did not keep him waiting a single moment, but mounted my horse at once, and we rode together through the gates of the fort.

The battalion was some five hundred yards ahead of us and looked like a dense, oscillating, black mass. It was only possible to guess that it was an infantry battalion by the bayonets which looked like needles standing close together, and by the sound of the soldiers' songs which occasionally reached us, the beating of a drum, and the delightful voice of the Sixth Company's second tenor, which had often charmed me at the fort. The road lay along the middle of a deep and broad ravine by the side of a stream which had overflowed its banks. Flocks of wild pigeons whirled above it, now alighting on the rocky banks, now turning in the air in rapid circles and vanishing out of sight. The sun was not yet visible, but the crest of the right side of the ravine was just beginning to be lit up. The grey and whitish rock, the yellowish-green moss, the dew-covered bushes of Christ's Thorn, dogberry, and dwarf elm, appeared extraordinarily distinct and salient in the golden morning light, but the other side and the valley, wrapped in thick mist which floated in uneven layers, were damp and gloomy and presented an indefinite mingling of colours: pale purple, almost black, dark green, and white. Right in front of us, strikingly distinct against the dark-blue horizon, rose the bright, dead-white masses of the snowy mountains, with their shadows and outlines fantastic and yet exquisite in every detail. Crickets, grasshoppers, and thousands of other insects, awoke in the tall grasses and filled the air with their clear and ceaseless sounds: it was as if innumerable tiny bells were ringing inside our very ears. The air was full of the scent of water, grass, and mist: the scent of a lovely early summer morning. The captain struck a light and lit his pipe, and the smell of his cheap tobacco and of the tinder seemed to me extraordinarily pleasant.

To overtake the infantry more quickly we left the road. The captain appeared more thoughtful than usual, did not take his Daghestan pipe from his mouth, and at every step touched with his heels his horse, which swaying from side to side left a scarcely perceptible green track in the tall wet grass. From under its very feet, with the cry and the whirr of wings which involuntarily sends a thrill through every sportsman, a pheasant rose, and flew slowly upwards. The captain did not take the least notice of it.

We had nearly overtaken the battalion when we heard the thud of a horse galloping behind us, and that same moment a good-looking youth in an officer's uniform and white sheepskin cap galloped past us. He smiled in passing, nodded to the captain, and flourished his whip. I only had time to notice that he sat his horse and held his reins with peculiar grace, that he had beautiful black eyes, a fine nose, and only the first indications of a moustache. What specially pleased me about him was that he could not repress a smile when he noticed our admiration. This smile alone showed him to be very young.

'Where is he galloping to?' muttered the captain with a dissatisfied air, without taking the pipe from his mouth.

'Who is he?' I replied.

'Ensign Alánin, a subaltern in my company. He came from the Cadet Corps only a month ago.'

'I suppose he is going into action for the first time,' I said.

'That's why he is so delighted,' answered the captain, thoughtfully shaking his head. 'Youth!'

'But how could he help being pleased? I can fancy how interesting it must be for a young officer.'

The captain remained silent for a minute or two.

'That is just why I say "youth",' he added in a deep voice. 'What is there to be pleased at without ever having seen the thing? When one has seen it many times one is not so pleased. There are now, let us say, twenty of us officers here: one or other is sure to be killed or wounded, that is quite certain. To-day it may be I, to-morrow he, the next day a third. So what is there to be pleased about?'

# CHAPTER III

As soon as the bright sun appeared above the hill and lit up the valley along which we were marching, the wavy clouds of mist cleared and it grew hot. The soldiers, with muskets and sacks on their shoulders, marched slowly along the dusty road. Now and then Ukrainian words and laughter could be heard in their ranks. Several old soldiers in white blouses (most of them non-commissioned officers) walked together by the roadside, smoking their pipes and conversing gravely. Heavily laden wagons drawn by three horses moved steadily along, raising thick clouds of dust that hung motionless in the air. The officers rode in front: some of them caracoled—whipping their horses, making them take three or four leaps and then, pulling their heads round, stopping abruptly. Others were occupied with the singers, who in spite of the heat and sultriness sang song after song.

With the mounted Tartars, about two hundred yards ahead of the infantry, rode a tall handsome lieutenant in Asiatic costume on a large white horse. He was known in the regiment as a desperate daredevil who would spit the truth out at anybody. He wore a black tunic trimmed with gold braid, leggings to match, soft closely fitting gold-braided oriental shoes, a yellow coat and a tall sheepskin cap pushed back from his forehead. Fastened to the silver strap that lay across his chest and back, he carried a powder-flask, and a pistol behind him. Another pistol and a silver-mounted dagger hung from his girdle, and above these a sword in a red leather sheath, and a musket in a black cover, were slung over his shoulder. By his clothing, by the way he sat his horse, by his general bearing, in fact by his every movement, one could see that he tried to resemble a Tartar. He even spoke to the Tartars with whom he was riding in a language I did not know, and from the bewildered and amused looks with which they glanced at one another I surmised that they did not understand him either. He was one of our young officers, daredevil braves who shape their lives on the model of Lérmontov's and Marlínsky's heroes. These officers see the Caucasus only through the prism of such books as *A Hero of our Time,* and *Mullah-Nur,*[1] and are guided in their actions not by their own inclinations but by the examples of their models.

The lieutenant, for instance, may perhaps have liked the company of well-bred women and men of rank: generals, colonels, and aides-de-camp (it is even my conviction that he liked such society very much, for he was exceedingly ambitious), but he considered it his imperative duty to turn his roughest side to all important men, though he was strictly moderate in his rudeness to them; and when any lady came to the fort he considered it his duty to walk before her window with his bosom friends, in a red shirt and with slippers on his bare feet, and shout and swear at the top of his voice. But all this he did not so much with the intention of offending her as to let her see what beautiful white feet he had, and how easy it would be to fall in love with him should he desire it. Or he would often go with two or three friendly Tartars to the hills at night to lie in ambush by the roadside to watch for passing hostile Tartars and kill them: and though his heart told him more than once that there was nothing valiant in this, he considered himself bound to cause suffering to people with whom he affected to be disillusioned and whom he chose to

---

[1] Novels by the above-mentioned authors.

hate and despise. He always carried two things: a large icon hanging round his neck, and a dagger which he wore over his shirt even when in bed. He sincerely believed that he had enemies. To persuade himself that he must avenge himself on someone and wash away some insult with blood was his greatest enjoyment. He was convinced that hatred, vengeance, and contempt for the human race were the noblest and most poetic of emotions. But his mistress (a Circassian of course) whom I happened to meet subsequently, used to say that he was the kindest and mildest of men, and that every evening he wrote down his dismal thoughts in his diary, as well as his accounts on ruled paper, and prayed to God on his knees. And how much he suffered merely to appear in his own eyes what he wished to be! For his comrades and the soldiers could never see him as he wished to appear. Once on one of his nocturnal expeditions on the road with his bosom friends he happened to wound a hostile Chechen with a bullet in the leg, and took him prisoner. After that the Chechen lived for seven weeks with the lieutenant, who attended to him and nursed him as he would have nursed his dearest friend, and when the Chechen recovered he gave him presents and set him free. After that, during one of our expeditions when the lieutenant was retreating with the soldiers of the cordon and firing to keep back the foe, he heard someone among the enemy call him by name, and the man he had wounded rode forward and made signs to the lieutenant to do the same. The lieutenant rode up to his friend and pressed his hand. The hillsmen stood some way back and did not fire, but scarcely had the lieutenant turned his horse to return before several men shot at him and a bullet grazed the small of his back. Another time, at night, when a fire had broken out in the fort and two companies of soldiers were putting it out, I myself saw the tall figure of a man mounted on a black horse and lit up by the red glow of the fire suddenly appeared among the crowd and, pushing through, rode up to the very flames. When quite close the lieutenant jumped from his horse and rushed into the house, one side of which was burning. Five

minutes later he came out with singed hair and scorched elbow, carrying in his bosom two pigeons he had rescued from
the flames.

His name was Rosenkranz, yet he often spoke of his de-
scent, deducing it somehow from the Varángians (the first
rulers of Russia), and clearly demonstrated that he and his
ancestors were pure Russians.

## *CHAPTER IV*

The sun had done half its journey, and cast its hot rays
through the glowing air onto the dry earth. The dark blue sky
was perfectly clear, and only the base of the snowy mountains began to clothe itself in lilac-tinged white clouds. The
motionless air seemed full of transparent dust, the heat was
becoming unbearable.

Half-way on their march the troops reached a small stream
and halted. The soldiers stacked their muskets and rushed to
the stream; the commander of the battalion sat down in the
shade on a drum, his full face assuming the correct expression
denoting the greatness of his rank. He, together with some
other officers, prepared to have a snack. The captain lay down
on the grass under his company's wagon. The brave Lieutenant Rosenkranz and some other young officers disposed themselves on their outspread cloaks and got ready for a drinking-bout, as could be gathered from the bottles and flasks
arranged round them, as well as from the peculiar animation
of the singers who, standing before them in a semicircle, sang
a Caucasian dance-song with a whistling obbligato interjected:

> *Shamyl, he began to riot*
> *In the days gone by,*
> *Try-ry-rataty,*
> *In the days gone by!*

Among these officers was the young ensign who had overtaken us in the morning. He was very amusing: his eyes

shone, he spoke rather thickly, and he wished to kiss and declare his love to everyone. Poor boy! He did not know that he might appear funny in such a situation, that the frankness and tenderness with which he assailed every one predisposed them not to the affection he so longed for, but to ridicule; nor did he know that when, quite heated, he at last threw himself down on the cloak and rested on his elbow with his thick black hair thrown back, he looked uncommonly charming.

[In a word, everyone was cheerful, except perhaps one officer who, sitting under his company's cart, had lost the horse he was riding to another officer at cards and had agreed to hand it over when they reached head-quarters. He was vainly trying to induce the other to play again, offering to stake a casket which everyone could confirm he had bought for thirty rubles from a Jew, but which—merely because he was in difficulties—he was now willing to stake for fifteen. His opponent looked casually into the distance and persistently remained silent, till at last he remarked that he was terribly anxious to have a doze.

I confess that from the time I started from the fort and decided to take part in this action, gloomy reflections involuntarily rose in my mind, and so—since one has a tendency to judge of others by oneself] I listened with curiosity to the conversation of the soldiers and officers and attentively watched the expression of their faces, but could find absolutely no trace of the anxiety I myself experienced: jokes, laughter and anecdotes, gambling and drunkenness, expressed the general carelessness and indifference to the impending danger [as if all these people had long ago finished their affairs in this world. What was this—firmness, habitation to danger, or carelessness and indifference to life? Or was it all these things together as well as others I did not know, forming a complex but powerful moral motive of human nature termed *esprit de corps*—a subtle code embracing within itself a general expression of all the virtues and vices of men banded together in any permanent condition, a code each new member involuntarily submits to unmurmuringly and which does not change with the individuals, since whoever they may

be the sum total of human tendencies everywhere and always
remains the same?]

## CHAPTER V

Towards seven that evening, dusty and tired, we entered the
wide fortified gate of Fort M. The sun was already setting
and threw its rosy slanting rays on the picturesque little batteries, on the gardens with their tall poplars which surrounded
the fortress, on the yellow gleaming cultivated fields, and on
the white clouds that crowding round the snowy peaks had,
as if trying to imitate them, formed a range not less fantastic
and beautiful. On the horizon the new moon appeared delicate as a little cloud. In the Tartar village, from the roof of a
hut, a Tartar was calling the faithful to prayer, and our singers raised their voices with renewed energy and vigour.

After a rest and after tidying myself up a bit, I went to an
adjutant of my acquaintance to ask him to let the general
know of my intention. On my way from the suburb where I
had put up I noticed in Fort M. something I did not at all
expect: a pretty little brougham overtook me, in which I
caught sight of a fashionable bonnet and from which I overheard some French words. The sounds of some 'Lizzie' or
'Kátenka' polka, played on a bad ramshackle piano, reached
me through the windows of the commander's house. In a little grocery and wine shop which I passed, some clerks with
cigarettes in their fingers sat drinking wine, and I heard one
of them say to another 'No, excuse me, as to politics, Mary
Gregórevna is first of our ladies.' A Jew in a worn-out coat,
with a bent back and sickly countenance, was dragging along
a wheezy barrel-organ and the whole suburb resounded to the
tones of the finale of 'Lucia'. Two women in rustling dresses
with silk kerchiefs on their heads and carrying bright-coloured
parasols passed by along the planks that did duty for a pavement. Two girls, one in a pink, the other in a blue dress, stood
bareheaded beside the earth-embankments of a low-roofed
house, and shrieked with high-pitched, forced laughter, evi-

dently to attract the attention of passing officers. Officers, dressed in new uniforms with glittering epaulettes and white gloves, flaunted along the street and on the boulevard.

I found my acquaintance on the ground floor of the general's house. I had scarcely had time to explain my wish to him and to get his reply that it could easily be fulfilled, when the pretty little brougham I had noticed outside rattled past the window we were sitting at. A tall, well-built man in an infantry major's uniform and epaulettes got out and entered the house.

'Oh, please excuse me,' said the adjutant, rising, 'I must go and announce them to the general.'

'Who is it?' I asked.

'The countess,' he replied, and buttoning his uniform he rushed upstairs.

A few minutes later a very handsome man in a frock coat without epaulettes and with a white cross in his buttonhole went out into the porch. He was not tall but remarkably good-looking. He was followed by the major, an adjutant, and a couple of other officers. The general's gait, voice, and all his movements, showed him to be a man well aware of his own value.

'*Bonsoir, madame la comtesse,*' [1] he said, offering his hand through the carriage window.

A small hand in a kid glove pressed his, and a pretty smiling face in a yellow bonnet appeared at the carriage window.

Of the conversation which lasted several minutes I only overheard the general say laughingly as I passed by:

'*Vous savez que j'ai fait voeu de combattre les infidèles; prenez donc garde de la devenir.*' [2]

A laugh replied from inside the carriage.

'*Adieu donc, cher général!*' [3]

'*Non, au revoir,*' said the general, ascending the steps of the

---

[1] 'Good evening, Countess.'
[2] 'You know I have sworn to fight the infidels (the unfaithful), so beware of becoming one.'
[3] 'Good-bye then, dear general.'

porch. '*N'oubliez pas, que je m'invite pour la soirée de de-
main.*' [4]

The carriage rattled off [and the general went into the
sitting-room with the major. Passing by the open window of
the adjutant's room, he noticed my uniformed figure and
turned his kind attention to me. Having heard my request he
announced his complete agreement with it and passed on
into his room.]

'There again,' I thought as I walked home, 'is a man who
possesses all that Russians strive after: rank, riches, distinction; and this man, the day before an engagement the out-
come of which is known only to God, jokes with a pretty
woman and promises to have tea with her next day, just as if
they had met at a ball!'

[I remembered a reflection I had heard a Tartar utter, to
the effect that only a pauper can be brave. '*Become rich,
become a coward,*' said he, not at all to offend his comrade
but as a common and unquestionable rule. But the general
could lose, together with his life, much more than anyone
else I had had an opportunity of observing and, contrary to
the Tartar's rule, no one had shown such a pleasant, graceful
indifference and confidence as he. My conceptions of courage
became completely confused.]

At that same adjutant's I met a young man who surprised
me even more. He was a young lieutenant of the K. regiment
who was noted for his almost feminine meekness and timidity
and who had come to the adjutant to pour out his vexation
and resentment against those who, he said, had intrigued
against him to keep him from taking part in the impending
action. He said it was mean to behave in that way, that it was
unfriendly, that he would not forget it, and so forth. Intently
as I watched the expression of his face and listened to the
sound of his voice, I could not help feeling convinced that he
was not pretending but was genuinely filled with indignation
and grief at not being allowed to go and shoot Circassians and

---

[4] 'No, *au revoir.* Don't forget that I am inviting myself for to-
morrow's soirée.'

expose himself to their fire. He was grieving like a little child
who has been unjustly birched . . . I could make nothing at
all of it.

## CHAPTER VI

The troops were to start at ten in the evening. At half-past
eight I mounted and rode to the general's, but thinking that
he and his adjutant were busy I tied my horse to the fence
and sat down on an earth-bank intending to catch the general when he came out.

The heat and glare of the sun were now replaced by the
coolness of night and the soft light of the young moon, which
had formed a pale glimmering semicircle around itself on the
deep blue of the starry sky and was already setting. Lights
appeared in the windows of the houses and shone through
cracks in the shutters of the earth huts. The stately poplars,
beyond the white moonlit earth huts with their rush-thatched
roofs, looked darker and taller than ever against the horizon.

The long shadows of the houses, the trees, and the fences,
stretched out daintily on the dusty road. . . . From the
river came the ringing of frogs;[1] along the street came the
sound of hurried steps and voices talking, or the gallop of a
horse, and from the suburb the tones of a barrel-organ playing now 'The winds are blowing', now some 'Aurora Waltz'.

I will not say in what meditations I was absorbed: first, because I should be ashamed to confess the gloomy waves of
thought that insistently flooded my soul while around me I
noticed nothing but gaiety and joy, and secondly, because it
would not suit my story. I was so absorbed in thought that I
did not even notice the bell strike eleven and the general with
his suite ride past me.

---

[1] Frogs in the Caucasus make a noise quite different from the
croaking of frogs elsewhere. L. T.

[Hastily mounting my horse I set out to overtake the detachment.]

The rear-guard was still within the gates of the fort. I had great difficulty in making my way across the bridge among the guns, ammunition wagons, carts of different companies, and officers noisily giving orders. Once outside the gates I trotted past the troops who, stretching out over nearly three-quarters of a mile, were silently moving on amid the darkness, and I overtook the general. As I rode past the guns drawn out in single file, and the officers who rode between them, I was hurt as by a discord in the quiet and solemn harmony by the German accents of a voice shouting, 'A linstock, you devil!' and the voice of a soldier hurriedly exclaiming, 'Shévchenko, the lieutenant wants a light!'

The greater part of the sky was now overcast by long strips of dark grey clouds; it was only here and there that a few stars twinkled dimly among them. The moon had already sunk behind the near horizon of the black hills visible to the right and threw a faint trembling light on their peaks, in sharp contrast to the impenetrable darkness enveloping their base. The air was so warm and still that it seemed as if not a single blade of grass, not a single cloudlet, was moving. It was so dark that even objects close at hand could not be distinguished. By the sides of the road I seemed to see now rocks, now animals, now some strange kind of men, and I discovered that they were merely bushes only when I heard them rustle, or felt the dew with which they were sprinkled.

Before me I saw a dense heaving wall followed by some dark moving spots; this was the cavalry vanguard and the general with his suite. Another similar dark mass, only lower, moved beside us; this was the infantry.

The silence that reigned over the whole division was so great that all the mingling sounds of night with their mysterious charm were distinctly audible: the far-off mournful howling of jackals, now like agonized weeping, now like chuckling; the monotonous resounding song of crickets, frogs, and quails; a sort of rumbling I could not at all account for but which seemed to draw nearer; and all those scarcely audible motions

of Nature which can neither be understood nor defined, mingled into one beautiful harmony which we call the stillness of
night. This stillness was interrupted by, or rather combined
with, the dull thud of hoofs and the rustling of the tall grass
caused by the slowly advancing detachment.

Only very occasionally could the clang of a heavy gun, the
sound of bayonets touching one another, hushed voices, or the
snorting of a horse, be heard. [By the scent of the wet juicy
grass which sank under our horses' feet, by the light steam
rising from the ground and by the horizons seen on two sides
of us, it was evident that we were moving across a wide,
luxuriant meadow.] Nature seemed to breathe with pacifying
beauty and power.

Can it be that there is not room for all men on this beautiful
earth under those immeasurable starry heavens? Can it be
possible that in the midst of this entrancing Nature feelings of
hatred, vengeance, or the desire to exterminate their fellows,
can endure in the souls of men? All that is unkind in the
hearts of men should, one would think, vanish at contact with
Nature—that most direct expression of beauty and goodness.

[War! What an incomprehensible phenomenon! When one's
reason asks: 'Is it just, is it necessary?' an inner voice always
replies 'No.' Only the persistence of this unnatural occurrence
makes it seem natural, and a feeling of self-preservation makes
it seem just.

Who will doubt that in the war of the Russians against the
mountain-tribes, justice—resulting from a feeling of self-preservation—is on our side? Were it not for this war, what would
secure the neighbouring rich and cultured Russian territories
from robbery, murder, and raids by wild and warlike tribes?
But consider two private persons. On whose side is the feeling of self-preservation and consequently of justice? Is it on
the side of this ragamuffin—some Djemi or other—who hearing of the approach of the Russians snatches down his old gun
from the wall, puts three or four charges (which he will only
reluctantly discharge) in his pouch and runs to meet the
giaours, and on seeing that the Russians still advance, approaching the fields he has sown which they will tread down

and his hut which they will burn, and the ravine where his
mother, his wife, and his children have hidden themselves,
shaking with fear—seeing that he will be deprived of all that
constitutes his happiness—in impotent anger and with a cry
of despair tears off his tattered jacket, flings down his gun,
and drawing his sheepskin cap over his eyes sings his death-
song and flings himself headlong onto the Russian bayonets
with only a dagger in his hand? Is justice on his side or on
that of this officer on the general's staff who is singing French
chansonettes so well just as he rides past us? He has a family in Russia, relations, friends, serfs, and obligations towards
them, but has no reason or desire to be at enmity with the
hillsmen, and has come to the Caucasus just by chance and
to show his courage. Or is it on the side of my acquaintance
the adjutant, who only wishes to obtain a captaincy and a
comfortable position as soon as possible and for that reason
has become the hillsmen's enemy? Or is it on the side of this
young German who, with a strong German accent, is demanding a linstock from the artillerymen? What devil has brought
him from his fatherland and set him down in this distant
region? Why should this Saxon, Kaspar Lavréntich, mix himself up in our blood-thirsty conflict with these turbulent neighbours?]

# CHAPTER VII

We had been riding for more than two hours. I was beginning to shiver and feel drowsy. Through the gloom I still
seemed to see the same indefinite forms; a little way in front
the same black wall and the moving spots. Close in front of
me I could see the crupper of a white horse which swung its
tail and threw its hind legs wide apart, the back of a white
Circassian coat on which could be discerned a musket in a
black case, and the glimmering butt of a pistol in an embroi-
dered holster; the glow of a cigarette lit up a fair moustache,
a beaver collar and a hand in a chamois glove. Every now
and then I leant over my horse's neck, shutting my eyes and

forgetting myself for a few minutes, then startled by the familiar tramping and rustling I glanced round, and felt as if
I were standing still and the black wall in front was moving
towards me, or that it had stopped and I should in a moment
ride into it. At one such moment the rumbling which increased and seemed to approach, and the cause of which I
could not guess, struck me forcibly: it was the sound of
water. We were entering a deep gorge and approaching a
mountain-stream that was overflowing its banks.[1] The rumbling increased, the damp grass became thicker and taller and
the bushes closer, while the horizon gradually narrowed. Now
and then bright lights appeared here and there against the
dark background of the hills, and vanished instantly.

'Tell me, please, what are those lights?' I asked in a whisper of a Tartar riding beside me.

'Don't you know?' he replied.

'No.'

'The hillsmen have tied straw to poles and are waving it
about alight.'

'Why are they doing that?'

'So that everyone should know that the Russians have
come. Oh, oh! What a bustle is going on now in the *aouls*!
Everybody's dragging his belongings into the ravine,' he said
laughing.

'Why, do they already know in the mountains that a detachment is on its way?' I asked him.

'How can they help knowing? They always know. Our people are like that.'

'Then Shamyl [2] too is preparing for action?' I asked.

'No,' he answered, shaking his head, 'Shamyl won't go into
action; Shamyl will send his *naibs*,[3] and he himself will look
on through a telescope from above.'

'Does he live far away?'

---

[1] In the Caucasus rivers are apt to overflow in July. L. T.
[2] Shamyl was the leader (in 1834-59) of the Caucasian hill-tribes
in their resistance to Russia.
[3] A *naib* was a man to whom Shamyl had entrusted some adminis-
trative office. L. T.

'Not far. Some eight miles to the left.'

'How do you know?' I asked. 'Have you been there?'

'I have. Our people have all been.'

'Have you seen Shamyl?'

'Such as we don't see Shamyl! There are a hundred, three hundred, a thousand *murids*[4] all round him, and Shamyl is in the centre,' he said, with an expression of servile admiration.

Looking up, it was possible to discern that the sky, now cleared, was beginning to grow lighter in the east and the pleiades to sink towards the horizon, but the ravine through which we were marching was still damp and gloomy.

Suddenly a little way in front of us several lights flashed through the darkness; at the same moment some bullets flew whizzing past amid the surrounding silence [and sharp abrupt firing could be heard and loud cries, as piercing as cries of despair but expressing instead of fear such a passion of brutal audacity and rage that one could not but shudder at hearing it.] It was the enemy's advanced picket. The Tartars who composed it whooped, fired at random, and then ran in different directions.

All became silent again. The general called up an interpreter. A Tartar in a white Circassian coat rode up to him and, gesticulating and whispering, talked with him for some time.

'Colonel Khasánov! Order the cordon to take open order,' commanded the general with a quiet but distinct drawl.

The detachment advanced to the river, the black hills and gorges were left behind, the dawn appeared. The vault of the heavens, in which a few pale stars were still dimly visible, seemed higher; the sunrise glow beyond shone brightly in the east, a fresh penetrating breeze blew from the west and the white mists rose like steam above the rushing stream.

---

[4] The word *murid* has several meanings, but here it denotes something between an adjutant and a bodyguard.

# CHAPTER VIII

Our guide pointed out a ford and the cavalry vanguard, followed by the general, began crossing the stream. The water
which reached to the horses' chests rushed with tremendous
force between the white boulders which here and there appeared on a level with its surface, and formed foaming and
gurgling ripples round the horses' legs. The horses, surprised
by the noise of the water, lifted their heads and pricked their
ears, but stepped evenly and carefully against the current on
the uneven bottom of the stream. Their riders lifted their feet
and their weapons. The infantry, literally in nothing but their
shirts, linked arm in arm by twenties and holding above the
water their muskets to which their bundles of clothing were
fastened, made great efforts (as the strained expression of
their faces showed) to resist the force of the current. The
mounted artillerymen with loud shouts drove their horses into
the water at a trot. The guns and green ammunition wagons,
over which the water occasionally splashed, rang against the
stony bottom, but the sturdy little horses, churning the water,
pulled at the traces in unison and with dripping manes and
tails clambered out on the opposite bank.

As soon as the crossing was accomplished the general's
face suddenly assumed a meditative and serious look and he
turned his horse and, followed by the cavalry, rode at a trot
down a broad glade which opened out before us in the midst
of the forest. A cordon of mounted Cossacks was scattered
along the skirts of the forest.

In the woods we noticed a man on foot dressed in a Circassian coat and wearing a tall cap—then a second and a third.
One of the officers said: 'Those are Tartars.' Then a puff of
smoke appeared from behind a tree, a shot, and another.
. . . Our rapid fire drowns the enemy's. Only now and then
a bullet, with a slow sound like the buzzing of a bee's wings,
passes by and proves that the firing is not all ours. Now the
infantry at a run and the guns at a trot pass into the cordon.
You can hear the boom of the guns, the metallic sounds of

flying grape-shot, the hissing of rockets, and the crackle of musketry. Over the wide glade on all sides you can see cavalry, infantry, and artillery. Puffs of smoke mingle with the dew-covered verdure and the mist. Colonel Khasánov, approaching the general at full gallop, suddenly reins in his horse.

'Your Excellency, shall we order the cavalry to charge?' he says, raising his hand to his cap. 'The enemy's colours [1] are in sight,' and he points with his whip to some mounted Tartars in front of whom ride two men on white horses with bits of blue and red stuff fastened to poles in their hands.

'Go, and God be with you, Iván Mikháylovich!' says the general.

The colonel turns his horse sharply round, draws his sword, and shouts 'Hurrah!'

'Hurrah! Hurrah! Hurrah!' comes from the ranks, and the cavalry gallop after him. . . .

Everyone looks on with interest: there is a colour, another, a third and a fourth. . . .

The enemy, not waiting for the attack, hides in the wood and thence opens a small-arms fire. Bullets come flying more and more frequently.

'*Quel charmant coup d'oeil!*' [2] says the general, rising slightly, English fashion, in his saddle on his slim-legged black horse.

'*Charmant!*' answers the major, rolling his r's, and striking his horse he rides up to the general: '*C'est un vrai plaisir que la guerre dans un aussi beau pays,*' [3] he says.

'*Et surtout en bonne compagnie,*' [4] replies the general with a pleasant smile.

The major bows.

At that moment a hostile cannon-ball flies past with a dis-

---

[1] The colours among the hillsmen correspond to those of our troops, except that every *dzhigit* or 'brave' among them may make his own colours and carry them. L. T.
[2] 'What a charming view.'
[3] 'Charming . . . War in such beautiful country is a real pleasure.'
[4] 'Especially in good company.'

agreeable whiz, and strikes something. We hear behind us the moan of a wounded man.

This moaning strikes me so strangely that the warlike scene instantly loses all its charm for me. But no one except myself seems to notice it: the major laughs with apparently greater gusto, another officer repeats with perfect calm the first words of a sentence he had just been saying, the general looks the other way and with the quietest smile says something in French.

'Shall we reply to their fire?' asks the commander of the artillery, galloping up.

'Yes, frighten them a bit!' carelessly replies the general, lighting a cigar.

The battery takes up its position and the firing begins. The earth groans under the shots, the discharges flash out incessantly, and smoke, through which it is scarcely possible to distinguish the artillerymen moving round their guns, veils your sight.

The *aoul* has been bombarded. Colonel Khasánov rides up again, and at the general's command gallops towards the *aoul*. The war-cry is again heard and the cavalry disappears in the cloud of dust it has raised.

The spectacle was truly magnificent. The one thing that spoilt the general impression for me—who took no part in the affair and was unaccustomed to it—was that this movement and the animation and the shouting appeared unnecessary. The comparison involuntarily suggested itself to me of a man swinging his arms vigorously to cut the air with an axe.

## CHAPTER IX

Our troops had taken possession of the village and not a single soul of the enemy remained in it when the general and his suite, to which I had attached myself, rode up to it.

The long clean huts, with their flat earthen roofs and shapely chimneys, stood on irregular stony mounds between which flowed a small stream. On one side were green gardens

with enormous pear and small plum trees brightly lit up by
the sun, on the other strange upright shadows, the perpen-
dicular stones of the cemetery, and long poles with balls and
many-coloured flags fastened to their ends. (These marked
the graves of *dzhigits*.)

The troops were drawn up outside the gates.

['Well, how about it, Colonel?' said the general. 'Let them
loot. I see they are terribly anxious to,' he added with a smile,
pointing at the Cossacks.

You cannot imagine how striking was the contrast between
the carelessness with which the general uttered these words,
and their import and the military surroundings.]

A moment later, dragoons, Cossacks, and infantry spread with
evident delight through the crooked lanes and in an instant
the empty village was animated again. Here a roof crashes,
an axe rings against the hard wood of a door that is being
forced open, here a stack of hay, a fence, a hut, is set on fire
and a pillar of thick smoke rises up in the clear air. Here is
a Cossack dragging along a sack of flour and a carpet, there a
soldier, with a delighted look on his face, brings a tin basin
and some rag out of a hut, another is trying with outstretched
arms to catch two hens that struggle and cackle beside a
fence, a third has somewhere discovered an enormous pot of
milk and after drinking some of it throws the rest on the
ground with a loud laugh.

The battalion with which I had come from Fort N. was also
in the *aoul*. The captain sat on the roof of a hut and sent thin
whiffs of cheap tobacco smoke through his short pipe with
such an expression of indifference on his face that on seeing
him I forgot that I was in a hostile *aoul* and felt quite at
home.

'Ah, you are here too?' he said when he noticed me.

The tall figure of Lieutenant Rosenkranz flitted here and
there in the village. He gave orders unceasingly and appeared
exceedingly engrossed in his task. I saw him with a trium-
phant air emerge from a hut followed by two soldiers leading
an old Tartar. The old man, whose only clothing consisted of

a mottled tunic all in rags and patchwork trousers, was so frail that his arms, tightly bound behind his bent back, seemed scarcely to hold onto his shoulders, and he could scarcely drag his bare crooked legs along. His face and even part of his shaven head were deeply furrowed. His wry toothless mouth kept moving beneath his close-cut moustache and beard, as if he were chewing something; but a gleam still sparkled in his red lashless eyes which clearly expressed an old man's indifference to life.

Rosenkranz asked him, through an interpreter, why he had not gone away with the others.

'Where should I go?' he answered, looking quietly away.

'Where the others have gone,' someone remarked.

'The *dzhigits* have gone to fight the Russians, but I am an old man.'

'Are you not afraid of the Russians?'

'What will the Russians do to me? I am old,' he repeated, again glancing carelessly round the circle that had formed about him.

Later, as I was returning, I saw that old man bareheaded, with his arms tied, being jolted along behind the saddle of a Cossack, and he was looking round with the same expression of indifference on his face. He was needed for the exchange of prisoners.

I climbed onto the roof and sat down beside the captain.

[A bugler who had vodka and provisions was sent for. The captain's calmness and equanimity involuntarily produced an effect on me. We ate roasted pheasant and chatted, without at all reflecting that the owners of that hut had not merely no desire to see us there but could hardly have imagined our existence.]

'There don't seem to have been many of the enemy,' I said, wishing to know his opinion of the action that had taken place.

'The enemy?' he repeated with surprise. 'The enemy was not there at all! Do you call those the enemy? . . . Wait till the evening when we go back, and you will see how they will speed us on our way: what a lot of them will pour out from there,' he said, pointing to a thicket we had passed in the morning.

'What is that?' I asked anxiously, interrupting the captain and pointing to a group of Don Cossacks who had collected round something not far from us.

A sound of something like a child's cry came from there, and the words:

'Stop . . . don't hack it . . . you'll be seen . . . Have you a knife, Evstignéich . . . Lend me a knife. . . .'

'They are up to something, the scoundrels . . .' replied the captain calmly.

But at that moment the young ensign, his comely face flushed and frightened, came suddenly running from behind a corner and rushed towards the Cossacks waving his arms.

'Don't touch it! Don't kill it!' he cried in a childish voice.

Seeing the officer, the Cossacks stepped apart and released a little white kid. The young ensign was quite abashed, muttered something, and stopped before us with a confused face. Seeing the captain and me on the roof he blushed still more and ran leaping towards us.

'I thought they were killing a child,' he said with a bashful smile.

## CHAPTER X

The general went ahead with the cavalry. The battalion with which I had come from Fort N. remained in the rear-guard. Captain Khlópov's and Lieutenant Rosenkranz's battalions retired together.

The captain's prediction was fully justified. No sooner had we entered the narrow thicket he had mentioned, than on both sides of us we caught glimpses of hillsmen mounted and on foot, and so near were they that I could distinctly see how some of them ran stooping, rifle in hand, from one tree to another.

The captain took off his cap and piously crossed himself,

some of the older soldiers did the same. From the wood were heard war-cries and the words '*Iay giaour*', '*Urus! iay!*' Sharp short rifle-shots, following one another fast, whizzed on both sides of us. Our men answered silently with a running fire, and only now and then remarks like the following were made in the ranks: 'See where *he*[1] fires from! It's all right for him inside the wood. We ought to use cannon,' and so forth.

Our ordnance was brought out, and after some grape-shot had been fired the enemy seemed to grow weaker, but a moment later and at every step taken by our troops, the enemy's fire again grew hotter and the shouting louder.

We had hardly gone seven hundred yards from the village before enemy cannon-balls began whistling over our heads. I saw a soldier killed by one. . . . But why should I describe the details of that terrible picture which I would myself give much to be able to forget!

Lieutenant Rosenkranz kept firing, and incessantly shouted in a hoarse voice at the soldiers and galloped from one end of the cordon to the other. He was rather pale and this suited his martial countenance very well.

The good-looking young ensign was in raptures: his beautiful dark eyes shone with daring, his lips were slightly smiling, and he kept riding up to the captain and begging permission to charge.

'We will repel them,' he said persuasively, 'we certainly will.'

'It's not necessary,' replied the captain abruptly. 'We must retreat.'

The captain's company held the skirts of the wood, the men lying down and replying to the enemy's fire. The captain in his shabby coat and shabby cap sat silent on his white horse, with loose reins, bent knees, his feet in his stirrups, and did not stir from his place. (The soldiers knew and did their work so well that there was no need to give them any orders.) Only at rare intervals he raised his voice to shout at those who ex-

---

[1] *He* is a collective noun by which the soldiers indicate the enemy. L. T.

posed their heads. There was nothing at all martial about the
captain's appearance, but there was something so sincere and
simple in it that I was unusually struck by it. 'It is he who is
really brave,' I involuntarily said to myself.

He was just the same as I had always seen him: the same
calm movements, the same guileless expression on his plain
but frank face, only his eyes, which were brighter than usual,
showed the concentration of one quietly engaged on his duties. 'As I had always seen him' is easily said, but how many
different shades have I noticed in the behaviour of others; one
wishing to appear quieter, another sterner, a third merrier,
than usual, but the captain's face showed that he did not even
see why he should appear anything but what he was.

The Frenchman at Waterloo who said, '*La garde meurt, mais
ne se rend pas*,' [2] and other, particularly French, heroes who
uttered memorable sayings were brave, and really uttered remarkable words, but between their courage and the captain's
there was this difference, that even if a great saying had in
any circumstance stirred in the soul of my hero, I am convinced that he would not have uttered it: first because by uttering a great saying he would have feared to spoil a great
deed, and secondly because when a man feels within himself
the capacity to perform a great deed no talk of any kind is
needed. That, I think, is a peculiar and a lofty characteristic of
Russian courage, and that being so, how can a Russian heart
help aching when our young Russian warriors utter trivial
French phrases intended to imitate antiquated French chiv-
alry?

Suddenly from the side where our young ensign stood with
his platoon we heard a not very hearty or loud 'Hurrah!' Looking round to where the shout came from, I saw some thirty
soldiers with sacks on their shoulders and muskets in their
hands managing with very great difficulty to run across a
ploughed field. They kept stumbling, but nevertheless ran on
and shouted. In front of them, sword in hand, galloped the
young ensign.

---

[2] 'The Guard dies, but does not surrender.'

They all disappeared into the wood. . . .

After a few minutes of whooping and clatter a frightened horse ran out of the wood, and soldiers appeared bringing back the dead and wounded. Among the latter was the young ensign. Two soldiers supported him under his arms. He was as pale as a sheet, and his pretty head, on which only a shadow remained of the warlike enthusiasm that had animated him a few minutes before, was dreadfully sunk between his shoulders and drooped on his chest. There was a small spot of blood on the white shirt beneath his unbuttoned coat.

'Ah, what a pity!' I said, involuntarily turning away from this sad spectacle.

'Of course it's a pity,' said an old soldier, who stood leaning on his musket beside me with a gloomy expression on his face. 'He's not afraid of anything. How can one do such things?' he added, looking intently at the wounded lad. 'He was still foolish and now he has paid for it!'

'And you?' I asked. 'Are you afraid?'

'What do you expect?'


## CHAPTER XI

Four soldiers were carrying the ensign on a stretcher and behind them an ambulance soldier was leading a thin, broken-winded horse with two green boxes on its back containing surgical appliances. They waited for the doctor. Some officers rode up to the stretcher and tried to cheer and comfort the wounded lad.

'Well, friend Alánin, it will be some time before you will dance again with castanets,' said Lieutenant Rosenkranz, riding up to the stretcher with a smile.

He probably supposed that these words would raise the young ensign's spirits, but as far as one could judge by the latter's coldly sad look the words had not the desired effect.

The captain rode up too. He looked intently at the wounded man and his usually calm and cold face expressed sincere

sympathy. 'Well, my dear Anatól Ivánich,' he said, in a voice
of tender sympathy such as I never expected from him, 'evidently it was God's will.'

The wounded lad looked round and his pale face lit up
with a sad smile. 'Yes, I disobeyed you.'

'Say rather, it was God's will,' repeated the captain.

The doctor when he arrived, [as far as could be judged by
the shakiness of his legs and the redness of his eyes, was in no
fit condition to bandage the patient: however, he] took from
his assistant bandages, a probe, and another instrument, rolled
up his sleeves and stepped up to the ensign with an encourag-
ing smile.

'So it seems they have made a hole in a sound spot for you
too,' he said in a carelessly playful tone. 'Let me see.'

The ensign obeyed, but the look he gave the merry doctor
expressed astonishment and reproof which the inebriated prac-
tioner did not notice. He touched the wound so awkwardly,
quite unnecessarily pressing on it with his unsteady fingers,
that the wounded ensign, driven beyond the limits of endurance, pushed away his hand with a deep groan.

'Let me alone!' he said in a scarcely audible voice. 'I shall
die anyway.'

[Then, addressing the captain, he said with difficulty:
'Please, Captain . . . yesterday I lost . . . twenty rubles to
Drónov. . . . When my things are sold . . . let him be
paid.']

With those words he fell back, and five minutes later when
I passed the group that had formed around him, and asked a
soldier, 'How is the ensign?' the answer was, 'Passing away.'

# CHAPTER XII

It was late in the day when the detachment, formed into a
broad column and singing, approached the Fort.

[The general rode in front and by his merry countenance
one could see that the raid had been successful. In fact, with

little loss, we had that day been in Mukay *aoul*—where from immemorial times no Russian foot had trod.

The Saxon, Kaspar Lavréntich, narrated to another officer that he had himself seen how three Chechens had aimed straight at his breast. In the mind of Ensign Rosenkranz a complete story of the day's action had formulated itself. Captain Khlópov walked with thoughtful face in front of his company, leading his little white horse by its bridle.]

The sun had hidden behind the snowy mountain range and threw its last rosy beams on a long thin cloud stretching motionless across the clear horizon. The snow peaks began to disappear in purple mist and only their top outline was visible, wonderfully distinct in the crimson sunset glow. The delicate moon, which had risen long since, began to grow pale against the deep azure. The green of the grass and trees was turning black and becoming covered with dew. The dark masses of troops moved with measured sounds over the luxuriant meadows. Tambourines, drums, and merry songs were heard from various sides. The voice of the second tenor of the Sixth Company rang out with full force and the sounds of his clear chest-notes, full of feeling and power, floated through the clear evening air.

# A BILLIARD-MARKER'S NOTES*

It was going on for three when it happened. The gentlemen
playing were 'the big guest' (as our people called him), the
prince (who always goes about with him), the gentleman with
whiskers, the little hussar, Oliver (the one who has been an
actor), and the *pan*.[1] There were a good many people.

The big guest was playing with the prince. I just go round
the table with the rest in my hand, counting 'ten and forty-
eight, twelve and forty-eight.' Everybody knows what it is to
be a billiard-marker. You haven't had a bite all day, nor slept
for two nights, but you must keep calling the score and taking
the balls out. I go on counting and look round—there's a new
gentleman coming in at the door. He looks and looks and then
sits down on the sofa. All right.

'Who may that be?—Of what class, I mean?' think I to myself. He was well dressed—oh, very smartly—all his clothes
looked as if they had just come out of a bandbox: fine cloth
checked trousers, short fashionable coat, a plush waistcoat, and
a gold chain with all sorts of little things hanging from it.

Handsomely dressed, but still handsomer himself: slim, tall,
hair brushed to the front, latest fashion, and with a red and
white complexion—in a word, a fine fellow.

Of course, in our business we see all sorts of people: the
grandest that ever were and much trash also, so that though

---

* While still in the Caucasus Tolstoy wrote this story with rapt concentration and enthusiasm in four days. He said he valued it more
highly than his two previously completed works—*Childhood* and
*The Raid*. It has a scant autobiographical framework in the external facts of gambling with a billiard-marker and in the hero's first
sexual experience.
[1] *Pan* in Polish and Ukrainian means 'squire' or 'gentleman.'

you are a marker you fit in with people, if you are artful
enough I mean.

I looked at the gentleman and noticed that he was sitting
quietly and did not know anybody, and his clothes were as
new as could be. So I think to myself: 'He is either a foreigner
—an Englishman—or some count who has turned up. He
bears himself well although he is young.' Oliver was sitting
beside him and even moved to make room for him.

The game was finished—the big guest had lost and shouted
at me:

'You always blunder! You keep looking at something else
instead of counting properly.'

He swore, threw down the cue, and went out. What can you
make of it? He'll play a fifty-ruble game with the prince of an
evening, but now when he loses a bottle of Burgundy he's
quite beside himself. He's that kind of character! Sometimes he
plays with the prince till two in the morning. They don't put
their stakes in the pockets,[2] and I know they haven't either of
them got any money, but they just swagger.

'Shall we play double or quits for twenty-five?'

'All right.'

But if you just dare to yawn or don't put a ball right—after
all, one is not made of stone—then they just jump down your
throat:

'We are not playing for chips, but for money!'

That one plagues me more than all the rest . . .

Well—so the prince says to the new gentleman, when the
big one has gone:

'Would you care to have a game with me?'

'With pleasure!' he says.

As long as he was sitting down he looked quite a sport, and
seemed to have plenty of confidence, but when he got up and
came to the table he was—not exactly timid—no, he was not
timid, but one could see he was upset. Whether he was uncomfortable in his new clothes, or frightened because every-

---

[2] The players put the money they staked in the pockets of the
billiard-table, and the player who pocketed a ball took the money
when he took the ball out.

body was looking at him, anyhow his confidence was gone. He walked somehow sideways, his pocket catching the table pockets. When chalking the cue he dropped the chalk, and when he did get a ball into a pocket he kept looking round and blushing. Not like the prince—he was used to it—he would chalk the cue and his hand, turn up his sleeve, and just smash the balls into the pockets, small as he was.

They played two or three games—I don't quite remember—and the prince put down the cue and said:

'Allow me to ask your name . . .'

'Nekhlyúdov,' he says.

'Didn't your father command a corps?'

'Yes,' he says.

Then they began talking quickly in French, and I didn't understand. Probably talking about their relations.

'*Au revoir*,' says the prince, 'I'm very glad to have made your acquaintance.'

He washed his hands and went out to get something to eat, but the other remained beside the table with his cue, shoving the balls about.

Of course everyone knows in our business that the ruder one is with a newcomer the better, so I began collecting the balls. He blushed and said:

'Can I go on playing?'

'Of course,' I says, 'that's what the billiard-table is for—to be played on.'

But I didn't look at him and put away the cues.

'Will you play with me?'

'Of course, sir,' say I.

I placed the balls.

'Is it to be a crawl?'

'What do you mean by a crawl?'

So I say: 'You pay half a ruble, and I crawl under the table if I lose.'

Of course never having seen such a thing it seemed funny to him and he laughed.

'Let's!' he says.

'All right. How much will you allow me?' I ask.

'Why, do you play worse than I?'

'Of course,' I say. 'I can see there are few players to match you.'

We began to play. He really thought himself a master at it. He banged the balls about dreadfully, and the *pan* sat there and kept saying:

'What a ball! What a stroke!'

What indeed! He could make strokes, but there was no calculation about it. Well, I lost the first game as is the usual thing, and began crawling under the table and groaning. Here Oliver and the *pan* jumped up and knocked with their cues.

'Splendid! Go on!' they said. 'Go on!'

Go on indeed! The *pan* especially . . . for half a ruble he would himself have been glad not only to crawl under the table but under the Blue Bridge. And then he shouted:

'Splendid!' he says. 'But you haven't swept up all the dust yet.'

I am Petrúshka the marker. Everybody knows me. It used to be Tyúrik the marker, but now it is Petrúshka.

But of course I did not show my game. I lost another one. 'I can't play level with you, sir,' I says.

He laughed. Then after I had won three games—and when he had a score of forty-nine and I nothing, I put my cue on the table and said: 'Will you make it double or quits, sir?'

'Quits, what do you mean?' he says.

'Either you'll owe me three rubles, or nothing,' I say.

'What?' he says. 'Am I playing you for money? You fool!' He even blushed.

Very well. He lost the game.

'Enough!' he says.

He got out his pocket-book, quite a new one bought at the *Magasin Anglais,* and opened it. I see that he wants to show off. It was chock full of notes, all hundred-ruble ones.

'No,' he says, 'there's no change there,' and he took three rubles out of his purse.

'There you are,' he says, 'two for the games, and the rest for you to have a drink.'

'Thank you very much,' I say. I saw he was a nice gentleman. One can do a little crawling for such as him. The pity was that he didn't want to play for money—'or else,' think I, 'I'd manage to get maybe twenty or even forty rubles of him.'

When the *pan* saw the young gentleman's money he says: 'Would you care to play a game with me? You play so splendidly!' he says, fawning on him like a fox.

'No,' he says, 'excuse me, please, I haven't time,' and he went away.

I don't know who that *pan* was. Someone nicknamed him 'the *pan*' and the name stuck to him. He'd sit all day long in the billiard-room looking on. He had been beaten and sworn at, and no one would play with him. He would bring his pipe and sit by himself and smoke. But he could play a careful game . . . the beast!

Well, Nekhlyúdov came a second and a third time and began coming often. He'd come in the morning and in the evening. Billiards, pool, snooker, he learnt them all. He grew bolder, got to know everybody, and began to play a decent game. Naturally, being a young man of good family and with money, everybody respected him. Only once he had a row with the big guest.

It was all about a trifle.

They played pool—the prince, the big guest, Nekhlyúdov, Oliver, and someone else. Nekhlyúdov stands by the stove talking to someone, it was the big one's turn to play. His ball happened to come just opposite the stove: there was not much room there, and he likes to play with a big swing.

Well, whether he didn't see Nekhlyúdov or did it on purpose, he took a big swing at the ball and hit Nekhlyúdov hard in the chest with the butt of his cue. The poor fellow even groaned a little. And what next? He didn't even say 'beg pardon'—the rude fellow—but went on without looking at him, and even muttered: 'Why do they shove themselves forward? It has made me lose a ball.' As if there was not plenty of room!

The other goes up to him, very pale, and says quite politely as if nothing had happened: 'You should apologize first, sir. You pushed me.'

'It's not the time for me to apologize. I ought to have won,' he says, 'and now that fellow will score off my ball.'

The other says again: 'You must apologize.'

'Be off!' he says. 'Pestering like this!' and keeps looking at his ball.

Nekhlyúdov came still nearer and took hold of his arm.

'You're a boor, sir,' he says.

For all that he's slim and young and rosy as a girl, yet his eyes glittered as fierce as if he were ready to eat him. The big guest is a strong man, and tall. Much bigger than Nekh- lyúdov.

'What?' he says. 'Do you call me a boor?'

And he shouts, and lifts his arm to strike him, but the others there jumped up, seized their arms, and dragged them apart.

They talk and talk—and Nekhlyúdov says:

'Let him give me satisfaction! He has insulted me,' he says —meaning that he wanted him to fight a duel. Of course they were gentlefolk—they have such customs . . . nothing can be done with them . . . in a word, they're gentlefolk!

'I won't give him any kind of satisfaction. He's only a boy— that's all he is. I'll pull his ears for him.'

'If you don't want to fight,' he says, 'you are not an honour- able man.' And he himself was almost weeping.

'And you're just an urchin—it's impossible for you to insult me!'

Well, they got them apart and took them into separate rooms, as is usually done. Nekhlyúdov was friendly with the prince.

'For God's sake go and persuade him to accept a duel,' he says. 'He was drunk, but he may have come to his senses by this time. The affair must not end like this.'

The prince went. The big one says:

'I have fought duels and I have fought in war, but I won't fight a mere lad—I don't want to: that's all about it.'

Well, they talked and talked and finally left off; only the big guest left off coming to our place.

As far as sensitiveness went Nekhlyúdov was like a cockerel, very ambitious, but in other matters he had no sense at all. I remember once the prince says to him: 'Whom have you with you here?'

'Nobody,' he says.

'How's that—nobody?'

'Why should there be anybody?'

'What do you mean by "Why should there be anybody?"'

'I've lived by myself up to now,' he says, 'so why is it impossible?'

'Lived by yourself? You don't mean it!'

And the prince roars with laughter, and the whiskered gentleman too. They did make fun of him!

'So you've never . . . ?' they say.

'Never!'

They died with laughter. Of course I understood at once why they laughed at him so. I watched to see what would come of it.

'Come along now,' says the prince. 'At once!'

'No, not on any account,' he says.

'Come, that's enough, it's too ridiculous,' he says. 'Have a drink to buck you up, and come along.'

I brought them a bottle of champagne. They drank it, and took the youngster along.

They returned after midnight and sat down to supper. There were a lot of them—all the very best: Atánov, Prince Rázin, Count Shustákh, and Mírtsov. They all congratulate Nekhlyúdov and laugh. They called me in, and I see they are all rather gay.

'Congratulate the gentleman!' they say.

'On what?' I ask.

Whatever did he call it? . . . On his *initiation* or *instigation*—I don't quite remember.

'I have the honour to congratulate you,' I say.

And he sits there, quite red, and only smiles. How they laughed!

Well, they come afterwards into the billiard-room all very merry, but Nekhlyúdov was unlike himself: his eyes were bleared, his lips twitching, and he kept hiccoughing and couldn't say a word properly. Of course, it being the first time, he was feeling bowled over. He went up to the table, put his elbows on it, and said:

'To you it seems funny, but I am sad. Why did I do it? I shall not forgive myself, or you, prince, for it all my life!'

And he bursts into tears and weeps. Of course he had drunk too much and didn't know himself what he was saying. The prince went up to him smiling.

'That's enough!' he says. 'It's a mere trifle! . . . Come home, Anatole.'

'I won't go anywhere. Why did I do it?' And he sobs. He wouldn't go away from the billiard-table, and that was all there was to it. What it is when a fellow is young and not used to it . . . And he spoilt the table there and then. Next day he paid eighty rubles for having cut the cloth.

So he often used to come to us. Once he came in with the prince and the whiskered gentleman who always went about with the prince. He was an official, or a retired officer— Heaven only knows—but the gentlemen all called him 'Fedót'. He had high cheekbones and was very ugly, but dressed well and came in a carriage. Why the gentlemen liked him so, God only knows. It's 'Fedót, Fedót,' and you see them treating him to food and drink, paying for him. But he was a desperate fellow! If he lost he did not pay, but if he won—that was different! The big guest has abused him and beaten him before my eyes, and challenged him to a duel. . . . But he always went about arm-in-arm with the prince. 'You'd be lost without me!' he says. 'I'm Fedót and the others are not.' Such a wag.

Well, so they come in, and say:

'Let's play pool, the three of us.'

'All right,' they say.

They began playing for three-ruble stakes. Nekhlyúdov and the prince jabber together. 'You should just see,' he says, 'what a foot she has!'

'Never mind her foot—it's her hair that's so beautiful.'

Of course they didn't attend to the game but only talked together. But Fedót knows his business and plays trickily while they miss or run in. And he wins six rubles of each of

them. Heaven only knows what accounts he had with the
prince—they never paid one another any money; but Nekhlyúdov got out two three-ruble notes and held them out to him.

'No,' he says, 'I won't take the money from you. Let's play
an ordinary game—double or quits, I mean either twice as
much or nothing.'

I placed the balls for them. Fedót took odds and they began
the game. Nekhlyúdov made strokes just to show off, and when
he had a chance to pocket a ball and run out, he says: 'No, I
don't want it—it's too easy,' but Fedót doesn't neglect his business and keeps on scoring. Of course he didn't show what he
could do, but won the game as if by chance.

'Let's play double or quits again,' he says.

'All right.'

He won again.

'We began with a trifle,' he says. 'I don't want to take so
much from you. Double or quits again, yes?'

'Yes.'

Say what one will one's sorry to lose fifty rubles, and Nekhlyúdov himself says: 'Let's have double or quits again.' So it
went on and on, more and more. At last he'd lost two hundred
and eighty rubles. Fedót knows all the tricks: he would lose
a single stake and win a double; and the prince sits there and
sees that things are getting serious.

'Assez,' he says, 'assez!'

Not a bit of it! They keep increasing the stakes.

At last Nekhlyúdov owed him over five hundred rubles.
Fedót puts down his cue and says:

'Haven't we had enough? I am tired,' he says.

But really he was ready to play till sunrise if there was
money in it—all his craftiness of course. The other was still
more anxious to go on. 'Let's play, let's play!' he says.

'No, really I'm tired . . . Come upstairs. You can take your
revenge there.'

At our place gentlemen played cards upstairs. They'd start
with preference and then go on to a gambling game.

Well, from that day on Fedót netted Nekhlyúdov so that

he began coming to us every day. They'd have a game or two, and then it was 'Upstairs, upstairs!'

What they did there Heaven only knows, but Nekhlyúdov became a different man, and everything was flourishing with Fedót.

Formerly Nekhlyúdov had been smart, clean, his hair well brushed; but now he was only like his real self in the morning; after having been upstairs he would come down dishevelled, with fluff on his coat and his hands dirty.

One day he comes down with the prince like that, pale, his lips trembling, and disputing about something.

'I won't permit *him*,' he says, 'to tell me I am . . .'—however did he put it? . . . 'unwell-mannered' or something like that—'and that *he* won't win against me. I have paid *him*,' he says, 'ten thousand rubles so *he* ought to be more careful before others.'

'Come now,' says the prince, 'is it worth being angry with Fedót?'

'No,' he says, 'I won't put up with it.'

'Stop!' he says. 'How can you lower yourself so far as to have an affair with Fedót?'

'But outsiders were present.'

'What if there were outsiders! If you like, I'll make him beg your pardon at once.'

'No,' says he.

And they jabbered something in French that I did not understand. Well, what do you think? That same evening they had supper with Fedót and the friendship continued.

Well, he'd sometimes come along.

'How is it?' he'd say. 'Do I play well?'

Of course it's our business to please everyone. 'Very well,' I say. But lord!—he just knocks the balls about without any kind of judgment. And ever since he got thick with Fedót he always played for money. Before that he did not like playing for any kind of stakes, not even for a lunch or champagne. Sometimes the prince would say:

'Let's play for a bottle of champagne.'

'No,' he'd say, 'I'd rather just order one. Hullo there! Bring a bottle of champagne!'

But now he began to play only for money. He'd walk up and down all day at our place either playing billiards with someone or going upstairs. So I thinks to myself: 'Why should others get it all, and not me?'

'Why haven't you played with me for such a long time, sir?' I says.

And we started playing.

When I had won some five rubles of him: 'Shall we play double or quits, sir?' I says.

He doesn't answer—doesn't say 'Fool!' as he did before. So we play double or quits again and again. I won some eighty rubles of him. Well, what d'you think? He played with me every day. Only he'd wait till no one else was there, because of course he was ashamed to play with a marker. One day he happened to get a bit excited when he already owed me some sixty rubles.

'Shall we play for the whole amount?' he says.

'All right,' I say.

I won.

'One hundred and twenty to one hundred and twenty?'

'All right.'

I won again.

'Two hundred and forty to two hundred and forty?'

'Isn't that too much?' I says.

He doesn't answer. We play. I win again.

'Four hundred and eighty to four hundred and eighty?'

I say: 'Why should I take advantage of you, sir? Play for a hundred rubles or leave it as it is.'

How he did shout! And how quiet he used to be!

'I'll knock you to bits!' he says. 'Either you play or you don't!'

Well, I see there is no help for it.

'Let it be three hundred and eighty,' I says.

Of course I meant to lose.

I allowed him forty points. His score was fifty-two and mine thirty-six. He potted the yellow and scored eighteen,[3] but left my ball standing well.

I struck the ball hard to make it rebound. No good, it cannoned and ran in and won the game again.

'Listen, Peter,' he says—he did not call me 'Petrúshka'—'I can't pay you the whole now, but in two months' time I could pay you three thousand, if necessary.'

And he flushed quite red and his voice even trembled.

'Very good, sir,' I says, and put down the cue. He paced up and down a bit and the perspiration just ran down his face.

'Peter,' he says, 'let's play for the whole amount!'

He was nearly crying.

I say:

'What, play again, sir?'

'Do please!'

And he hands me the cue himself. I took the cue and flung the balls on the table so that they fell onto the floor—of course I had to show off—and I say: 'All right, sir!'

He was in such a hurry that he himself picked a ball up. I thought to myself: 'I shan't get the seven hundred away, so I might as well lose.' So I purposely played badly. And what do you think?

'Why,' he says, 'do you play badly on purpose?'

And his hands tremble, and when a ball rolls towards a pocket he spreads out his fingers, his mouth goes awry, and he stretches his head and his hands towards the pocket. So that I say:

'That won't help, sir!'

Well, when he had won that game, I says:

'You'll owe me a hundred and eighty rubles and a hundred and fifty games—and I'll go and have supper.'

I put down my cue and went away.

I sit down at a little table by the door and look to see what he'll do. What d'you think? He walks up and down—thinking

---

[3] In the game of 'five balls' to pot the yellow ball in the middle pocket scores twelve, and to run in off it counts six, so that the two together at one stroke scores eighteen.

I expect that nobody sees him—and pulls so at his hair! Then he walks about again muttering to himself, and suddenly gives another pull!

After that we didn't see him for eight days or so. Then he came in once into the dining-room, looking as gloomy as anything, but didn't go into the billiard-room.

The prince noticed him.

'Come, let's have a game!' he said.

'No,' he says, 'I won't play any more.'

'Oh, nonsense! Come along!'

'No,' he says, 'I won't. It would do you no good for me to come and it would do me harm.'

So he didn't come for another ten days. Then in the holidays he looked in one day in a dress suit—evidently he had been paying calls—and remained for the rest of the day playing all the time: next day he came again, and the day after, and then things went on in the old way. I wanted to play with him again.

'No, I won't play with you,' he says, 'but come to me in a month's time for the hundred and eighty rubles I owe you and you shall have them.'

All right. A month later I went to him.

'On my word,' he says, 'I haven't got it, but come back on Thursday.'

I went on the Thursday. He had such an excellent little flat.

'Is the master at home?' I says.

'Not up yet,' they tell me.

'All right. I'll wait.'

His valet was a serf of his own—an old, grey-haired fellow, simple and not up to any tricks. So we had a talk together.

'What are we living here for?' he says. 'My master is running quite to waste, and we get no honour nor profit in this Petersburg of yours. When we came from the country we thought we'd be as it used to be when the old master—the Kingdom of Heaven be his!—was alive; visiting princes, counts, and generals. We thought we'd get some queenly countess with a dowry, and live like a nobleman; but it turns out that we do nothing but run from one restaurant to another—quite bad!

Princess Rtíshcheva, you know, is an aunt of ours, and Prince Borotýnzev is our godfather. What d'you think? He's only been to see them once, at Christmas, and hasn't shown his nose there since. Even their servants laugh at me: "Seems your master doesn't take after his papa!" they say. I once said to him:

' "Why don't you go to see your auntie, sir? She is sad at not having seen you so long."

' "It's dull there, Demyánych!" he says.

'Just look at that! The only pleasure he's found is at the restaurants. If only he were in public service somewhere— but no, he is only interested in cards and the like, and such doings never lead to any good . . . Eh, eh, we're ruining ourselves—ruining ourselves for nothing! We inherited from our deceased mistress—the Kingdom of Heaven be hers!—a very rich estate: more than a thousand serfs and more than three hundred thousand rubles' worth of forest land. He's mortgaged it all now, sold the forest, ruined the peasants, and nothing comes of it. In the master's absence a steward is more than a master, as is well known. What does the steward care? He skins the peasants completely, and there's an end of it. All he wants is to stuff his own pockets, though they all die of hunger. The other day two peasants came here to complain from the whole commune.

' "He's ruined the serfs completely," they said.

'Well, he read the complaints, gave the peasants ten rubles each and said: "I shall come myself soon. As soon as I receive money I'll settle up and leave town."

'But "settle up" indeed, when we keep making debts! Why, we have lived here the winter and have got through some eighty thousand rubles, and now there's not a ruble left in the house! And it's all because of his charitableness. Oh, what a simple gentleman he is—there are no words for it. It's because of that he is perishing, perishing just for nothing!'

And the old man almost wept.

Nekhlyúdov woke up about eleven and called me in.

'They haven't sent me the money, but it is not my fault,' he says. 'Shut the door.'

I shut it.

'Here,' he says, 'take this watch or this diamond pin and pawn it. They'll give you more than a hundred and eighty rubles for it, and when I get the money I will buy them out,' he says.

'All right, sir,' I say. 'If you have no money it can't be helped: let me have the watch—I'll pawn it for you.'

I could see myself that the watch was worth three hundred rubles.

Well, I pawned it for a hundred rubles and brought him the ticket.

'You'll owe me eighty rubles, and you can redeem the watch yourself,' I says.

Those eighty rubles are still owing me to this day!

So he kept coming to us every day again. I don't know what arrangements there were between them but he and the prince always went about together, or they went upstairs with Fedót to play cards. And they had some queer accounts among the three of them! One gave to another, the other to the third, but you could not at all make out who was owing whom.

And he came to us in this way almost every day for two years. Only he had lost his old manner: he became bold, and it got to such a pitch that at times he'd borrow a ruble from me to pay his cab fare; yet he still played with the prince for a hundred rubles a game.

He grew thin, sallow, and gloomy. He'd come in, order a glass of absinthe at once, have a snack, and wash it down with port wine, and then he would seem a bit brighter.

He came one day during Carnival, and began playing with some hussar.

'Do you want to have something on the game?' says the hussar.

'Certainly,' he says. 'How much?'

'Shall it be a bottle of burgundy?'

'All right.'

Well, the hussar won, and they sat down to dinner. They sat down, and Nekhlyúdov says at once:

'Simon, a bottle of Clos Vougeot—and mind it's properly warmed.'

Simon went out and brought some food, but no bottle.

'Well, and the wine?'

Simon ran out and brought the joint.

'Bring the wine,' says Nekhlyúdov.

Simon says nothing.

'Have you gone mad? We're finishing dinner and there's no wine. Who drinks it with the dessert?'

Simon ran out.

'The proprietor would like to see you,' he says.

Nekhlyúdov went quite red and jumped up from the table—

'What does he want?' he says.

The proprietor was standing at the door.

'I can't give you any more credit unless you pay me what you owe.'

'But I told you I'd pay at the beginning of next month!'

'As you please, but I can't go on giving credit and not receiving anything. As it is I lose tens of thousands by bad debts.'

'Oh, come, *mon cher*,' he says, 'surely you can trust me! Send up the bottle, and I will try to pay you as soon as possible.'

And he ran back.

'What did they call you away for?' asked the hussar.

'Just to ask me about something.'

'A little warm wine now would be just the thing,' says the hussar.

'Well, Simon, how about it?'

Poor Simon ran out again. Again there was no wine or anything. It was a bad lookout. Nekhlyúdov got up from the table and came to me.

'For God's sake, Petrúshka,' he says, 'let me have six rubles.'

He looked beside himself.

'I haven't got it, sir, on my word! As it is you're owing me a lot.'

'I'll give you forty rubles in a week's time for the six!'

'If I had it,' I says, 'I wouldn't dare refuse you, but really I haven't got it.'

And what do you think? He rushed out, clenching his teeth, and ran up and down the corridor like a madman, banging himself on the forehead.

'Oh, my God!' he says. 'What does it mean?'

He didn't even go back to the dining-room, but jumped into a carriage and drove off.

How they laughed! The hussar says:

'Where's the gentleman who was dining with me?'

'Gone,' they say.

'What do you mean—gone? What message did he leave?'

'He didn't leave any message,' they tell him. 'He just got in and drove away.'

'A fine goose!' he says.

'Well,' I think to myself, 'now he won't come for a long time, after such a disgrace.' But next day towards evening he came again, just the same. He went to the billiard-room with a box of some kind he had brought with him. He took off his overcoat.

'Let's play!' he says, looking from under his brows very cross.

We played a game.

'That's enough,' he says. 'Go and get me a pen and paper. I have to write a letter.'

Thinking nothing and guessing nothing, I brought the paper and put it on the table in the little room.

'It's all ready, sir,' I says.

Well, so he sat down at the table and wrote and wrote something; then he jumped up frowning.

'Go and see if my carriage has come!'

It happened on the Friday in Carnival Week, so none of our gentlemen were there: they had all gone to balls.

I was just going to find out about the carriage, but was hardly out of the door when he cried: 'Petrúshka! Petrúshka!' as if frightened of something.

I came back, and there he stood as white as a sheet, looking at me.

'You were pleased to call me, sir?' I says.

He was silent.

'What is it you want, sir?'

He was still silent.

'Oh, yes! Let's have another game,' he says.

Well, he won the game.

'Have I learnt to play well?' he says.

'Yes,' says I.

'That's it,' he says. 'Now go and find out about my carriage.'

And he paces up and down the room.

Without thinking anything, I went out onto the porch and saw that there was no carriage there at all, and went back.

As I go back it sounds as if someone had given a knock with a cue.

I go into the billiard-room—there's a strange smell.

I look: and there he lies on the floor covered with blood, with a pistol thrown down beside him. I was so frightened that I could not say a word.

He jerked his leg again and again and stretched himself. Then his throat rattled, and he stretched out like this.

And why such a sinful thing happened to him—I mean, why he ruined his soul—God alone knows: he left nothing but this paper behind, but I can't understand it at all.

Really, what things gentlemen do! . . . Gentlefolk—that's it—gentlefolk!


'God gave me everything man can desire: wealth, a name, intelligence, and noble aspirations. I wanted to enjoy myself and trampled in the mire all that was good in me.

'I am not dishonoured, not unfortunate, have committed no crime; but I have done worse—I have killed my feelings, my reason, my youth.

'I am enmeshed in a dirty net from which I cannot free myself and to which I cannot get used. I continually fall and fall, feel myself falling, and cannot stop.

'It would be easier if I were dishonoured, unfortunate, or a criminal. Then there would be some consolation of gloomy greatness in my despair. If I were dishonoured I could raise myself above the perception of honour held in our society and could despise it.

'If I were unfortunate I could complain. If I had committed a crime I might redeem it by repentance or by suffering punishment: but I am merely base, nasty—I know it and cannot raise myself.

'And what has ruined me? Had I some strong passion which could be my excuse? No.

'Sevens, aces, champagne, the yellow in the middle pocket, grey or rainbow-coloured currency notes, cigarettes, women who could be bought—those are my recollections!

'One terrible moment when I forgot myself, a humiliation I shall never wipe out, has made me recollect myself. I was horrified when I saw what an immeasurable gulf separates me from what I wished to be and might have been. In my imagination the dreams and thoughts of my youth reappeared.

'Where are those bright thoughts of life, of eternity, of God, which filled my soul so clearly and powerfully? Where is that force of love—not confined to any person—that filled my soul with such joyful warmth? Where is my hope of development, my sympathy with all that is excellent, my love of my relations, neighbours, work, and fame? Where is my sense of duty?

'I was insulted—and challenged the man to a duel and thought I had fully satisfied the demands of honour. I needed money to satisfy my vices and vanity, and I ruined a thousand families entrusted to me by God and did it without shame— I who so well understood those sacred obligations. A dishonourable man told me that I had no conscience and that I wished to steal—and I remained friends with him because he was a dishonourable man and told me that he had not meant to offend me. I was told that it was ridiculous to be chaste and I abandoned without regret the flower of my soul —my innocence—to a purchasable woman.

'And how good and happy I might have been had I trodden the path which on entering life my fresh mind and my child-

like, genuine feeling indicated to me! More than once I tried to
escape from the rut in which my life was moving and get back
to that bright path. I told myself: I will use all the will I have
—but I could not. When I remained alone I felt awkward and
afraid of myself. When I was with others I no longer heard
the inner voice at all, and sank lower and lower.

'At last I reached the terrible conviction that I could not
rise, and left off thinking of doing so and tried to forget myself; but hopeless remorse tormented me still more. Then the
idea—terrible to others but comforting to me—of suicide first
occurred to me. But in that respect also I was mean and base.
Only yesterday's stupid affair with the hussar gave me sufficient resolution to carry out my intention. Nothing honourable
remained in me—only vanity, and out of vanity I am doing
the one good action of my life. I formerly thought that the
proximity of death would uplift my soul. I was mistaken. In
a quarter of an hour I shall be no more, yet my views have
not changed at all. I still see, still hear, still think, in the same
way. There is the same strange inconsistency, inconsequence,
vacillation, and levity in my thoughts—so contrary to the
unity and clarity that man is—God knows why—able to con-
ceive of. Thoughts of what will be beyond the tomb and of
what will be said tomorrow about my death at Aunt Rtíshcheva's present themselves to me with equal force.'

# THE WOOD-FELLING

## A Cadet's Story*

◇◇◇◇◇◇

### CHAPTER I

In the middle of the winter of 185– a division of one battery
was on service with the detachment operating in that part of
the Térek Territory[1] called the Great Chéchnya. On the evening of February 14, knowing that the platoon which I, in the
absence of any officer was commanding, was to join a column
told off to fell wood next day, and having given and received
the necessary orders, I retired to my tent earlier than usual.
As I had not contracted the bad habit of warming my tent
with hot charcoal, I lay down without undressing on my bed,

---

* Tolstoy finished the third draft of this story in 1854 and it was
published the following year. It describes a military action that
took place at the beginning of 1853, in which Shamyl, leader of
the Caucasian hill tribes, opposed the attempt of a large Russian
force to cut down the forests from Khobi-Shavdonsky heights to
the Argunskoye gorge, in an effort to kill off the Chechenians in
this territory or drive them into the Black Mountains. Tolstoy distinguished himself in a major attack of this campaign in which his
battery silenced the guns of the enemy.

[1] The Térek Territory lies to the north-east of the Caucasian
Mountains. The Great and Little Chéchnya are districts in the
southern part of it.

which was supported on stakes driven into the ground, drew my fur cap over my eyes, tucked myself up in my sheepskin cloak, and fell into that peculiar, heavy, and deep sleep which comes at times of anxiety and when one is awaiting danger. The expectation of the next day's affair had this effect on me.

At three next morning, while it was still quite dark, the warm sheepskin was pulled off me and my eyes, heavy with sleep, were unpleasantly struck by the red light of a candle.

'Get up, please,' said a voice. I shut my eyes, unconsciously pulled the sheepskin back over myself, and again fell asleep. 'Get up, please,' said Dmítry once more, remorselessly shaking me by the shoulder: 'the infantry are starting.' The reality suddenly flashed on my mind, I sat up and jumped to my feet. After hurriedly drinking a glass of tea and washing myself with icy water I crept out of the tent and went to the 'park" (the place where the cannon were). It was dark, misty, and cold. The dim red light of the night-fires, which gleaming here and there in the camp showed up the figures of the sleepy soldiers who lay near them, seemed only to make the darkness more intense.

Near by, quiet regular snoring could be heard, and from farther off, sounds of movements, voices, and the clatter of the muskets of the infantry preparing to start. There was a smell of smoke, manure, torches, and mist; the morning air caused cold shivers to run down one's back, and one's teeth chattered involuntarily.

It was only by the snorting and occasional stamping of the horses harnessed to them that we could tell where the limbers and ammunition wagons stood in the impenetrable darkness; and only the fiery dots of the linstocks showed where the guns were. 'God be with us!' With these words came the clanging sound of the first gun moving, then the noise of the ammunition wagon—and the platoon started. We all took off our caps and crossed ourselves. Having occupied the interval between the infantry companies, the platoon stopped and waited a quarter of an hour for the whole column to collect and for the commander to appear.

'One of our men is missing, Nicholas Petróvich.' With these

words a black figure approached me, whom I only knew by
the voice to be the gun-sergeant of the platoon, Maksímov.

'Who is it?'

'Velenchúk is missing. He was there all the time they were
harnessing—I saw him myself—but now he's gone.'

As the column could not be expected to start at once, we
decided to send Corporal Antónov to look for Velenchúk.
Directly after that, several horsemen trotted past us in the
dark. They were the commander and his suite; and immediately the head of the column moved and started and so at
last did we also, but Antónov and Velenchúk were still ab-
sent. We had, however, hardly gone a hundred yards before
they both overtook us.

'Where was he?' I asked Antónov.

'Asleep in the "park".'

'Why, has he had a drop too much?'

'Oh, no.'

'Then how is it he fell asleep?'

'I can't make out.'

For about three hours we moved slowly on in silence and
darkness over some unploughed fields bare of snow and over
low bushes that crackled under the wheels of the gun-carriages.
At last, after we had crossed a shallow but extremely rapid
stream, we were stopped, and we heard the abrupt reports of
*vintóvkas*[2] in the direction of the vanguard.

These sounds as usual had a most exhilarating effect on
everyone. The detachment seemed to wake up: sounds of talking, movement, and laughter were heard in the ranks. Here
a soldier wrestled with a comrade, there another hopped from
foot to foot. Here was one chewing hard-tack, or to while
away the time shouldering and grounding arms. Meanwhile
the mist began to grow distinctly whiter in the east, the damp
became more intense, and the surrounding objects gradually
emerged from the gloom. I could already discern the green
gun-carriages and ammunition wagons, the brass of the guns

---

[2] The *vintóvka* was a long Asiatic rifle used by the Circassians
(Cherkéses). When firing, they rested the barrel on a support
formed by two thin spiked sticks tied at the top by a strap.

covered with moisture by the mist, the familiar figures of my soldiers, every minute detail of which I had involuntarily studied, the bay horses, and the lines of infantry with their bright bayonets, their bags, their ramrods, and the kettles they carried on their backs.

We were soon again moved forward a few hundred yards where there was no road, and then we were shown our position. To the right one could see the steep bank of a winding stream and the high wooden posts of a Tartar cemetery; to the left and in front a black strip was visible through the mist. The platoon unlimbered. The Eighth Company, which covered us, piled their muskets, and a battalion with axes and muskets went to the forest.

Before five minutes were over fires were crackling and smoking in all directions. The soldiers dispersed, blew the fires and stirred them with hands and feet, dragged logs and branches, while the forest resounded with the unceasing noise of hundreds of axes and the crashing of falling trees.

The artillery, with a certain rivalry of the infantry, heaped their pile high, and though it was already burning so that one could hardly come within two paces of it and thick black smoke was rising through the frozen branches, which the soldiers pressed down into the fire (and from which drops fell sizzling into the flames), and though the charcoal was glowing beneath and the grass was scorched all around, the soldiers were not satisfied, but kept throwing great logs on to the pile, feeding it with dry grass beneath and heaping it higher and higher.

When I came up to the fire to smoke a cigarette, Velenchúk, always officious, but to-day feeling guilty and bustling about more than any one, in a fit of zeal snatched a piece of charcoal from the fire with his bare hand and, after tossing it from hand to hand a couple of times, dropped it on the ground.

'Light a twig and hold it up,' said a soldier.

'No, better get a linstock, lad,' said another.

When I had at length lit my cigarette without the aid of Velenchúk, who was again trying to take a piece of charcoal in his hand, he rubbed his burnt fingers on the skirts of his sheepskin coat and then, probably for want of something else to do, lifted a large piece of plane-tree wood and swung it into the fire. When at last he felt free to rest a bit, he came close up to the fire, threw open his cloak which he wore like a mantle fastened by one button, spread out his legs, held out his big, black hands, and drawing his mouth a bit to one side, screwed up his eyes.

'Ah, I've gone and forgot my pipe. Here's a go, lads!' said he after a short silence, not addressing any one in particular.

## CHAPTER II

In Russia there are three predominant types of soldier under which the men of all our forces—whether line, guards, infantry, cavalry, artillery, army of the Caucasus, or what not—may be classified.

These principal types, including many sub-divisions and combinations, are:

1. The submissive;
2. The domineering;
3. The reckless.

The submissive are divided into (*a*) the calmly submissive and (*b*) the bustlingly submissive.

The domineering are divided into (*a*) the sternly domineering and (*b*) the diplomatically domineering.

The reckless are divided into (*a*) the amusingly reckless and (*b*) the viciously reckless.

The type most often met with—a type more lovable and attractive than the others and generally accompanied by the best Christian virtues,—meekness, piety, patience, and devotion to the will of God,—is the submissive type in general. The distinctive feature of the calmly submissive is his invincible resignation to and contempt for all the reverses of fate which may befall him; the distinctive features of the submissive drunkard are a mild, poetic disposition and sensibility; the distinctive feature of the bustlingly submissive is limited mental capacity combined with purposeless industry and zeal.

The domineering type in general is found chiefly among the higher grade of soldiers: the corporals, sergeants, sergeant-majors and so on. The first sub-division, the sternly domineering, is a noble, energetic, pre-eminently military type and does not exclude high poetic impulses (Corporal Antónov, with whom I wish to acquaint the reader, belonged to this type). The second sub-division, formed by the diplomatically domineering, has for some time past been increasing largely. A man of this type is always eloquent and literate,[1] wears pink shirts, won't eat out of the common pot, sometimes smokes tobacco of Mousátov's brand, and thinks himself much superior to the common soldier, but is rarely himself as good a soldier as the domineering of the first sub-division.

The reckless type, like the domineering type, is good in its first sub-division, the amusingly reckless, whose characteristic traits are irresistible mirth, great capacity of all kinds, and a highly gifted and daring nature. As with the domineering class, the second sub-division is bad; the viciously reckless are terribly bad, but to the honour of the Russian army it must be said that this type is very rare, and when found it is excluded from companionship by the public opinion of the soldiers themselves. Unbelief and a kind of boldness in vice are the chief traits characteristic of this class.

Velenchúk belonged to the bustlingly submissive. He was an Ukrainian by birth, had already served for fifteen years, and although not a showy or smart soldier he was simple-minded, kindly, extremely though often inopportunely zealous, and also exceedingly honest. I say exceedingly honest, because an incident had occurred the year before which made this characteristic quality of his very evident. It must be remembered that almost every soldier knows a trade. The most usual trades are tailoring and boot-making. Velenchúk taught himself the former, and judging from the fact that even Michael Doroféich, the sergeant-major, ordered clothes from him, he must have attained some proficiency at his craft. Last year,

---

[1] A distinction very frequently met with in Russian is between *literate* and *illiterate* people; i.e. between those who can and those who cannot read and write.

in camp, Velenchúk undertook to make a fine cloth coat for
Michael Doroféich; but that very night after he had cut out
the coat and measured out the trimmings and put them all under his pillow in the tent, a misfortune befell him: the cloth
that had cost *seven rubles*, disappeared during the night! Velenchúk, with tears in his eyes, trembling white lips and suppressed sobs, informed the sergeant-major of the occurrence.
Michael Doroféich was enraged. In the first moment of irritation he threatened the tailor; but afterwards, being a man
with means and kindly, he just waved his hand and did not
demand from Velenchúk payment of the value of the cloth. In
spite of all the fuss made by the fussy Velenchúk, in spite of
all the tears he shed when telling of his mishap, the thief was
not found. A strong suspicion fell on the viciously reckless soldier Chernóv, who slept in the same tent; but there were no
positive proofs. The diplomatically domineering Michael Doroféich, being a man with means and having some little business
transactions with the master-at-arms and the caterer of the
mess (the aristocracy of the battery), very soon forgot all
about the loss of his mufti coat. Not so Velenchúk. He did not
forget his misfortune. The soldiers said they feared at the time
that he might commit suicide or run away into the mountains,
so great was the effect of his mishap upon him. He neither ate
nor drank and could not even work, but was continually crying. When three days had passed he appeared, quite pale,
before Michael Doroféich, took with trembling fingers a gold
coin from under his cuff and gave it him. 'Heaven's my witness, Michael Doroféich, that it's all I have, and even that I
borrowed from Zhdánov,' said he, sobbing again; 'and the
other two rubles I swear I will also return as soon as I have
earned them. He' (whom 'he' meant Velenchúk did not himself know) 'has made me appear like a rascal before you. He—
with his loathsome, viper soul—he takes the last morsel from
his brother soldier, after I have served for fifteen years. . . .'
To the honour of Michael Doroféich be it said, he did not take
the remaining two rubles, though Velenchúk brought them to
him two months later.

## CHAPTER III

Besides Velenchúk, five other soldiers of my platoon sat warming themselves by our fire.

In the best place, on a butt with his back to the wind, sat
Maksímov, the gun-sergeant of the platoon, smoking a pipe.
The habit of commanding and the consciousness of his dignity
were betrayed by the pose, the look, and by every movement
of this man, not to mention his nankeen-covered sheepskin
coat and the butt he was sitting on, which latter is an emblem
of power at a halting-place.

When I came up he turned his head towards me without
removing his eyes from the fire, and his look, following the
direction his head had taken, only fell on me some time later.
Maksímov was not a serf but a peasant-yeoman; he had some
money, had qualified to take a class in the school-brigade,
and had stuffed his head with erudition. He was awfully rich
and awfully learned, so the soldiers said. I remember how once
when we were practising plunging fire with a quadrant, he
explained to the soldiers gathered round, that a spirit level
*is nothing but as it occurs that atmospheric mercury has its
motion.* In reality, Maksímov was far from being stupid, and
understood his work thoroughly; but he had the unfortunate
peculiarity of sometimes purposely speaking so that there was
no possibility of understanding him and so that, I am convinced, he did not understand his own words. He was particularly fond of the words 'as it occurs' and 'continues', so
that when I heard him say 'as it occurs' or 'continues', I knew
beforehand that I should understand nothing of what followed.
The soldiers on the other hand, as far as I could judge, liked
to hear his 'as it occurs' and suspected it of being fraught
with deep meaning, though they did not understand a word
of it any more than I did. This they attributed entirely to
their own stupidity, and respected Theodor Maksímov all the
more. In a word, Maksímov was one of the diplomatically
domineering.

The soldier next to him, who had bared his sinewy red legs

and was putting on his boots again by the fire, was Antónov,— that same Corporal Antónov who in 1837, remaining with only two others in charge of an exposed gun, persisted in firing back at a powerful enemy and, with two bullets in his leg, continued to serve his gun and to reload it.

The soldiers used to say that he would have been made a gun-sergeant long ago but for his character. And his character really was very peculiar. No one could have been calmer, gentler, or more accurate than he was when sober; but when he had a fit of drinking he became quite another man; he would not submit to authority, fought, brawled, and became a perfectly good-for-nothing soldier. Only the week before this, during the Carnival, he had had a drinking-bout, and in spite of all threats, persuasions, and being tied to a cannon, he went on drinking and brawling up to the first day of Lent. During the whole of Lent, though the division had been ordered not to fast, he fed on dried bread, and during the first week would not even drink the regulation cup of vodka. But one had to see his sturdy thick-set figure, as of wrought iron, on its stumpy bandy legs, and his shiny moustached visage when in a tipsy mood he took the *balaláyka* in his sinewy hands and looking carelessly round played *Lady*, or walked down the street with his cloak thrown loosely over his shoulders, his medals dangling, his hands in the pockets of his blue nankeen trousers, and a look on his countenance of soldierly pride and of contempt for all that was not of the artillery —one had to see all this in order to understand how impossible it was for him at such a moment to abstain from fighting an orderly, a Cossack, an infantry-man, a peasant (in fact, anyone not of the artillery) who was rude to him or happened merely to be in his way. He fought and rioted not so much for his own pleasure as to maintain the spirit of soldiership in general, of which he felt himself to be the representative.

The third soldier, who sat on his heels smoking a clay pipe, was the artillery driver Chíkin. He had an ear-ring in one of his ears, bristling little moustaches, and the physiognomy of a bird. 'Dear old Chíkin,' as the soldiers called him, was a wit. During the bitterest frost, or up to his knees in mud, or after going two days without food, on the march, on parade, or at drill, the 'dear fellow' was always and everywhere making faces, twisting his legs about, or cracking jokes that convulsed the whole platoon with laughter. At every halting-place, and in the camp, there was always a circle of young soldiers collected round Chíkin, who played *Fílka*[1] with them, told them stories about the cunning soldier and the English *milord*, personated a Tartar or a German, or simply made remarks of his own at which everyone roared with laughter. It is true that his reputation as a wit was so well established in the battery that it was sufficient for him to open his mouth and wink in order to produce a general guffaw, but really there was much in him that was truly humorous and surprising. He saw something special, something that never entered anybody else's head, in everything, and above all, this capacity for seeing the funny side of things was proof against any and every trial.

The fourth soldier was an insignificant-looking boy recruited the year before and this was his first campaign. He stood surrounded by the smoke and so near the flames that his threadbare cloak seemed in danger of catching fire, yet judging by the way he extended the skirts of his cloak and bent out his calves, and by his quiet self-satisfied pose, he was feeling highly contented.

The fifth and last of the soldiers was Daddy Zhdánov. He sat a little way off, cutting a stick. Zhdánov had been serving in the battery longer than anyone else, had known all the others as recruits, and they were all in the habit of calling him 'daddy'. It was said of him that he never drank, smoked, or played cards (not even 'noses'), and never used bad language. He spent all his spare time boot-making, went to church on holidays where that was possible, or else put a farthing taper before his icon and opened the book of psalms, the only book he could read. He seldom kept company with the other soldiers. To those who were his seniors in rank though his juniors in years he was coldly respectful; with his equals he had few opportunities of mixing, not being a drinker. He liked the re-

---

[1] A soldier's card game.—L. T.

cruits and the youngest soldiers best: he always took them under his protection, admonished them, and often helped them. Everyone in the battery considered him a capitalist because he had some twenty-five rubles, out of which he was always ready to lend something to a soldier in real need.

The same Maksímov who was now gun-sergeant told me that ten years ago, when he first came as a recruit and drank all he had with the old soldiers who were in the habit of drinking, Zhdánov, noticing his unfortunate position, called him up, severely reprimanded him for his conduct and even beat him, delivered a lecture on how one should live in the army, and sent him away after giving him a shirt (which Maksímov lacked) and half-a-ruble in money. 'He made a man of me,' Maksímov always used to say with respect and gratitude. He also helped Velenchúk (whom he had taken under his protection since he was a recruit) at the time of his misfortune. When the coat was stolen he helped him as he had helped many and many another during the twenty-five years of his service.

One could not hope to find a man in the service who knew his work more thoroughly or was a better or more conscientious soldier than he; but he was too meek and insignificant-looking to be made a gun-sergeant, though he had been bombardier for fifteen years. Zhdánov's one enjoyment and passion was song. He had a few favourite songs, always collected a circle of singers from among the younger soldiers, and though he could not sing himself he would stand by them, his hands in the pockets of his cloak, his eyes closed, showing sympathy by the movements of his head and jaw. I don't know why, but that regular movement of the jaws below the ears, which I never noticed in anyone else, seemed to me extremely expressive. His snow-white head, his blackened moustaches, and his sunburnt, wrinkled face, gave him at first sight a stern and harsh expression; but on looking closer into his large round eyes, especially when they smiled (he never laughed with his lips), you were suddenly struck by something remarkable in their unusually mild, almost childlike look.

## CHAPTER IV

'I'll be blowed! I've gone and forgot my pipe. Here's a go, lads!' repeated Velenchúk.

'You should smoke *cikars*, old fellow!' began Chíkin, drawing his mouth to one side and winking. 'There, now, I always smoke *cikars* when I'm at home—them's sweeter.'

Of course everybody burst out laughing.

'Forgot your pipe, indeed!' interrupted Maksímov without heeding the general mirth, and beating the tobacco out of his pipe into the palm of his left hand with the proud air of a superior; 'where did you vanish to—eh, Velenchúk?'

Velenchúk, half turning round to him, was about to raise his hand to his cap, but dropped it again.

'Seems to me you hadn't your sleep out after yesterday— falling asleep when you are once up! It's not thanks the likes of you get for such goings on.'

'May I die, Theodor Maksímov, if a drop has passed my lips; I don't myself know what happened to me,' answered Velenchúk. 'Much cause I had for revelling,' he muttered.

'Just so; but we have to answer to the authorities because of the likes of you, and you continue—it's quite scandalous!' the eloquent Maksímov concluded in a calmer tone.

'It's quite wonderful, lads,' Velenchúk went on after a moment's silence, scratching his head and addressing no one in particular; 'really quite wonderful, lads! Here have I been serving for the last sixteen years and such a thing never happened to me. When we were ordered to appear for muster I was all right, but at the "park", there *it* suddenly clutches hold of me, and clutches and clutches, and down it throws me, down on the ground and no more ado—and I did not myself know how I fell asleep, lads! That must have been the trances,' he concluded.

'True enough, I hardly managed to wake you,' said Antónov as he pulled on his boot. 'I had to push and push just as if you'd been a log!'

'Fancy now,' said Velenchúk, 'if I'd been drunk now! . . .'

'That's just like a woman we had at home,' began Chíkin; 'she hardly got off the stove for two years. Once they began waking her—they thought she was asleep—and she was already dead. She used to be taken sleepy that way. That's what it is, old fellow!'

'Now then, Chíkin, won't you tell us how you set the tone during your leave of absence?' said Maksímov, looking at me with a smile as if to say: 'Would you, too, like to hear the stupid fellow?'

'What tone, Theodor Maksímov?' said Chíkin, giving me a rapid side-glance. 'In course I told them what sort of a *Caw-cusses* we'd got here.'

'Well, yes, how did you do it? There! don't give yourself airs; tell us how you *administrated* it to them.'

'How should I administrate it? In course they asked me how we live,' Chíkin began rapidly with the air of a man recounting something he had repeated several times before. ' "We live well, old fellow," says I. "Provisions in plenty we get: morning and night a cup of *chokelad* for every *soldier lad,* and at noon barley broth before us is set, such as gentle-folks get, and instead of vodka we get a pint of Modera wine from Devirier, such as costs forty-four—with the bottle ten more!" '

'Fine Modera,' Velenchúk shouted louder than anyone, rolling with laughter: 'that's Modera of the right sort!'

'Well, and what did you tell them about the Asiaites?' Maksímov went on to ask when the general mirth had sub-sided a little.

Chíkin stooped over the fire, poked out a bit of charcoal with a stick, put it to his pipe, and long continued puffing at his shag as though not noticing the silent curiosity awakened in his hearers. When he had at last drawn enough smoke he threw the bit of charcoal away, pushed his cap yet farther back, and, stretching himself, continued with a slight smile—

'Well, so they asked, "What's that Cherkés fellow or Turk as you've got down in your Cawcusses", they say, "as fights?" and so I says, "Them's not all of one sort; there's different Cherkéses, old fellow. There's the Wagabones, them as lives in the stony mountains and eat stones instead of bread. They're big," says I, "as big as a good-sized beam, they've one eye in the forehead and wear burning red caps," just such as yours, old fellow,' he added, turning to the young recruit, who really wore an absurd cap with a red crown.

At this unexpected sally the recruit suddenly collapsed, slapped his knees, and burst out laughing and coughing so that he hardly managed to utter in a stifled voice, 'Them Wagabones is the right sort!'

' "Then", says I, "there's also the Mopingers," ' continued Chíkin, making his cap slip onto his forehead with a movement of his head: ' "These others are little twins, so big . . . all in pairs," says I, "they run about hand in hand at such a rate," says I, "that you couldn't catch 'em on a horse!"— "Then how's it, lad," they say, "how's them Mopingers, be they born hand in hand?" ' He said this in a hoarse bass, pretending to imitate a peasant. ' "Yes," says I, "he's naturally like that. Tear their hands apart and they'll bleed just like a Chinaman: take a Chinaman's cap off and it'll bleed."—"And tell us, lad, how do they fight?"—"That's how," says I, "they catch you and rip your belly up and wind your bowels round your arm, and wind and wind. They go on winding and you go on laughing till your breath all goes." '

'Well, and did they believe you, Chíkin?' said Maksímov with a slight smile, while all the rest were dying with laughter.

'Such queer people, Theodor Maksímych, they believe everything. On my word they do. But when I told them about Mount Kazbék and said that the snow didn't melt on it all the summer, they mocked at me! "What are you bragging for, lad," they says; "a big mountain and the snow on it don't melt? Why, lad, when the thaw sets in here every tiny bit of a hillock thaws first while the snow still lies in the hollows." There now!' Chíkin concluded with a wink.

## CHAPTER V

The bright disk of the sun shining through the milky-white
mist had already risen to a considerable height. The purple-
grey horizon gradually widened, but though it had receded
considerably it was still as sharply outlined by a deceptive
white wall of mist.

Beyond the felled wood a good-sized plain now opened in
front of us. The black or milky-white or purple smoke of the
fires expanded and fantastic shapes of white mist-clouds floated
above the plain. An occasional group of mounted Tartars appeared far in the distance before us and at rare intervals the
reports of our rifles[1] and of their *vintóvkas* and cannon were
to be heard.

This, as Captain Khlópov said, was 'not yet business, but
only play.'

The commander of the 9th Company of Chasseurs, that
formed our support, came up to our guns, pointed to three
Tartars[2] on horseback skirting the forest some 1,400 yards
from us, and with the fondness for artillery fire common
among infantry officers in general, asked me to let off a ball
or bomb at them.

'Do you see?' he said with a kind and persuasive smile as
he stretched his hand from behind my shoulder, 'in front of
those big trees there . . . one on a white horse and in a black
Circassian cloak and two others behind. Do you see? Could
you not, please?'

'And there are three more riding at the outskirt of the
forest,' said Antónov, who had astonishingly sharp eyesight,
coming up to us, and hiding behind his back the pipe he had

[1] Most of the Russian army at that time were armed with smooth-
bore muskets, but a few had wide-calibred muzzle-loading rifles
(*stútzers*), which were difficult to handle and slow to load. *Vintóvkas* were also rifles.

[2] Russians in the Caucasus used the word 'Tartar' loosely for any of
the native Mohammedan tribes (Circassians, Kabardáns, &c.),
much as among ourselves the word 'Niggers' is used to denote
almost any dark race.

been smoking. 'There, the one in front has taken his gun out of its case. They can be seen distinctly, y'r honor!'

'Look there! he's fired, lads. D'ye see the white smoke?' said Velenchúk, who was one of a group of soldiers standing a little behind us.

'At our line surely, the blackguard!' remarked another.

'See what a lot of 'em come streaming out of the forest. Must be looking round . . . want to place a gun,' said a third.

'Supposing now a bomb was sent right into that lot, wouldn't they spit!'

'And what d'ye think, old fellow—that it would just reach 'em?' said Chíkin.

'Twelve hundred or twelve hundred and fifty yards: not more than that,' said Maksímov calmly and as if speaking to himself, though it was evident he was just as anxious to fire as the rest: 'if we were to give an elevation of forty-five lines to our "unicorn" [3] we could hit the very point, that is to say, perfectly.'

'D'ye know, if you were now to aim at that group you would be sure to hit somebody. There now, they are all together— please be quick and give the order to fire,' the company commander continued to entreat me.

'Are we to point the gun?' suddenly asked Antónov in an abrupt bass with a look as if of gloomy anger.

I must admit that I also felt a strong wish to fire, so I ordered the second gun to be trained.

I had hardly given the order before the shell was charged and rammed in and Antónov, leaning against the cheek of the gun-carriage and holding two of his thick fingers to the base-ring, was directing the movement of the tail of the gun. 'Right, left—a bit to the left, a wee bit—more—more—right!' he said, stepping from the gun with a look of pride.

The infantry officer, I, and Maksímov, one after the other, approached, put our heads to the sights, and expressed our various opinions.

---

[3] The 'unicorn' was a type of gun, narrowing towards the muzzle, used in the Russian artillery at that time.

'By Heavens, it will shoot over,' remarked Velenchúk, clicking his tongue, though he was only looking over Antónov's
shoulder and therefore had no grounds for this supposition. 'By
Hea—vens it will shoot over; it will hit that there tree, my
lads!'

I gave the order: 'Two.'

The men stepped away from the gun. Antónov ran aside to
watch the flight of the shot. The touch-hole flashed and the
brass rang. At the same moment we were enveloped in a cloud
of powder-smoke and, emerging from the overpowering boom
of the discharge, the humming, metallic sound of the flying
shot receded with the swiftness of lightning and died away in
the distance amid general silence.

A little beyond the group of horsemen a white cloudlet appeared; the Tartars galloped away in all directions and the
report of the explosion reached us. 'That was very fine!' 'Ah,
how they galloped!' 'The devils don't like that!' came the words
of approval and ridicule from the ranks of the artillery and infantry.

'If we had had the gun pointed only a touch lower we
should just have caught him. I said it would hit the tree and
sure enough it did go to the right,' remarked Velenchúk.

## CHAPTER VI

Leaving the soldiers to discuss how the Tartars galloped off
when they saw the shell, why they had been riding there, and
whether there were many of them in the forest, I went and sat
down with the company commander under a tree a few steps
off to wait while the cutlets he had invited me to share were
being warmed up. The company commander, Bólkhov, was
one of the officers nicknamed 'bonjourists' in the regiment. He
was a man of some means, had formerly served in the Guards,
and spoke French. But in spite of all this his comrades liked
him. He was clever enough, and had tact enough, to wear a
coat of Petersburg make, to eat a good dinner, and to speak
French, without too much offending his fellow officers. After

talking about the weather, the military operations, our mutual acquaintances among the officers, and having assured ourselves of the satisfactory state of each other's ideas by questions and answers and the views expressed, we involuntarily passed to more intimate conversation. And when people belonging to the same circle meet in the Caucasus a very evident, even if unspoken, question arises: 'Why are you here?' and it was to this silent question of mine that, as it seemed to me, my companion wished to reply.

'When will this expedition end?' he said lazily. 'It is so dull.'

'I don't think it dull,' said I. 'It's much worse on the staff.'

'Oh, it's ten thousand times worse on the staff,' he said irascibly. 'No, I mean when will the whole thing end?'

'What is it you want to end?' I asked.

'Everything,—the whole affair! . . . Are the cutlets ready, Nikoláyev?'

'Then why did you come to serve here if you so dislike the Caucasus?' I said.

'Do you know why?' he answered with resolute frankness. 'In obedience to tradition! You know there exists in Russia a most curious tradition about the Caucasus, making it out to be a "promised land" for all unfortunates.'

'Yes, that is almost true,' said I. 'Most of us——'

'But the best of it is,' he said, interrupting me, 'that all of us who came to the Caucasus in obedience to the tradition made a terrible mistake in our calculations and I can't for the life of me see why one should, in consequence of an unfortunate love affair or of financial troubles, choose to go and serve in the Caucasus rather than in Kazán or Kalúga. Why in Russia they imagine the Caucasus to be something majestic: eternal virgin ice, rushing torrents, daggers, mantles, fair Circassians, and an atmosphere of terror and romance; but in reality there is nothing amusing in it. If they only realized that we never get to the virgin ice, that it would not be at all amusing if we did, and that the Caucasus is divided into governments—Stavrópol, Tiflís, and so on.'

'Yes,' said I, laughing, 'we look very differently at the Caucasus when we are in Russia and when we are here. It is like what you may have experienced when reading verses in a language you are not familiar with; you imagine them to be much better than they are.'

'I really don't know; but I dislike this Caucasus awfully,' he said interrupting me.

'Well, no; I still like the Caucasus only in a different way.'

'Perhaps it is all right,' he continued irritably; 'all I know is that I'm not all right in the Caucasus.'

'Why is that?' I asked, to say something.

'Well, first because it has deceived me. All that I, in obedience to tradition, came to the Caucasus to be cured of has followed me here, only with the difference that there it was all on a big scale and now it is on a little dirty one where at each step I find millions of petty anxieties, shabbinesses, and insults; and next because I feel that I am sinking, morally, lower and lower every day; but chiefly, because I do not feel fit for the service here. I can't stand running risks. The fact of the matter is simply that I am not brave.'

He stopped and looked at me, not joking.

Though this unasked-for confession surprised me very much, I did not contradict him as he evidently wished me to do, but waited for his own refutation of his words, which always follows in such cases.

'Do you know, in coming on this expedition I am taking part in an action for the first time,' he continued, 'and you can't think what was going on in me yesterday. When the sergeant-major brought the order that my company was to join the column, I turned as white as a sheet and could not speak for excitement. And if you only knew what a night I had! If it were true that one's hair turns white from fear, mine ought to be perfectly white to-day, because I don't think any one condemned to death ever suffered more in a night than I did; and even now, though I feel a bit easier than in the night, this is what goes on inside!' he added, turning his fist about before his chest. 'And what is funny is that while a most fearful tragedy is being enacted, here one sits eating cutlets and onions and making believe that it is great fun.—Have we any wine, Nikoláyev?' he added, yawning.

'That's *him*, my lads!' came the excited voice of one of the soldiers, and all eyes turned towards the border of the distant forest.

In the distance a puff of bluish smoke expanded and rose, blown about by the wind. When I had understood that this was a shot fired at us by the enemy, all before my eyes at the moment assumed a sort of new and majestic character. The piles of arms, the smoke of the fires, the blue sky, the green gun-carriages, Nikoláyev's sunburnt, moustached face—all seemed telling me that the ball that had already emerged from the smoke and was at that moment flying through space might be directed straight at my breast.

'Where did you get the wine?' I asked Bólkhov lazily, while deep in my soul two voices spoke with equal clearness. One said, 'Lord receive my soul in peace,' the other, 'I hope I shall not stoop, but smile, while the ball is passing,' and at that moment something terribly unpleasant whistled past our heads and a cannon ball crashed down a couple of paces from us.

'There now, had I been a Napoleon or a Frederick I should certainly have paid you a compliment,' Bólkhov remarked, turning towards me quite calmly.

'You have done so as it is,' I answered, with difficulty hiding the excitement produced in me by the danger just passed.

'Well, what if I have?—no one will write it down.'

'Yes, I will.'

'Well, if you do put it down, it will only be "for criticism", as Míschenkov says,' he added with a smile.

'Ugh! the damned thing!' just then remarked Antónov behind us, as he spat over his shoulder with vexation, 'just missed my legs!'

All my attempts to seem calm, and all our cunning phrases, suddenly seemed to me insufferably silly after that simple exclamation.

## CHAPTER VII

The enemy had really placed two guns where we had seen the
Tartars riding, and they fired a shot every twenty or thirty
minutes at our men who were felling the wood. My platoon
was ordered forward to the plain to answer the enemy's fire.
A puff of smoke appeared on the outskirts of the forest, then
followed a report and a whistle, and a ball fell in front or behind us. The enemy's shots fell fortunately for us and we sustained no losses.

The artillerymen behaved splendidly as they always do;
loaded quickly, pointed carefully at the spots where the puffs
of smoke were, and quietly joked with one another.

The infantry supports lay near in silent inaction awaiting
their turn. The wood-fellers went on with their work, the axes
rang faster and more unintermittently through the forest; but
when the whistle of a shot became audible all were suddenly
silent and, in the midst of the deathly stillness, voices not quite
calm exclaimed, 'Scatter, lads!' and all eyes followed the ball
ricochetting over wood piles and strewn branches.

The mist had now risen quite high and, turning into clouds,
gradually disappeared into the dark-blue depths of the sky; the
unveiled sun shone brightly, throwing sparkling reflections
from the steel bayonets, the brass of the guns, the thawing
earth, and the glittering hoar-frost. In the air one felt the freshness of the morning frost together with the warmth of the
spring sunshine; thousands of different hues and tints mingled
in the dry leaves of the forest, and the shining, beaten track
plainly showed the traces left by wheels and the marks of
rough-shod horses' feet.

The movement became greater and more noticeable between the two forces. On all sides the blue smoke of the guns
appeared more and more frequently. Dragoons rode forward,
the streamers of their lances flying; from the infantry companies one heard songs, and the carts laden with firewood
formed into a train in our rear. The general rode up to our
platoon and ordered us to prepare to retire. The enemy settled

in the bushes on our left flank and their snipers began to molest us seriously. A bullet came humming from the woods to the left and struck a gun-carriage, then came another, and a third. . . . The infantry supports that had been lying near us rose noisily, took up their muskets and formed into line.

The small-arm firing increased and bullets flew more and more frequently. The retreat commenced and consequently the serious part of the action, as is usual in the Caucasus.

Everything showed that the artillerymen liked the bullets as little as the infantry had liked the cannonballs. Antónov frowned, Chíkin imitated the bullets and joked about them, but it was easy to see he did not like them. 'It's in a mighty hurry,' he said of one of them; another he called 'little bee'; a third, which seemed to fly slowly past overhead with a kind of piteous wail, he called an 'orphan', which caused general laughter.

The recruit who, unaccustomed to such scenes, bent his head to one side and stretched his neck every time a bullet passed, also made the soldiers laugh. 'What, is that a friend of yours you're bowing to?' they said to him. Velenchúk also, usually quite indifferent to danger, was now excited: he was evidently vexed that we did not fire case-shot in the direction whence the bullets came. He repeated several times in a discontented tone, 'Why is *he* allowed to go for us and gets nothing in return. If we turned a gun that way and gave them a taste of case-shot they'd hold their noise, no fear!'

It was true that it was time to do this, so I ordered them to fire a last bomb and then to load with case-shot.

'Case-shot!' Antónov called out briskly as he went through the thick of the smoke to sponge out the gun as soon as it was discharged.

At that moment I heard just behind me the rapid whiz of a bullet suddenly stopped by something, with a dull thud. My heart ceased beating. 'Someone of the men has been hit,' I thought, while a sad presentiment made me afraid to turn round. And really that sound was followed by the heavy fall of a body, and the heart-rending 'Oh-o-oh' of someone who had been wounded. 'I'm hit, lads!' a voice I knew exclaimed with an effort. It was Velenchúk. He was lying on his back between the limbers and a cannon. The cartridge-bag he had been carrying was thrown to one side. His forehead was covered with blood, and a thick red stream was running down over his right eye and nose. He was wounded in the stomach but hardly bled at all there; his forehead he had hurt against a log in falling.

All this I made out much later; the first moment I could only see an indistinct mass and, as it seemed to me, a tremendous quantity of blood.

Not one of the soldiers who were loading said a word, only the young recruit muttered something that sounded like 'Dear me! he's bleeding', and Antónov, frowning, gave an angry grunt; but it was clear that the thought of death passed through the soul of each. All set to work very actively and the gun was loaded in a moment, but the ammunition-bearer bringing the case-shot went two or three steps round the spot where Velenchúk still lay groaning.

## CHAPTER VIII

Everyone who has been in action undoubtedly knows that strange and though illogical yet powerful feeling of aversion for the spot where some one has been killed or wounded. It was evident that for a moment my men gave way to this feeling when Velenchúk had to be taken to the cart that came up to fetch him. Zhdánov came up angrily to the wounded man and, taking him under the arms, lifted him without heeding his loud screams. 'Now then, what are you standing there for? take hold!' he shouted, and about ten assistants, some of them superfluous, immediately surrounded Velenchúk. But hardly had they moved him when he began screaming and struggling terribly.

'What are you screaming like a hare for?' said Antónov roughly, holding his leg; 'mind, or we'll just leave you.'

And the wounded man really became quiet and only now and then uttered, 'Oh, it's my death! Oh, oh, oh, lads!'

When he was laid in the cart he even stopped moaning and I heard him speak to his comrades in low clear tones, probably saying farewell to them.

No one likes to look at a wounded man during an action and, instinctively hurrying to end this scene, I ordered him to be taken quickly to the ambulance, and returned to the guns. But after a few minutes I was told that Velenchúk was asking for me, and I went up to the cart.

The wounded man lay at the bottom of the cart holding on to the sides with both hands. His broad healthy face had completely changed during those few moments; he seemed to have grown thinner and years older, his lips were thin and pale and pressed together with an evident strain. The hasty and dull expression of his glance was replaced by a kind of bright clear radiance, and on the bloody forehead and nose already lay the impress of death. Though the least movement caused him excruciating pain, he nevertheless asked to have a small *chérez*[1] with money taken from his left leg.

The sight of his bare, white, healthy leg, when his jack-boot had been taken off and the purse untied, produced on me a terribly sad feeling.

'Here are three rubles and a half,' he said, as I took the purse: 'you'll take care of them.'

The cart was starting, but he stopped it.

'I was making a cloak for Lieutenant Sulimóvsky. He gave me two rubles. I bought buttons for one and a half, and half a ruble is in my bag with the buttons. Please let him have it.'

'All right! all right!' said I. 'Get well again, old fellow.'

He did not answer; the cart started and he again began to groan and cry out in a terrible, heart-rending voice. It was as if, having done with the business of this life, he did not think it necessary to restrain himself and considered it permissible to allow himself this relief.

---

[1] The *chérez* is a purse in the form of a garter, usually worn by soldiers below the knee.—L. T.

# CHAPTER IX

'Where are you off to? Come back! Where are you going?' I
shouted to the recruit, who with his reserve linstock under his
arm and a stick of some sort in his hand was, in the coolest
manner, following the cart that bore the wounded man.

But the recruit only looked at me lazily, muttered something
or other, and continued his way, so that I had to send a soldier
to bring him back. He took off his red cap and looked at me
with a stupid smile.

'Where were you going?' I asked.

'To the camp.'

'Why?'

'Why? . . . Velenchúk is wounded,' he said, again smiling.

'What's that to you? You must stay here.'

He looked at me with surprise, then turned quietly round,
put on his cap, and went back to his place.

The affair in general was successful. The Cossacks, as we
heard, had made a fine charge and brought back three dead
Tartars;[1] the infantry had provided itself with firewood and
had only half-a-dozen men wounded; the artillery had lost only
Velenchúk and two horses. For that, two miles of forest had
been cut down and the place so cleared as to be unrecogniz-
able. Instead of the thick outskirts of the forest you saw before
you a large plain covered with smoking fires and cavalry and
infantry marching back to camp.

Though the enemy continued to pursue us with artillery and
small-arm fire up to the cemetery by the little river we had
crossed in the morning, the retirement was successfully accomplished. I was already beginning to dream of the cabbage-soup
and mutton-ribs with buckwheat that were awaiting me in

---

[1] The 'Tartars,' being Mohammedans, made a point of not letting
the bodies of their slain fall into the hands of the 'unbelievers,' but
removed them and buried them as heroes. The capture of three
bodies therefore indicates the vigour of the attack and the demor-
alization of the enemy.

camp, when a message came from the General ordering a redoubt to be constructed by the river, and the 3rd battalion of
the K—— Regiment and the platoon of the 4th Battery to remain there till next day.

The carts with the wood and the wounded, the Cossacks,
the artillery, the infantry with muskets and faggots on their
shoulders, all passed us with noise and songs. Every face expressed animation and pleasure caused by the escape from
danger and the hope of rest. Only we and the 3rd battalion
had to postpone those pleasant feelings till to-morrow.

## CHAPTER X

While we of the artillery were busy with the guns—parking
the limbers and the ammunition wagons and arranging the
picket-ropes—the infantry had already piled their muskets,
made up camp-fires, built little huts of branches and maize
straw, and begun boiling their buckwheat.

The twilight had set in. Bluish white clouds crept over the
sky. The mist, turning into fine dank drizzle, wetted the earth
and the soldiers' cloaks; the horizon narrowed and all the surroundings assumed a gloomier hue. The damp I felt through
my boots and on my neck, the ceaseless movement and talk in
which I took no part, the sticky mud on which my feet kept
slipping, and my empty stomach, all combined to put me into
the dreariest, most unpleasant frame of mind after the physical
and moral weariness of the day. I could not get Velenchúk out
of my head. The whole simple story of his soldier-life depicted
itself persistently in my imagination.

His last moments were as clear and calm as his whole life
had been. He had lived too honestly and been too artless for
his simple faith in a future heavenly life to be shaken at the
decisive moment.

'Your honour!' said Nikoláyev, coming up to me, 'the Captain asks you to come and have tea with him.'

Having scrambled through, as best I could, between the
piles of arms and the camp-fires, I followed Nikoláyev to

where Bólkhov was, thinking with pleasure of a tumbler of hot tea and a cheerful conversation which would disperse my gloomy thoughts.

'Have you found him?' I heard Bólkhov's voice say from inside a maize-hut in which a light was burning.

'I've brought him, y'r honour,' answered Nikoláyev's bass voice.

Inside the hut Bólkhov was sitting on a dry mantle, with unbuttoned coat and no cap. A samovar stood boiling by his side and on a drum were light refreshments. A bayonet holding a candle was stuck into the ground.

'What do you think of it?' he asked, looking proudly round his cosy establishment. It really was so nice inside the hut that at tea I quite forgot the damp, the darkness, and Velenchúk's wound. We talked of Moscow and of things that had not the least relation to the war or to the Caucasus.

After a moment of silence such as sometimes occurs in the most animated conversation, Bólkhov looked at me with a smile.

'I think our conversation this morning struck you as being very strange,' he said.

'No, why do you think so? It only seemed to me that you were too frank; there are things which we all know, but which should never be mentioned.'

'Why not? If there were the least possibility of changing this life for the lowest and poorest without danger and without service, I should not hesitate a moment.'

'Then why don't you return to Russia?' I asked.

'Why?' he repeated. 'Oh, I have thought about that long ago. I can't return to Russia now until I have the Anna and Vladímir orders: an Anna round my neck and the rank of major, as I planned when I came here.'

'Why?—if, as you say, you feel unfit for the service here.'

'But what if I feel still more unfit to go back to Russia to the same position that I left? That is also one of the traditions in Russia, confirmed by Pássek, Sleptsóv and others, that one need only go to the Caucasus to be laden with rewards. Everyone expects and demands it of us; and I have been here for two years, have been on two expeditions, and have got nothing. But still I have so much ambition that I won't leave on any account until I am a major with a Vladímir and Anna round my neck. I have become so concerned about it that it upsets me when Gnilokíshkin gets a reward and I don't. And then how am I to show myself in Russia, to the village elder, to the merchant Kotélnikov to whom I sell my corn, to my Moscow aunt, and to all those good people, if after two years spent in the Caucasus I return without any reward? It is true I don't at all wish to know all those people, and they no doubt care very little about me either; but man is so made that, though I don't want to know them, yet on account of them I'm wasting the best years of my life, all my life's happiness, and am ruining my future.'

## CHAPTER XI

Just then we heard the voice of the commander of the battalion outside, addressing Bólkhov.

'Who is with you, Nicholas Fëdorovich?'

Bólkhov gave him my name, and then three officers scrambled into the hut—Major Kirsánov; the adjutant of his battalion; and Captain Trosénko.

Kirsánov was not tall but stout, he had black moustaches, rosy cheeks, and oily little eyes. These eyes were his most remarkable feature. When he laughed nothing remained of them but two tiny moist stars, and these little stars together with his widestretched lips and outstretched neck often gave him an extraordinarily senseless look. In the regiment Kirsánov behaved himself and bore himself better than anyone else; his subordinates did not complain of him and his superiors respected him—though the general opinion was that he was very limited. He knew the service, was exact and zealous, always had ready money, kept a carriage and a man-cook, and knew how to make an admirable pretence of being proud.

'What were you talking about, Nicholas Fëdorovich?'

'Why, about the attractions of the service here.'

But just then Kirsánov noticed me, a cadet, and to impress me with his importance he paid no attention to Bólkhov's reply, but looked at the drum and said—

'Are you tired, Nicholas Fëdorovich?'

'No, you see we———' Bólkhov began.

But again the dignity of the commander of the battalion seemed to make it necessary to interrupt, and to ask another question.

'That was a famous affair to-day, was it not?'

The adjutant of the battalion was a young ensign recently promoted from being a cadet, a modest, quiet lad with a bashful and kindly-pleasant face. I had met him at Bólkhov's before. The lad would often come there, bow, sit down in a corner, and remain silent for hours making cigarettes and smoking them; then he would rise, bow, and go away. He was the type of a poor Russian nobleman's son who had chosen the military career as the only one possible to him with his education, and who esteemed his position as an officer above everything else in the world—a simple-minded and lovable type notwithstanding the comical appurtenances inseparable from it: the tobacco-pouch, dressing-gown, guitar, and little moustache-brush we are accustomed to associate with it. It was told of him in the regiment that he bragged about being just but strict with his orderly, and that he used to say, 'I punish seldom, but when I am compelled to do it it's no joke,' but that when his tipsy orderly robbed him outrageously and even began to insult him, he, the master, took him to the guard-house and ordered everything to be prepared for a flogging, but was so upset at the sight of the preparations that he could only say, 'There now, you see, I could———' and becoming quite disconcerted, ran home in great confusion and was henceforth afraid to look his man Chernóv in the eyes. His comrades gave the simple-minded boy no rest but teased him continually about this episode, and more than once I heard how he defended himself, and blushing to the tips of his ears assured them that it was not true, but just the contrary.

The third visitor, Captain Trosénko, was a thoroughgoing old Caucasian—that is, a man for whom the company he commanded had become his family; the fortress where the staff was, his home; and the soldiers' singing his only pleasure in life. He was a man for whom everything unconnected with the Caucasus was contemptible and scarcely worthy of being considered probable, and everything connected with the Caucasus was divided into two halves: ours and not ours. The first he loved, the second he hated with all the power of his soul; but above all he was a man of steeled, calm courage, wonderfully kind in his behaviour to his comrades and subordinates and desperately frank and even rude to aides-de-camp and 'bonjourists', for whom for some reason he had a great dislike. On entering the hut he nearly caved the roof in with his head, then suddenly sank down and sat on the ground.

'Well?' he said, and then suddenly remarking me whom he did not know, he stopped and gazed at me with a dull, fixed look.

'Well, and what have you been conversing about?' asked the major, taking out his watch and looking at it, though I am perfectly certain he had no need to.

'Why, I've been asked my reasons for serving here——'

'Of course, Nicholas Fëdorovich wishes to distinguish himself here, and then to return home,' said the major.

'Well, and you, Abram Ilých,' said Bólkhov, addressing Kirsánov, 'tell me why you are serving in the Caucasus.'

'I serve because in the first place, as you know, it is everyone's duty to serve. . . . What?' he then added, though no one had spoken. 'I had a letter from Russia yesterday, Nicholas Fëdorovich,' he continued, evidently wishing to change the subject; 'they write that . . . they ask such strange questions.'

'What questions?' asked Bólkhov.

The major began laughing.

'Very queer questions. . . . They ask, can jealousy exist where there is no love. . . . What?' he asked, turning round and glancing at us all.

'Dear me!' said Bólkhov, with a smile.

'Yes, you know, it is nice in Russia,' continued the major, just as if his sentences flowed naturally from one another. 'When I was in Tambóv in '52 they received me everywhere

as if I had been some emperor's aide-de-camp. Will you believe it that at a ball at the Governor's, when I came in, you
know . . . well, they received me very well. The General's
wife herself, you know, talked to me and asked me about the
Caucasus, and everybody was . . . so that I hardly knew.
. . . They examined my gold sabre as if it were some curiosity; they asked for what I had received the sabre, for what the
Anna, for what the Vladímir . . . so I just told them. . . .
What? That's what the Caucasus is good for, Nicholas Fëdorovich!' he continued without waiting for any reply:—'There
they think very well of us Caucasians. You know a young man
that's a staff-officer and has an Anna and a Vladímir . . . that
counts for a good deal in Russia. . . . What?'

'And you, no doubt, piled it on a bit, Abram Ilých?' said
Bólkhov.

'He—he!' laughed the major stupidly. 'You know one has to
do that. And didn't I feed well those two months!'

'And tell me, is it nice there in Russia?' said Trosénko, in-
quiring about Russia as though it were China or Japan.

'Yes, and the champagne we drank those two months, it was
awful!'

'Eh, nonsense! You'll have drunk nothing but lemonade.
There now, I'd have burst to let them see how Caucasians
drink. I'd have given them something to talk about. I'd have
shown them how one drinks; eh, Bólkhov?' said Trosénko.

'But you, Daddy, have been more than ten years in the
Caucasus,' said Bólkhov, 'and you remember what Ermólov[1]
said? . . . And Abram Ilých has been only six.'

'Ten indeed! . . . nearly sixteen. . . . Well, Bólkhov, let
us have some sage-vodka. It's damp, b-r-r-r! . . . Eh?' said
Trosénko, smiling, 'Will you have a drink, Major?'

But the major had been displeased by the old captain's first
remarks to him, and plainly drew back and sought refuge in

---

[1] General A. P. Ermólov (1772-1861), who was renowned for his
firmness and justness as a ruler in the Caucasus, and who subdued
Chéchnya and Daghestán, used to say that after ten years in the
Caucasus an officer 'either takes to drink or marries a loose woman.'

his own grandeur. He hummed something, and again looked
at his watch.

'For my part I shall never go there!' Trosénko continued
without heeding the major's frowns. 'I have lost the habit of
speaking and walking in the Russian way. They'd ask, "What
curious creature is this coming here? Asia, that's what it is."
Am I right, Nicholas Fëdorovich? Besides, what have I to go
to Russia for? What does it matter? I shall be shot here some
day. They'll ask, "Where's Trosénko?" "Shot!" What will you
do with the 8th Company then, eh?' he added, always addressing the major.

'Send the officer on duty!' shouted the major, without answering the captain, though I again felt sure there was no
need for him to give any orders.

'And you, young man, are glad, I suppose, to be drawing
double pay?' [2] said the major, turning to the adjutant of the
battalion after some moments of silence.

'Yes, sir, very glad of course.'

'I think our pay now very high, Nicholas Fëdorovich,' continued the major; 'a young man can live very decently and
even permit himself some small luxuries.'

'No, really, Abram Ilých,' said the adjutant bashfully.
'Though it's double it's barely enough. You see one must have
a horse.'

'What are you telling me, young man? I have been an ensign myself and know. Believe me, one can live very well with
care. But there! count it up,' added he, bending the little finger of his left hand.

'We always draw our salaries in advance; isn't that account
enough for you?' said Trosénko, emptying a glass of vodka.

'Well, yes, but what do you expect. . . . What?'

Just then a white head with a flat nose thrust itself into the
opening of the hut and a sharp voice said with a German accent—

---

[2] An officer's allowance in Russia proper was very small, but when
on service in Poland, the Caucasus, Siberia, &c., they received a
higher rate of pay.

'Are you there, Abram Ilých? The officer on duty is looking for you.'

'Come in, Kraft!' said Bólkhov.

A long figure in the uniform of the general staff crept in at the door and began shaking hands all round with peculiar fervour.

'Ah, dear Captain, are you here too?' said he, turning to Trosénko.

In spite of the darkness the new visitor made his way to the captain and to the latter's extreme surprise and dismay as it seemed to me, kissed him on the lips.

'This is a German trying to be hail fellow well met,' thought I.


## CHAPTER XII

My surmise was at once confirmed. Captain Kraft asked for vodka, calling it a 'warmer,' croaked horribly, and throwing back his head emptied the glass.

'Well, gentlemen, we have scoured the plains of Chéchnya to-day, have we not?' he began, but seeing the officer on duty, stopped at once to allow the major to give his orders.

'Have you been round the lines?'

'Yes, sir.'

'Have the ambuscades been placed?'

'Yes, sir.'

'Then give the company commanders orders to be as cautious as possible.'

'Yes, sir.'

The major screwed up his eyes in profound contemplation.

'Yes, and tell the men they may now boil their buckwheat.'

'They are already boiling it, sir.'

'All right! You may go, sir.'

'Well, we were just reckoning up how much an officer needs,' continued the major, turning to us with a condescending smile. 'Let us count. You want a uniform and a pair of trousers, don't you?'

'Certainly.'

'That, let us say, is 50 rubles for two years; therefore 25 rubles a year for clothes. Then for food, 40 kopeks a day—is that right?'

'Oh yes, that is even too much.'

'Well, never mind, I'll leave it so. Then for a horse and repair of harness and saddle—30 rubles. And that is all. So it's 25, and 120, and 30—that's 175 rubles. So you have for luxuries—tea, sugar, tobacco—a matter of 20 rubles left. So you see . . . Isn't it so, Nicholas Fëdorovich?'

'No, but excuse me, Abram Ilých,' said the adjutant timidly, 'nothing remains for tea and sugar. You allow one suit in two years; but it's hardly possible to keep oneself in trousers with all this marching. And boots? I wear out a pair almost every month. Then underclothing—shirts, towels, leg-bands,[1]—it all has to be bought. When one comes to reckon it all up nothing remains over. That's really so, Abram Ilých.'

'Ah, it's splendid to wear leg-bands,' Kraft suddenly remarked after a moment's silence, uttering the word 'leg-bands' in specially tender tones. 'It's so simple, you know; quite Russian!'

'I'll tell you something,' Trosénko remarked. 'Reckon what way you like and you'll find we might as well put our teeth away on a shelf, and yet here we are all alive, drinking tea, smoking tobacco, and drinking vodka. When you've served as long as I have,' he went on, turning to the ensign, 'you'll have also learned how to live. Why, gentlemen, do you know how he treats the orderlies?'

And Trosénko, dying with laughter, told us the whole story about the ensign and his orderly, though we had all heard it hundreds of times.

'Why do you look so like a rose, old chap?' continued he, addressing the ensign, who blushed, perspired, and smiled, so that it was pitiful to see him. 'Never mind, old chap! I was

---

[1] It is customary, especially among the peasants and soldiers, to wrap long strips of linen round the feet and legs instead of wearing stockings.

just like you once and now look what a fine fellow I am. You let a young fellow straight from Russia in here—haven't we seen them?—and he gets spasms or rheumatism or something; and here am I settled here, and it's my house and my bed and all, d'you see?'

And thereupon he drank another glass of vodka and looking fixedly at Kraft, said, 'Eh?'

'That is what I respect! Here's a genuine old Caucasian! Permit me to shake hands.'

And Kraft, pushing us all aside, forced his way to Trosénko and catching hold of his hand shook it with peculiar emotion.

'Yes,' continued Kraft, 'we may say we have gone through every kind of experience here. In '45 you were present, Captain, were you not?—you remember the night between the 12th and 13th, when we spent the night knee-deep in mud and next day captured the barricades they had made of felled trees. I was attached to the commander-in-chief at the time and we took fifteen barricades that one day,—you remember, Captain?'

Trosénko nodded affirmatively, stuck out his nether lip and screwed up his eyes.

'You see . . .' began Kraft with great animation, making unsuitable gestures with his hands and addressing the major.

But the major, who had in all probability heard the story more than once, suddenly looked at the speaker with such dim, dull eyes that Kraft turned away from him and addressed me and Bólkhov, looking alternately at one and the other. But he did not give a single glance at Trosénko during the whole of his narration.

'Well then, you see, when we went out in the morning the commander-in-chief said to me, "Kraft, take those barricades!" Well, you know, a soldier's duty is not to reason—it's hand to cap, and "Yes, your Excellency!" and off. Only as we drew near the first barricade I turned and said to the soldiers, "Now then, lads, don't funk it but look sharp. If anyone hangs back I'll cut him down myself!" With Russian soldiers, you know, one has to speak straight out. Suddenly a bomb . . . I look, one soldier down, another, a third, . . . then bullets came whizzing . . . vzin! . . . vzin! . . . vzin! . . . "On!" I cry, "On, follow me!" Just as we got there I look and see a . . . a . . . you know . . . what do you call it?' and the narrator flourished his arms, trying to find the word he wanted.

'A scarp?' suggested Bólkhov.

'No . . . Ach! what is the word? Good heavens, what is it? . . . A scarp!' he said quickly. 'So, "fix bayonets! Hurrah! ta-ra, ta-ta-ta!" not a sign of the enemy! Everybody was surprised, you know. Well, that's all right; we go on to the second barricade. Ah, that was a totally different matter. Our mettle was now up, you know. Just as we reached it I look and see the second barricade, and we could not advance. There was a what's-its-name . . . now what do you call it? Ach, what is it? . . .'

'Another scarp, perhaps,' I suggested.

'Not at all,' he said crossly: 'not a scarp but—oh dear, what do you call it?' and he made an awkward gesture with his hands. 'Oh, good heavens, what is it?' He seemed so distressed that one involuntarily wished to help him.

'A river, perhaps,' said Bólkhov.

'No, only a scarp! Hardly had we got down, when, will you believe it, such a hell of fire . . .'

At this moment someone outside the tent asked for me. It was Maksímov. And as after having heard the different histories of these two barricades there were still thirteen left, I was glad to seize the excuse to return to my platoon. Trosénko came out with me.

'It's all lies,' he said to me when we were a few steps from the hut; 'he never was near those barricades at all,' and Trosénko laughed so heartedly that I, too, enjoyed the joke.

# CHAPTER XIII

It was already dark and only the watch-fires dimly lit up the camp when, after the horses were groomed, I rejoined my men. A large stump lay smouldering on the charcoal. Only three men sat round it: Antónov, who was turning a little pot of *ryábco*[1] on the fire; Zhdánov, who was dreamily poking the embers with a stick, and Chíkin, with his pipe, which never would draw well. The rest had already lain down to sleep—some under the ammunition wagons, some on the hay, some by the camp-fires. By the dim light of the charcoal I could distinguish familiar backs, legs, and heads, and among the latter that of the young recruit who, drawn close to the fire, seemed to be already sleeping. Antónov made room for me. I sat down by him and lit a cigarette. The smell of mist and the smoke of damp wood filled the air and made one's eyes smart and, as before, a dank drizzle kept falling from the dismal sky.

One could hear the regular sound of snoring near by, the crackling of branches in the fire, a few words now and then, and the clattering of muskets among the infantry. The camp watch-fires glowed all around, lighting up within narrow circles the dark shadows of the soldiers near them. Where the light fell by the nearest fires I could distinguish the figures of naked soldiers waving their shirts close over the fire. There were still many who had not lain down, but moved and spoke, collected on a space of some eighty square yards; but the gloomy dull night gave a peculiar mysterious character to all this movement as if each one felt the dark silence and feared to break its calm monotony.

When I began to speak I felt that my voice sounded strange, and I discerned the same frame of mind reflected in the faces of all the soldiers sitting near me. I thought that before I joined them they had been talking about their wounded comrade, but it had not been so at all. Chíkin had been telling them about receiving supplies at Tiflís and about the scamps there.

I have noticed always and everywhere, but especially in the Caucasus, the peculiar tact with which our soldiers avoid mentioning anything that might have a bad effect on a com-

---

[1] *Ryábco*, soldier's food, made of soaked hard-tack and dripping.— L. T.

rade's spirits. A Russian soldier's spirit does not rest on easily inflammable enthusiasm which cools quickly like the courage of Southern nations; it is as difficult to inflame him as it is to depress him. He does not need scenes, speeches, war-cries, songs, and drums; on the contrary he needs quiet, order, and an absence of any affectation. In a Russian, a real Russian, soldier you will never find any bragging, swagger, or desire to befog or excite himself in time of danger; on the contrary, modesty, simplicity, and a capacity for seeing in peril something quite else than the danger, are the distinctive features of his character. I have seen a soldier wounded in the leg, who in the first instant thought only of the hole in his new sheepskin cloak; and an artillery outrider who, creeping from beneath a horse that was killed under him, began unbuckling the girths to save the saddle. Who does not remember the incident at the siege of Gergebel when the fuse of a loaded bomb caught fire in the laboratory and an artillery sergeant ordered two soldiers to take the bomb and run to throw it into the ditch, and how the soldiers did not run to the nearest spot by the colonel's tent, which stood over the ditch, but took it farther on so as not to wake the gentlemen asleep in the tent and were consequently both blown to pieces? I remember also how, in the expedition of 1852, something led a young soldier while in action to say he thought the platoon would never escape, and how the whole platoon angrily attacked him for such evil words which they did not like even to repeat. And now, when the thought of Velenchúk must have been in the mind of each one and when we might expect Tartars to steal up at any moment and fire a volley at us, everyone listened to Chíkin's sprightly stories and no one referred either to the day's action, or to the present danger, or to the wounded man; as if it had all happened goodness knows how long ago or had never happened at all. But it seemed to me that their faces were rather sterner than usual, that they did not listen to Chíkin so very attentively, and that even Chíkin himself felt he was not being listened to, but talked for the sake of talking.

Maksímov joined us at the fire and sat down beside me. Chíkin made room for him, stopped speaking, and started sucking at his pipe once more.

'The infantry have been sending to the camp for vodka,' said Maksímov after a considerable silence; 'they have just returned.' He spat into the fire. 'The sergeant says they saw our man.'

'Is he alive?' asked Antónov, turning the pot.

'No, he's dead.'

The young recruit suddenly raised his head in the little red cap, looked intently for a minute over the fire at Maksímov and at me, then quickly let his head sink again and wrapped himself in his cloak.

'There now, it wasn't for naught that death had laid its hand on him when I had to wake him in the "park" this morning,' said Antónov.

'Nonsense!' said Zhdánov, turning the smouldering log, and all were silent.

Then, amid the general silence, came the report of a gun from the camp behind us. Our drummers beat an answering tattoo. When the last vibration ceased Zhdánov rose first, taking off his cap. We all followed his example.

Through the deep silence of the night rose an harmonious choir of manly voices:

'Our Father which art in heaven, hallowed be Thy name. Thy kingdom come. Thy will be done as in heaven so on earth. Give us day by day our daily bread. And forgive us our debts as we forgive our debtors. And lead us not into temptation; but deliver us from the evil one.'

'We had a man in '45 who was wounded in the same place,' said Antónov when we had put on our caps and again sat down by the fire. 'We carried him about with us on a gun for two days—do you remember Shévchenko, Zhdánov?—and then we just left him there under a tree.'

At this moment an infantryman with tremendous whiskers

and moustaches came up to our fire, carrying a musket and pouch.

'Give me a light for my pipe, comrades,' said he.

'All right, smoke away: there's fire enough,' remarked Chíkin.

'I suppose it's about Dargo[2] you are telling, comrade,' said the infantry soldier to Antónov.

'Yes, about Dargo in '45,' Antónov replied.

The infantryman shook his head, screwed up his eyes, and sat down on his heels near us.

'Yes, all sorts of things happened there,' he remarked.

'Why did you leave him behind?' I asked Antónov.

'He was suffering a lot with his stomach. As long as we halted it was all right, but as soon as we moved on he screamed aloud and asked for God's sake to be left behind—but we felt it a pity. But when *he* began to give it us hot, killed three of our men from the guns and an officer besides and we somehow got separated from our battery. . . . It was such a go! We thought we shouldn't get our guns away. It was muddy and no mistake!'

'The mud was worst under the Indéysky[3] Mountain,' remarked one of the soldiers.

'Yes, it was there he got more worse! So we considered it with Anóshenka—he was an old artillery sergeant. "Now really he can't live and he's asking for God's sake to be left behind; let us leave him here." So we decided. There was a tree, such a branchy one, growing there. Well, we took some soaked hard-tack Zhdánov had, and put it near him, leant him against the tree, put a clean shirt on him, and said good-bye,—all as it should be—and left him.'

'And was he a good soldier?'

'Yes, he was all right as a soldier,' remarked Zhdánov.

'And what became of him God only knows,' continued Antónov; 'many of the likes of us perished there.'

---

[2] Dargo, in the Térek Territory, was the head-quarters of Shamyl until 1845.

[3] The soldier miscalls the Andíysky chain of mountains 'Indéysky,' apparently connecting them with India.

'What, at Dargo?' said the infantryman as he rose, scraping out his pipe and again half-closing his eyes and shaking his head; 'all sorts of things happened there.'

And he left us.

'And have we many still in the battery who were at Dargo?' I asked.

'Many? Why, there's Zhdánov, myself, Patsán who is now on furlough, and there may be six others, not more.'

'And why's our Patsán holiday-making all this time?' said Chíkin, stretching out his legs and lying down with his head on a log. 'I reckon he's been away getting on for a year.'

'And you, have you had your year at home?' I asked Zhdánov.

'No, I didn't go,' he answered unwillingly.

'You see, it's all right to go,' said Antónov, 'if they're well off at home or if you are yourself fit to work; then it's tempting to go and they're glad to see you.'

'But where's the use of going when one's one of two brothers?' continued Zhdánov. 'It's all they can do to get their bread; how should they feed a soldier like me? I'm no help to them after twenty-five years' service. And who knows whether they're alive still?'

'Haven't you ever written?' I asked.

'Yes, indeed! I wrote two letters, but never had an answer. Either they're dead, or simply won't write because they're living in poverty themselves; so where's the good?'

'And is it long since you wrote?'

'I wrote last when we returned from Dargo . . . Won't you sing us "The Birch-Tree"?' he said, turning to Antónov, who sat leaning his elbows on his knees and humming a song.

Antónov began to sing 'The Birch-Tree'.

'This is the song Daddy Zhdánov likes most best of all,' said Chíkin to me in a whisper, pulling at my cloak. 'Sometimes he right down weeps when Philip Antónych sings it.'

Zhdánov at first sat quite motionless with eyes fixed on the glimmering embers, and his face, lit up by the reddish light, seemed very gloomy; then his jaws below his ears began to move faster and faster, and at last he rose, and spreading out his cloak, lay down in the shadow behind the fire. Either it was his tossing and groaning as he settled down to sleep, or it may have been the effect of Velenchúk's death and of the dull weather, but it really seemed to me that he was crying.

The bottom of the charred log, bursting every now and then into flames, lit up Antónov's figure with his grey moustaches, red face, and the medals on the cloak that he had thrown over his shoulders, or it lit up someone's boots, head, or back. The same gloomy drizzle fell from above, the air was still full of moisture and smoke, all around were the same bright spots of fires, now dying down, and amid the general stillness came the mournful sound of Antónov's song; and when that stopped for an instant the faint nocturnal sounds of the camp—snoring, clanking of sentries' muskets, voices speaking in low tones—took part.

'Second watch! Makatyúk and Zhdánov!' cried Maksímov. Antónov stopped singing. Zhdánov rose, sighed, stepped across the log, and went slowly towards the guns.

15 *June* 1855.

# SEVASTOPOL IN DECEMBER 1854*

The early dawn is just beginning to colour the horizon above the Sapún Hill. The dark blue surface of the sea has already thrown off the gloom of night and is only awaiting the first ray of the sun to begin sparkling merrily. A current of cold misty air blows from the bay; there is no snow on the hard black ground, but the sharp morning frost crunches under your feet and makes your face tingle. The distant, incessant murmur of the sea, occasionally interrupted by the reverberating boom of cannon from Sevastopol, alone infringes the stillness of the morning. All is quiet on the ships. It strikes eight bells.

On the north side the activity of day is beginning gradually to replace the quiet of night: here some soldiers with clanking muskets pass to relieve the guard, there a doctor is already hurrying to the hospital, and there a soldier, having crept out of his dug-out, washes his weather-beaten face with icy water and then turning to the reddening horizon says his prayers, rapidly crossing himself: a creaking Tartar cart drawn by camels crawls past on its way to the cemetery to bury the blood-stained dead with which it is loaded almost to the top. As you approach the harbour you are struck by the peculiar smell of coal-smoke, manure, dampness, and meat. Thousands

---

* When this first of Tolstoy's three accounts of the siege of Sevastopol during the Crimean War was published in 1855, it aroused much favorable comment. Alexander II read it with emotion, had it translated into French, and is reported to have dispatched an order to 'guard well the life of that young man.'

of different objects are lying in heaps by the harbour: firewood, meat, gabions, sacks of flour, iron, and so on. Soldiers of various regiments, some carrying bags and muskets and others empty-handed, are crowded together here, smoking, quarrelling, and hauling heavy loads onto the steamer which lies close to the wharf, its funnel smoking. Private boats crowded with all sorts of people—soldiers, sailors, merchants, and women—keep arriving at the landing stage or leaving it.

'To the Gráfskaya, your Honour? Please to get in!' Two or three old salts offer you their services, getting out of their boats.

You choose the one nearest to you, step across the half-decayed carcass of a bay horse that lies in the mud close to the boat, and pass on towards the rudder. You push off from the landing stage, and around you is the sea, now glittering in the morning sunshine. In front of you the old sailor in his camel-hair coat, and a flaxen-haired boy, silently and steadily ply the oars. You gaze at the enormous striped ships scattered far and wide over the bay, at the ships' boats that move about over the sparkling azure like small black dots, at the opposite bank where the handsome light-coloured buildings of the town are lit up by the rosy rays of the morning sun, at the foaming white line by the breakwater and around the sunken vessels, the black tops of whose masts here and there stand mournfully out of the water, at the enemy's fleet looming on the crystal horizon of the sea, and at the foaming and bubbling wash of the oars. You listen to the steady sound of voices that reaches you across the water, and to the majestic sound of firing from Sevastopol which as it seems to you is growing more intense.

It is impossible for some feeling of heroism and pride not to penetrate your soul at the thought that you, too, are in Sevastopol, and for the blood not to run faster in your veins.

'Straight past the *Kistentin*,[1] your Honour!' the old sailor tells you, turning round to verify the direction towards the right in which you are steering.

---

[1] The vessel, the *Constantine*.

'And she's still got all her guns!'[2] says the flaxen-headed boy, examining the ship in passing.

'Well, of course. She's a new one. Kornílov lived on her,' remarks the old seaman, also looking up at the ship.

'Look where it's burst!' the boy says after a long silence, watching a small white cloud of dispersing smoke that has suddenly appeared high above the South Bay accompanied by the sharp sound of a bursting bomb.

'That's *him* firing from the new battery to-day,' adds the old seaman, calmly spitting on his hand. 'Now then, pull away Míshka! Let's get ahead of that long-boat.' And your skiff travels faster over the broad swell of the roadstead, gets ahead of the heavy long-boat laden with sacks and unsteadily and clumsily rowed by soldiers, and making its way among all sorts of boats moored there, is made fast to the Gráfsky landing.

Crowds of grey-clad soldiers, sailors in black, and gaily-dressed women, throng noisily about the quay. Here are women selling buns, Russian peasants with samovars[3] are shouting, 'Hot sbíten!',[4] and here too on the very first steps lie rusty cannon-balls, bombs, grape-shot, and cannon of various sizes. A little farther on is a large open space where some enormous beams are lying, together with gun carriages and sleeping soldiers. Horses, carts, cannon, green ammunition wagons, and stacked muskets, are standing there. Soldiers, sailors, officers, women, children, and tradespeople, are moving about, carts loaded with hay, sacks, and casks, are passing, and now and then a Cossack, a mounted officer, or a general in a vehicle. To the right is a street closed by a barricade on which some small guns are mounted in embrasures and beside which sits a sailor smoking a pipe. To the left is a handsome building with Roman figures engraved on its frontage and before which soldiers are standing with blood-stained

---

[2] The guns were removed from most of the ships for use on the fortifications.

[3] The samovár, or 'self-boiler,' is an urn in which water can be boiled and kept hot without any other fire having to be lit.

[4] A hot drink made with treacle and lemon, or honey and spice.

stretchers. Everywhere you will see the unpleasant indications of a war camp. Your first impressions will certainly be most disagreeable: the strange mixture of camp-life and town-life —of a fine town and a dirty bivouac—is not only ugly but looks like horrible disorder: it will even seem to you that every one is scared, in a commotion, and at a loss what to do. But look more closely at the faces of these people moving about around you and you will get a very different impression. Take for instance this convoy soldier muttering something to himself as he goes to water those three bay horses, and doing it all so quietly that he evidently will not get lost in this motley crowd which does not even exist as far as he is concerned, but will do his job be it what it may—watering horses or hauling guns—as calmly, self-confidently, and unconcernedly as if it were all happening in Túla or Saránsk. You will read the same thing on the face of this officer passing by in immaculate white gloves, on the face of the sailor who sits smoking on the barricade, on the faces of the soldiers waiting in the portico of what used to be the Assembly Hall, and on the face of that girl who, afraid of getting her pink dress muddy, is jumping from stone to stone as she crosses the street.

Yes, disenchantment certainly awaits you on entering Sevastopol for the first time. You will look in vain in any of these faces for signs of disquiet, perplexity, or even of enthusiasm, determination, or readiness for death—there is nothing of the kind. What you see are ordinary people quietly occupied with ordinary activities, so that perhaps you may reproach yourself for having felt undue enthusiasm and may doubt the justice of the ideas you had formed of the heroism of the defenders of Sevastopol, based on the tales and descriptions and sights and sounds seen and heard from the North Side. But before yielding to such doubts go to the bastions and see the defenders of Sevastopol at the very place of the defence, or better still go straight into that building opposite which was once the Sevastopol Assembly Rooms and in the portico of which stand soldiers with stretchers. There you will see the defenders of Sevastopol and will see terrible and lamentable, solemn and amusing, but astounding and soul-elevating sights.

You enter the large Assembly Hall. As soon as you open the door you are struck by the sight and smell of forty or fifty amputation and most seriously wounded cases, some in cots but most of them on the floor. Do not trust the feeling that checks you at the threshold, it is a wrong feeling. Go on, do not be ashamed of seeming to have come to *look* at the sufferers, do not hesitate to go up and speak to them. Sufferers like to see a sympathetic human face, like to speak of their sufferings, and to hear words of love and sympathy. You pass between the rows of beds and look for a face less stern and full of suffering, which you feel you can approach and speak to.

'Where are you wounded?' you inquire hesitatingly and timidly of an emaciated old soldier who is sitting up in his cot and following you with a kindly look as if inviting you to approach him. I say 'inquire timidly' because, besides strong sympathy, sufferings seem to inspire a dread of offending, as well as a great respect for him who endures them.

'In the leg,' the soldier replies, and at the same moment you yourself notice from the fold of his blanket that one leg is missing from above the knee. 'Now, God be thanked,' he adds, 'I am ready to leave the hospital.'

'Is it long since you were wounded?'

'Well, it's over five weeks now, your Honour.'

'And are you still in pain?'

'No, I'm not in any pain now; only when it's bad weather I seem to feel a pain in the calf, else it's all right.'

'And how did it happen that you were wounded?'

'It was on the Fifth Bastion, your Honour, at the first *bond-barment*. I trained the gun and was stepping across to the next embrasure, when *he* hits me in the leg, just as if I had stumbled into a hole. I look—and the leg is gone.'

'Do you mean to say you felt no pain the first moment?'

'Nothing much, only as if something hot had shoved against my leg.'

'And afterwards?'

'And nothing much afterwards except when they began to

draw the skin together, then it did seem to smart. The chief
thing, your Honour, is *not to think;* if you don't think it's
nothing much. It's most because of a man thinking.'

At this moment a woman in a grey striped dress and with a
black kerchief tied round her head comes up to you and
enters into your conversation with the sailor. She begins telling you about him, about his sufferings, the desperate condition he was in for four weeks, and of how when he was
wounded he stopped his stretcher-bearers that he might see
a volley fired from our battery; and how the Grand Duke
spoke to him and gave him twenty-five rubles, and how he
had told them he wanted to go back to the bastion to teach
the young ones, if he could not himself work any longer. As
she says all this in a breath, the woman keeps looking now at
you and now at the sailor, who having turned away is picking
lint on his pillow as if not listening, and her eyes shine with
a peculiar rapture.

'She's my missus, your Honour!' he remarks with a look
that seems to say: 'You must excuse her. It's a woman's way
to talk nonsense.'

You begin now to understand the defenders of Sevastopol,
and for some reason begin to feel ashamed of yourself in the
presence of this man. You want to say too much, in order to
express your sympathy and admiration, but you can't find the
right words and are dissatisfied with those that occur to you,
and so you silently bow your head before this taciturn and
unconscious grandeur and firmness of spirit—which is ashamed
to have its worth revealed.

'Well, may God help you to get well soon,' you say to him,
and turn to another patient who is lying on the floor apparently awaiting death in unspeakable torment.

He is a fair-haired man with a puffy pale face. He is lying
on his back with his left arm thrown back in a position that
indicates cruel suffering. His hoarse breathing comes with
difficulty through his parched, open mouth; his leaden blue
eyes are rolled upwards, and what remains of his bandaged
right arm is thrust out from under his tumbled blanket. The

oppressive smell of mortified flesh assails you yet more strongly, and the feverish inner heat in all the sufferer's limbs seems to penetrate you also.

'Is he unconscious?' you ask the woman who follows you and looks at you kindly as at someone akin to her.

'No, he can still hear, but not at all well,' and she adds in a whisper: 'I gave him some tea to drink to-day—what if he is a stranger, one must have pity—but he hardly drank any of it.'

'How do you feel?' you ask him.

The wounded man turns his eyes at the sound of your voice, but neither sees nor understands you.

'My heart's on fire,' he mumbles.

A little farther on you see an old soldier who is changing his shirt. His face and body are a kind of reddish brown and as gaunt as a skeleton. Nothing is left of one of his arms. It has been amputated at the shoulder. He sits up firmly, he is convalescent; but his dull, heavy look, his terrible emaciation and the wrinkles on his face, show that the best part of this man's life has been consumed by his sufferings.

In a cot on the opposite side you see a woman's pale, delicate face, full of suffering, a hectic flush suffusing her cheek.

'That's the wife of one of our sailors: she was hit in the leg by a bomb on the 5th,' [5] your guide will tell you. 'She was taking her husband's dinner to him at the bastion.'

'Amputated?'

'Yes, cut off above the knee.'

Now, if your nerves are strong, go in at the door to the left; it is there they bandage and operate. There you will see doctors with pale, gloomy faces, and arms red with blood up to the elbows, busy at a bed on which a wounded man lies under chloroform. His eyes are open and he utters, as if in delirium, incoherent but sometimes simple and pathetic words. The doctors are engaged on the horrible but beneficent work of amputation. You will see the sharp curved knife enter

---

[5] The first bombardment of Sevastopol was on the 5th of October 1854, old style, that is, the 17th of October, new style.

the healthy white flesh; you will see the wounded man come back to life with terrible, heart-rending screams and curses. You will see the doctor's assistant toss the amputated arm into a corner and in the same room you will see another wounded man on a stretcher watching the operation, and writhing and groaning not so much from physical pain as from the mental torture of anticipation. You will see ghastly sights that will rend your soul; you will see war not with its orderly beautiful and brilliant ranks, its music and beating drums, its waving banners, its generals on prancing horses, but war in its real aspect of blood, suffering, and death. . . .

On coming out of this house of pain you will be sure to experience a sense of relief, you will draw deeper breaths of the fresh air, and rejoice in the consciousness of your own health. Yet the contemplation of those sufferings will have made you realize your own insignificance, and you will go calmly and unhesitatingly to the bastions.

'What matters the death and suffering of so insignificant a worm as I, compared to so many deaths, so much suffering?' But the sight of the clear sky, the brilliant sun, the beautiful town, the open church, and the soldiers moving in all directions, will soon bring your spirit back to its normal state of frivolity, its petty cares and absorption in the present. You may meet the funeral procession of an officer as it leaves the church, the pink coffin accompanied by waving banners and music, and the sound of firing from the bastions may reach your ears. But these things will not bring back your former thoughts. The funeral will seem a very beautiful military pageant, the sounds very beautiful warlike sounds; and neither to these sights nor these sounds will you attach the clear and personal sense of suffering and death that came to you in the hospital.

Passing the church and the barricade you enter that part of the town where everyday life is most active. On both sides of the street hang the signboards[6] of shops and restaurants.

---

[6] Among a population largely illiterate, the signboards were usually pictorial. The bakers showed loaves and rolls, the bootmakers boots and shoes, and so on.

Tradesmen, women with bonnets or kerchiefs on their heads, dandified officers—everything speaks of the firmness, self-confidence, and security of the inhabitants.

If you care to hear the conversation of army and navy officers, enter the restaurant on the right. There you are sure to hear them talk about last night, about Fanny, about the affair of the 24th,[7] about how dear and badly served the cutlets are, and how such and such of their comrades have been killed.

'Things were confoundedly bad at our place today!' a fair beardless little naval officer with a green knitted scarf round his neck says in a bass voice.

'Where was that?' asks another.

'Oh, in the Fourth Bastion,' answers the young officer, and at the words 'Fourth Bastion' you will certainly look more attentively and even with a certain respect at this fair-complexioned officer. The excessive freedom of his manner, his gesticulations, and his loud voice and laugh, which had appeared to you impudent before, now seem to indicate that peculiarly combative frame of mind noticeable in some young men after they have been in danger, but all the same you expect him to say how bad the bombs and bullets made things in the Fourth Bastion. Not at all! It was the mud that made things so bad. 'One can scarcely get to the battery,' he continues, pointing to his boots, which are muddy even above the calves. 'And I have lost my best gunner,' says another, 'hit right in the forehead.' 'Who's that? Mitúkhin?' 'No . . . but am I ever to have my veal, you rascal?' he adds, addressing the waiter. 'Not Mitúkhin but Abrámov—such a fine fellow. He was out in six sallies.'

At another corner of the table sit two infantry officers with plates of cutlets and peas before them and a bottle of sour Crimean wine called 'Bordeaux'. One of them, a young man with a red collar and two little stars on his cloak, is talking to the other, who has a black collar and no stars, about the

---

[7] The 24th October o.s. = 5th November n.s., the date of the Battle of Inkerman.

Alma affair. The former has already been drinking and the pauses he makes, the indecision in his face—expressive of his doubt of being believed—and especially the fact that his own part in the account he is giving is too important and the thing is too terrible, show that he is diverging considerably from the strict truth. But you do not care much for the stories of this kind, which will long be current all over Russia; you want to get quickly to the bastions, especially to that Fourth Bastion about which you have been told so many and such different tales. When anyone says: 'I am going to the Fourth Bastion' he always betrays a slight agitation or too marked an indifference; if anyone wishes to chaff you, he says: 'You should be sent to the Fourth Bastion.' When you meet someone carried on a stretcher and ask, 'Where from?' the answer usually is, 'From the Fourth Bastion'. Two quite different opinions are current concerning this terrible bastion[8]: that of those who have never been there and who are convinced it is a certain grave for any one who goes, and that of those who, like the fair-complexioned midshipman, live there and who when speaking of the Fourth Bastion will tell you whether it is dry or muddy, whether it is cold or warm in the dug-outs, and so forth.

During the half-hour you have spent in the restaurant the weather has changed. The mist that spread over the sea has gathered into dull grey moist clouds which hide the sun, and a kind of dismal sleet showers down and wets the roofs, the pavements, and the soldiers' overcoats.

Passing another barricade you go through some doors to the right and up a broad street. Beyond this barricade the houses on both sides of the street are unoccupied: there are no sign-boards, the doors are boarded up, the windows smashed, here a corner of the wall is knocked down and there a roof is broken in. The buildings look like old veterans who have borne much sorrow and privation; they even seem to gaze proudly and somewhat contemptuously at you. On the road you stumble over cannon-balls that lie about, and into holes

[8] Called by the English the 'Flagstaff Bastion.'

made in the stony ground by bombs and full of water. You
meet and overtake detachments of soldiers, Cossacks, officers,
and occasionally a woman or a child; only it will not be a
woman wearing a bonnet, but a sailor's wife wearing an old
cloak and soldiers' boots. After you have descended a little
slope farther down the same street you will no longer see any
houses, but only ruined walls amid strange heaps of bricks,
boards, clay, and beams, and before you, up a steep hill, you
see a black untidy space cut up by ditches. This space you
are approaching is the Fourth Bastion. . . . Here you will
meet still fewer people and no women at all, the soldiers walk
briskly by, there are traces of blood on the road, and you are
sure to meet four soldiers carrying a stretcher and on the
stretcher probably a pale yellow face and a blood-stained
overcoat. If you ask, 'Where is he wounded?' the bearers without looking at you will answer crossly, 'in the leg' or 'in the
arm' if the man is not severely wounded, or will remain
sternly silent if no head is raised on the stretcher and the
man is either dead or seriously wounded.

The whiz of cannon-ball or bomb near by impresses you
unpleasantly as you ascend the hill, and the meaning of the
sounds is very different from what it seemed to be when they
reached you in the town. Some peaceful and joyous memory
will suddenly flash through your mind; self-consciousness begins to supersede the activity of your observation: you are
less attentive to all that is around you and a disagreeable feeling of indecision suddenly seizes you. But silencing this despicable little voice that has suddenly made itself heard within
you at the sight of danger—especially after seeing a soldier
run past you laughing, waving his arms, and slipping downhill through the yellow mud—you involuntarily expand your
chest, raise your head higher, and clamber up the slippery
clay hill. You have climbed only a little way before bullets
begin to whiz past you to the right and left, and you will perhaps consider whether you had not better walk inside the
trench which runs parallel to the road; but the trench is full
of such yellow liquid stinking mud, more than knee deep, that
you are sure to choose the road, especially as *everybody* does

so. After walking a couple of hundred yards you come to a muddy place much cut up, surrounded by gabions, cellars, platforms, and dug-outs, and on which large cast-iron cannon are mounted and cannon-balls lie piled in orderly heaps. It all seems placed without any plan, aim, connexion, or order. Here a group of sailors are sitting in the battery; here in the middle of the open space, half sunk in mud, lies a shattered cannon; and there a foot-soldier is crossing the battery, drawing his feet with difficulty out of the sticky mud. Everywhere, on all sides and all about, you see fragments of bombs, unexploded bombs, cannon balls, and various traces of an encampment, all sunk in the liquid, sticky mud. You think you hear the thud of a cannon-ball not far off and you seem to hear the different sounds of bullets all around, some humming like bees, some whistling, and some rapidly flying past with a shrill screech like the string of some instrument. You hear the dreadful boom of a shot that sends a shock all through you and seems most terrible.

'So this is the Fourth Bastion! This is that terrible, truly dreadful spot!' So you think, experiencing a slight feeling of pride and a strong feeling of suppressed fear. But you are mistaken, this is not the Fourth Bastion yet. This is only Yazónovsky Redoubt—comparatively a very safe and not at all dreadful place. To get to the Fourth Bastion you must turn to the right along that narrow trench where a foot-soldier has just passed, stooping down. In this trench you may again meet men with stretchers and perhaps a sailor or a soldier with a spade. You will see the mouths of mines, dug-outs into which only two men can crawl, and there you will see the Cossacks of the Black Sea battalions changing their boots, eating, smoking their pipes, and in short living. And again you will see the same stinking mud, the traces of camp life and cast-iron refuse of every shape and form. When you have gone some three hundred steps more you will come out at another battery—a flat space with many holes, surrounded with gabions filled with earth, and cannons on platforms, and the whole walled in with earthworks. Here you will perhaps see four or five soldiers playing cards under shelter of the breastworks, and a naval officer, noticing that you are a stranger and inquisitive, will be pleased to show you his 'household' and everything that can interest you. This officer sits on a cannon rolling a yellow cigarette so composedly, walks from one embrasure to another so quietly, talks to you so calmly and with such an absence of affectation, that in spite of the bullets whizzing around you oftener than before you yourself grow cooler, question him carefully and listen to his stories. He will tell you (but only if you ask) about the bombardment on the 5th of October; will tell you that only one gun of his battery remained usable and only eight gunners of the crew were left, and that nevertheless he fired all his guns next morning, the 6th. He will tell you how a bomb dropped into one of the dug-outs and knocked over eleven sailors; from an embrasure he will show you the enemy's batteries and trenches which are here not more than seventy-five to eighty-five yards distant. I am afraid though, that when you lean out of the embrasure to have a look at the enemy the whiz of the flying bullets will hinder you from seeing anything, but if you do see anything you will be much surprised to find that this whitish stone wall—which is so near you and from which puffs of white smoke keep bursting—is the enemy: *he,* as the soldiers and sailors say.

It is even very likely that the naval officer from vanity, or merely for a little recreation, will wish to show you some firing. 'Call the gunner and crew to the cannon!' and fourteen sailors—their hob-nailed boots clattering on the platform, one putting his pipe in his pocket, another still chewing a rusk—will quickly and cheerfully man the gun and begin loading. Look well into these faces and note the bearing and carriage of these men. In every wrinkle of that tanned face with its high cheek-bones, in every muscle, in the breadth of those shoulders, the thickness of those legs in their enormous boots, in every movement, quiet, firm, and deliberate, can be seen the chief characteristic of the strength of the Russian—his simplicity and obstinacy.

Suddenly the most fearful roar strikes not only your ears

but your whole being and makes you shudder all over. It is followed by the whistle of the departing ball, and a thick cloud of powder-smoke envelops you, the platform, and the black moving figures of the sailors. You will hear various comments made by the sailors concerning this shot of ours and you will notice their animation, the evidences of a feeling you had not perhaps expected: the feeling of animosity and thirst for vengeance which lies hidden in each man's soul. You will hear joyful exclamations: 'It's gone right into the embrasure! It's killed two, I think. . . . There, they're carrying them off!' 'And now *he's* riled and will send one this way,' some one remarks; and really, soon after, you will see before you a flash and some smoke; the sentinel standing on the breastwork will call out 'Ca-n-non!', and then a ball will whiz past you and bury itself in the earth, throwing out a circle of stones and mud. The commander of the battery will be irritated by this shot and will give orders to fire another and another cannon, the enemy will reply in like manner, and you will experience interesting sensations and see interesting sights. The sentinel will again call 'Cannon!' and you will have the same sound and shock, and the mud will be splashed around as before. Or he will call out 'Mortar!' and you will hear the regular and rather pleasant whistle—which is difficult to connect with the thought of anything dreadful—of a bomb; you will hear this whistle coming nearer and faster towards you, then you will see a black ball, feel the shock as it strikes the ground, and will hear the ringing explosion. The bomb will fly apart into whizzing and shrieking fragments, stones will rattle in the air, and you will be bespattered with mud.

At these sounds you will experience a strange feeling of mingled pleasure and fear. At the moment you know the shot is flying towards you, you are sure to imagine that it will kill you, but a feeling of pride will support you and no one will know of the knife that cuts at your heart. But when the shot has flown past without hitting you, you revive and are seized, though only for a moment, by an inexpressibly joyful emotion, so that you feel a peculiar delight in the danger—in this game of life and death—and wish the bombs and balls to fall nearer and nearer to you.

But again the sentinel in his loud gruff voice shouts 'Mortar!', again a whistle, a fall, an explosion; and mingled with this last you are startled by a man's groans. You approach the wounded sailor just as the stretchers are brought. Covered with blood and dirt he presents a strange, scarcely human, appearance. Part of his breast has been torn away. For the first few moments only terror and the kind of feigned, premature, look of suffering, common to men in this state, appear on his mud-besprinkled face, but when the stretcher is brought and he himself lies down on it on his healthy side you notice that his expression changes. His eyes shine more brightly, his teeth are clenched, he raises his head higher with difficulty, and when the stretcher is lifted he stops the bearers for a moment and turning to his comrades says with an effort, in a trembling voice, 'Forgive me, brothers!' [9] He wishes to say more, something pathetic, but only repeats, 'Forgive me, brothers!' At this moment a sailor approaches him, places the cap on the head the wounded man holds up towards him, and then placidly swinging his arms returns quietly to his cannon.

'That's the way with seven or eight every day,' the naval officer remarks to you, answering the look of horror on your face, and he yawns as he rolls another yellow cigarette.

So now you have seen the defenders of Sevastopol where they are defending it, and somehow you return with a tranquil heightened spirit, paying no heed to the balls and bombs whose whistle accompanies you all the way to the ruined theatre. The principal thought you have brought away with you is a joyous conviction of the strength of the Russian people; and this conviction you have gained not by looking at all those traverses, breastworks, cunningly interlaced trenches, mines, cannon, one after another, of which you

---

[9] 'Forgive me' and 'farewell' are almost interchangeable expressions in Russian. 'Good-bye' (*prostcháyte*) etymologically means 'forgive.' The form (*prostíte*) here used, however, means primarily 'forgive me.'

could make nothing; but from the eyes, words, and actions—
in short from seeing what is called the 'spirit'—of the defenders of Sevastopol. What they do is all done so simply,
with so little effort, that you feel convinced that they could
do a hundred times as much. . . . You understand that the
feeling which actuates them is not that petty ambition or
forgetfulness which you yourself experienced, but something
more powerful, which has made them able to live so quietly
under the flying balls, exposed to a hundred chances of death
besides the one all men are subject to—and this amid conditions of constant toil, lack of sleep, and dirt. Men could not
accept such terrible conditions of life for the sake of a cross,
or promotion, or because of a threat: there must be some
other and higher motive power.

It is only now that the tales of the early days of the siege
of Sevastopol are no longer beautiful historical legends for
you, but have become realities: the tales of the time when it
was not fortified, when there was no army to defend it, when
it seemed a physical impossibility to retain it and yet there was
not the slightest idea of abandoning it to the enemy—of the
time when Kornílov, that hero worthy of ancient Greece, making his round of the troops, said, 'Lads, we will die, but will
not surrender Sevastopol!' and our Russians, incapable of
phrase-making, replied, 'We will die! Hurrah!' You will clearly
recognize in the men you have just seen those heroes who
gladly prepared for death and whose spirits did not flag during those dismal days, but rose.

The evening is closing in. Just before setting, the sun
emerges from behind the grey clouds that covered the sky
and suddenly lights up with its bright red glow the purple
clouds, the greenish sea with the ships and boats rocking on
its broad even swell, the white buildings of the town, and the
people moving in the streets. The sound of some old valse
played by a military band on the boulevard is carried across
the water and mingles strangely with the sound of firing on
the bastions.

*Sevastopol, 25 April o.s. 1855.*

# SEVASTOPOL IN MAY 1855*

## I

Six months have passed since the first cannon-ball went whistling from the bastions of Sevastopol and threw up the earth of the enemy's entrenchments. Since then bullets, balls, and bombs by the thousand have flown continually from the bastions to the entrenchments and from the entrenchments to the bastions, and above them the angel of death has hovered unceasingly.

Thousands of human ambitions have had time to be mortified, thousands to be gratified and extend, thousands to be lulled to rest in the arms of death. What numbers of pink coffins and linen palls! And still the same sounds from the bastions fill the air; the French still look from their camp with involuntary trepidation and fear at the yellowy earth of the bastions of Sevastopol and count the embrasures from which the iron cannon frown fiercely; as before, through the fixed telescope on the elevation of the signal-station the pilot still watches the bright-coloured figures of the French, their batteries, their tents, their columns on the green hill, and the puffs of smoke that rise from the entrenchments; and as before, crowds of different men, with a still greater variety of

* In May 1855 Tolstoy was transferred from the Fourth Bastion to the Belbek River where he commanded a battery of mountain guns. In July he sent to his publisher this second Sevastopol piece. With Tolstoy's longer service and broader experience, the idealizing patriotism of his first Sevastopol narrative vanished and he now described war with all its cruelty, stupidity and heroism. The censor made a number of alterations, but in the present translation Tolstoy's original manuscript has been followed.

desires, stream with the same ardour from many parts of the world to this fatal spot. But the question the diplomatists did not settle still remains unsettled by powder and blood.

## II

A regimental band was playing on the boulevard near the pavilion in the besieged town of Sevastopol, and crowds of women and military men strolled along the paths making holiday. The bright spring sun had risen in the morning above the English entrenchments, had reached the bastions, then the town and the Nicholas Barracks, shining with equal joy on all, and was now sinking down to the distant blue sea which, rocking with an even motion, glittered with silvery light.

A tall infantry officer with a slight stoop, drawing on a presentable though not very white glove, passed out of the gate of one of the small sailors' houses built on the left side of the Morskáya Street and gazing thoughtfully at the ground ascended the hill towards the boulevard. The expression of his plain face did not reveal much intellectual power, but rather good-nature, common sense, honesty, and an inclination to respectability. He was badly built, and seemed rather shy and awkward in his movements. His cap was nearly new, a gold watch-chain showed from under his thin cloak of a rather peculiar lilac shade, and he wore trousers with foot-straps, and clean, shiny calf-skin boots. He might have been a German (but that his features indicated his purely Russian origin), an adjutant, or a regimental quartermaster (but in that case he would have worn spurs), or an officer transferred from the cavalry or the Guards for the duration of the war. He was in fact an officer who had exchanged from the cavalry, and as he ascended the hill towards the boulevard he was thinking of a letter he had received from a former comrade now retired from the army, a landed proprietor in the government of T———, and of his great friend, the pale, blue-eyed Natásha, that comrade's wife. He recalled a part of the letter where his comrade wrote:

'When we receive the *Invalide*,[1] Púpka' (so the retired Uhlan called his wife) 'rushes headlong into the hall, seizes the paper, and runs with it to a seat in the arbour or the drawing-room—in which, you remember, we spent such jolly winter evenings when your regiment was stationed in our town—and reads of *your* heroic deeds with an ardour you cannot imagine. She often speaks of you. "There now," she says, "Mikháylov is a *darling*. I am ready to cover him with kisses when I see him. He [is fighting on the bastions and] is certain to receive a St. George's Cross, and they'll write about him in the papers," &c., &c., so that I am beginning to be quite jealous of you.'

In another place he wrote: 'The papers reach us awfully late, and though there are plenty of rumours one cannot believe them all. For instance, those musical young ladies you know of, were saying yesterday that Napoleon has been captured by our Cossacks and sent to St. Petersburg, but you can imagine how much of this I believe. One fresh arrival from Petersburg tells us for certain (he is a capital fellow, sent by the Minister on special business—and now there is no one in the town you can't think what a *resource* he is to us), that we have taken Eupatoria [so that the French are cut off from Balaclava], and that we lost two hundred in the affair and the French as many as fifteen thousand. My wife was in such raptures that she *caroused* all night and said that a presentiment assured her that you distinguished yourself in that affair.'

In spite of the words and expressions I have purposely italicized, and the whole tone of the letter, Lieutenant-Captain Mikháylov thought with an inexpressibly melancholy pleasure about his pale-faced provincial friend and how he used to sit with her of an evening in the arbour, talking *sentiment*. He thought of his kind comrade the Uhlan: how the latter used to get angry and lose when they played cards in the study for kopek points and how his wife used to laugh at him. He recalled the friendship these people had for him (perhaps

[1] The Army and Navy Gazette.

he thought there was something more on the side of the pale-faced friend): these people and their surroundings flitted through his memory in a wonderfully sweet, joyously rosy light and, smiling at the recollection, he put his hand to the pocket where this *dear* letter lay.

From these recollections Lieutenant-Captain Mikháylov involuntarily passed to dreams and hopes. 'How surprised and pleased Natásha will be,' he thought as he passed along a narrow side-street, 'when she reads in the *Invalide* of my being the first to climb on the cannon, and receiving the St. George! I ought to be made full captain on that former recommendation. Then I may easily become a major this year by seniority, because so many of our fellows have been killed and no doubt many more will be killed this campaign. Then there'll be more fighting and I, as a well-known man, shall be entrusted with a regiment . . . then a lieutenant-colonel, the order of St. Anna . . . a colonel' . . . and he was already a general, honouring with a visit Natásha, the widow of his comrade (who would be dead by that time according to his daydream)—when the sounds of the music on the boulevard reached his ears more distinctly, a crowd of people appeared before his eyes, and he realized that he was on the boulevard and a lieutenant-captain of infantry as before.

### III

He went first to the pavilion, beside which stood the band with soldiers of the same regiment acting as music-stands and holding open the music books, while around them clerks, cadets, nursemaids, and children formed a circle, looking on rather than listening. Most of the people who were standing, sitting, and sauntering round the pavilion were naval officers, adjutants, and white-gloved army officers. Along the broad avenue of the boulevard walked officers of all sorts and women of all sorts—a few of the latter in hats, but the greater part with kerchiefs on their heads, and some with neither kerchiefs nor hats—but it was remarkable that there was not a single old woman amongst them—all were young.

Lower down, in the scented alleys shaded by the white acacias, isolated groups sat or strolled.

No one was particularly glad to meet Lieutenant-Captain
Mikháylov on the boulevard, except perhaps Captain Obzhógov of his regiment and Captain Súslikov who pressed his
hand warmly, but the first of these wore camel-hair trousers,
no gloves, and a shabby overcoat, and his face was red and
perspiring, and the second shouted so loud and was so free
and easy that one felt ashamed to be seen walking with him,
especially by those white-gloved officers—to one of whom,
an adjutant, Mikháylov bowed, and he might have bowed to
another, a Staff officer whom he had twice met at the house
of a mutual acquaintance. Besides, what was the fun of walking with Obzhógov and Súslikov when as it was he met them
and shook hands with them six times a day? Was this what
he had come to hear *the music* for?

He would have liked to accost the adjutant whom he had
bowed to and to talk with those gentlemen, not at all that he
wanted Captains Obzhógov and Súslikov and Lieutenant Pash-
tétski and others to see him talking to them, but simply because they were pleasant people who knew all the news and
might have told him something.

But why is Lieutenant-Captain Mikháylov afraid and unable to muster courage to approach them? 'Supposing they
don't return my greeting,' he thinks, 'or merely bow and go
on talking among themselves as if I were not there, or simply
walk away and leave me standing among the aristocrats?' The
word aristocrats (in the sense of the highest and most select
circle of any class) has lately gained great popularity in Russia, where one would think it ought not to exist. It has made
its way to every part of the country, and into every grade
of society which can be reached by vanity—and to what conditions of time and circumstance does this pitiful propensity
not penetrate? You find it among merchants, officials, clerks,
officers—in Sarátov, Mamadíshi, Vínnitza, in fact wherever
men are to be found. And since there are many men, and
consequently much vanity, in the besieged town of Sevastopol,

aristocrats are to be found here too, though death hangs over everyone, be he aristocrat or not.

To Captain Obzhógov, Lieutenant-Captain Mikháylov was an aristocrat, and to Lieutenant-Captain Mikháylov, Adjutant Kalúgin was an aristocrat, because he was an adjutant and intimate with another adjutant. To Adjutant Kalúgin, Count Nórdov was an aristocrat, because he was an aide-de-camp to the Emperor.

Vanity! vanity! vanity! everywhere, even on the brink of the grave and among men ready to die for a noble cause. Vanity! It seems to be the characteristic feature and special malady of our time. How is it that among our predecessors no mention was made of this passion, as of small-pox and cholera? How is it that in our time there are only three kinds of people: those who, considering vanity an inevitably existing fact and therefore justifiable, freely submit to it; those who regard it as a sad but unavoidable condition; and those who act unconsciously and slavishly under its influence? Why did the Homers and Shakespeares speak of love, glory, and suffering, while the literature of to-day is an endless story of snobbery and vanity?

Twice the lieutenant-captain passed irresolutely by the group of his aristocrats, but drawing near them for the third time he made an effort and walked up to them. The group consisted of four officers: Adjutant Kalúgin, Mikháylov's acquaintance, Adjutant Prince Gáltsin who was rather an aristocrat even for Kalúgin himself, Lieutenant-Colonel Nefërdov, one of the so-called 'two hundred and twenty-two' society men, who being on the retired list re-entered the army for this war, and Cavalry-Captain Praskúkhin, also of the 'two hundred and twenty-two'. Luckily for Mikháylov, Kalúgin was in splendid spirits (the General had just spoken to him in a very confidential manner, and Prince Gáltsin who had arrived from Petersburg was staying with him), so he did not think it beneath his dignity to shake hands with Mikháylov, which was more than Praskúkhin did though he had often met Mikháylov on the bastion, had more than once drunk his wine and vodka, and even owed him twelve and a half rubles lost at cards. Not being yet well acquainted with Prince Gáltsin he did not like to appear to be acquainted with a mere lieutenant-captain of infantry. So he only bowed slightly.

'Well, Captain,' said Kalúgin, 'when will you be visiting the bastion again? Do you remember our meeting at the Schwartz Redoubt? Things were hot, weren't they, eh?'

'Yes, very,' said Mikháylov, and he recalled how when making his way along the trench to the bastion he had met Kalúgin walking bravely along, his sabre clanking smartly.

'My turn's to-morrow by rights, but we have an officer ill', continued Mikháylov, 'so———'

He wanted to say that it was not his turn but as the Commander of the 8th Company was ill and only the ensign was left in the company, he felt it his duty to go in place of Lieutenant Nepshisétski and would therefore be at the bastion that evening. But Kalúgin did not hear him out.

'I feel sure that something is going to happen in a day or two,' he said to Prince Gáltsin.

'How about to-day? Will nothing happen to-day?' Mikháylov asked shyly, looking first at Kalúgin and then at Gáltsin.

No one replied. Prince Gáltsin only puckered up his face in a curious way and looking over Mikháylov's cap said after a short silence:

'Fine girl that, with the red kerchief. You know her, don't you, Captain?'

'She lives near my lodgings, she's a sailor's daughter,' answered the lieutenant-captain.

'Come, let's have a good look at her.'

And Prince Gáltsin gave one of his arms to Kalúgin and the other to the lieutenant-captain, being sure he would confer great pleasure on the latter by so doing, which was really quite true.

The lieutenant-captain was superstitious and considered it a great sin to amuse himself with women before going into action; but on this occasion he pretended to be a *roué*, which Prince Gáltsin and Kalúgin evidently did not believe and which greatly surprised the girl with the red kerchief, who had more than once noticed how the lieutenant-captain blushed when he passed her window. Praskúkhin walked behind them, and kept touching Prince Gáltsin's arm and making various remarks in French, but as four people could not walk abreast on the path he was obliged to go alone until, on the second round, he look the arm of a well-known brave naval officer, Servyágin, who came up and spoke to him, being also anxious to join the aristocrats. And the well-known hero gladly passed his honest muscular hand under the elbow of Praskúkhin, whom everybody, including Servyágin himself, knew to be no better than he should be. When, wishing to explain his acquaintance with this sailor, Praskúkhin whispered to Prince Gáltsin that this was the well-known hero, Prince Gáltsin—who had been in the Fourth Bastion the day before and seen a shell burst at some twenty yards' distance—considering himself not less courageous than the newcomer, and believing that many reputations are obtained by luck, paid not the slightest attention to Servyágin.

Lieutenant-Captain Mikháylov found it so pleasant to walk in this company that he forgot the nice letter from T——— and his gloomy forebodings at the thought of having to go to the bastion. He remained with them till they began talking exclusively among themselves, avoiding his eyes to show that he might go, and at last walked away from him. But all the same the lieutenant-captain was contented, and when he passed Cadet Baron Pesth—who was particularly conceited and self-satisfied since the previous night, when for the first time in his life he had been in the bomb-proof of the Fifth Bastion and had consequently become a hero in his own estimation—he was not at all hurt by the suspiciously haughty expression with which the cadet saluted him.

## IV

But the lieutenant-captain had hardly crossed the threshold of his lodgings before very different thoughts entered his head. He saw his little room with its uneven earth floor, its crooked windows, the broken panes mended with paper, his old bedstead with two Túla pistols and a rug (showing a lady on horseback) nailed to the wall beside it,[1] as well as the dirty bed of the cadet who lived with him, with its cotton quilt. He saw his man Nikíta, with his rough greasy hair, rise from the floor scratching himself, he saw his old cloak, his common boots, a little bundle tied in a handkerchief ready for him to take to the bastion, from which peeped a bit of cheese and the neck of a porter bottle containing vodka—and he suddenly remembered that he had to go with his company to spend the whole night at the lodgements.

'I shall certainly be killed to-night,' thought he, 'I feel I shall. And there was really no need for me to go—I offered to do it of my own accord. And it always happens that the one who offers himself gets killed. And what is the matter with that confounded Nepshisétski? He may not be ill at all, and they'll go and kill me because of him—they're sure to. Still, if they don't kill me I shall certainly be recommended for promotion. I saw how pleased the regimental commander was when I said: "Allow me to go if Lieutenant Nepshisétski is ill." If I'm not made a major then I'll get the Order of Vladímir for certain. Why, I am going to the bastion for the thirteenth time. Oh dear, the thirteenth! Unlucky number! I am certain to be killed. I feel I shall . . . but somebody had to go: the company can't go with only an ensign. Supposing something were to happen. . . . Why, the honour of the regiment, the honour of the army is at stake. It is my *duty* to go. Yes, my sacred duty. . . . But I have a presentiment.'

The lieutenant-captain forgot that it was not the first time he had felt this presentiment: that in a greater or lesser degree he had it whenever he was going to the bastion, and he did not know that before going into action everyone has such forebodings more or less strongly. Having calmed himself by appealing to his sense of duty—which was highly developed and very strong—the lieutenant-captain sat down at the table

---

[1] A common way in Russia of protecting a bed from the damp or cold of a wall, is to nail a rug or carpet to the wall by the side of the bed.

and began writing a farewell letter to his father. Ten minutes later, having finished his letter, he rose from the table his eyes wet with tears, and repeating mentally all the prayers he knew he began to dress. His rather tipsy and rude servant lazily handed him his new cloak—the old one which the lieutenant-captain usually wore at the bastion not being mended.

'Why isn't my cloak mended? You do nothing but sleep,' said Mikháylov angrily.

'Sleep indeed!' grumbled Nikíta, 'I do nothing but run about like a dog the whole day, and when I get fagged I mayn't even go to sleep!'

'I see you are drunk again.'

'It's not at your expense if I am, so you needn't complain.'

'Hold your tongue, you dolt!' shouted the lieutenant-captain, ready to strike the man.

Already upset, he now quite lost patience and felt hurt by the rudeness of Nikíta, who had lived with him for the last twelve years and whom he was fond of and even spoilt.

'Dolt? Dolt?' repeated the servant. 'And why do you, sir, abuse me and call me a dolt? You know in times like these it isn't right to abuse people.'

Recalling where he was about to go Mikháylov felt ashamed.

'But you know, Nikíta, you would try anyone's patience!' he said mildly. 'That letter to my father on the table you may leave where it is. Don't touch it,' he added reddening.

'Yes, sir,' said Nikíta, becoming sentimental under the influence of the vodka he had drunk, as he said, at his own expense, and blinking with an evident inclination to weep.

But at the porch, when the lieutenant-captain said, 'Good-bye, Nikíta,' Nikíta burst into forced sobs and rushed to kiss his master's hand, saying, 'Good-bye, sir,' in a broken voice. A sailor's widow who was also standing in the porch could not, as a woman, help joining in this tender scene, and began wiping her eyes on her dirty sleeve, saying something about people who, though they were gentlefolk, took such sufferings upon themselves while she, poor woman, was left a widow.

And she told the tipsy Nikíta for the hundredth time about her sorrows; how her husband had been killed in the first *bondbarment*, and how her hut had been shattered (the one she lived in now was not her own) and so on. After his master was gone Nikíta lit his pipe, asked the landlady's little girl to get some vodka, very soon left off crying, and even had a quarrel with the old woman about a pail he said she had smashed for him.

'But perhaps I shall only be wounded,' reasoned the lieutenant-captain as he drew near the bastion with his company when twilight had already begun to fall. 'But where, and how? Here or here?' he said to himself, mentally passing his chest, his stomach, and his thighs in review. 'Supposing it's here' (he thought of his thighs) 'and goes right round. . . . Or goes here with a piece of a bomb, then it will be all up.'

The lieutenant-captain passed along the trenches and reached the lodgements safely. In perfect darkness he and an officer of Engineers set the men to their work, after which he sat down in a pit under the breastwork. There was little firing; only now and again there was a lightning flash on our side or *his*, and the brilliant fuse of a bomb formed a fiery arc on the dark, star-speckled sky. But all the bombs fell far beyond or far to the right of the lodgement where the lieutenant-captain sat in his pit. He drank some vodka, ate some cheese, smoked a cigarette, said his prayers, and felt inclined to sleep for a while.

## V

Prince Gáltsin, Lieutenant-Colonel Neferdov, and Praskúkhin —whom no one had invited and to whom no one spoke, but who still stuck to them—went to Kalúgin's to tea.

'But you did not finish telling me about Váska Méndel,' said Kalúgin, when he had taken off his cloak and sat in a soft easy chair by the window unbuttoning the collar of his clean starched shirt. 'How did he get married?'

'It was a joke, my boy! . . . *Je vous dis, il y avait un*

*temps, on ne parlait que de ça à Pétersbourg,'* [1] said Prince
Gáltsin, laughing as he jumped up from the piano-stool and
sat down near Kalúgin on the window-sill,[2] 'a capital joke. I
know all about it.'

And he told, amusingly, cleverly, and with animation, a
love story which, as it has no interest for us, we will omit.

It was noticeable that not only Prince Gáltsin but each of
these gentlemen who established themselves, one on the
window-sill, another with his legs in the air, and a third by
the piano, seemed quite different people now from what they
had been on the boulevard. There was none of the absurd
arrogance and haughtiness they had shown towards the infantry officers; here among themselves they were natural,
and Kalúgin and Prince Gáltsin in particular showed themselves very pleasant, merry, and good-natured young fellows.
Their conversation was about their Petersburg fellow officers
and acquaintances.

'What of Máslovski?'

'Which one—the Leib-Uhlan, or the Horse Guard?'

'I know them both. The one in the Horse Guards I knew
when he was a boy just out of school. But the eldest—is he a
captain yet?'

'Oh yes, long ago.'

'Is he still fussing about with his gipsy?'

'No, he has dropped her. . . .' And so on in the same
strain.

Later on Prince Gáltsin went to the piano and gave an
excellent rendering of a gipsy song. Praskúkhin, chiming in
unasked, put in a second and did it so well that he was invited to continue, and this delighted him.

A servant brought tea, cream, and cracknels on a silver
tray.

'Serve the prince,' said Kalúgin.

---

[1] 'I tell you, at one time it was only the only thing talked of in Petersburg.'

[2] The thick walls of Russian houses allow ample space to sit or
lounge at the windows.

'Isn't it strange to think that we're in a besieged town,' said Gáltsin, taking his tea to the window, 'and here's a *pianer-forty*, tea with cream, and a house such as I should really be glad to have in Petersburg?'

'Well, if we hadn't even that much,' said the old and ever-dissatisfied lieutenant-colonel, 'the constant uncertainty we are living in—seeing people killed day after day and no end to it—would be intolerable. And to have dirt and discomfort added to it——.'

'But our infantry officers live at the bastions with their men in the bomb-proofs and eat the soldiers' soup', said Kalúgin, 'what of them?'

'What of them? Well, though it's true they don't change their shirts for ten days at a time, they are heroes all the same—wonderful fellows.'

Just then an infantry officer entered the room.

'I . . . I have orders . . . may I see the Gen . . . his Excellency? I have come with a message from General N.,' he said with a timid bow.

Kalúgin rose and without returning the officer's greeting asked with an offensive, affected, official smile if he would not have the goodness to wait; and without asking him to sit down or taking any further notice of him he turned to Gáltsin and began talking French, so that the poor officer left alone in the middle of the room did not in the least know what to do with himself.

'It is a matter of the utmost urgency, sir,' he said after a short silence.

'Ah! Well then, please come with me,' said Kalúgin, putting on his cloak and accompanying the officer to the door.

.     .     .     .     .     .

'*Eh bien, messieurs, je crois que cela chauffera cette nuit,*' [3] said Kalúgin when he returned from the General's.

'Ah! What is it—a sortie?' asked the others.

---

[3] 'Well, gentlemen, I think there will be warm work to-night.'

'That I don't know. You will see for yourselves,' replied Kalúgin with a mysterious smile.

'And my commander is at the bastion, so I suppose I must go too,' said Praskúkhin, buckling on his sabre.

No one replied, it was his business to know whether he had to go or not.

Praskúkhin and Nefërdov left to go to their appointed posts.

'Good-bye gentlemen. *Au revoir!* We'll meet again before the night is over,' shouted Kalúgin from the window as Praskúkhin and Nefërdov, stooping on their Cossack saddles, trotted past. The tramp of their Cossack horses soon died away in the dark street.

'*Non, dites-moi, est-ce qu'il y aura véritablement quelque chose cette nuit?*' [4] said Gáltsin as he lounged in the window-sill beside Kalúgin and watched the bombs that rose above the bastions.

'I can tell *you*, you see . . . you have been to the bastions?' (Gáltsin nodded, though he had only been once to the Fourth Bastion). 'You remember just in front of our lunette there is a trench,'—and Kalúgin, with the air of one who without being a specialist considers his military judgement very sound, began, in a rather confused way and misusing the technical terms, to explain the position of the enemy, and of our own works, and the plan of the intended action.

'But I say, they're banging away at the lodgements! Oho! I wonder if that's ours or *his*? . . . Now it's burst,' said they as they lounged on the window-sill looking at the fiery trails of the bombs crossing one another in the air, at flashes that for a moment lit up the dark sky, at puffs of white smoke, and listened to the more and more rapid reports of the firing.

'*Quel charmant coup d'oeil! a?*' [5] said Kalúgin, drawing his guest's attention to the really beautiful sight. 'Do you know, you sometimes can't distinguish a bomb from a star.'

---

[4] 'No, tell me, will there really be anything to-night?'
[5] 'What a charming sight, eh?'

'Yes, I thought that was a star just now and then saw it fall . . . there! it's burst. And that big star—what do you call it?—looks just like a bomb.'

'Do you know I am so used to these bombs that I am sure when I'm back in Russia I shall fancy I see bombs every star-light night—one gets so used to them.'

'But hadn't I better go with this sortie?' said Prince Gáltsin after a moment's pause.

'Humbug, my dear fellow! Don't think of such a thing. Be-sides, I won't let you,' answered Kalúgin. 'You will have plenty of opportunities later on.'

'Really? You think I need not go, eh?'

At that moment, from the direction in which these gen-tlemen were looking, amid the boom of the cannon came the terrible rattle of musketry, and thousands of little fires flaming up in quick succession flashed all along the line.

'There! Now it's the real thing!' said Kalúgin. 'I can't keep cool when I hear the noise of muskets. It seems to seize one's very soul, you know. There's an *hurrah!*' he added, listening intently to the distant and prolonged roar of hundreds of voices—'Ah—ah—ah'—which came from the bastions.

'Whose *hurrah* was it? Theirs or ours?'

'I don't know, but it's hand-to-hand fighting now, for the firing has ceased.'

At that moment an officer followed by a Cossack galloped under the window and alighted from his horse at the porch.

'Where are you from?'

'From the bastion. I want the General.'

'Come along. Well, what's happened?'

'The lodgements have been attacked—and occupied. The French brought up tremendous reserves—attacked us—we had only two battalions,' said the officer, panting. He was the same officer who had been there that evening, but though he was now out of breath he walked to the door with full self-possession.

'Well, have we retired?' asked Kalúgin.

'No,' angrily replied the officer, 'another battalion came up in time—we drove them back, but the colonel is killed and many officers. I have orders to ask for reinforcements.'

And saying this he went with Kalúgin to the General's, where we shall not follow him.

Five minutes later Kalúgin was already on his Cossack horse (again in the semi-Cossack manner which I have noticed that all adjutants, for some reason, seem to consider the proper thing), and rode off at a trot towards the bastion to deliver some orders and await the final result of the affair. Prince Gáltsin, under the influence of that oppressive excitement usually produced in a spectator by proximity to an action in which he is not engaged, went out, and began aimlessly pacing up and down the street.

## VI

Soldiers passed carrying the wounded on stretchers or supporting them under their arms. It was quite dark in the streets, lights could be seen here and there, but only in the hospital windows or where some officers were sitting up. From the bastions still came the thunder of cannon and the rattle of muskets,[1] and flashes kept on lighting up the dark sky as before. From time to time the tramp of hoofs could be heard as an orderly galloped past, or the groans of a wounded man, the steps and voices of stretcher-bearers, or the words of some frightened women who had come out onto their porches to watch the cannonade.

Among the spectators were our friend Nikíta, the old sailor's widow with whom he had again made friends, and her ten-year-old daughter.

'O Lord God! Holy Mary, Mother of God!' said the old woman, sighing as she looked at the bombs that kept flying

---

[1] Rifles, except some clumsy *stutzers,* had not been introduced into the Russian army, but were used by the besiegers, who had a still greater advantage in artillery. It is characteristic of Tolstoy that, occupied with men rather than mechanics, he does not in these sketches dwell on this disparity of equipment.

across from side to side like balls of fire; 'What horrors! What horrors! Ah, ah! Oh, oh! Even at the first *bondbarment* it wasn't like that. Look now where the cursed thing has burst just over our house in the suburb.'

'No, that's further, they keep tumbling into Aunt Irene's garden,' said the girl.

'And where, where, is master now?' drawled Nikíta, who was not quite sober yet. 'Oh! You don't know how I love that master of mine! I love him so that if he were killed in a sinful way, which God forbid, then would you believe it, granny, after that I myself don't know what I wouldn't do to myself! I don't! . . . My master is that sort, there's only one word for it. Would I change him for such as them there, playing cards? What are they? Ugh! There's only one word for it!' concluded Nikíta, pointing to the lighted window of his master's room to which, in the absence of the lieutenant-captain, Cadet Zhvadchévski had invited Sub-Lieutenants Ugróvich and Nepshisétski—the latter suffering from face-ache—and where he was having a spree in honour of a medal he had received.

'Look at the stars! Look how they're rolling!' the little girl broke the silence that followed Nikíta's words as she stood gazing at the sky. 'There's another rolled down. What is it a sign of, mother?'

'They'll smash up our hut altogether,' said the old woman with a sigh, leaving her daughter unanswered.

'As we went there to-day with uncle, mother,' the little girl continued in a sing-song tone, becoming loquacious, 'there was such a b—i—g cannon-ball inside the room close to the cupboard. Must have smashed in through the passage and right into the room! Such a big one—you couldn't lift it.'

'Those who had husbands and money all moved away,' said the old woman, 'and there's the hut, all that was left me, and that's been smashed. Just look at *him* blazing away! The fiend! . . . O Lord! O Lord!'

'And just as we were going out, comes a bomb fly-ing, and goes and bur-sts and co-o-vers us with dust. A bit of it nearly hit me and uncle.'

## VII

Prince Gáltsin met more and more wounded carried on stretchers or walking supported by others who were talking loudly.

'Up they sprang, friends,' said the bass voice of a tall soldier with two guns slung from his shoulder, 'up they sprang, shouting "Allah! Allah!" [1] and just climbing one over another. You kill one and another's there, you couldn't do anything; no end of 'em——'

But at this point in the story Gáltsin interrupted him.

'You are from the bastion?'

'Yes, your Honour.'

'Well, what happened? Tell me.'

'What happened? Well, your Honour, such a force of 'em poured down on us over the rampart, it was all up. They quite overpowered us, your Honour!'

'Overpowered? . . . But you repulsed them?'

'How could we repulse them when *his* whole force came on, killed all our men, and no re'forcements were given us?'

The soldier was mistaken, the trench had remained ours; but it is a curious fact which anyone may notice, that a soldier wounded in action always thinks the affair lost and imagines it to have been a very bloody fight.

'How is that? I was told they had been repulsed,' said Gáltsin irritably. 'Perhaps they were driven back after you left? Is it long since you came away?'

'I am straight from there, your Honour,' answered the soldier, 'it is hardly possible. They must have kept the trench, *he* quite overpowered us.'

'And aren't you ashamed to have lost the trench? It's terrible!' said Gáltsin, provoked by such indifference.

'Why, if the strength is on their side . . . ' muttered the soldier.

[1] Our soldiers fighting the Turks have become so accustomed to this cry of the enemy that they now always say that the French also shout 'Allah!' L. T.

'Ah, your Honour,' began a soldier from a stretcher which had just come up to them, 'how could we help giving it up when *he* had killed almost all our men? If we'd had the strength we wouldn't have given it up, not on any account. But as it was, what could we do? I stuck one, and then something hits me. Oh, oh-h! Steady, lads, steady! Oh, oh!' groaned the wounded man.

'Really, there seem to be too many men returning,' said Gáltsin, again stopping the tall soldier with the two guns. 'Why are you retiring? You there, stop!'

The soldier stopped and took off his cap with his left hand.

'Where are you going, and why?' shouted Gáltsin severely, 'you scoun——'

But having come close up to the soldier, Gáltsin noticed that no hand was visible beneath the soldier's right cuff and that the sleeve was soaked in blood to the elbow.

'I am wounded, your Honour.'

'Wounded? How?'

'Here. Must have been with a bullet,' said the man, pointing to his arm, 'but I don't know what struck my head here,' and bending his head he showed the matted hair at the back stuck together with blood.

'And whose is this other gun?'

'It's a French rifle I took, your Honour. But I wouldn't have come away if it weren't to lead this fellow—he may fall,' he added, pointing to a soldier who was walking a little in front leaning on his gun and painfully dragging his left leg.

Prince Gáltsin suddenly felt horribly ashamed of his unjust suspicions. He felt himself blushing, turned away, and went to the hospital without either questioning or watching the wounded men any more.

Having with difficulty pushed his way through the porch among the wounded who had come on foot and the bearers who were carrying in the wounded and bringing out the dead, Gáltsin entered the first room, gave a look round, and involuntarily turned back and ran out into the street: it was too terrible.

## VIII

The large, lofty, dark hall, lit up only by the four or five candles with which the doctors examined the wounded, was quite full. Yet the bearers kept bringing in more wounded— laying them side by side on the floor which was already so packed that the unfortunate patients were jostled together, staining one another with their blood—and going to fetch more wounded. The pools of blood visible in the unoccupied spaces, the feverish breathing of several hundred men, and the perspiration of the bearers with the stretchers, filled the air with a peculiar, heavy, thick, fetid mist, in which the candles burnt dimly in different parts of the hall. All sorts of groans, sighs, death-rattles, now and then interrupted by shrill screams, filled the whole room. Sisters with quiet faces, expressing no empty feminine tearful pity, but active practical sympathy, stepped here and there across the wounded with medicines, water, bandages, and lint, flitting among the blood-stained coats and shirts. The doctors, kneeling with rolled-up sleeves beside the wounded, by the light of the candles their assistants held, examined, felt, and probed their wounds, heedless of the terrible groans and entreaties of the sufferers. One doctor sat at a table near the door and at the moment Gáltsin came in was already entering No. 532.

'Iván Bogáev, Private, Company Three, S— Regiment, *fractura femuris complicata!*' shouted another doctor from the end of the room, examining a shattered leg. 'Turn him over.'

'Oh, oh, fathers! Oh, you're our fathers!' screamed the soldier, beseeching them not to touch him.

'*Perforatio capitis!*'

'Simon Neferdov, Lieutenant-Colonel of the N— Infantry Regiment. Have a little patience, Colonel, or it is quite impossible: I shall give it up!' said a third doctor, poking about with some kind of hook in the unfortunate colonel's skull.

'Oh, don't! Oh, for God's sake be quick! Be quick! Ah——!'

'*Perforatio pectoris* . . . Sebastian Seredá, Private . . . what regiment? But you need not write that: *moritur*. Carry him away,' said the doctor, leaving the soldier, whose eyes turned up and in whose throat the death-rattle already sounded.

About forty soldier stretcher-bearers stood at the door waiting to carry the bandaged to the wards and the dead to the chapel. They looked on at the scene before them in silence, only broken now and then by a heavy sigh.

## IX

On his way to the bastion Kalúgin met many wounded, but knowing by experience that in action such sights have a bad effect on one's spirits, he did not stop to question them but tried on the contrary not to notice them. At the foot of the hill he met an orderly-officer galloping fast from the bastion.

'Zóbkin! Zóbkin! Wait a bit!'

'Well, what is it?'

'Where are you from?'

'The lodgements.'

'How are things there—hot?'

'Oh, awful!'

And the orderly galloped on.

In fact, though there was now but little small-arm firing, the cannonade had recommenced with fresh heat and persistence.

'Ah, that's bad!' thought Kalúgin with an unpleasant sensation, and he too had a presentiment—a very usual thought, the thought of death. But Kalúgin was ambitious and blessed with nerves of oak—in a word, he was what is called brave. He did not yield to the first feeling but began to nerve himself. He recalled how an adjutant, Napoleon's he thought, having delivered an order, galloped with bleeding head full speed to Napoleon, *'Vous êtes blessé?'* [1] said Napoleon. *'Je vous demande pardon, sire, je suis mort,'* [2] and the adjutant fell from his horse, dead.

---

[1] 'You are wounded?'

[2] 'Excuse me, sire, I am dead.'

That seemed to him very fine, and he pictured himself for
a moment in the role of that adjutant. Then he whipped his
horse, assuming a still more dashing Cossack seat, looked back
at the Cossack who, standing up in his stirrups, was trotting
behind, and rode quite gallantly up to the spot where he had
to dismount. Here he found four soldiers sitting on some stones
smoking their pipes.

'What are you doing there?' he shouted at them.

'Been carrying off a wounded man and sat down to rest a
bit, your Honour,' said one of them, hiding his pipe behind his
back and taking off his cap.

'Resting, indeed! . . . To your places, march!'

And he went up the hill with them through the trench,
meeting wounded men at every step.

After ascending the hill he turned to the left, and a few
steps farther on found himself quite alone. A splinter of a
bomb whizzed near him and fell into the trench. Another
bomb rose in front of him and seemed flying straight at him.
He suddenly felt frightened, ran a few steps at full speed,
and lay down flat. When the bomb burst a considerable distance off he felt exceedingly vexed with himself and rose,
looking round to see if anyone had noticed his downfall, but
no one was near.

But when fear has once entered the soul it does not easily
yield to any other feeling. He, who always boasted that he
never even stooped, now hurried along the trench almost on
all fours. He stumbled, and thought, 'Oh, it's awful! They'll
kill me for certain!' His breath came with difficulty, and perspiration broke out over his whole body. He was surprised at
himself but no longer strove to master his feelings.

Suddenly he heard footsteps in front. Quickly straightening
himself he raised his head, and boldly clanking his sabre
went on more deliberately. He felt himself quite a different
man. When he met an officer of the Engineers and a sailor,
and the officer shouted to him to lie down, pointing to a
bright spot which growing brighter and brighter approached
more and more swiftly and came crashing down close to the

trench, he only bent a little, involuntarily influenced by the frightened cry, and went on.

'That's a brave one,' said the sailor, looking quite calmly at the bomb and with experienced eye deciding at once that the splinters could not fly into the trench, 'he won't even lie down.'

It was only a few steps across open ground to the bomb-proof shelter of the Commander of the bastion, when Kalúgin's mind again became clouded and the same stupid terror seized him: his heart beat more violently, the blood rushed to his head, and he had to make an effort to force himself to run to the bomb-proof.

'Why are you so out of breath?' said the General, when Kalúgin had reported his instructions.

'I walked very fast, your Excellency!'

'Won't you have a glass of wine?'

Kalúgin drank a glass of wine and lit a cigarette. The action was over, only a fierce cannonade still continued from both sides. In the bomb-proof sat General N—, the Commander of the bastion, and some six other officers among whom was Praskúkhin. They were discussing various details of the action. Sitting in this comfortable room with blue wall-paper, a sofa, a bed, a table with papers on it, a wall-clock with a lamp burning before it, and an icón[3]—looking at these signs of habitation, at the beams more than two feet thick that formed the ceiling, and listening to the shots that sounded faint here in the shelter, Kalúgin could not understand how he had twice allowed himself to be overcome by such unpardonable weakness. He was angry with himself and wished for danger in order to test his nerve once more.

'Ah! I'm glad you are here, Captain,' said he to a naval officer with big moustaches who wore a staff-officer's coat with a St. George's Cross and had just entered the shelter and asked the General to give him some men to repair two em-

---

[3] The Russian icóns are paintings in Byzantine style of God, the Holy Virgin, Christ, or some saint, martyr, or angel. They are usually on wood and often covered over, except the face and hands, with an embossed gilt cover.

brasures of his battery which had become blocked. When the General had finished speaking to the captain, Kalúgin said: 'The Commander-in-Chief told me to ask if your guns can fire case-shot into the trenches.'

'Only one of them can,' said the captain sullenly.

'All the same, let us go and see.'

The captain frowned and gave an angry grunt.

'I have been standing there all night and have come in to get a bit of rest—couldn't you go alone?' he added. 'My assistant, Lieutenant Kartz, is there and can show you everything.'

The captain had already been more than six months in command of this, one of the most dangerous batteries. From the time the siege began, even before the bomb-proof shelters were constructed, he had lived continuously on the bastion and had a great reputation for courage among the sailors. That is why his refusal struck and surprised Kalúgin. 'So much for reputation,' thought he.

'Well then, I will go alone if I may,' he said in a slightly sarcastic tone to the captain, who however paid no attention to his words.

Kalúgin did not realize that whereas he had spent some fifty hours all in all at different times on the bastions, the captain had lived there for six months. Kalúgin was still actuated by vanity, the wish to shine, the hope of rewards, of gaining a reputation, and the charm of running risks. But the captain had already lived through all that: at first he had felt vain, had shown off his courage, had been foolhardy, had hoped for rewards and reputation and had even gained them, but now all these incentives had lost their power over him and he saw things differently. He fulfilled his duty exactly, but quite understanding how much the chances of life were against him after six months at the bastion, he no longer ran risks without serious need, and so the young lieutenant who had joined the battery a week ago and was now showing it to Kalúgin, with whom he vied in uselessly leaning out of the embrasures and climbing out on the banquette, seemed ten times braver than the captain.

Returning to the shelter after examining the battery, Kalúgin in the dark came upon the General, who accompanied by
his staff officers was going to the watch-tower.

'Captain Praskúkhin,' he heard the General say, 'please go
to the right lodgement and tell the second battalion of the
M— Regiment which is at work there to cease their work,
leave the place, and noiselessly rejoin their regiment which is
stationed in reserve at the foot of the hill. Do you understand?
Lead them yourself to the regiment.'

'Yes, sir.'

And Praskúkhin started at full speed towards the lodgements.

The firing was now becoming less frequent.

X

'Is this the second battalion of the M— Regiment?' asked
Praskúkhin, having run to his destination and coming across
some soldiers carrying earth in sacks.

'It is, your Honour.'

'Where is the Commander?'

Mikháylov, thinking that the commander of the company
was being asked for, got out of his pit and taking Praskúkhin
for a commanding officer saluted and approached him.

'The General's orders are . . . that you . . . should go
. . . . quickly . . . and above all quietly . . . back—no
not back, but to the reserves,' said Prashkúkhin, looking askance in the direction of the enemy's fire.

Having recognized Praskúkhin and made out what was
wanted, Mikháylov dropped his hand and passed on the order. The battalion became alert, the men took up their muskets, put on their cloaks, and set out.

No one without experiencing it can imagine the delight a
man feels when, after three hours' bombardment, he leaves so
dangerous a spot as the lodgements. During those three hours
Mikháylov, who more than once and not without reason had
thought his end at hand, had had time to accustom himself
to the conviction that he would certainly be killed and that

he no longer belonged to this world. But in spite of that he
had great difficulty in keeping his legs from running away
with him when, leading the company with Praskúkhin at his
side, he left the lodgement.

'Au revoir!' said a major with whom Mikháylov had eaten
bread and cheese sitting in the pit under the breastwork and
who was remaining at the bastion in command of another
battalion. 'I wish you a lucky journey.'

'And I wish you a lucky defence. It seems to be getting
quieter now.'

But scarcely had he uttered these words before the enemy,
probably observing the movement in the lodgement, began
to fire more and more frequently. Our guns replied and a
heavy firing recommenced.

The stars were high in the sky but shone feebly. The night
was pitch dark, only the flashes of the guns and the bursting
bombs made things around suddenly visible. The soldiers
walked quickly and silently, involuntarily outpacing one another; only their measured footfall on the dry road was heard
besides the incessant roll of the guns, the ringing of bayonets
when they touched one another, a sigh, or the prayer of some
poor soldier lad: 'Lord, O Lord! What does it mean?' Now
and again the moaning of a man who was hit could be heard,
and the cry, 'Stretchers!' (In the company Mikháylov commanded artillery fire alone carried off twenty-six men that
night.) A flash on the dark and distant horizon, the cry,
'Can-n-on!' from the sentinel on the bastion, and a ball flew
buzzing above the company and plunged into the earth, making the stones fly.

'What the devil are they so slow for?' thought Praskúkhin,
continually looking back as he marched beside Mikháylov.
'I'd really better run on. I've delivered the order. . . . But
no, they might afterwards say I'm a coward. What must be
will be. I'll keep beside him.'

'Now why is he walking with me?' thought Mikháylov on
his part. 'I have noticed over and over again that he always
brings ill luck. Here it comes, I believe, straight for us.'

After they had gone a few hundred paces they met Kalú-

gin, who was walking briskly towards the lodgements clanking his sabre. He had been ordered by the General to find
out how the works were progressing there. But when he met
Mikháylov he thought that instead of going there himself
under such a terrible fire—which he was not ordered to do—
he might just as well find out all about it from an officer who
had been there. And having heard from Mikháylov full details
of the work and walked a little way with him, Kalúgin turned
off into a trench leading to the bomb-proof shelter.

'Well, what news?' asked an officer who was eating his supper there all alone.

'Nothing much. It seems that the affair is over.'

'Over? How so? On the contrary, the General has just gone
again to the watch-tower and another regiment has arrived.
Yes, there it is. Listen! The muskets again! Don't you go—
why should you?' added the officer, noticing that Kalúgin
made a movement.

'I certainly ought to be there,' thought Kalúgin, 'but I have
already exposed myself a great deal to-day: the firing is awful!'

'Yes, I think I'd better wait here for him,' he said.

And really about twenty minutes later the General and the
officers who were with him returned. Among them was Cadet
Baron Pesth but not Praskúkhin. The lodgements had been
retaken and occupied by us.

After receiving a full account of the affair Kalúgin, accompanied by Pesth, left the bomb-proof shelter.

## XI

'There's blood on your coat! You don't mean to say you were
in the hand-to-hand fight?' asked Kalúgin.

'Oh, it was awful! Just fancy——'

And Pesth began to relate how he had led his company,
how the company-commander had been killed, how he himself had stabbed a Frenchman, and how if it had not been
for him we should have lost the day.

This tale was founded on fact: the company-commander

had been killed and Pesth had bayoneted a Frenchman, but in recounting the details the cadet invented and bragged.

He bragged unintentionally, because during the whole of the affair he had been as it were in a fog and so bewildered that all he remembered of what had happened seemed to have happened somewhere, at some time, and to somebody. And very naturally he tried to recall the details in a light advantageous to himself. What really occurred was this:

The battalion the cadet had been ordered to join for the sortie stood under fire for two hours close to some low wall. Then the battalion-commander in front said something, the company-commanders became active, the battalion advanced from behind the breastwork, and after going about a hundred paces stopped to form into company columns. Pesth was told to take his place on the right flank of the second company.

Quite unable to realize where he was and why he was there, the cadet took his place, and involuntarily holding his breath while cold shivers ran down his back he gazed into the dark distance expecting something dreadful. He was however not so much frightened (for there was no firing) as disturbed and agitated at being in the field beyond the fortifications.

Again the battalion-commander in front said something. Again the officers spoke in whispers passing on the order, and the black wall, formed by the first company, suddenly sank out of sight. The order was to lie down. The second company also lay down and in lying down Pesth hurt his hand on a sharp prickle. Only the commander of the second company remained standing. His short figure brandishing a sword moved in front of the company and he spoke incessantly.

'Mind lads! Show them what you're made of! Don't fire, but give it them with the bayonet—the dogs!—when I cry "Hurrah!" Altogether, mind, that's the thing! We'll let them see who we are. We won't disgrace ourselves, eh lads? For our father the Tsar!'

'What's your company-commander's name?' asked Pesth of a cadet lying near him. 'How brave he is!'

'Yes he always is, in action,' answered the cadet. 'His name is Lisinkóvski.'

Just then a flame suddenly flashed up right in front of the company, who were deafened by a resounding crash. High up in the air stones and splinters clattered. (Some fifty seconds later a stone fell from above and severed a soldier's leg.) It was a bomb fired from an elevated stand, and the fact that it reached the company showed that the French had noticed the column.

'You're sending bombs, are you? Wait a bit till we get at you, then you'll taste a three-edged Russian bayonet, damn you!' said the company-commander so loud that the battalion-commander had to order him to hold his tongue and not make so much noise.

After that the first company got up, then the second. They were ordered to fix bayonets and the battalion advanced. Pesth was in such a fright that he could not in the least make out how long it lasted, where he went, or who was who. He went on as if he were drunk. But suddenly a million fires flashed from all sides, and something whistled and clattered. He shouted and ran somewhere, because everyone shouted and ran. Then he stumbled and fell over something. It was the company-commander, who had been wounded at the head of his company, and who taking the cadet for a Frenchman had seized him by the leg. Then when Pesth had freed his leg and got up, someone else ran against him from behind in the dark and nearly knocked him down again. 'Run him through!' someone else shouted. 'Why are you stopping?' Then someone seized a bayonet and stuck it into something soft. 'Ah Dieu!' came a dreadful, piercing voice and Pesth only then understood that he had bayoneted a Frenchman. A cold sweat covered his whole body, he trembled as in a fever and threw down his musket. But this lasted only a moment; the thought immediately entered his head that he was a hero. He again seized his musket, and shouting 'Hurrah!' ran with the crowd away from the dead Frenchman. Having run twenty paces he came to a trench. Some of our men were there with the battalion-commander.

'And I have killed one!' said Pesth to the commander.

'You're a fine fellow, Baron!'

## XII

'Do you know Praskúkhin is killed?' said Pesth, while accompanying Kalúgin on his way home.

'Impossible!'

'It is true. I saw him myself.'

'Well, good-bye . . . I must be off.'

'This is capital!' thought Kalúgin, as he came to his lodgings. 'It's the first time I have had such luck when on duty. It's first-rate. I am alive and well, and shall certainly get an excellent recommendation and am sure of a gold sabre. And I really have deserved it.'

After reporting what was necessary to the General he went to his room, where Prince Gáltsin, long since returned, sat awaiting him, reading a book he had found on Kalúgin's table.

It was with extraordinary pleasure that Kalúgin found himself safe at home again, and having put on his night-shirt and got into bed he gave Gáltsin all the details of the affair, telling them very naturally from a point of view where those details showed what a capable and brave officer he, Kalúgin, was (which it seems to me it was hardly necessary to allude to, since everybody knew it and had no right or reason to question it, except perhaps the deceased Captain Praskúkhin who, though he had considered it an honour to walk arm in arm with Kalúgin, had privately told a friend only yesterday that though Kalúgin was a first-rate fellow, yet, 'between you and me, he was awfully disinclined to go to the bastions').

Praskúkhin, who had been walking beside Mikháylov after Kalúgin had slipped away from him, had scarcely begun to revive a little on approaching a safer place, than he suddenly saw a bright light flash up behind him and heard the sentinel shout 'Mortar!' and a soldier walking behind him say: 'That's coming straight for the bastion!'

Mikháylov looked round. The bright spot seemed to have stopped at its zenith, in the position which makes it absolutely impossible to define its direction. But that only lasted a moment: the bomb, coming faster and faster, nearer and nearer, so that the sparks of its fuse were already visible and its fatal whistle audible, descended towards the centre of the battalion.

'Lie down!' shouted someone.

Mikháylov and Praskúkhin lay flat on the ground. Praskúkhin, closing his eyes, only heard the bomb crash down on the hard earth close by. A second passed which seemed an hour: the bomb had not exploded. Praskúkhin was afraid. Perhaps he had played the coward for nothing. Perhaps the bomb had fallen far away and it only seemed to him that its fuse was fizzing close by. He opened his eyes and was pleased to see Mikháylov lying immovable at his feet. But at that moment he caught sight of the glowing fuse of the bomb which was spinning on the ground not a yard off. Terror, cold terror excluding every other thought and feeling, seized his whole being. He covered his face with his hands.

Another second passed—a second during which a whole world of feelings, thoughts, hopes, and memories flashed before his imagination.

'Whom will it hit—Mikháylov or me? Or both of us? And if it's me, where? In the head? Then I'm done for. But if it's the leg, they'll cut it off (I'll certainly ask for chloroform) and I may survive. But perhaps only Mikháylov will be hit. Then I will tell how we were going side by side and how he was killed and I was splashed with his blood. No, it's nearer to me . . . it will be I.'

Then he remembered the twelve rubles he owed Mikháylov, remembered also a debt in Petersburg that should have been paid long ago, and the gipsy song he had sung that evening. The woman he loved rose in his imagination wearing a cap with lilac ribbons. He remembered a man who had insulted him five years ago and whom he had not yet paid out. And yet, inseparable from all these and thousands of other recollections, the present thought, the expectation of death, did not leave him for an instant. 'Perhaps it won't explode,' and with desperate decision he resolved to open his eyes. But at that instant a red flame pierced through the still closed lids and something struck him in the middle of his chest with a terrible crash. He jumped up and began to run, but stumbling over the sabre that got between his legs he fell on his side.

'Thank God, I'm only bruised!' was his first thought, and he was about to touch his chest with his hand, but his arms seemed tied to his sides and he felt as if a vice were squeezing his head. Soldier's flitted past him and he counted them unconsciously: 'One, two, three soldiers! And there's an officer with his cloak tucked up,' he thought. Then lightning flashed before his eyes and he wondered whether the shot was fired from a mortar or a cannon. 'A cannon, probably. And there's another shot and here are more soldiers—five, six, seven soldiers. . . . They all pass by!' He was suddenly seized with fear that they would crush him. He wished to shout that he was hurt, but his mouth was so dry that his tongue clove to the roof of his mouth and a terrible thirst tormented him. He felt a wetness about his chest and this sensation of being wet made him think of water, and he longed to drink even this that made him feel wet. 'I suppose I hit myself in falling and made myself bleed,' thought he, and giving way more and more to fear lest the soldiers who kept flitting past might trample on him, he gathered all his strength and tried to shout, 'Take me with you!' but instead of that he uttered such a terrible groan that the sound frightened him. Then some other red fires began dancing before his eyes and it seemed to him that the soldiers put stones on him. The fires danced less and less but the stones they put on him pressed more and more heavily. He made an effort to push off the stones, stretched himself, and saw and heard and felt nothing more. He had been killed on the spot by a bomb-splinter in the middle of his chest.

## XIII

When Mikháylov dropped to the ground on seeing the bomb he too, like Praskúkhin, lived through an infinitude of thoughts and feelings in the two seconds that elapsed before the bomb burst. He prayed mentally and repeated, 'Thy will be done.' And at the same time he thought, 'Why did I enter the army? And why did I join the infantry to take part in this campaign? Wouldn't it have been better to have remained with the Uhlan regiment at T—— and spent my time with my friend Natásha? And now here I am . . ." and he began to count, 'One, two, three, four,' deciding that if the bomb burst at an even number he would live but if at an odd number he would be killed. 'It is all over, I'm killed!' he thought when the bomb burst (he did not remember whether at an odd or even number) and he felt a blow and a cruel pain in his head. 'Lord, forgive me my trespasses!' he muttered, folding his hands. He rose, but fell on his back senseless.

When he came to, his first sensations were that of blood trickling down his nose, and the pain in his head which had become much less violent. 'That's the soul passing,' he thought. 'How will it be *there*? Lord, receive my soul in peace! . . . Only it's strange,' thought he, 'that while dying I should hear the steps of the soldiers and the sounds of the firing so distinctly.'

'Bring stretchers! Eh, the Captain has been hit!' shouted a voice above his head, which he recognized as the voice of the drummer Ignátyev.

Someone took him by the shoulders. With an effort he opened his eyes and saw above him the sky, some groups of stars, and two bombs racing one another as they flew over him. He saw Ignátyev, soldiers with stretchers and guns, the embankment, the trenches, and suddenly realized that he was not yet in the other world.

He had been slightly wounded in the head by a stone. His first feeling was one almost of regret: he had prepared himself so well and so calmly to go *there* that the return to reality, with its bombs, stretchers, and blood, seemed unpleasant. The second feeling was unconscious joy at being alive, and the third a wish to get away from the bastion as quickly as possible. The drummer tied a handkerchief round his commander's head and taking his arm led him towards the ambulance station.

'But why and where am I going?' thought the lieutenant-captain when he had collected his senses. 'My duty is to re-

main with the company and not leave it behind—especially,'
whispered a voice, 'as it will soon be out of range of the guns.'

'Don't trouble about me, my lad,' said he, drawing his hand
away from the attentive drummer. 'I won't go to the ambulance station: I'll stay with the company.'

And he turned back.

'It would be better to have it properly bandaged, your
honour,' said Ignátyev. 'It's only in the heat of the moment
that it seems nothing. Mind it doesn't get worse. . . . And
just see what warm work it is here. . . . Really, your honour——'

Mikháylov stood for a moment undecided, and would probably have followed Ignátyev's advice had he not reflected how
many severely wounded there must be at the ambulance station. 'Perhaps the doctors will smile at my scratch,' thought
the lieutenant-captain, and in spite of the drummer's arguments he returned to his company.

'And where is the orderly officer Praskákhin, who was with
me?' he asked when he met the ensign who was leading the
company.

'I don't know. Killed, I think,' replied the ensign unwillingly.

'Killed? Or only wounded? How is it you don't know?
Wasn't he going with us? And why didn't you bring him
away?'

'How could we, under such a fire?'

'But how could you do such a thing, Michael Iványch?'
angrily. 'How could you leave him supposing he is alive?
Even if he's dead his body ought to have been brought away.'

'Alive indeed, when I tell you I went up and saw him
myself!' said the ensign. 'Excuse me. . . . It's hard enough
to collect our own. There, those villains are at it again!' he
added. 'They're sending up cannon-balls now.'

Mikháylov sat down and lifted his hands to his head, which
ached terribly when he moved.

'No, it is absolutely necessary to go back and fetch him,' he
said. He may still be alive. It is our *duty*, Michael Iványch.'

Michael Iványch did not answer.

'O Lord! Just because he didn't bring him in at the time, soldiers will have to be sent back alone now . . . and yet can I possibly send them under this terrible fire? They may be killed for nothing,' thought Mikháylov.

'Lads! Someone will have to go back to fetch the officer who was wounded out there in the ditch,' said he, not very loudly or peremptorily, for he felt how unpleasant it would be for the soldiers to execute this order. And he was right. Since he had not named any one in particular no one came forward to obey the order.

'And after all he may be dead already. It isn't worth exposing men uselessly to such danger. It's all my fault, I ought to have seen to it. I'll go back myself and find out whether he is alive. It is my *duty*,' said Mikháylov to himself.

'Michael Iványch, you lead the company, I'll catch you up,' said he, and holding up his cloak with one hand while with the other he kept touching a small icón of St. Metrophanes that hung round his neck and in which he had great faith, he ran quickly along the trench.

Having convinced himself that Praskúkhin was dead he dragged himself back panting, holding the bandage that had slipped on his head, which was beginning to ache very badly. When he overtook the battalion it was already at the foot of the hill and almost beyond the range of the shots. I say 'almost', for a stray bomb reached even here now and then.

'To-morrow I had better go and be entered at the ambulance station,' thought the lieutenant-captain, while a medical assistant, who had turned up, was bandaging his head.

## XIV

Hundreds of bodies, which a couple of hours before had been men full of various lofty or trivial hopes and wishes, were lying with fresh bloodstains on their stiffened limbs in the dewy, flowery valley which separated the bastions from the trenches and on the smooth floor of the mortuary chapel in Sevastopol. Hundreds of men with curses or prayers on their parched lips, crawled, writhed, and groaned, some among the dead in the flowery valley, some on stretchers, or beds, or on the blood-stained floor of the ambulance station. Yet the dawn broke behind the Sapún hill, the twinkling stars grew pale and the white mists spread from the dark roaring sea just as on other days, and the rosy morning glow lit up the east, long streaks of red clouds spread along the pale-blue horizon, and just as in the old days the sun rose in power and glory, promising joy, love, and happiness to all the awakening world.

## XV

Next evening the Chasseurs' band was again playing on the boulevard, and officers, cadets, soldiers, and young women, again promenaded round the pavilion and along the side-walks under the acacias with their sweet-scented white blossoms.

Kalúgin was walking arm in arm with Prince Gáltsin and a colonel near the pavilion and talking of last night's affair. The main theme of their conversation, as usual in such cases, was not the affair itself, but the part each of the speakers had taken in it. Their faces and the tone of their voices were serious, almost sorrowful, as if the losses of the night had touched and saddened them all. But to tell the truth, as none of them had lost any one very dear to him, this sorrowful expression was only an official one they considered it their duty to exhibit.

Kalúgin and the colonel in fact, though they were first-rate fellows, were ready to see such an affair every day if they could gain a gold sword and be made major-general each time. It is all very well to call some conqueror a monster because he destroys millions to gratify his ambition, but go and ask any Ensign Petrúshev or Sub-Lieutenant Antónov on their conscience, and you will find that everyone of us is a little Napoleon, a petty monster ready to start a battle and kill a hundred men merely to get an extra medal or one-third additional pay.

'No, I beg your pardon,' said the colonel. 'It began first on the left side. I was there myself.'

'Well, perhaps,' said Kalúgin. 'I spent more time on the

right. I went there twice: first to look for the General, and
then just to see the lodgements. It was hot there, I can tell
you!'

'Kalúgin ought to know,' said Gáltsin. 'By the way, V—
told *me* to-day that you are a trump————'

'But the losses, the losses are terrible!' said the colonel. 'In
my regiment we had four hundred casualties. It is astonishing that I'm still alive.'

Just then the figure of Mikháylov, with his head bandaged,
appeared at the end of the boulevard walking towards these
gentlemen.

'What, are you wounded, Captain?' asked Kalúgin.

'Yes, slightly, with a stone,' answered Mikháylov.

'*Est-ce que le pavillon est baissé déjà?*' [1] asked Prince Gáltsin, glancing at the lieutenant-captain's cap and not addressing anyone in particular.

'*Non, pas encore,*' [2] answered Mikháylov, wishing to show
that he understood and spoke French.

'Do you mean to say the truce still continues?' said Gáltsin,
politely addressing him in Russian and thereby (so it seemed
to the lieutenant-captain) suggesting: 'It must no doubt be
difficult for you to have to speak French, so hadn't we better
simply . . .' and with that the adjutants went away. The
lieutenant-captain again felt exceedingly lonely, just as he had
done the day before. After bowing to various people—some
of whom he did not wish and some of whom he did not ven-
ture to join—he sat down near the Kazárski monument and
smoked a cigarette.

Baron Pesth also turned up on the boulevard. He mentioned
that he had been at the parley and had spoken to the French
officers. According to his account one of them had said to
him: '*S'il n'avait pas fait clair encore pendant une demi-heure,
les ambuscades auraient été reprises,*' [3] and he replied, '*Monsieur, je ne dis pas non, pour ne pas vous donner un dé-*

---

[1] 'Is the flag (of truce) lowered already?'

[2] 'No, not yet.'

[3] 'Had it remained dark for another half-hour, the ambuscades
would have been recaptured.'

*menti,'* [4] and he told how pat it had come out, and so on.

But though he had been at the parley he had not really managed to say anything in particular, though he much wished to speak with the French ('for it's awfully jolly to speak to those fellows'). He had paced up and down the line for a long time asking the Frenchmen near him: *'De quel régiment êtes-vous?'* [5] and had got his answer and nothing more. When he went too far beyond the line, the French sentry, not suspecting that 'that soldier' knew French, abused him in the third person singular: *'Il vient regarder nos travaux, ce sacré ——'* [6] in consequence of which Cadet Baron Pesth, finding nothing more to interest him at the parley, rode home, and on his way back composed the French phrases he now repeated.

On the boulevard was Captain Zóbov talking very loud, and Captain Obzhógov, the artillery captain who never curried favour with anyone, was there too, in a dishevelled condition, and also the cadet who was always fortunate in his love affairs, and all the same people as yesterday, with the same motives as always. Only Praskúkhin, Nefërdov, and a few more were missing, and hardly anyone now remembered or thought of them, though there had not yet been time for their bodies to be washed, laid out, and put into the ground.

## XVI

White flags are hung out on our bastions and on the French trenches, and in the flowery valley between them lie heaps of mangled corpses without boots, some clad in blue and others in grey, which workmen are removing and piling onto carts. The air is filled with the smell of decaying flesh. Crowds of people have poured out from Sevastopol and from the French camp to see the sight, and with eager and friendly curiosity draw near to one another.

---

[4] 'Sir, I will not say no, lest I give you the lie.'
[5] 'What regiment do you belong to?'
[6] 'He's come to look at our works, the confounded ——'

Listen to what these people are saying.

Here, in a circle of Russians and Frenchmen who have collected round him, a young officer, who speaks French badly but sufficiently to be understood, is examining a guardsman's pouch.

'*Eh sussy, poor quah se waso lié?*' [1]

'*Parce que c'est une giberne d'un régiment de la garde, monsieur, qui porte l'aigle impérial.*' [2]

'*Eh voo de la guard?*' [3]

'*Pardon, monsieur, du 6-ème de ligne.*' [4]

'*Eh sussy oo ashtay?*' [5] pointing to a cigarette-holder of yellow wood, in which the Frenchman is smoking a cigarette.

'*A Balaclava, monsieur. C'est tout simple en bois de palme.*' [6]

'*Joli,*' [7] says the officer, guided in his remarks not so much by what he wants to say as by the French words he happens to know.

'*Si vous voulez bien garder cela comme souvenir de cette rencontre, vous m'obligerez.*' [8]

And the polite Frenchman puts out his cigarette and presents the holder to the officer with a slight bow. The officer gives him his, and all present, both French and Russian, smile and seem pleased.

Here is a bold infantryman in a pink shirt with his cloak thrown over his shoulders, accompanied by other soldiers standing near him with their hands folded behind their backs and with merry inquisitive faces. He has approached a Frenchman and asked for a light for his pipe. The Frenchman

---

[1] 'And what is this tied bird for?'
[2] 'Because this is a cartridge pouch of a guard regiment, monsieur, and bears the Imperial eagle.'
[3] 'And do you belong to the Guards?'
[4] 'No, monsieur, to the 6th regiment of the line.'
[5] 'And where did you buy this?'
[6] 'At Balaclava, monsieur. It's only made of palm wood.'
[7] 'Pretty.'
[8] 'If you will be so good as to keep it as a souvenir of this meeting you will do me a favour.'

draws at and stirs up the tobacco in his own short pipe and shakes a light into that of the Russian.

'*Tabac boon?*' says the soldier in the pink shirt, and the spectators smile. '*Oui, bon tabac, tabac turc,*' says the Frenchman. '*Chez vous autres tabac—Russe? Bon?*' [9]

'*Roos boon,*' says the soldier in the pink shirt while the onlookers shake with laughter. '*Fransay* not *boon. Bongjour, mossier!*', and having let off his whole stock of French at once, he slaps the Frenchman on the stomach and laughs. The French also laugh.

'*Ils ne sont pas jolis ces b—— de Russes,*' [10] says a Zouave among the French.

'*De quoi est-ce qu'ils rient donc?*' [11] says another with an Italian accent, a dark man, coming up to our men.

'*Coat boon,*' says the cheeky soldier, examining the embroidery of the Zouave's coat, and everybody laughs again.

'*Ne sors pas de ta ligne, à vos places, sacré nom!*' [12] cries a French corporal, and the soldiers separate with evident reluctance.

And here, in the midst of a group of French officers, one of our young cavalry officers is gushing. They are talking about some Count Sazónov, '*que j'ai beaucoup connu, monsieur,*' says a French officer with only one epaulette—'*c'est un de ces vrais comtes russes, comme nous les aimons.*' [13]

'*Il y a un Sazónoff, que j'ai connu,*' says the cavalry officer, '*mais il n'est pas comte, à moins que je sache, un petit brun de votre âge à peu près.*' [14]

'*C'est ça, monsieur, c'est lui. Oh! que je voudrais le voir, ce cher comte. Si vous le voyez, je vous prie bien de lui faire*

---

[9] 'Yes, good tobacco, Turkish tobacco . . . You others have Russian tobacco. Is it good?'
[10] 'They are not handsome, these d—— Russians.'
[11] 'What are they laughing about?'
[12] 'Don't leave your ranks. To your places, damn it!'
[13] 'Whom I knew very intimately, monsieur. He is one of those real Russian counts of whom we are so fond.'
[14] 'I am acquainted with a Sazónov, but he is not a count, as far as I know—a small dark man, of about your age.'

*mes compliments—Capitaine Latour,'* [15] he said, bowing.

*'N'est-ce pas terrible la triste besogne que nous faisons? Ça chauffait cette nuit, n'est-ce pas?'* [16] said the cavalry officer, wishing to maintain the conversation and pointing to the corpses.

*'Oh, monsieur, c'est affreux! Mais quels gaillards vos soldats, quels gaillards! C'est un plaisir que de se battre avec des gaillards comme eux.'* [17]

*'Il faut avouer que les vôtres ne se mouchent pas du pied non plus,'* [18] said the cavalry officer, bowing and imagining himself very agreeable.

But enough.

Let us rather look at this ten-year-old boy in an old cap (probably his father's), with shoes on his stockingless feet and nankeen trousers held up by one brace. At the very beginning of the truce he came over the entrenchments, and has been walking about the valley ever since, looking with dull curiosity at the French and at the corpses that lie on the ground and gathering the blue flowers with which the valley is strewn. Returning home with a large bunch of flowers he holds his nose to escape the smell that is borne towards him by the wind, and stopping near a heap of corpses gazes for a long time at a terrible headless body that lies nearest to him. After standing there some time he draws nearer and touches with his foot the stiff outstretched arm of the corpse. The arm trembles a little. He touches it again more boldly; it moves and falls back to its old position. The boy gives a sudden scream, hides his face in his flowers, and runs towards the fortifications as fast as his legs can carry him.

Yes, there are white flags on the bastions and the trenches

---

[15] 'Just so, monsieur, that is he. Oh, how I should like to meet the dear count. If you should see him, please be so kind as to give him my compliments—Captain Latour.'

[16] 'Isn't it terrible, this sad duty we are engaged in? It was warm work last night, wasn't it?'

[17] 'Ah, monsieur, it is terrible! But what fine fellows your men are, what fine fellows! It is a pleasure to fight with such fellows!'

[18] 'It must be admitted that yours are no fools either.' (Literally, 'don't wipe their noses with their feet').

but the flowery valley is covered with dead bodies. The glorious sun is sinking towards the blue sea, and the undulating blue sea glitters in the golden light. Thousands of people crowd together, look at, speak to, and smile at one another. And these people—Christians professing the one great law of love and self-sacrifice—on seeing what they have done do not at once fall repentant on their knees before Him who has given them life and laid in the soul of each a fear of death and a love of the good and the beautiful, and do not embrace like brothers with tears of joy and gladness.

The white flags are lowered, the engines of death and suffering are sounding again, innocent blood is flowing and the air is filled with moans and curses.

———

There, I have said what I wished to say this time. But I am seized by an oppresive doubt. Perhaps I ought to have left it unsaid. What I have said perhaps belongs to that class of evil truths that lie unconsciously hidden in the soul of each man and should not be uttered lest they become harmful, as the dregs in a bottle must not be disturbed for fear of spoiling the wine. . . .

Where in this tale is the evil that should be avoided, and where the good that should be imitated? Who is the villain and who the hero of the story? All are good and all are bad.

Not Kalúgin, with his brilliant courage—*bravoure de gentilhomme*—and the vanity that influences all his actions, not Praskúkhin, the empty harmless fellow (though he fell in battle for faith, throne, and fatherland), not Mikháylov with his shyness, nor Pesth, a child without firm principles or convictions, can be either the villain or the hero of the tale.

The hero of my tale—whom I love with all the power of my soul, whom I have tried to portray in all his beauty, who has been, is, and will be beautiful—is Truth.

# SEVASTOPOL IN AUGUST
## 1855*

### I

Towards the end of August, through the hot thick dust of the
rocky and hilly highway between Duvánka[1] and Bakhchisaráy,
an officer's vehicle was slowly toiling towards Sevastopol (that
peculiar kind of vehicle you never meet anywhere else—something between a Jewish *britzka*, a Russian cart, and a basket).

In the front of the trap, pulling at the reins, squatted an
orderly in a nankeen coat and wearing a cap, now quite limp,
that had once belonged to an officer: behind, on bundles and
bales covered with a soldier's overcoat, sat an infantry officer
in a summer cloak. The officer, as far as one could judge while
he was sitting, was not tall but very broad and massive, not
across the shoulders so much as from back to chest. His neck
and the back of his head were much developed and very solid.
He had no waist, and yet his body did not appear to be stout
in that part: on the contrary he was rather lean, especially in
the face, which was burnt to an unwholesome yellow. He
would have been good-looking had it not been for a certain
puffiness and the broad soft wrinkles, not due to age, that
blurred the outlines of his features, making them seem larger
and giving the face a general look of coarseness and lack of
freshness. His small eyes were hazel, with a daring and even
insolent expression: he had very thick but not wide mous-

* The Russian forces abandoned Sevastopol in August 1855 and in
November Tolstoy was sent as a courier to St. Petersburg. Then, in
December of that year, he finished this last piece on Sevastopol.
[1] The last posting-station north of Sevastopol. L. T.

taches the ends of which were bitten off, and his chin and especially his jaws were covered with an exceedingly strong, thick, black stubble of two days' growth.

This officer had been wounded in the head by a bomb splinter on 10 May[2] and still wore a bandage, but having felt well again for the past week, he had left the hospital at Simferópol and was now on his way to rejoin his regiment stationed somewhere in the direction of the firing—but whether in Sevastopol itself, on the North Side, or at Inkerman, no one had yet been able to tell him for certain. The sound of frequent firing, especially at times when no hills intercepted it and the wind carried it this way, was already very distinct and seemed quite near. Now an explosion shook the air and made one start involuntarily, now less violent sounds followed one another in quick succession like the roll of drums, broken now and then by a startling boom, and now again all these sounds mingled into a kind of rolling crash, like peals of thunder when a storm is raging in all its fury and rain has just begun to fall in torrents. Everyone was remarking (and one could moreover hear for oneself) that a terrific bombardment was going on. The officer kept telling his orderly to drive faster; he seemed in a hurrry to get to his destination. They met a train of Russian peasant-carts that had taken provisions to Sevastopol and were now returning laden with sick and wounded soldiers in grey uniforms, sailors in black cloaks, volunteers with red fezes on their heads, and bearded militiamen. The officer's trap had to stand still in the thick motionless cloud of dust raised by this train of carts and, frowning and blinking at the dust that filled his eyes, he sat looking at the faces of the sick and wounded as they drove past.

'There's a soldier of our company—that one who is so weak!' said the orderly, turning to his master and pointing to a cart laden with wounded men which had just come up to them.

A bearded Russian in a felt hat sat sideways in the front

---

[2] There were a series of desperate night conflicts on the 9 to 11 May o.s. (21 to 23 May n.s.)

of the cart plaiting the lash of a whip, the handle of which he
held to his side with his elbow. Behind him in the cart five
or six soldiers were being jolted along, some lying and some
sitting in different positions. One with a bandaged arm and his
cloak thrown loosely over his very dirty shirt, though he
looked pale and thin, sat upright in the middle of the cart and
raised his hand as if to salute the officer, but probably remembering that he was wounded, pretended that he only meant
to scratch his head. Beside him on the bottom of the cart lay
a man of whom all that was visible was his two hands holding
on to the sides of the cart and his lifted knees swaying to and
fro like rags. A third, whose face was swollen and who had a
soldier's cap stuck on the top of his bandaged head, sat on
the side of the cart with his legs hanging down over the
wheel, and, resting his elbows on his knees, seemed to be
dozing. The officer addressed him; 'Dolzhnikóv!' he cried.

'Here!' answered the soldier, opening his eyes and taking
off his cap and speaking in such a deep and abrupt bass that
it sounded as if twenty soldiers had shouted all together.

'When were you wounded, lad?'

The soldier's leaden eyes with their swollen lids brightened.
He had evidently recognized his officer.

'Good-day, your honour!' said he in the same abrupt bass.

'Where is your regiment stationed now?'

'In Sevastopol. We were going to move on Wednesday,
your honour!'

'Where to?'

'Don't know, your honour—to the North Side, maybe. . . .
Now they're firing right across, your honour!' he added in a
long-drawn tone, replacing his cap. 'Mostly bombs—they
reach us right across the bay. *He's* giving it us awful hot
now . . .'

What the soldier said further could not be heard, but the
expression of his face and his pose showed that his words,
spoken with the bitterness of one suffering, were not reassur-
ing.

The officer in the trap, Lieutenant Kozeltsóv, was not an

ordinary type of man. He was not one of those who live and act this way or that because others live and act so: he did what he chose, and others followed his example and felt sure it was right. He was by nature endowed with many minor gifts: he sang well, played the guitar, talked to the point, and wrote very easily (especially official papers—a knack for writing which he had acquired when he was adjutant of his battalion), but his most remarkable characteristic was his ambitious energy, which though chiefly founded on those same minor talents was in itself a marked and striking feature. He had ambition of a kind most frequently found among men and especially in military circles, and this had become so much a part of his life that he could imagine no other course than to lead or to perish. Ambition was at the root of his innermost impulses and even in his private thoughts he liked to put himself first when he compared himself with others.

'It's likely I should pay attention to the chatter of a private!' he muttered, with a feeling of heaviness and apathy at heart and a certain dimness of thought left by the sight of the convoy of wounded men and the words of the soldier, enforced as they were by the sounds of the cannonade.

'Funny fellow, that soldier! Now then, Nikoláev, get on! . . . Are you asleep?' he added rather fretfully as he arranged the skirt of his cloak.

Nikoláev jerked the reins, clicked his tongue, and the trap rolled on at a trot.

'We'll only stop just to feed the horse, and then go on at once, to-night,' said the officer.

## II

When he was entering what was left of a street of ruined stone Tartar houses in Duvánka, Lieutenant Kozeltsóv was stopped by a convoy of bombs and cannon-balls on its way to Sevastopol, that blocked the road.

Two infantrymen sat on the stones of a ruined wall amid a cloud of dust, eating a water-melon and some bread.

'Going far, comrade?' asked one of them, with his mouth full of bread, as another soldier with a little bag on his back stopped beside them.

'Going to join our regiment,' answered the soldier, looking past the water-melon and readjusting his bag. 'We've been nearly three weeks in the province looking for hay for our company, and now we've all been recalled, but we don't know where the regiment is. Some say it crossed to the Korábelnaya last week. Perhaps you have heard, friends?'

'In the town, mate. It's quartered in the town,' muttered the other, an old convoy soldier who was digging a clasp-knife into an unripe, whitish water-melon. 'We only left there this afternoon. [It's so awful there, mate, you'd better not go, but fall down here somewhere among the hay and lie there for a day or two!]'

'What do you mean, friend?'

'Why, can't you hear? They're firing from all sides to-day, there's not a place left whole. As for the likes of us as has been killed—there's no counting 'em!' And making an expressive gesture with his hand, the speaker set his cap straight.

The soldier who had stopped shook his head thoughtfully and clicked his tongue, then he took a pipe out of the leg of his boot, and not filling it but merely loosening the scorched tobacco in it, he lit a bit of tinder at the pipe of one of the others. Then he raised his cap and said:

'One can't get away from God, friends! Good-bye.' And straightening his bag with a jerk he went his way.

'It would be far better to wait!' the man who was digging into the water-melon said with conviction.

'It can't be helped!' muttered the newcomer, as he squeezed between the wheels of the crowded carts. ['It seems I too must buy a water-melon for my supper. Just think what people are saying!']

## III

The post-station was full of people when Kozeltsóv drove up. The first one he met in the porch was a very thin young man, the superintendent, bickering with two officers who were following him.

'It's not only three days you'll have to wait but maybe ten. . . . Even generals have to wait, my good sir!' said the superintendent, evidently wishing to hurt the travellers' feelings. 'I can't hitch myself to a cart for you, can I?'

'Then don't give horses to anyone, if you have none! Why did you give them to that lackey with the baggage?' shouted the elder of the officers, who had a tumbler of tea in his hand.

'Just consider a moment, Mr. Superintendent,' said the other, a very young officer, hesitatingly. 'We are not going for our own pleasure. You see, we are evidently wanted there, since we have been summoned. I shall really have to report it to the general. It will never do, you know. . . . It seems you don't respect an officer's position.'

But the elder man interrupted him crossly. 'You always spoil everything! You only hinder me . . . a man has to know how to speak to these people. There you see, he has lost all respect. . . . Horses, I say, this very minute!'

'Willingly, my dear sir, but where am I to get them from?' The superintendent was silent for a few minutes. Then he suddenly flared up and waving his arms began:

'I know it all very well, my dear sir, and fully understand it, but what am I to do? You give me but' (a ray of hope showed itself on the faces of the officers) . . . 'let me but hold out to the end of the month, and I'll stay here no longer. I'd rather go to the Malákhov Hill than remain here, I swear I would! Let them do what they please. There's not a single sound vehicle left in the whole place, and it's the third day the horses haven't had a wisp of hay.' And the superintendent disappeared through the gate.

Kozeltsóv entered the room together with the officers.

'Well,' said the elder calmly to the younger, though the

moment before he had seemed quite beside himself, 'we've been three months on the road already and can wait a bit longer. No matter, we'll get there soon enough!'

The dirty, smoky room was so full of officers and trunks that Kozeltsóv had some difficulty in finding a seat on the window-sill. While observing the faces and listening to the conversation of the others he began rolling himself a cigarette. To the right of the door sat the principal group round a crooked, greasy table on which stood two samovars with verdigris showing on them here and there, and with sugar spread on various bits of paper. A young officer who had not yet grown a moustache, in a new, quilted Caucasian coat which had certainly been made out of a woman's dressing-gown, was filling a teapot, and there were four other equally young officers in different parts of the room. One of them lay asleep on the sofa with a fur coat of some kind rolled up under his head; another was standing at the table cutting up some roast mutton for a one-armed officer who sat there. Two offi-cers, one in an adjutant's cloak, the other in infantry uniform made of fine cloth and with a satchel across his shoulders, were sitting by the stove, and from the way they looked at the others and the manner in which the one with the satchel smoked his cigar, it was plain that they were not officers of the line and were glad they were not. Their manner did not show contempt so much as a certain calm self-satisfaction founded partly on money and partly on intimacy with generals —a consciousness of superiority extending even to a desire to conceal it. Then there was a thick-lipped young doctor and an artillery officer who looked like a German—these were sitting on the sofa almost on the feet of the sleeping officer, counting money. There were also several orderlies, some dozing, others near the door busy with bundles and portman-teaux. Among all these people Kozeltsóv did not recognize a single acquaintance, but he listened with interest to their conversation. He liked the young officers who, as he at once concluded from their appearance, had come straight from the Cadet College; they reminded him of the fact that his brother,

who was coming straight from the College too, ought to reach
one of the batteries in Sevastopol in a few days' time. But he
did not like the officer with the satchel, whose face he had
seen somewhere before—everything about him seemed insolent and repellent. 'We'll put him down if he ventures to say
anything!' he thought, and he even moved from the window
to the stove and sat down there. Belonging to a line regiment
and being a good officer, he had a general dislike for those
'on the Staff', and such he at once recognized these officers to
be.

## IV

'I say, isn't it an awful nuisance that being so near we can't
get there?' said one of the young officers. 'There may be an
action to-day and we shan't be in it.'

The high-pitched voice and the fresh rosy spots which appeared on his face betrayed the charming youthful bashfulness
of one in constant fear of not saying the right thing.

The officer who had lost an arm looked at him with a smile.
'You'll get there soon enough, believe me,' he said.

The young officer looked respectfully at the crippled man,
whose emaciated face suddenly lit up with a smile, and then
silently turned his attention to making his tea. And really the
face, the attitude, and especially the empty sleeve of the
officer expressed a kind of calm indifference that seemed to
say in reply to every word and action: 'Yes, all that is admirable, but I know it all, and can do it all if only I wish to.'

'Well, and how shall we decide it?' the young officer began
again, turning to his comrade in the Caucasian coat. 'Shall
we stay the night here or go on with our own horse?'

His comrade decided to stay.

'Just fancy, Captain,' continued the one who was making
the tea, addressing the one-armed officer and handing him a
knife he had dropped, 'we are told that horses were awfully
dear in Sevastopol, so we two bought one together in Sim-
feropól.'

'I expect they made you pay a stiff price.'

'I really don't know, Captain. We paid ninety rubles for it with the trap. Is that very much?' he said, turning to the company in general, including Kozeltsóv, who was loooking at him.

'It's not much if it's a young horse,' said Kozeltsóv.

'You think not? . . . And we were told it was too much. Only it limps a bit, but that will pass. We were told it's strong.'

'What Cadet College were you at?' asked Kozeltsóv, who wished to get news of his brother.

'We are now from the Nobles' Regiment. There are six of us and we are all going to Sevastopol—by our own desire,' said the talkative young officer. 'Only we don't know where our battery is. Some say it is Sevastopol, but those fellows there say it's in Odessa.'

'Couldn't you have found out in Simferópol?' asked Kozeltsóv.

'They didn't know. . . . Only think, one of our comrades went to the Chancellery there and got nothing but rudeness. Just think how unpleasant! Would you like a ready-made cigarette?' he said to the one-armed officer who was trying to get out his cigar-case.

He attended to this officer's wants with a kind of servile enthusiasm.

'And are you from Sevastopol too?' he continued. 'How wonderful it is! How all of us in Petersburg used to think about you all and all our heroes!' he said, addressing Kozeltsóv with respect and kindly affection.

'Well then, you may find that you have to go back?' asked the lieutenant.

'That's just what we are afraid of. Just fancy, when we had bought the horse and got all we needed—a coffee-pot with a spirit-lamp and other necessary little things—we had no money left at all,' he said in a low tone, glancing at his comrade, 'so that if we have to return we don't at all know how we are to manage.'

'Didn't you receive your travelling allowance, then?' asked Kozeltsóv.

'No,' answered the young officer in a whisper, 'they promised to give it us here.'

'Have you the certificate?'

'I know that a certificate is the principal thing, but when I was in Moscow, a senator—he's my uncle and I was at his house—told me they would give it to me here, or else he would have given it me himself. But will they give me one in Sevastopol?'

'Certainly they will.'

'Yes, I think so too,' said the lad in a tone which showed that, having asked the same question at some thirty other post-stations and having everywhere received different answers, he did not now quite believe anyone.

## V

## [*Previously Suppressed by the Censor*]

['How can they help giving it?' suddenly remarked the officer who had quarrelled with the station-master on the porch and had now approached the speakers, addressing himself partly to the staff-officers who were sitting near by, as to listeners more worthy of attention. 'Why, I myself wanted to join the active army just as these gentlemen do. I even gave up a splendid post and asked to be sent right into Sevastopol. And they gave me nothing but a hundred and thirty-six rubles for post-horses from Petersburg and I have already spent more than a hundred and fifty rubles of my own money. Only think of it! It's only eight hundred versts and this is the third month we have been on the way. I have been travelling with these gentlemen here for two months. A good thing I had money of my own, but suppose I hadn't had any?'

'The third month? Is it possible?' someone asked.

'Yes, and what can one do?' the speaker continued. 'You see if I had not wanted to go I would not have volunteered and left a good post, so I haven't been stopping at places on the road because I was afraid. . . . It was just impossible. For instance I lived a fortnight in Perekóp, and the station-master wouldn't even speak to me. . . . "Go when you like; here are a whole pile of requisition forms for couriers alone." . . . It must be my fate. . . . You see I want—but it's just my fate. It's not because there's a bombardment going on, but it evidently makes no difference whether one hurries or not—and yet how I should like. . . .'

The officer was at such pains to explain his delays and seemed so keen to vindicate himself that it involuntarily occurred to one that he was afraid. This was still more evident when he began to ask where his regiment was, and whether it was dangerous there. He even grew pale and his voice faltered when the one-armed officer, who belonged to the same regiment, told him that during those last two days they had lost seventeen officers.

In fact this officer was just then a thorough coward, though six months previously he had been very different. A change had come over him which many others experienced both before and after him. He had had an excellent and quiet post in one of our provincial towns in which there is a Cadet College, but reading in the papers and in private letters of the heroic deeds performed at Sevastopol by his former comrades, he was suddenly inspired by ambition and still more by patriotic heroism.

He sacrificed much to this feeling: his well-established position, his little home with its comfortable furniture painstakingly acquired by five years' effort, his acquaintances, and his hopes of making a good marriage. He threw all this up, and in February already had volunteered for active service, dreaming of deathless honours and of a general's epaulettes. Two months after he had sent in his application he received an official inquiry whether he would require assistance from the government. He replied in the negative, and continued to wait patiently for an appointment, though his patriotic ardour had had time to cool considerably during those eight weeks. After another two months he received an inquiry as to

whether he belonged to a Freemasons' Lodge,[1] and other
similar questions, and having replied in the negative, he at
last, in the fifth month, received his appointment. But all that
time his friends, and still more that subconscious feeling which
always awakens at any change in one's position, had had
time to convince him that he was committing an act of extreme folly by entering the active army. And when he found
himself alone, with a dry throat and his face covered with
dust, at the first post-station—where he met a courier from
Sevastopol who told him of the horrors of the war, and where
he had to spend twelve hours waiting for relay horses—he
quite repented of his thoughtlessness, reflecting with vague
horror on what awaited him, and without realizing it continued on his way as to a sacrifice. This feeling constantly
increased during his three months' travelling from station to
station, at which he always had to wait and where he met
officers returning from Sevastopol with dreadful stories, and
at last this poor officer—far from being a hero prepared for
desperate deeds, as in the provincial town he had imagined
himself to be—arrived in Djánka a wretched coward, and
having a month ago come across some young fellows from the
Cadet College, he tried to travel as slowly as possible, considering these days to be his last on earth, and at every station
put up his bed, unpacked his canteen, played preference,
looked through the station complaint-book for amusement,
and felt glad when horses were not to be had.

Had he gone at once from home to the bastions he would
really have been a hero, but now he would have to go through
much moral suffering before he could become such a calm,
patient man, facing toil and danger, as Russian officers generally are. But it would by this time have been difficult to
reawaken enthusiasm in him.]

---

[1] A number of Freemasons were involved in the Decembrist mutiny
in 1825, when Nicholas I ascended the throne. He was consequently very suspicious of that organization, which at the time of
the Crimean War was prohibited in Russia. The inquiry made
would therefore be offensive to a loyal and patriotic volunteer.

## VI

'Who ordered soup?' demanded the landlady, a rather dirty, fat woman of about forty, as she came into the room with a tureen of cabbage-soup.

The conversation immediately stopped, and everyone in the room fixed his eyes on the landlady. One officer even winked to another with a glance at her.

'Oh, Kozeltsóv ordered it,' said the young officer. 'We must wake him up. . . . Get up for dinner!' he said, going up to the sofa and shaking the sleeper's shoulder. A lad of about seventeen, with merry black eyes and very rosy cheeks, jumped up energetically and stepped into the middle of the room rubbing his eyes.

'Oh, I beg your pardon,' he said to the doctor, whom he had knocked against in rising.

Lieutenant Kozeltsóv at once recognized his brother and went up to him.

'Don't you know me?' he asked with a smile.

'Ah-h-h!' cried the younger Kozeltsóv. 'This is wonderful!' And he began kissing his brother.

They kissed three times, but hesitated before the third kiss, as if the thought, 'Why has it to be just three times?' had struck them both.

'Well, I *am* glad!' said the elder, looking into his brother's face. 'Come out into the porch and let's have a chat.'

'Yes, come along. I don't want any soup. You eat it, Féderson,' he said to his comrade.

'But you wanted something to eat.'

'I don't want anything now.'

Out on the porch the younger one kept asking his brother: 'Well, and how are you? Tell me how things are!' and saying how glad he was to see him, but he did not tell him anything about himself.

When five minutes had passed and they had paused for a moment, the elder brother asked why the younger had not entered the Guards as everyone had expected him to do.

['Oh, yes!' the younger replied, blushing at the very recollection, 'that upsets me terribly. I never expected such a thing
could happen. Just imagine, at the very end of the term three
of us went to have a smoke—you remember that little room
by the hall-porter's lodge? It must have been there in your
time—but just imagine, that beast of a hall-porter saw us
and ran to tell the officer on duty (though we had tipped that
porter several times) and the officer crept up on tiptoe. As
soon as we noticed him the others threw away their cigarettes
and bolted out by the side door—you know—but I hadn't the
chance. The officer was very nasty to me, and of course I
answered him back. Well, he told the Inspector, and there was
a row. Because of that, you see, they didn't give me full marks
for conduct, though for everything else my marks were excellent, except for mechanics, for which I got twelve. And so
they wouldn't let me enter the Guards. They promised to
transfer me later . . . but I no longer wanted it, and applied
to be sent to the front.'

'Dear me!'

'Really, I tell you seriously, I was so disgusted with everything that] I wanted to get to Sevastopol as quickly as possible. And you see, if things turn out well here one can get
on quicker than in the Guards. There it takes ten years to
become a colonel, but here in two years Todleben from a
lieutenant-colonel has become a general. And if one gets
killed—well, it can't be helped.'

'So that's the sort of stuff you are made of!' said his brother,
with a smile.

'But the chief thing, you know,' said the younger brother,
smiling and blushing as if he were going to say something
very shameful—'the chief thing was that I felt rather ashamed
to be living in Petersburg while here men are dying for the
Fatherland. And besides, I wanted to be with you,' he added,
still more shyly.

The other did not look at him. 'What a funny fellow you
are!' he said, taking out his cigarette-case. 'Only the pity is
that we shan't be together.'

'I say, tell me quite frankly: is it very dreadful at the bastions?' asked the younger suddenly.

'It seems dreadful at first but one gets used to it. You'll see for yourself.'

'Yes . . . and another thing: Do you think they will take Sevastopol? I don't think they will. I'm certain they won't.'

'Heaven only knows.'

'It's so provoking. . . . Just think what a misfortune! Do you know, we've had a whole bundle of things stolen on the way and my shako was inside so that I am in a terrible position. Whatever shall I appear in? [You know we have new shakos now, and in general there are many changes, all improvements. I can tell you all about it. I have been everywhere in Moscow.']

The younger Kozeltsóv, Vladímir, was very like his brother Michael, but it was the likeness of an opening rosebud to a withered dog-rose. He had the same fair hair as his brother, but it was thick and curled about his temples, and a little tuft of it grew down the delicate white nape of his neck—a sign of luck according to the nurses. The delicate white skin of his face did not always show colour, but the full young blood rushing to it betrayed his every emotion. His eyes were like his brother's, but more open and brighter, and seemed especially so because a slight moisture often made them glisten. Soft, fair down was beginning to appear on his cheeks and above the red lips, on which a shy smile often played disclosing his white and glistening teeth. Straight, broad-shouldered, the uniform over his red Russian shirt unbuttoned— as he stood there before his brother, cigarette in hand, leaning against the banisters of the porch, his face and attitude expressing naïve joy, he was such a charming, handsome boy that one could not help wishing to look at him. He was very pleased to see his brother, and looked at him with respect and pride, imagining him to be a hero; but in some respects, namely, in what in society is considered good form (being able to speak good French, knowing how to behave in the presence of people of high position, dancing, and so on) he was rather ashamed of his brother, looked down on him, and even hoped if possible to educate him. All his views were still those he had acquired in Petersburg, particularly in the house of a lady who liked good-looking lads and had got him to spend his holidays at her house; and at a senator's house in Moscow, where he had once danced at a grand ball.

## VII

Having talked almost their fill, and reached that stage which often comes when two people find that though they are fond of one another they have little in common, the brothers remained silent for some time.

'Well then, collect your things and let us be off!' said the elder.

The younger suddenly blushed and became confused.

'Do we go straight to Sevastopol?' he asked after a moment's silence.

'Well of course. You haven't got much luggage, I suppose. We'll get it all in.'

'All right! Let's start at once,' said the younger with a sigh, and went towards the room.

But he stopped in the passage without opening the door, hung his head sorrowfully and began thinking.

'Now, at once, straight to Sevastopol . . . into that hell . . . terrible! Ah well, never mind. It had to be sooner or later. And now at least I'll have my brother with me. . . .'

In fact, only now, at the thought that after getting into the trap there would be nothing more to detain him and that he would not alight again before reaching Sevastopol, did he clearly realize the danger he had been seeking, and he grew confused and frightened at the mere thought of the nearness of that danger. Having mastered himself as well as he could, he went into the room; but a quarter of an hour passed and he did not return to his brother, so the latter at last opened the door to call him. The younger Kozeltsóv, in the attitude of a guilty schoolboy, was talking to an officer. When his brother opened the door he seemed quite disconcerted.

'Yes, yes, I'm just coming!' he cried, waving his hand to

prevent his brother coming in. 'Please wait for me there.'

A few minutes later he came out and went up to his brother with a sigh. 'Just fancy,' he said, 'it turns out that I can't go with you, after all!'

'What? What nonsense!'

'I'll tell you the whole truth, Misha . . . none of us have any money left and we are all in debt to that lieutenant-captain whom you saw in there. It's such a shame!'

The elder brother frowned, and remained silent for some time.

'Do you owe much?' he asked at last, looking at his brother from under his brows.

'Much? No, not very much, but I feel terribly ashamed. He paid for me at three post-stations, and the sugar was always his, so that I don't. . . . Yes, and we played prefer-ence . . . and I lost a little to him.'

'That's bad, Volódya! Now what would you have done if you hadn't met me?' the elder remarked sternly without look-ing at him.

'Well, you see, I thought I'd pay when I got my travelling allowance in Sevastopol. I could do that, couldn't I? . . . So I'd better drive on with him to-morrow.'

The elder brother drew out his purse and with slightly trembling fingers produced two ten-ruble notes and one of three rubles.

'There's the money I have,' he said. 'How much do you owe?'

Kozeltsóv did not speak quite truly when he made it ap-pear as if this were all the money he had. He had four gold coins sewn into his cuff in case of special need, but he had resolved not to touch them.

As it turned out the younger Kozeltsóv owed only eight rubles, including the sugar and the preference, his brother gave them to him, merely remarking that it would never do to go playing preference when one had no money.

'How high did you play?'

The younger brother did not reply. The question seemed to suggest a doubt of his honour.

Vexed with himself, ashamed of having done anything that could give rise to such suspicions, and hurt at such offensive words from the brother he so loved, his impressionable nature suffered so keenly that he did not answer. Feeling that he could not suppress the sobs that were gathering in his throat he took the money without looking at it and returned to his comrades.

## VIII

Nikoláev, who had fortified himself in Duvánka with two cups of vodka[1] sold by a soldier he had met on the bridge, kept pulling at the reins, and the trap bumped along the stony road that leads by the Belbék[2] to Sevastopol. The two brothers, their legs touching as they jolted along, sat in obstinate silence though they never ceased to think about each other.

'Why did he say that?' thought the younger. 'Couldn't he have left it unsaid? Just as if he thought me a thief! And I believe he's still angry, so that we have gone apart for good. And yet how fine it would have been for us to be together in Sevastopol! Two brothers, friends with one another, fighting the enemy side by side: one, the elder, not highly educated but a brave warrior, and the other young but . . . also a fine fellow. . . . In a week's time I would have proved to everybody that I am not so very young! I shall leave off blushing and my face will look manly; my moustaches, too, will have grown by that time—not very big but quite sufficiently,' and he pulled at the short down that showed at the corners of his mouth. 'Perhaps when we get there to-day we may go straight into action, he and I together. And I'm certain he is very brave and steadfast—a man who says little, but does more than others. I wonder whether he is pushing me to the very edge of the trap on purpose? I expect he knows I am uncomfortable but pretends he doesn't notice me.' Pressing close to the edge of the trap for fear of his brother's noticing

---

[1] Vodka is a spirit distilled from rye. It is the commonest form of strong drink in Russia.
[2] The Belbék is a river.

his discomfort, he continued his meditations: 'Well then, we shall get there to-day, and then perhaps straight to the bastion—I with the guns and my brother with his company, both together. Suddenly the French will fall upon us. I shall fire and fire. I shall kill quite a lot of them, but they will still keep coming straight at me. I can no longer fire and of course there is no escape for me, but suddenly my brother rushes to the front with his sword drawn and I seize a musket, and we run on with the soldiers. The French attack my brother: I run forward, kill one Frenchman, then another, and save my brother. I am wounded in the arm, I seize the gun in the other hand and still run on. Then my brother falls at my side, shot dead by a bullet. I stop for a moment, bend sadly over him, draw myself up and cry: "Follow me, we will avenge him! I loved my brother more than anything on earth," I shall say. "I have lost him. Let us avenge him, let us annihilate the foe or let us all die here!" They will all rush after me shouting. Then all the French army, with Pélissier himself, will advance. We shall slaughter them, but at last I shall be wounded a second and a third time and shall fall down dying. Then they will all rush to me and Gorchakóv himself will come and ask if I want anything. I shall say that I want nothing—only to be laid near my brother: that I wish to die beside him. They will carry me and lay me down by the blood-stained corpse of my brother. I shall raise myself, and say only, "Yes, you did not know how to value two men who really loved the Fatherland: now they have both fallen. May God forgive you!" . . . and then I'll die.'

Who knows how much of those dreams will come true?

'I say, have you ever been in a hand-to-hand fight?' he suddenly asked, having quite forgotten that he was not going to speak to his brother.

'No, never,' answered the elder. 'We lost two thousand men from the regiment, but it was all at the trenches, and I was wounded while doing my work there. War is not carried on at all in the way you imagine, Volódya.'

The pet name Volódya touched the younger brother. He

longed to put matters right with the elder, who had no idea
that he had given offence.

'You are not angry with me, Mísha?' he asked after a minute's pause.

'Angry? What for?'

'Oh, nothing . . . only because of what happened . . .
it's nothing.'

'Not at all,' answered the other, turning towards him and
slapping him on the the knee.

'Then forgive me if I have pained you, Mísha!' And the
younger brother turned away to hide the tears that suddenly
filled his eyes.

## IX

'Can this be Sevastopol already?' asked the younger brother
when they reached the top of the hill.

Spread out before them they saw the Roadstead with the
masts of the ships, the sea with the enemy's fleet in the distance, the white shore-batteries, the barracks, the aqueducts,
the docks, the buildings of the town, and the white and purple clouds of smoke that, rising continually from the yellow
hills surrounding the town, floated in the blue sky lit up by
the rosy rays of the sun, which was reflected brilliantly in
the sea towards whose dark horizon it was already sinking.

Volódya looked without the slightest trepidation at the
dreadful place that had so long been in his mind. He even
gazed with concentrated attention at this really splendid and
unique sight, feeling aesthetic pleasure and an heroic sense of
satisfaction at the thought that in another half-hour he would
be there, and he continued gazing until they came to the commissariat of his brother's regiment, on the North Side, where
they had to ascertain the exact location of the regiment and
of the battery.

The officer in charge of the commissariat lived near the so-
called 'new town' (a number of wooden sheds constructed by
the sailors' families) in a tent connected with a good-sized

shed constructed of green oak branches that had not yet had time to dry completely.

The brothers found the officer seated at a dirty table on which stood a tumbler of cold tea, a tray with a vodka bottle, and bits of dry caviare and bread. He was wearing a dirty yellowish shirt, and, with the aid of a big abacus, was counting an enormous pile of bank-notes. But before speaking of the personality of this officer and of his conversation, we must examine the interior of the shed more attentively and see something of his occupations and way of living. His newly built shed was as big, as strongly wattled, and as conveniently arranged with tables and seats made of turf, as though it were built for a general or the commander of a regiment. To keep the dry leaves from falling in, the top and sides were lined with three carpets, which though hideous were new and must have cost money. On the iron bedstead, beside which a most striking carpet was fastened to the wall (the pattern of which represented a lady on horseback), lay a bright red plush coverlet, a torn and dirty leather pillow, and an overcoat lined with raccoon fur. On the table was a looking-glass in a silver frame, an exceedingly dirty silver-backed hairbrush, a broken horn comb full of greasy hair, a silver candlestick, a bottle of liqueur with an enormous red and gold label, a gold watch with a portrait of Peter I, two gold rings, a box of some kind of capsules, a crust of bread, and a scattered pack of old cards. Bottles, full and empty, were stowed away under the bed. This officer was in charge of the regimental commissariat and the forage for the horses. With him lived his great friend, the commissioner employed on contracts. When the brothers entered, the latter was asleep in the tent while the commissariat officer was making up the regimental accounts for the month. He had a very handsome and military appearance: tall, with large moustaches and a portly figure. What was unpleasant about him was merely that his white face was so puffy as almost to hide his small grey eyes (as if he were filled with porter), and his extreme lack of cleanliness, from his thin greasy hair to his big bare feet thrust into ermine-lined slippers of some kind.

'What a heap of money!' said the elder Kozeltsóv on entering the shed, as he fixed his eyes eagerly on the pile of banknotes. 'If only you'd lend me half, Vasíli Mikháylovich!'

The commissariat officer shrank back when he saw his visitor, as if caught stealing, and gathering up the money bowed without rising.

'Oh, if it were mine! But it's Government money, my dear fellow. . . . And who is that with you?' he asked, placing the money in a cash-box that stood near him and looking at Volódya.

'It's my brother, straight from the training college. We've come to learn from you where our regiment is stationed.'

'Take a seat, gentlemen. Won't you have something to drink? A glass of porter perhaps?' he said, and without taking any further notice of his visitors he rose and went out into the tent.

'I don't mind if I do, Vasíli Mikháylovich.'

Volódya was struck by the grandeur of the commissariat officer, his off-hand manner, and the respect with which his brother addressed him.

'I expect this is one of their best officers, whom they all respect—probably simple-minded but hospitable and brave,' he thought as he sat down modestly and shyly on the sofa.

'Then where is our regiment stationed?' shouted the elder brother across to the tent.

'What?'

The question was repeated.

'Seifert was here this morning. He says the regiment has gone over to the Fifth Bastion.'

'Is that certain?'

'If I say so of course it's certain. Still, the devil only knows if he told the truth! It wouldn't take much to make him tell a lie either. Well, will you have some porter?' said the commissariat officer, still speaking from the tent.

'Well, yes, I think I will,' said Kozeltsóv.

'And you, Osip Ignátevich, will you have some?' continued the voice from the tent, apparently addressing the sleeping contractor. 'Wake up, it's past four!'

'Why do you bother me? I'm not asleep,' answered a thin voice lazily, pronouncing the *ls* and *rs* with a pleasant lisp.

'Well, get up, it's dull without you,' and the commissariat officer came out to his visitors.

'A bottle of Simferópol porter!' he cried.

The orderly entered the shed with an expression of pride as it seemed to Volódya, and in getting the porter from under the seat he even jostled Volódya.

['Yes, sir,' said the commissariat officer, filling the glasses. 'We have a new commander of the regiment now. Money is needed to get all that is required.'

'Well, this one is quite a special type of the new generation,' remarked Kozeltsóv, politely raising his glass.

'Yes, of a new generation! He'll be just as close-fisted as the battalion-commander was. How he used to shout when he was in command! But now he sings a different tune.'

'Can't be helped, old fellow. It just is so.'

The younger brother understood nothing of what was being said, but vaguely felt that his brother was not expressing what he thought, and spoke in that way only because he was drinking the commissariat officer's porter.]

The bottle of porter was already emptied and the conversation had continued for some time in the same strain, when the flap of the tent opened and out stepped a rather short, fresh-looking man in a blue satin dressing-gown with tassels and a cap with a red band and a cockade. He came in twisting his little black moustaches, looking somewhere in the direction of one of the carpets, and answered the greetings of the officers with a scarcely perceptible movement of the shoulders.

'I think I'll have a glass too,' he said, sitting down to the table.

'Have you come from Petersburg, young man?' he remarked, addressing Volódya in a friendly manner.

'Yes, sir, and I'm going to Sevastopol.'

'At your own request?'

'Yes, sir.'

'Now why do you do it, gentlemen? I don't understand it,'

remarked the commissioner. 'I'd be ready to walk to Petersburg on foot, I think, if they'd let me go. My God, I'm sick
of this damned life!'

'What have you to complain of?' asked the elder Kozeltsóv—'As if you weren't well enough off here!'

The contractor gave him a look and turned away.

'The danger, privations, lack of everything,' he continued,
addressing Volódya. 'Whatever induces you to do it? I don't
at all understand you, gentlemen. If you got any profit out
of it—but no! Now would it be pleasant, at your age, to be
crippled for life?'

'Some want to make a profit and others serve for honour,'
said the elder Kozeltsóv crossly, again intervening in the conversation.

'Where does the honour come in if you've nothing to eat?'
said the contractor, laughing disdainfully and addressing the
commissariat officer, who also laughed. 'Wind up and let's
have the tune from Lucia,' he added, pointing to a musical
box. 'I like it.'

'What sort of a fellow is that Vasíli Mikháylovich?' asked
Volódya when he and his brother had left the shed and were
driving to Sevastopol in the dusk of the evening.

'So-so, but terribly stingy! [You know he gets at least three
hundred rubles a month, but lives like a pig, as you saw.]
But that contractor I can't bear to look at. I'll give him a
thrashing some day! [Why, that rascal carried off some twelve
thousand rubles from Turkey. . . .'

And Kozeltsóv began to enlarge on the subject of usury,
rather (to tell the truth) with the bitterness of one who con-
demns it not because it is an evil, but because he is vexed
that there are people who take advantage of it.]

## X

It was almost night when they reached Sevastopol. Driving
towards the large bridge across the Roadstead Volódya was
not exactly dispirited, but his heart was heavy. All he saw

and heard was so different from his past, still recent, experience: the large, light examination hall with its parquet floor,
the jolly, friendly voices and laughter of his comrades, the
new uniform, the beloved Tsar he had been accustomed to
see for the past seven years, and who at parting from them
with tears in his eyes had called them his children—all he
saw now was so little like his beautiful, radiant, high-souled
dreams.

'Well, here we are,' said the elder brother when they
reached the Michael Battery and dismounted from their trap.
'If they let us cross the bridge we will go at once to the
Nicholas Barracks. You can stay there till the morning, and
I'll go to the regiment and find out where your battery is and
come for you to-morrow.'

'Oh, why? Let's go together,' said Volódya. 'I'll go to the
bastion with you. It doesn't matter. One must get used to it
sooner or later. If you go, so can I.'

'Better not.'

'Yes, please! I shall at least find out how. . . .'

'My advice is don't go . . . however——'

The sky was clear and dark. The stars, the flash of the
guns and the continual flare of the bombs already showed up
brightly in the darkness, and the large white building of the
battery and the entry to the bridge[1] loomed out. The air was
shaken every second by a quick succession of artillery shots
and explosions which became ever louder and more distinct.
Through this roar, and as if answering it, came the dull murmur of the Roadstead. A slight breeze blew in from the sea
and the air smelt moist. The brothers reached the bridge. A
recruit, awkwardly striking his gun against his hand, called
out, 'Who goes there?'

'Soldier!'

'No one's allowed to pass!'

---

[1] This pontoon bridge was erected during the summer of 1855. At
first it was feared that the water was too rough in the Roadstead
for a secure bridge to be built, but it served its purpose, and later
on even stood the strain put upon it by the retreat of the Russian
army to the North Side.

'How is that? We must.'

'Ask the officer.'

The officer, who was sitting on an anchor dozing, rose and ordered that they should be allowed to pass.

'You may go there, but not back.'

'Where are you driving, all of a heap?' he shouted to the regimental wagons which, laden high with gabions, were crowding the entrance.

As the brothers were descending to the first pontoon, they came upon some soldiers going the other way and talking loudly.

'If he's had his outfit money his account is squared—that's so.'

'Ah, lads,' said another, 'when one gets to the North Side one sees light again. It's a different air altogether.'

'Is it though?' said the first. 'Why, only the other day a damned ball flew over and tore two soldiers' legs off for them, even there. . . .'

Waiting for the trap the brothers after crossing the first pontoon stopped on the second, which was washed here and there by the waves. The wind which seemed gentle on land was strong and gusty here; the bridge swayed and the waves broke noisily against beams, anchors, and ropes, and washed over the boards. To the right, divided from the light blue-grey starry horizon by a smooth, endless black line, was the sea, dark, misty, and with a hostile sullen roar. Far off in the distance gleamed the lights of the enemy's fleet. To the left loomed the black hulk of one of our ships, against whose sides the waves beat audibly. A steamer too was visible moving quickly and noisily from the North Side. The flash of a bomb exploding near the steamer lit up for a moment the gabions piled high on its deck, two men standing on the paddle-box, and the white foam and splash of the greenish waves cut by the vessel. On the edge of the bridge, his feet dangling in the water, a man in his shirt sat chopping something on the pontoon. In front, above Sevastopol, similar flashes were seen, and the terrible sounds became louder and louder. A wave flowing in from the sea washed over the right

side of the bridge and wetted Volódya's boots, and two soldiers passed by him splashing their feet through the water.
Suddenly something came crashing down which lit up the
bridge ahead of them, a cart driving over it, and a horseman,
and fragments of a bomb fell whistling and splashing into the
water.

'Ah, Michael Semënich!' [2] said the rider, stopping his horse
in front of the elder Kozeltsóv. 'Have you recovered?'

'As you see. And where is fate taking you?'

'To the North Side for cartridges. You see I'm taking the
place of the regimental adjutant to-day. . . . We're expecting an attack from hour to hour.'

'And where is Mártsov?'

'His leg was torn off yesterday while he was sleeping in his
room in town. . . . Did you know him?'

'Is it true that the regiment is at the Fifth Bastion now?'

'Yes, we have replaced the M— regiment. You'd better call
at the Ambulance, you'll find some of our fellows there—
they'll show you the way.'

'And my lodgings in the Morskáya Street, are they safe?'

'Safe, my dear fellow! They've long since been shattered
by bombs. You won't know Sevastopol again. Not a woman
left, not a restaurant, no music! The last brothel left yesterday.
It's melancholy enough now. Good-bye!'

And the officer trotted away.

Terrible fear suddenly overcame Volódya. He felt as if a
ball or a bomb-splinter would come the next moment and hit
him straight on the head. The damp darkness, all these
sounds, especially the murmur of the splashing water—all
seemed to tell him to go no farther, that no good awaited him

---

2 In addressing anyone in Russian, it is usual to employ the Christian name and patronymic: i.e. to the Christian name (in this case
Michael) the father's Christian name is joined (in this case Semën)
with the termination *vich* (*o-vich* or *e-vich*) which means 'son of.'
The termination is often shortened to *ich*, and colloquially to *ych*.
Surnames are less used than in English, for the patronymic is suit-
able for all circumstances of life—both for speaking to and of any
one—except that people on very intimate terms use only the Christian name, or a pet name.

here, that he would never again set foot on this side of the
bay, that he should turn back at once and run somewhere as
far as possible from this dreadful place of death. 'But perhaps
it is too late, it is already decided now,' thought he shuddering, partly at that thought and partly because the water had
soaked through his boots and was making his feet wet.

He sighed deeply and moved a few steps away from his
brother.

'O Lord! Shall I really be killed—just I? Lord, have mercy
on me!' he whispered, and made the sign of the cross.

'Well, Volódya, come on!' said the elder brother when the
trap had driven on to the bridge. 'Did you see the bomb?'

On the bridge they met carts loaded with wounded men,
with gabions, and one with furniture driven by a woman. No
one stopped them at the farther side.

Keeping instinctively under the wall of the Nicholas Battery and listening to the bombs that here were bursting overhead, and to the howling of the falling fragments, the brothers came silently to that part of the battery where the icon
hangs. Here they heard that the Fifth Light Artillery, to which
Volódya was appointed, was stationed at the Korábelnaya[1]
and they decided that Volódya, in spite of the danger, should
spend the night with his elder brother at the Fifth Bastion
and go from there to his battery next morning. After turning
into a corridor and stepping across the legs of the soldiers who
lay sleeping all along the wall of the battery they at last
reached the Ambulance Station.

## XI

On entering the first room, full of beds on which lay wounded
men and permeated by a horribly disgusting hospital smell,
they met two Sisters of Mercy just going out.

One, a woman of fifty, with black eyes and a stern expres-

[1] The Korábelnaya was a suburb of Sevastopol lying to the east of
the South Bay and to the south of the Roadstead. Like the 'North
Side' it was connected with Sevastopol by a floating bridge. (See
map, p. vi.)

sion, was carrying bandages and lint and giving orders to a young lad, a medical assistant, who was following her. The other, a very pretty girl of about twenty whose pale, delicate, fair face looked from under her white cap with a peculiarly sweet helplessness, was walking by the side of the older woman with her hands in her apron pockets, and seemed afraid of being left behind.

Kozeltsóv asked them if they knew where Mártsov was, whose leg had been torn off the day before.

'He is of the P— regiment, I think?' asked the elder. 'Is he a relation of yours?'

'No, just a comrade.'

'Take them to him,' she said to the young sister in French. 'It is this way,' and she herself went up to one of the patients, followed by the assistant.

'Come along, what are you looking at?' said Kozeltsóv to Volódya, who stood with raised eyebrows and a look of suffering on his face, unable to tear his eyes from the wounded. 'Come now!'

Volódya followed his brother but still kept looking back and repeating unconsciously, 'O, my God! My God!'

'I suppose he has not been here long?' the sister remarked to Kozeltsóv, indicating Volódya, who followed them along the corridor with exclamations and sighs.

'He has only just come.'

The pretty sister looked as Volódya and suddenly began to cry.

'My God! My God! When will it all end?' she said in a despairing voice.

They entered the officers' ward. Mártsov was lying on his back, his sinewy arms bare to the elbow thrown back behind his head, and on his yellow face the expression of one who has clenched his teeth to prevent himself from screaming with pain. His sound leg with a stocking on showed from under the blanket and one could see the toes moving spasmodically.

'Well, how are you?' asked the sister, raising his slightly bald head with her slender delicate fingers (on one of which Volódya noticed a gold ring) and arranging his pillow.

'In pain of course!' he answered angrily. 'That'll do—the pillow's all right!' and the toes in the stocking moved still faster. 'How d'you do? What's your name?' . . . 'Excuse me,' he added, when Kozeltsóv had told him. 'Ah yes, I beg your pardon. One forgets everything here. Why, we lived together,' he remarked without any sign of pleasure, and looked inquiringly at Volódya.

'This is my brother, arrived to-day from Petersburg.'

'H'm! And I have got my discharge!' said the wounded man, frowning. 'Oh, how it hurts! If only it would be over quicker!'

He drew up his leg and, moving his toes still more rapidly, covered his face with his hands.

'He must be left alone,' said the sister in a whisper while tears filled her eyes. 'He is very ill.'

While still on the North Side the brothers had agreed to go to the Fifth Bastion together, but as they passed out of the Nicholas Battery it was as if they had agreed not to run unnecessary risks and for each to go his own way.

'But how will you find it, Volódya?' said the elder. 'Look here! Nikoláev shall take you to the Korábelnaya and I'll go on alone and come to you to-morrow.'

Nothing more was said at this last parting between the brothers.

## XII

The thunder of the cannonade continued with unabated violence. Ekaterína Street, down which Volódya walked followed by the silent Nikoláev, was quiet and deserted. All he could distinguish in the dark was the broad street with its large white houses, many of them in ruins, and the stone pavement along which he was walking. Now and then he met soldiers and officers. As he was passing by the left side of the Admiralty Building, a bright light inside showed him the acacias planted along the side-walk of the streets with green stakes to support them and sickly, dusty leaves. He distinctly heard his own footsteps and those of Nikoláev, who followed him breathing heavily. He was not thinking of anything: the pretty Sister of Mercy, Mártsov's foot with the toes moving in the stocking, the darkness, the bombs, and different images of death, floated dimly before his imagination. His whole young impressionable soul was weighed down and crushed by a sense of loneliness and of the general indifference shown to his fate in these dangerous surroundings. 'I shall be killed, I shall suffer, endure torments, and no one will shed a tear!' And all this instead of the heroic life abounding in energy and sympathy of which he had had such glorious dreams. The bombs whistled and burst nearer and nearer. Nikoláev sighed more and more often, but did not speak. As they were crossing the bridge that led to the Korábelnaya he saw a whistling something fall and disappear into the water near by, lighting the purple waves to a flaming red for a second and then come splashing up again.

'Just look! Not quenched!' said Nikoláev in a hoarse voice.

'No,' answered Volódya in an involuntarily high-pitched plaintive tone which surprised him.

They met wounded men carried on stretchers and more carts loaded with gabions. In the Korábelnaya they met a regiment, and men on horseback rode past. One of these was an officer followed by a Cossack. He was riding at a trot, but seeing Volódya he reined up his horse, looked in his face, turned away, and rode on, touching his horse with the whip.

'Alone, alone! No one cares whether I live or not,' thought the lad, and felt inclined to cry in real earnest.

Having gone up the hill past a high white wall he came into a street of small shattered houses, continually lit up by the bombs. A dishevelled, tipsy woman, coming out of a gate with a sailor, knocked up against Volódya.

'Because if he'sh an on'ble man,' she muttered—'pardon y'r exshensh offisher!'

The poor lad's heart ached more and more. On the dark horizon the lightnings flashed oftener and oftener and the bombs whistled and exploded more and more frequently around them. Nikoláev sighed and suddenly began to speak in what seemed to Volódya a lifeless tone.

'There now, and we were in such a hurry to leave home! "We must go! We must go!" Fine place to hurry to! [Wise gentlemen when they are the least bit wounded lie up quietly in 'orspital. It's so nice, what better can you want?]'

'Well, but if my brother had recovered his health,' answered Volódya, hoping by conversation to disperse the dreadful feeling that had seized him.

'Health indeed! Where's his health, when he's quite ill? Even them as is really well had best lie in 'orspital these times. Not much pleasure to be got. All you get is a leg or an arm carried off. It's done before you know where you are! It's horrible enough even here in the town, but what's it like at the *baksions*! You say all the prayers you know when you're going there. See how the beastly thing twangs past you!' he added, listening to the buzzing of a flying fragment.

'Now,' he continued, 'I'm to show y'r honour the way. Our business is o' course to obey orders: what's ordered has to be done. But the trap's been left with some private or other, and the bundle's untied. . . . "Go, go!" but if something's lost, why Nikoláev answers for it!'

A few more steps brought them to a square. Nikoláev did not speak but kept sighing. Then he said suddenly:

'There, y'r honour, there's where your *antillary's* stationed. Ask the sentinel, he'll show you.'

A few steps farther on Volódya no longer heard Nikoláev sighing behind him. He suddenly felt himself utterly and finally deserted. This sense of loneliness, face to face as it seemed to him with death, pressed like a heavy, cold stone on his heart. He stopped in the middle of the square, glanced round to see if anyone was looking, seized his head and thought with horror:

'O Lord, am I really a vile, miserable coward . . . when it's for my Fatherland, for the Tsar for whom I used to long to die? Yes! I am a miserable, wretched being!' And Volódya, filled with despair and disappointed at himself, asked the sen-

tinel the way to the house of the commander of the battery
and went where he was directed.


## XIII

The commander of the battery lived in a small two-storied
house with an entrance from the yard, which the sentinel
pointed out. The faint light of a candle shone through a window patched up with paper. An orderly, who sat on the steps
smoking his pipe, went in to inform the commander of the
battery of Volódya's arrival and then showed him into the
room. In the room, under a broken mirror between two windows, was a table littered with official papers; there were also
several chairs and an iron bedstead with clean bedding, with
a small rug beside it.

Just beside the door stood a handsome sergeant-major with
large moustaches, wearing side-arms, and with a cross and
an Hungarian medal [1] on his uniform. A staff-officer, a short
man of about forty in a thin old cloak and with a swollen
cheek tied round with a bandage, was pacing up and down
the room.

'I have the honour to report myself, Ensign Kozeltsóv, se-
cundus, ordered to join the Fifth Light Artillery,' said Volódya
on entering the room, repeating the sentence he had been
taught.

The commander answered his greeting dryly and without
shaking hands asked him to take a seat.

Volódya sat down shyly on a chair by the writing table,
and began playing with a pair of scissors his hand happened
to fall on. The commander, with his hands at his back and
with drooping head, continued to pace the room in silence as
if trying to remember something, only now and then glancing at the hand that was playing with the scissors.

The commander of the battery was rather stout, with a
large bald patch on his head, thick moustaches hanging

---

[1] That is, a medal granted for service in the suppression of the
Hungarian rising in 1849, when Nicholas I helped Austria to suppress the insurgent Hungarians.

straight down over his mouth, and pleasant hazel eyes. His hands were plump, well-shaped, and clean, his small feet were much turned out and he trod with firmness in a way that indicated that he was not a diffident man.

'Yes,' he said, stopping opposite the sergeant-major, 'the ammunition horses must have an extra peck beginning from to-morrow. They are getting very thin. Don't you think so?'

'Well, we can manage an extra peck, your honour! Oats are a bit cheaper now,' answered the sergeant-major, standing at attention but moving his fingers, which evidently liked to aid his conversation by gestures. 'Then our forage-master, Frantchúk, sent me a note from the convoy yesterday that we must be sure, your Excellency, to buy axles there. They say they can be got cheap. Will you give the order?'

'Well, let him buy them—he has the money,' said the commander, and again began to pace the room. 'And where are your things?' he suddenly asked, stopping short in front of Volódya.

Poor Volódya was so oppressed by the thought that he was a coward, that he saw contempt for himself as a miserable craven in every look and every word. He felt as if the commander of the battery had already discerned his secret, and was chaffing him. He was abashed, and replied that his things were at the Gráfskaya and that his brother had promised to send them on next day.

The commander did not stop to hear him out, but turning to the sergeant-major asked, 'Where could we put the ensign up?'

'The ensign, sir?' said the sergeant-major, making Volódya still more confused by casting a rapid glance at him which seemed to ask: 'What sort of an ensign is he?'

'Why, downstairs, your Excellency. We can put his honour up in the lieutenant-captain's room,' he continued after a moment's thought. 'The lieutenant-captain is at the *baksion* at present, so there's his bed empty.'

'Well then, if you don't mind for the present,' said the commander. 'I should think you are tired, and we'll make better arrangements to-morrow.'

Volódya rose and bowed.

'Would you like a glass of tea?' said the commander of the battery when Volódya had nearly reached the door. 'The samovar can be lit.'

Volódya bowed and went out. The colonel's orderly showed him downstairs into a bare, dirty room, where all sorts of rubbish was lying about and a man in a pink shirt and covered with a thick coat lay asleep on a bed without sheets or blankets. Volódya took him for a soldier.

'Peter Nikoláevich!' said the orderly, shaking the sleeper by the shoulder. 'The ensign will sleep here. . . . This is our cadet,' he added, turning to Volódya.

'Oh, please don't let me disturb you!' said Volódya, but the cadet, a tall, solid young man with a handsome but very stupid face, rose from the bed, threw the cloak over his shoulders, and evidently not yet quite awake, left the room saying: 'Never mind, I'll lie down in the yard.'

## XIV

Left alone with his thoughts Volódya's first feeling was one of fear at the disordered and cheerless state of his own soul. He longed to fall asleep, to forget all that surrounded him and especially himself. Putting out the candle, he took off his cloak and lay down on the bed, drawing the cloak over his head to shut out the darkness, of which he had been afraid from childhood. But suddenly the thought occurred to him that now, immediately, a bomb would crash through the roof and kill him, and he began listening. Just above his head he heard the steps of the commander of the battery.

'If it does come,' he thought, 'it will first kill those upstairs and then me—anyway not me alone.' This thought comforted him a little and he was about to fall asleep.

'But supposing that suddenly, to-night, Sevastopol is taken and the French break in here? What shall I defend myself with?' He rose and paced up and down the room. The fear of real danger drove away the fanciful fear of the darkness.

A saddle and a samovar were the only hard things in the room.

'What a wretch I am—a coward, a despicable coward!' he thought again, and once more the oppressive feeling of contempt and even disgust for himself came over him. He lay down again and tried not to think. Then, under the influence of the unceasing noise which made the panes rattle in the one window of the room, the impressions of the day rose in his imagination, reminding him of danger. Now he seemed to see wounds and blood, then bombs and splinters flying into the room, then the pretty Sister of Mercy bandaging his wounds and crying over him as he lay dying, then his mother seeing him off in the little country town and praying fervently with tears in her eyes before the wonder-working icon—and again sleep seemed impossible. But suddenly the thought of God Almighty, who can do anything and hears every prayer, came clearly into his mind. He knelt down, crossed himself, and folded his hands as he had been taught to do when a child. This attitude suddenly brought back to him an old, long-forgotten sense of comfort.

'If I must die, if I must cease to exist, then do it, Lord,' he thought, 'do it quickly, but if courage is needed and firmness, which I lack, grant them to me! Deliver me from the shame and disgrace which are more than I can bear, and teach me what I must do to fulfil Thy Will.'

The frightened, cramped, childish soul suddenly matured, brightened, and became aware of new, bright, and broad horizons. He thought and felt many things during the short time this state continued, but soon fell into a sweet untroubled slumber, amid the continued booming of the cannonade and rattle of the window-panes.

O Lord Almighty! Thou alone hast heard and knowest the simple yet burning and desperate prayers of ignorance, of confused repentance, prayers for bodily health and for spiritual enlightenment, that have risen to Thee from this dreadful place of death: from the general who, an instant after his mind has been absorbed by the Order of St. George upon his neck, feels with trepidation the nearness of Thy presence—to the private soldier prostrate on the bare floor of the Nicholas Battery, who prays for the future reward he dimly expects for all his sufferings.

## XV

The elder Kozeltsóv happening to meet a soldier of his regiment in the street went with him straight to the Fifth Bastion.

'Keep to the wall, your honour!' said the soldier.

'Why?'

'It's dangerous, your honour. There it is, flying over us!' said the soldier, listening to the sound of a ball that whistled past and fell on the hard ground on the other side of the road.

[Without heeding the soldier's words Kozeltsóv went boldly down the middle of the road.]

Here were still the same streets, the same or even more frequent firing, the same sounds, the same groans from the wounded one met on the way, and the same batteries, breastworks, and trenches, as when he was in Sevastopol in the spring; but somehow it all seemed more melancholy now and yet more vigorous. There were more holes in the houses, there were no lights in any of the windows except those of Kústchin's house (a hospital), not a woman was to be seen, and the place no longer bore its former customary character and air of unconcern, but seemed burdened with heavy suspense and weariness.

But here is the last trench and the voice of a soldier of the P— regiment who has recognized his former company-commander, and there stands the third battalion, pressing against the wall in the darkness, now and then lit up for an instant by the firing, and sounds are heard, subdued talking and the clatter of muskets.

'Where is the commander of the regiment?' asked Kozeltsóv.

'In the naval officers' casemate, your honour,' answers an obliging soldier. 'Let me show you the way.'

Passing from trench to trench, the soldier led the way to a

cutting in the trench. A sailor sat there smoking a pipe. Behind him with a door through a chink in which a light shone.

'Can I go in?'

'I'll announce you at once,' and the sailor went in at the door.

Two voices were heard talking inside.

'If Prussia remains neutral,' said one voice, 'Austria will too. . . .'

'What does Austria matter?' said the other, 'when the Slavonic lands. . . . Well, ask him in.'

Kozeltsóv had never been in this casemate and was struck by its elegance. It had a parquet floor and a screen in front of the door, two beds stood against the walls, and in a corner of the room there was a large icon—the Mother of God with an embossed gilt cover—with a pink lamp alight before it. A naval officer, fully dressed, was lying asleep on one of the beds. On the other, before a table on which stood two uncorked bottles of wine, sat the speakers—the new regimental commander and his adjutant. Though Kozeltsóv was far from being a coward and was not at all guilty of any offence either against the government or the regimental commander, still he felt abashed in the presence of his former comrade the colonel, so proudly did that colonel rise and give him his attention.

[And the adjutant who was sitting there also made Kozeltsóv feel abashed by his pose and look, that seemed to say: 'I am only a friend of your regimental commander's. You have not come to present yourself to me, and I can't and don't wish to demand any deference from you.']

'How strange!' thought Kolzeltsóv as he looked at his commander, 'It's only seven weeks since he took the command, and yet all his surroundings—his dress, manner, and looks—already indicate the power a regimental commander has: [a power based not so much on his age, seniority, or military worth, as on his wealth as a regimental commander.] It isn't long since this same Batríshchev used to hobnob with us, wore one and the same dark cotton print shirt a whole week, ate rissoles and curd dumplings every day, never asking any one to share them—but look at him now! [A fine linen shirt show-ing from under his wide-sleeved cloth coat, a ten-ruble cigar in his hand, a six-ruble bottle of claret on the table—all bought at incredible prices through the quartermaster at Sim-ferópol—and] in his eyes that look of the cold pride of a wealthy aristocrat, which says: though as a regimental com-mander of the new school I am your comrade [don't forget that your pay is sixty rubles once in four months, while tens of thousands pass through my hands, and] believe me I know very well that you'd give half your life to be in my place!'

'You have been under treatment a long time,' said the colo-nel, with a cold look at Kozeltsóv.

'I have been ill, Colonel. The wound is not thoroughly closed even now.'

'Then it's a pity you've come,' said the colonel, looking sus-piciously at the officer's solid figure. 'But still, you are capable of taking duty?'

'Certainly sir, I am.'

'I am very glad to hear it. Then you'll take over from En-sign Záytsev the Ninth Company that you had before. You will receive your orders at once.'

'Yes, sir.'

'Be so good as to send the regimental adjutant to me when you go.' The commander finished with a slight bow, thereby intimating that the audience was at an end.

On leaving the casemate Kozeltsóv muttered something to himself several times, and shrugged his shoulders as if he were hurt, or uncomfortable, or provoked—and provoked not with the colonel (he had no ground to be so) but with himself, and he felt dissatisfied with everything around him.

[Discipline and the subordination that goes with it, like every legalized relationship, is pleasant only when it rests on a mutual consciousness of its necessity, and of a superiority in experience, military worth, or simply on a moral superiority recognized by the inferior. But if the discipline is founded on arbitrary or pecuniary considerations, as is often the case among us, it always turns into pretentiousness on the one side and into suppressed envy and irritation on the other, and in-

stead of a useful influence uniting the mass into one whole
it produces a quite opposite effect. A man who does not feel
that he can inspire respect by his own worth, instinctively
fears intimacy with his subordinates and tries by ostentation
to keep criticism at a distance. The subordinates, seeing only
this external side which is offensive to themselves, suppose
(often unjustly) that there is nothing good behind it.]

## XVI

Before going to join his fellow officers Kozeltsóv went to greet
the men of his company and to see where it was stationed.
The breastworks of gabions, the plan of the trenches, the
cannon he passed, and even the fragments and bombs he
stumbled over on the way, all lit up incessantly by the flashes
of the firing, were quite familiar to him. All this had vividly
impressed itself on his memory three months before, when he
had spent two consecutive weeks at this bastion. Though
there was much that was dreadful in the recollection, a certain
charm of old times was mingled with it and he recognized all
the familiar places and objects with pleasure, as if the fortnight spent there had been an agreeable one. His company
was stationed against the wall of defence on the side towards
the Sixth Bastion.

Kozeltsóv entered a long bomb-proof, quite open on the entrance side, where he was told he would find the Ninth Company. There was literally no room to set one's foot in the
whole shelter: it was crowded with soldiers from the very
entrance. At one side burned a crooked tallow candle which
a soldier, lying on the ground, held over the book another
was reading from, spelling out the words. Through the smoky
atmosphere of the place, in the dim light near the candle,
heads were visible, raised eagerly to listen to the reader. The
book was a primer, and on entering the bomb-proof Kozeltsóv
heard the following:

'Pra-yer af-ter les-sons. We Thank Thee, O Cre-a-tor. . . .'
'Snuff the candle!' said a voice. 'It's a fine book.'
'God . . . is' . . . continued the reader.

When Kozeltsóv asked for the sergeant-major the reader stopped and the soldiers began moving, coughing and blowing their noses, as is usual after a restrained silence. The sergeant-major, buttoning his uniform, rose not far from the reader's group, and stepping over and onto the legs of those who could not get out of his way for lack of room, came up to the officer.

'Good evening, friend! Is this the whole of our company?'

'We wish your honour health. Welcome back, your honour!' answered the sergeant-major with a cheerful and friendly look at Kozeltsóv. 'How is your health getting on, your honour? Thank God you're better! We have missed you.'

It was easy to see that Kozeltsóv was liked by his company.

Far back in the bomb-proof voices were heard saying: 'Our old company-commander has come back!' 'Him that was wounded.' 'Kozeltsóv.' 'Michael Semënich,' and so on. Some men even moved nearer to him, and the drummer greeted him.

'How do you do, Obantchúk?' said Kozeltsóv. 'Still whole? Good evening, lads!' he added, raising his voice.

The answer, 'Wish your honour health!' resounded through the casemate.

'How are you getting on, lads?'

'Badly, your honour. The French are getting the better of us. They give it us hot from behind their 'trenchments, but don't come out into the open.'

'Perhaps it will be my luck to see them coming out into the open, lads,' said Kozeltsóv. 'It won't be the first time . . . you and I will give them a thrashing.'

'We'll do our best, your honour,' several voices replied.

'Yes, he's really brave!' said a voice.

'Awfully brave!' said the drummer to another soldier, not loud but so as to be heard, and as if justifying the commander's words to himself and proving that there was nothing boastful or unlikely in what he had said.

From the soldiers, Kozeltsóv went to join his fellow officers in the Defence Barracks.

## XVII

In the large caserne there was a crowd of naval, artillery, and infantry officers. Some slept, others talked, sitting on a chest of some kind and on the carriage of a garrison gun, but the largest and noisiest group sat on two Cossack cloaks spread out on the floor beyond the arch, and were drinking porter and playing cards.

'Ah, Kozeltsóv! Kozeltsóv! . . . So you've come! That's good. . . . You're a brick. . . . How's your wound?' It was evident that he was liked here also, and that his return gave pleasure.

When he had shaken hands with those he knew, Kozeltsóv joined the noisy group of officers playing cards. With some of them he was acquainted. A thin, dark, handsome man, with a long thin nose and large moustaches which joined his whiskers, was keeping the bank and dealt the cards with thin white fingers on one of which he wore a large seal-ring with a crest. He dealt straight ahead and carelessly, being evidently excited about something, and only trying to appear at ease. On his right lay a grey-haired major leaning on his elbows who with affected coolness kept staking half-rubles and paying at once. On his left squatted an officer with a red perspiring face, smiling unnaturally and joking. When his cards lost he kept fumbling with one hand in his empty trouser pocket. He was playing high, but evidently no longer for ready money, and it was this that upset the handsome dark man. A bald, thin, pale officer with a huge nose and mouth paced the room with a large bundle of paper money in his hand and continually staked *va-banque* for ready money and won. Kozeltsóv drank a glass of vodka and sat down with the players.

'Stake something, Michael Seménich!' said the banker. 'You must have brought back heaps of money.'

'Where should I get money? On the contrary, what I had I've spent in the town.'

'Never! . . . You've surely cleared someone out in Simferópol!'

'I've really very little,' said Koseltsóv, but evidently not wishing to be believed he unbuttoned his uniform and took up an old pack of cards.

'Well, suppose I have a try! Who knows what the devil may do for one? Even a mosquito, you know, wins his battles sometimes. But I must have a drink to keep up my courage.'

And having drunk another glass of vodka and some porter he soon lost his last three rubles.

A hundred and fifty rubles were noted down against the perspiring little officer.

'No, I've no luck,' he said, carelessly preparing another card.

'I'll trouble you to hand up the money,' said the banker, ceasing to deal the cards for a moment and looking at him.

'Allow me to send it to-morrow,' replied the other, rising and fumbling with renewed vigour in his empty pocket.

The banker cleared his throat loudly, and angrily throwing the cards right and left finished the deal.

'But this won't do. I give up the bank. This won't do, Zakhár Ivánich,' he repeated. 'We were playing for cash, not on credit.'

'What? Don't you trust me? It's really too ridiculous!'

'Who am I to receive from?' muttered the major, who was quite drunk by this time and had won some eight rubles. 'I have paid up more than twenty rubles and when I win I get nothing.'

'What am I to pay with,' said the banker, 'when there's no money on the board?'

'That's not my business,' shouted the major, rising. 'I'm playing with you, *with honest people,* and not with him.'

The perspiring officer suddenly flared up:

'I shall pay to-morrow, I tell you. How dare you insult me?'

'I shall say what I please! *Honest people don't behave like that.* So there!' shouted the major.

'That's enough, Fëdor Fëdorich!' said everybody, trying to pacify him.

But let us hasten to drop the curtain on this scene. To-morrow or to-day, perhaps, each of these men will cheerfully and proudly go to face death, and die steadfastly and calmly; but the only relief in these inhuman conditions, horrible even to the coldest imagination and from which there is no hope of escape, is to forget and to suppress consciousness. Deep in each soul is a noble spark capable of making its possessor a hero, but it wearies of burning brightly—till a fateful moment comes when it will flash into flame and illumine great deeds.

## XVIII

The bombardment continued with equal vigour the next day. At about eleven o'clock Volódya Kozeltsóv was sitting among the officers of his battery whom he was already beginning to get used to. He was examining the new faces, observing, asking questions, and talking. The modest conversation, with some pretension to knowledge, of these artillery officers inspired him with respect and pleased him, and on the other hand, Volódya's bashful and innocent good looks inclined the officers in his favour. The senior of the battery, a captain, a short man with reddish hair standing up in a tuft above his forehead and brushed smooth on his temples, brought up in the old artillery traditions, a ladies' man with pretensions to scientific knowledge, questioned Volódya about what he knew of artillery and new inventions, joked in a friendly manner about his youth and his pretty face, and in general treated him like a son—and this pleased Volódya very much. Sub-lieutenant Dyádenko, a young officer who spoke with an Ukrainian accent and who wore a torn cloak and had dishevelled hair—though he talked loudly, snatched every opportunity to begin a hot dispute, and was abrupt in his movements—nevertheless seemed attractive to Volódya, for he could not help seeing that a very kind heart and much that was good lay beneath this rough exterior. Dyádenko kept offering to be of use to Volódya, and demonstrating to him that none of the guns in Sevastopol were placed according to rule.

The only one Volódya did not like was Lieutenant Tchernovítski with his arched eyebrows, though he was the most polite of them all, and wore a coat which was clean enough and

neatly patched if not very new, and though he displayed a
gold chain over his satin waistcoat. He kept asking what the
Emperor and the Minister of War were doing, and told him
with unnatural rapture of feats of valour performed in Sevastopol, regretted [the ill-advised arrangements that were being
made, and] that there were so few real patriots, and in general displayed much knowledge, intelligence, and noble feeling; but for some reason it all seemed unnatural and unpleasant. Volódya noticed in particular that the other officers
hardly spoke to Tchernovítski. Cadet Vlang, whom Volódya
had disturbed the night before, was also there. He did not
speak, but sitting modestly in a corner laughed when there
was anything funny, helped to recall anything that was forgotten, handed the vodka bottle, and made cigarettes for all
the officers. Whether it was the modest, courteous manner of
Volódya, who treated him as an officer and did not order him
about as if he were a boy, or whether Volódya's attractive appearance charmed Vlánga (as the soldiers called him, giving
a feminine form to his name), at any rate he did not take his
large kindly eyes from the new officer, foresaw and anticipated
his wants, and was all the time in a state of enamoured ec-
stasy which of course the officers noticed and made fun of.

Before dinner the lieutenant-captain was relieved from the
bastion and joined them. Lieutenant-Captain Kraut was a fair-
haired, handsome, vivacious officer with big sandy moustaches
and whiskers. He spoke Russian excellently, but too accurately
and elegantly for a Russian. In the service and in his life he
was just the same as in his speech: he served admirably, was
a first-rate comrade, most reliable in money matters, but as a
man he seemed to lack something just because everything
about him was so satisfactory. Like all Russo-Germans, in
strange contradistinction to the idealist German-Germans, he
was *praktisch* in the extreme.

'Here he comes—our hero!' said the captain, as Kraut entered the room swinging his arms and jingling his spurs. 'What
will you take, Friedrich Christiánich, tea or vodka?'

'I have already ordered some tea,' answered Kraut, 'but
meanwhile I do not mind taking a drop of vodka as a refresh-

ment for my soul. . . . Very pleased to make your acquaintance. I hope you will favour me with your company and your
friendship,' he added, turning to Volódya, who rose and bowed
to him. 'Lieutenant-Captain Kraut. . . . The master-gunner
at out bastion told me yesterday that you had arrived!'

'I am very grateful to you for your bed: I slept on it.'

'But were you comfortable? One of the legs is broken; no
one has time to mend it in this state of siege, it has to be
propped up.'

'Well, what luck have you had on duty?' asked Dyádenko.

'Oh, all right; only Skvortsóv was hit, and yesterday we
had to mend a gun-carriage—the cheek was blown to shivers.'

He rose and began to walk up and down. It was evident
that he was under the influence of that pleasant feeling men
experience who have just left a post of danger.

'Well, Dmítri Gavrílich,' he said, shaking the captain by
his knee, 'how are you getting on? What of your recommendation? Is it still silent?'

'There's no news as yet.'

'And there won't be any,' began Dyádenko. 'I told you so
before.'

'Why won't there be?'

'Because the report was not written properly.'

'Ah, you wrangler! You wrangler!' said Kraut, smiling
merrily. 'A real obstinate Ukrainian! There now, just to spite
you you'll get a lieutenancy.'

'No I shan't!'

'Vlang, get me my pipe and fill it,' said Kraut, turning to
the cadet, who rose at once and readily ran for the pipe.

Kraut brightened them all up: he talked of the bombardment, asked what had been going on in his absence, and
spoke to everybody.


## XIX

'Well, have you established yourself satisfactorily among us?'
Kraut asked Volódya. 'Excuse me, what is your name and

patronymic? You know that's our custom in the artillery. . . . Have you a horse?'

'No,' said Volódya, 'I don't know what I'm to do. I was telling the captain . . . I have no horse nor any money until I get my forage-money and travelling expenses paid. I thought meanwhile of asking the commander of the battery to let me have a horse, but I'm afraid he'll refuse.'

'Apollón Sergéich . . . ?' and Kraut made a sound with his lips expressive of strong doubt, and looking at the captain added, 'Hardly!'

'Well, if he does refuse there'll be no harm done,' said the captain. 'To tell you the truth, a horse is not much wanted here. Still, it's worth trying. I will ask him to-day.'

'How little you know him,' Dyádenko put in: 'he might refuse anything else, but not that. . . . Will you bet?'

'Oh, we know you can't help contradicting!'

'I contradict because I know. He's close in other matters, but he'll give a horse because he gains nothing by refusing.'

'Gains nothing when oats are eight rubles?' said Kraut. 'The gain is not having to keep an extra horse.'

'You ask for Skvoréts, Vladímir Semënich,' said Vlang, returning with Kraut's pipe. 'He's a capital horse.'

'Off which you fell into a ditch in Soróki, eh, Vlánga?' remarked the lieutenant-captain.

'What does it matter if oats are eight rubles, when in his estimates they figure at ten and a half?[1] That's where the gain comes in,' said Dyádenko, continuing to argue.

'Well naturally you can't expect him to keep nothing. When you're commander of a battery I daresay you won't let a man have a horse to ride into town.'

'When I'm commander of a battery my horses will get four measures each and I shan't make an income, no fear!'

'We shall see if we live . . .' said the lieutenant-captain.

---

[1] Referring to the custom of charging the government more than the actual price of supplies, and thereby making an income which was supposed to go for the benefit of the regiment, but part of which frequently remained unaccounted for.

'You'll act in just the same way—and so will he,' pointing to Volódya.

'Why do you think that he too would wish to make a profit?' said Tchernovítski to Kraut. 'He may have private means, then why should he want to make a profit?'

'Oh no, I . . . excuse me, Captain,' said Volódya, blushing up to his ears, 'but I should think such a thing dishonourable.'

'Dear me! What a severe fellow he is!' said Kraut.

'No, I only mean that I think that if the money is not mine I ought not to take it.'

'But I'll tell you something, young man,' began the lieutenant-captain in a more serious tone. 'Do you know that if you are commanding a battery you have to conduct things properly, and that's enough. The commander of a battery doesn't interfere with the soldiers' supplies: that's always been the custom in the artillery. If you are a bad manager you will have no surplus. But you have to spend over and above what's in the estimates: for shoeing—that's one' (he bent down one finger), 'and for medicine—that's two' (and he bent down another finger), 'for office expenses—that's three: then for off-horses one has to pay up to five hundred rubles my dear fellow—that's four: you have to supply the soldiers with new collars, spend a good bit on charcoal for the samovars, and keep open table for the officers. If you are in command of a battery you must live decently: you must have a carriage and a fur coat, and one thing and another. . . . It's quite plain!'

'And above all,' interrupted the captain, who had been silent all the time, 'look here, Vladímir Semënich—imagine a man like myself say, serving for twenty years with a pay of first two hundred, then three hundred rubles a year. Can one refuse him a crust of bread in his old age, after all his service?'

'Ah, what's the good of talking,' began the lieutenant-captain again. 'Don't be in a hurry to judge, but live and serve.'

Volódya felt horribly confused and ashamed of what he had so thoughtlessly said. He muttered something, and then listened in silence while Dyádenko began very irritably to

224 ))                                   Sevastopol in August 1855

dispute and to argue the contrary of what had been said. The
dispute was interrupted by the colonel's orderly who came to
call them to dinner.

'Ask Appollón Sergéich to give us some wine to-day,' said
Tchernovítski to the captain, buttoning his uniform. 'Why
is he so stingy? If we get killed, it will all be wasted.'

'Ask him yourself.'

'Oh no, you're the senior officer. We must observe order in
everything.'

<h2 style="text-align:center">XX</h2>

In the room where Volódya had presented himself to the
colonel the evening before, the table had been moved away
from the wall and covered with a dirty table-cloth. To-day
the commander of the battery shook hands with him and
asked him for the Petersburg news, and about his journey.

'Well, gentlemen, who takes vodka? Please help yourselves.
. . . Ensigns don't take any,' he added with a smile.

Altogether he did not seem at all as stern as the night
before; on the contrary he seemed a kind and hospitable host
and an elder comrade among fellow officers. But in spite of
it all, the officers from the old captain down to Ensign
Dyádenko showed him great respect, if only by the way they
addressed him, politely looking him straight in the eyes, and
by the timid way they came up one by one to the side-table
to drink their glass of vodka.

The dinner consisted of Polish cutlets with mustard, dumplings with butter that was not very fresh, and a large tureen
of cabbage-soup in which floated pieces of fat beef with an
enormous quantity of pepper and bay-leaves. There were no
napkins, the spoons were of tin or wood, there were only two
tumblers, and there was only water on the table, in a bottle
with a broken neck; but the meal was not dull and the conversation never flagged. At first they talked about the battle
of Inkerman, in which the battery had taken part, and each
gave his own impressions of it and reasons for our reverse,

but all were silent as soon as the commander spoke. Then the conversation naturally passed to the insufficient calibre of our field-guns, and to the subject of the new lighter guns, which gave Volódya an opportunity to show his knowledge of artillery. But the conversation never touched on the present terrible condition of Sevastopol: it was as if each man had thought so much on this subject that he did not wish to speak of it. Nor to Volódya's great surprise and regret was there any mention at all of the duties of the service he would have to perform. It was as if he had come to Sevastopol solely to discuss lighter guns and to dine with the commander of the battery. During dinner a bomb fell near the house they were in. The floor and walls shook as if from an earthquake, and the windows were darkened by the powder smoke.

'You didn't see that sort of thing in Petersburg, I fancy, but here we get many such surprises,' said the commander of the battery. 'Vlang, go and see where it burst.'

Vlang went out to see, and reported that it had fallen in the square, and no more was said about the bomb.

Just before dinner ended, a little old man, the battery clerk, came into the room with three sealed envelopes and handed them to the commander: 'This one is very important: a Cossack has just brought it from the Chief of the Artillery.'

The officers all watched with eager impatience as the commander with practised fingers broke the seal and drew out the *very important* paper. 'What can it be?' each one asked himself. It might be an order to retire from Sevastopol to recuperate, or the whole battery might be ordered to the bastions.

'Again!' said the commander, angrily throwing the paper on the table.

'What is it, Apollón Sergéich?' asked the senior officer.

'They order an officer and men to some mortar-battery or other. . . . As it is I have only four officers, and not enough men for the gun detachments,' grumbled the commander of the battery, 'and here they are taking more away. . . . However, gentlemen, some one will have to go,' he said after a short silence, 'the order is, to be at the outpost at seven. Send the sergeant-major to me. Well, who will go? Decide, gentlemen.'

'There's your man—he's not been anywhere yet,' said Tchernovítski, pointing to Volódya.

The commander of the battery did not answer.

'Yes, I should like to go,' said Volódya, feeling a cold sweat break out on his back and neck.

'No, why should he?' interrupted the captain. 'Of course no one would refuse, but one need not offer oneself either: if Apollón Sergéich leaves it to us, let us cast lots as we did last time.'

All agreed. Kraut cut up some paper, rolled up the pieces, and threw them into a cap. The captain joked and on this occasion even ventured to ask the colonel for some wine—to keep up their courage, as he said. Dyádenko sat looking grim, something made Volódya smile. Tchernovítski declared he was sure to draw it. Kraut was perfectly calm. Volódya was allowed to draw first. He took a roll of paper a bit longer than the others but then decided to change it, and taking a thinner and shorter one unrolled it and read, 'Go.'

'It's I,' he said with a sigh.

'Well, God be with you! You'll get your baptism of fire at once,' said the commander, looking at the ensign's perturbed face with a kindly smile. 'But make haste and get ready, and to make it more cheerful for you, Vlang shall go with you as gun-sergeant.'

## XXI

Vlang was extremely pleased with his appointment, ran off quickly to get ready, and when dressed came to help Volódya, trying to persuade him to take with him a bed, a fur coat, some back numbers of *Fatherland Records*, the coffee-pot with the spirit lamp, and other unnecessary things. The captain advised Volódya to read up in the Handbook (Bezák's *Artillery Officer's Handbook*) about firing mortars, and especially to copy out the tables in it. Volódya set to work at once and noticed to his surprise and joy that his fear of the danger and even greater fear that he was a coward, though it still troubled him a little, was far from what it had been the night before. This was partly the effect of daylight and activity, but was chiefly due to the fact that fear, like every strong feeling, cannot long continue with the same intensity. In short he had already had time to live through the worst of it. At about seven o'clock, just as the sun began to disappear behind the Nicholas Barracks, the sergeant-major came and announced that the men were ready and waiting.

'I have given Vlánga the list, your honour will please receive it from him,' said he.

About twenty artillerymen, with side-arms only, stood behind the corner of the house. Volódya and the cadet walked up to them. 'Shall I make them a little speech or simply say "Good-day lads," or say nothing at all?' he thought. 'But why not say "Good-day lads", it is even right that I should,' and he cried boldly with his ringing voice, 'Good-day lads!' The soldiers answered gaily. The fresh young voice sounded pleasantly in the ears of each. Volódya went briskly in front of the soldiers, and though his heart beat as fast as if he had run full-speed for miles his step was light and his face cheerful. As they approached the Malákhov Redoubt and mounted the hill he noticed that Vlang, who kept close to him all the time and had seemed so brave before leaving the house, was continually dodging and stooping, as if all the bombs and cannon-balls, which whistled past very frequently here, were flying straight at him. Some of the soldiers did the same, and in general most of the faces expressed uneasiness if not exactly alarm. These circumstances emboldened Volódya and completely comforted him.

'So here am I too on the Malákhov mound, which I fancied a thousand times more terrible. And I get along without bowing to the balls, and am even much less frightened than the others. So I am no coward,' he thought with pleasure, and even with a certain self-complacent rapture.

This feeling however was quickly shaken by a sight he came upon in the twilight at the Kornílov Battery while look-

ing for the commander of the bastion. Four sailors stood by
the breastwork holding by its arms and legs the blood-
stained corpse of a man without boots or coat and swinging
it before heaving it over. (On the second day of this bombardment it was found impossible in some parts to clear away
the corpses from the bastions, and they were therefore thrown
out into the ditch so as not to be in the way at the batteries.)
Volódya felt stunned for a moment when he saw the body
bump on the top of the breastwork and then roll down into
the ditch, but luckily for him the commander of the bastion
met him just then and gave him his orders and a guide to
show him the way to the battery and to the bomb-proof as-
signed to his men. We will not speak of all the dangers and
disenchantments our hero lived through that evening: how—
instead of the firing he was used to on the Vólkov field amid
conditions of perfect exactitude and order which he had expected to meet with here also—he found two damaged mortars, one with its muzzle battered in by a ball, the other
standing on the splinters of its shattered platform; how he
could not get workmen before the morning to mend the platform; how not a single charge was of the weight specified in
the Handbook; how two of the men under him were wounded,
and how he was twenty times within a hair's-breadth of death.
Fortunately a gigantic gunner, a seaman who had served with
the mortars since the commencement of the siege, had been
appointed to assist Volódya, and convinced him of the possibility of using the mortars. By the light of a lantern this gunner showed him all over the battery as he might have shown
him over his own kitchen-garden, and undertook to have
everything right by the morning. The bomb-proof to which
his guide led him was an oblong hole dug in the rocky
ground, twenty-five cubic yards in size and covered with oak
beams two and a half feet thick. He and all his soldiers in-
stalled themselves in it.

As soon as he discovered the little door, not three feet high,
Vlang rushed in headlong before anyone else, and at the risk
of breaking his limbs against the stone bottom squeezed into
the farthest corner and remained there. Volódya, when all

the soldiers had settled on the ground along the walls and some had lit their pipes, made up his own bed in a corner, lit a candle, and after lighting a cigarette, lay down.

The reports of continuous firing could be heard overhead but not very distinctly, except from one cannon which stood quite close and shook the bomb-proof with its thunder. In the bomb-proof all was quiet, except when one or other of the soldiers, still rather shy in the presence of the new officer, spoke, asking a neighbour to move a little or to give him a light for his pipe, when a rat scratched somewhere among the stones, or when Vlang, who had not yet recovered and was still looking wildly around him, heaved a deep sigh.

Volódya, on his bed in this quiet corner crammed with people and lighted by a solitary candle, experienced a sensation of cosiness such as he had felt as a child when, playing hide-and-seek, he used to creep into a cupboard or under his mother's skirt and sit listening in breathless silence, afraid of the dark yet conscious of enjoyment. It felt rather uncanny, yet his spirits were high.

## XXII

After ten minutes or so the soldiers grew bolder and began to talk. The more important ones—two non-commissioned officers: an old grey-haired one with every possible medal and cross except the St. George, and a young one, a Cantonist,[1] who was smoking cigarettes he had rolled himself— settled nearest to the light and to the officer's bed. The drummer had as usual assumed the duty of waiting upon the officer. The bombardiers and those who had medals came next, and farther off, in the shadow nearer the entrance, sat the humbler folk. It was these last who started a conversation, caused by the noise a man made who came tumbling hurriedly into the bomb-proof.

---

[1] The Cantonists, under serfdom, which still prevailed at the time of the Crimean War, were the sons of soldiers, condemned by law and heredity to be soldiers also.

'Hullo, old fellow! Why don't you stay outside? Don't the lasses play merrily enough out there?' said a voice.

'They're playing such tunes as we never hear in our village,' laughingly replied the man who had just run in.

'Ah, Vásin don't like bombs—that he don't!' said some one in the aristocratic corner.

'If it was necessary, that would be a different matter,' replied Vásin slowly, and when he spoke all the others were silent. 'On the 24th we were at least firing, but why grumble at me now? The authorities won't thank the likes of us for getting killed uselessly.'

At these words everyone laughed.

'There's Mélnikov—he's out there now, I fancy,' said some-one.

'Go and send Mélnikov in here,' said the old sergeant, 'or else he really will get killed uselessly.'

'Who is Mélnikov?' asked Volódya.

'Oh, he's a poor silly soldier of ours, your honour. He's just afraid of nothing, and he's walking about outside now. You should have a look at him, he's just like a bear.'

'He knows a charm,' came Vásin's long-drawn accents from the other corner.

Mélnikov entered the bomb-proof. He was stout (an extremely rare thing among soldiers), red-haired and red-faced, with an enormous bulging forehead and prominent pale-blue eyes.

'Aren't you afraid of the bombs?' asked Volódya.

'What's there to be afraid of in them bombs?' answered Mélnikov, wriggling and scratching himself. 'They won't kill me with a bomb, I know.'

'So you'd like to live here?'

''Course I should. It's jolly here,' he said and burst out laughing.

'Oh, then they should take you for a sortie! Shall I speak to the general about it?' said Volódya, though he did not know a single general in the place.

'Like, indeed! 'Course I should!' And Mélnikov hid behind the others.

'Let's have a game of "noses" lads! Who has the cards?' his voice was heard to say hurriedly.

And soon the game had started in the far corner: laughter could be heard, and noses being smacked and trumps declared. The drummer having heated the samovar for him, Volódya drank some tea, treated the non-commissioned officers to some, and, wishing to gain popularity, joked and talked with them and felt very pleased at the respect paid him. The soldiers, seeing that the gentleman gave himself no airs, became talkative too. One of them explained that the siege of Sevastopol would not last much longer, because a reliable fellow in the fleet had told him that Constantine, the Tsar's brother, was coming with the 'merican fleet to help us, and also that there would soon be an agreement not to fire for a fortnight, but to have a rest, and that if anyone did fire, he'd have to pay a fine of seventy-five kopéks for each shot. Vásin, who was a small man with whiskers and large kind eyes, as Volódya had already noticed, related, first amid general silence and then amid roars of laughter, how he had gone home on leave and at first everyone was glad to see him, but then his father had begun sending him to work while the forester-lieutenant sent a horse and trap to fetch his wife! All this amused Volódya very much. He not only felt no fear or annoyance because of the overcrowding and bad air in the bomb-proof, but on the contrary felt exceedingly bright and contented.

Many of the soldiers were already snoring. Vlang had also stretched himself out on the floor, and the old sergeant having spread his cloak on the ground was crossing himself and muttering prayers before going to sleep, when Volódya felt moved to go out of the bomb-proof and see what was happening outside.

'Draw in your legs!' the soldiers called to one another as soon as he rose, and the legs were drawn in to make room for him.

Vlang, who had seemed to be asleep, suddenly raised his head and seized Volódya by the skirts of his cloak.

'Don't go! Don't go—how can you?' he began in a tearfully

persuasive voice. 'You don't know what it's like. Cannon-balls are falling all the time out there. It's better in here.'

But in spite of Vlang's entreaties Volódya made his way out of the bomb-proof and sat down on the threshold, where Mélnikov was already sitting making his feet comfortable.

The air was pure and fresh, especially after that of the bomb-proof, and the night was clear and calm. Mingling with the booming of the cannon could be heard the rumbling of the wheels of carts bringing gabions, and voices of men at work in the powder-vault. High overhead stretched the starry sky, across which the fiery trails of the bombs ran incessantly. On the left was another bomb-proof, through the three-foot opening of which the legs and backs of the sailors who lived there could be seen and their voices heard. In front was the roof of the powder-vault, past which flitted the figures of stooping men, while on the top of it, under the bullets and bombs that kept flying past, was a tall figure in a black cloak with its hands in its pockets, treading down the earth the others carried up in sacks. Many a bomb flew past and exploded very near the vault. The soldiers who were carrying the earth stooped and stepped aside, but the black figure continued calmly to stamp the earth down with its feet and remained on the spot in the same position.

'Who is that black fellow there?' said Volódya to Mélnikov.

'Can't say. I'll go and see.'

'No, don't. There's no need.'

But Mélnikov rose without heeding him, approached the black figure, and for a long time stood beside it just as indifferent and immovable.

'That's the powder-master, your honour!' he said when he returned. 'The vault has been knocked in by a bomb, so the infantry are carrying earth there.'

Now and then a bomb seemed to fly straight at the door of the bomb-proof. Then Volódya pressed behind the corner, but soon crept out again looking up to see if another was coming that way. Though Vlang from inside the bomb-proof again and again entreated him to come in, Volódya sat at the

threshold for about three hours, finding a kind of pleasure
in tempting fate and watching the flying bombs. By the end
of the evening he knew how many guns were firing, from
which positions, and where their shots fell.

## XXIII

The next morning, 27 August, Volódya, fresh and vigorous
after ten hours' sleep, stepped across the threshold of the
bomb-proof. Vlang too came out, but at the first sound of a
bullet rushed wildly back to the entrance, pushing his way
through the crowd with his head amid the general laughter
of the soldiers, most of whom had also come out into the
fresh air.

Vlang, the old sergeant, and a few others only came out
into the trench at rare intervals, but the rest could not be
kept inside: they all crept out of the stuffy bomb-proof into
the fresh morning air and in spite of the firing, which continued as violently as on the day before, settled themselves—
some by the threshold of the bomb-proof and some under the
breastwork. Mélnikov had been strolling about from battery
to battery since early dawn, looking calmly upwards.

Near the threshold sat two old soldiers and one young
curly-haired one, a Jew transferred to the battery from an
infantry regiment. This latter had picked up one of the bullets
that were lying about, and after flattening it out on a stone
with the fragment of a bomb, was now carving out a cross
like the Order of St. George. The others sat talking and
watching his work. The cross was really turning out very
well.

'I say,' said one of them, 'if we stay here much longer
we shall all have served our time and get discharged when
there's peace.'

'You're right. Why I had only four years left to serve, and
I've been five months already in Sevastopol.'

'That won't be reckoned specially towards our discharge,
it seems,' said another.

At that moment a cannon-ball flew over the heads of the speakers and fell a couple of feet from Mélnikov, who was coming towards them through the trench.

'That one nearly killed Mélnikov,' said one of them.

'It won't kill me,' said Mélnikov.

'Then I present you with this cross for your courage,' said the young soldier, giving him the cross he had made.

'. . . No, my lad, a month's service here counts as a year for everything—that was said in the proclamation,' continued one of the soldiers.

'You may say what you like, but when we have peace we're sure to have an Imperial review at Warsaw, and then if we don't all get our discharge we shall be put on the permanent reserve.'

Just then a shrieking, glancing rifle-bullet flew just over the speakers' heads and struck a stone.

'Look out, or you'll be getting your discharge in full before to-night,' said one of the soldiers.

They all laughed.

And not only before night, but before two hours had passed, two of them had got their discharge in full and five more were wounded, but the rest went on joking just the same.

By the morning the two mortars had really been put into such a condition that they could be fired, and at ten o'clock Volódya called out his company and marched with it to the battery, in accordance with the order he had received from the commander of the bastion.

Not a trace of the fear noticeable the day before remained among the men as soon as they were actively engaged. Only Vlang could not master himself, but hid and ducked in the same old way, and Vásin lost some of his composure, fidgetted, and kept dodging. Volódya was in ecstasies, the thought of danger never entered his head. Joy at fulfilling his duty, at finding that not only was he no coward but that he was even quite brave, the sense of commanding and being in the presence of twenty men who were he knew watching him with curiosity, made him quite valiant. He was even vain of his

courage and showed off before the soldiers, climbing out onto
the banquette and unfastening his cloak on purpose to be
more conspicuous. The commander of the bastion making the
round of his 'household' as he expressed it, accustomed as
he had grown during the last eight months to courage of all
kinds, could not help admiring this handsome lad, with his
coat unbuttoned showing a red shirt fitting close to his delicate
white neck, who with flushed face and shining eyes clapped
his hands, gave the order, 'One—two!' in ringing tones, and
ran gaily onto the breastwork to see where his bombs were
falling. At half-past eleven the firing slackened on both sides,
and at twelve o'clock precisely the storming of the Malákhov
Redoubt, and of the Second, Third (the Redan), and Fifth
Bastions, began.

## XXIV

On the North Side of the Roadstead, towards midday, two
sailors were standing on the telegraph hill between Inkerman
and the Northern entrenchment: one of them, an officer, was
looking at Sevastopol through the telescope fixed there. Another officer with a Cossack had just ridden up to the signal-
post.

The sun shone brightly high above the Roadstead, and with
its warm bright light played on the stationary vessels, the
flapping sails, and the rowing boats. A light wind scarcely
swayed the withering leaves of the oak-scrub near the telegraph post, filled the sails of the boats, and ruffled the waves.
Sevastopol, still the same, with its unfinished church, its
column, its quay, its boulevard showing green on the hill, and
the elegant building of its library; with its little azure creeks
bristling with masts, the picturesque arches of its aqueducts,
and with clouds of blue powder-smoke now and then lit up
by red flashes from the guns—this same beautiful, festive,
proud Sevastopol, surrounded on one side by yellow smoking
hills and on the other by the bright blue sea playing in the
sunlight—could still be seen on the opposite side of the
Roadstead. Above the rim of the sea, along which spread a

streak of black smoke from a steamer, drifted long white clouds that portended rain. Along the whole line of entrenchments, especially on the hills to the left, compressed puffs of thick white smoke continually appeared several at a time, accompanied by flashes that sometimes gleamed like lightning even in the noontide light; and these puffs grew larger and assumed various shapes, rising and seeming darker against the sky.

They started now here now there from the hills, from the enemy's batteries, from the town, and high up in the sky. The noise of the reports never ceased, and mingling with one another they shook the air.

Towards noon the cloudlets of smoke showed less and less often and the air was less shaken by the booming.

'There now, the Second Bastion doesn't reply at all!' said the mounted hussar officer. 'It's absolutely knocked to bits. It's terrible!'

'Yes, and the Malákhov hardly fires one shot for three of theirs,' replied the man who was looking through the telescope. 'It makes me mad that ours are silent. They are firing straight into the Kornílov Battery and it doesn't reply at all.'

'But look here, I told you they always stop bombarding at noon. And it's the same to-day. We'd better go to lunch . . . they'll be waiting for us as it is. . . . There's nothing to look at now.'

'Wait a bit! Don't bother me!' said the man in possession of the telescope, looking eagerly at Sevastopol.

'What is it? What?'

'A movement in the trenches—dense columns advancing.'

'Yes, one can see it with the naked eye,' said the sailor. 'They are advancing in columns. We must give the alarm.'

'Look! Look! They have left the trenches.'

And one could really see with the naked eye what seemed like dark spots coming down the hill, across the ravine from the French batteries towards our bastions. In front of these spots, dark streaks could already be seen near our lines. From our bastions white cloudlets of firing burst out at different points as if crossing one another. The wind brought a sound of small-arm firing, like rain pelting against window-panes. The dark streaks were moving nearer and nearer right amid the smoke. The sounds of firing grew louder and louder and merged into a prolonged rumbling peal. The smoke, rising more and more often, spread rapidly along the lines and at last merged into one light-purple cloud curling and uncurling, amid which here and there flashes just flickered and dark dots appeared: all the separate sounds blended into one thundering crash.

'An assault!' said the officer, growing pale and letting the sailor have the telescope.

Cossacks galloped down the road, officers on horseback passed by, and the commander-in-chief in a carriage accompanied by his suite. On every face there was an expression of painful agitation and expectancy.

'They can't have taken it!' cried the mounted officer.

'By God, a standard! Look! Look!' said the officer, panting and moving away from the telescope—'A French standard on the Malákhov!'

'Impossible!'


## XXV

The elder Kozeltsóv, who had found time that night to win back his money and to lose it all again, including the gold pieces sewn in his cuff, was lying towards morning in a heavy, unhealthy, and deep sleep in the Defence Barracks of the Fifth Bastion, when a desperate cry arose, repeated by many voices—

'The alarm!'

'Why are you sleeping, Michael Semënich? We are attacked!' shouted someone.

'It must be a hoax,' he said, opening his eyes incredulously.

Then he saw an officer running from one corner of the barracks to the other without any apparent reason and with such a pale face that he realized it all. The thought that they might take him for a coward who did not wish to be with his company at a critical moment upset him terribly, and he rushed full speed to join it. The artillery firing had ceased, but the clatter of musketry was at its height. The bullets did not whistle as single ones do but came in swarms like a flock of autumn birds flying overhead.

The whole place where his battalion had been stationed the day before was hidden in smoke, and enemy shouts and exclamations could be heard. As he went he met crowds of wounded and unwounded soldiers. Having run another thirty paces he saw his own company pressed to the wall.

'The Schwartz Redoubt is taken!' said a young officer, whose teeth were chattering. 'All is lost!'

'Nonsense!' said Kozeltsóv angrily, and [wishing to rouse himself by a gesture] he drew his blunt little iron sword and cried:

'Forward, lads! Hurrah!'

His voice sounded loud and clear and roused Kozeltsóv himself. He ran forward along the traverse, and about fifty soldiers ran shouting after him. From the traverse he ran out into the open ground. The bullets fell just like hailstones. Two hit him, but where, and what they had done—bruised him or wounded him—he had no time to determine. Before him through the smoke he could already see blue coats and red trousers, and hear shouts that were not Russian. One Frenchman stood on the breastwork waving his cap and shouting something. Kozeltsóv felt sure he would be killed, and this increased his courage. He ran on and on. Several soldiers outran him, others appeared from somewhere else and also ran. The blue uniforms were always at the same distance from him, running back to their trenches, but there were dead and wounded on the ground under his feet. When he had run to the outer ditch, everything became blurred in Kozeltsóv's eyes and he felt a pain in his chest.

Half an hour later he was lying on a stretcher near the Nicholas Barracks and knew that he was wounded, but felt hardly any pain. He only wished for something cool to drink, and to lie more comfortably.

A plump little doctor with large black whiskers came up to him and unbuttoned his cloak. Kozeltsóv looked over his chin to see the doctor's face and what he was doing to his wound, but he still felt no pain. The doctor covered the wound with the shirt, wiped his fingers on the skirt of his cloak and silently, without looking at the wounded man, passed on to another patient. Kozeltsóv unconsciously watched what was going on around him and, remembering what had happened at the Fifth Bastion with exceedingly joyful self-satisfaction, felt that he had performed his duty well—that for the first time in the whole of his service he had acted as well as it was possible to act, and that he had nothing to reproach himself with. The doctor, bandaging another man, pointed to Kozeltsóv and said something to a priest with a large red beard, who stood near by with a cross.

'Am I dying?' asked Kozeltsóv when the priest approached him.

The priest did not reply, but said a prayer and held a cross to the wounded man's lips.

Death did not frighten Kozeltsóv. He took the cross with his weak hands, pressed it to his lips, and began to weep.

'Were the French driven back?' he asked the priest firmly.

'The victory is ours at all points,' answered the latter to console the wounded man, concealing from him the fact that a French standard was already waving from the Malákhov Redoubt.

'Thank God!' exclaimed the dying man, not feeling the tears that ran down his cheeks, [and experiencing inexpressible delight at the consciousness of having performed an heroic deed].

The thought of his brother flashed through his brain. 'God grant him as good a fate!' thought he.

## XXVI

But a different fate awaited Volódya. He was listening to a tale Vásin was telling when he heard the cry 'The French are coming!' The blood suddenly rushed to his heart and he felt his cheeks grow cold and pale. He remained immovable for a moment, but glancing round saw the soldiers fastening their uniforms and crawling out one after the other fairly coolly.

One of them—Mélnikov probably—even joked, saying, 'Take them some bread and salt.' [1]

Volódya, and Vlang who followed him like a shadow, climbed out of the bomb-proof and ran to the battery. There was no artillery firing at all from either side. The coolness of the soldiers did less to rouse Volódya than the pitiful coward-ice of the cadet. 'Can I possibly be like him?' he thought, and ran gaily to the breastwork where his mortars stood. He could plainly see the French running straight towards him across the open ground, and crowds of them moving in the nearer trenches, their bayonets glittering in the sunshine. One short, broad-shouldered fellow in a Zouave uniform was running in front, sword in hand, jumping across the pits.

'Fire case-shot!' cried Volódya, running back from the ban-quette, but the soldiers had already arranged matters without him and the metallic ring of the discharged case-shot whistled over his head first from one mortar and then from the other. 'One—Two!' ordered Volódya, running the distance between the two mortars and quite forgetting the danger. From one side and near at hand was heard the clatter of the musketry of our supports, and excited cries.

Suddenly a wild cry of despair arose on the left. 'They're behind us! Behind us!' repeated several voices. Volódya looked round. About twenty Frenchmen appeared behind him. One of them, a handsome man with a black beard, was in front of the rest, but having run up to within ten paces of the battery he stopped, fired point-blank at Volódya, and then again started running towards him. For a moment Volódya stood petrified, unable to believe his eyes. When he recovered and glanced round he saw French uniforms on the breastwork before him; two Frenchmen were even spiking a cannon some ten paces from him. No one was near but Mélnikov, who had fallen at his side killed by a bullet, and Vlang, who had seized a linstock and was rushing forward with a furious look on his face, roll-ing his eyes and shouting.

'Follow me, Vladímir Seménich! . . . Follow me!' he cried

---

[1] It is a Russian custom to offer bread and salt to new arrivals.

in a desperate voice, brandishing his linstock at the Frenchmen who had appeared from behind. The furious figure of the
cadet perplexed them. Vlang hit the front one on the head,
the others involuntarily hesitated, and he ran to the trench
where our infantry lay firing at the French, continually looking back and shouting desperately, 'Come with me, Vladímir
Seménich! Why are you stopping? Run!' Having jumped in, he
climbed out again to see what his adored ensign was doing.
Something in a cloak lay prostrate where Volódya had stood,
and that whole place was occupied by Frenchmen firing at
our men.

## XXVII

Vlang found his battery at the second line of defence. Of the
twenty soldiers belonging to the mortar battery only eight
were left.

Towards nine in the evening Vlang crossed over with the
battery to the North Side on a steamer crowded with soldiers,
cannon, horses, and wounded men. There was no firing anywhere. The stars shone as brightly in the sky as they had done
the night before, but the sea was rocked by a strong wind. On
the First and Second Bastions flames kept bursting up along
the ground, explosions rent the air and lit up strange dark objects and the stones flying in the air around them. Something
was burning near the docks and the red glare was reflected on
the water. The bridge thronged with people was illuminated
by a fire at the Nicholas Battery. A large flame seemed to
stand above the water on the distant little headland of the
Alexander Battery, lighting up from below the clouds of smoke
that hung above it, and quiet, bold lights gleamed over the
sea, as they had done yesterday, from the distant enemy fleet,
and the fresh wind raised waves in the Roadstead. By the glar-
ing light of the conflagration one could see the masts of our
sinking ships as they slowly descended deeper and deeper into
the water. There was no talking on board, only words of command given by the captain, the snorting and stamping of the
horses on the vessel, and the moaning of the wounded, could

be heard above the steam and the regular swish of the parting waters. Vlang, who had had nothing to eat all day, took a piece of bread from his pocket and began munching it, but suddenly remembering Volódya he began to sob so loud that the soldiers near him heard it.

'Look! He's eating bread and yet he's sobbing, is our Vlánga!' said Vásin.

'That's queer!' said another.

'Look! Our barrack's been set on fire too,' he continued with a sigh. 'What a lot of the likes of us perished there; and now the Frenchmen have got it for nothing.'

'At all events we have got off alive, thank God!' said Vásin.

'All the same, it's a shame.'

'Where's the shame? D'you think they'll get a chance of amusing themselves there? See if ours don't retake it. No matter how many of the likes of us are lost; if the Emperor gives the word, as sure as there's a God we'll take it back. You don't suppose we'll leave it like that? No fear! There, take the bare walls. . . . The 'trenchments are all blown up. . . . Yes, I daresay. . . . *He's* stuck his flag on the mound, but he's not shoved himself into the town. . . .You wait a bit! The real reckoning will come yet—only wait a bit!' he concluded, admonishing the French.

'Of course it will!' said another with conviction.

Along the whole line of the Sevastopol bastions—which for so many months had been seething with such extraordinary life and energy, for so many months had seen heroes relieved by death as they fell one after another, and for so many months had aroused the fear, the hatred, and at last the admiration of the enemy—no one was now to be seen: all was dead, ghastly, terrible. But it was not silent: destruction was still going on. Everywhere on the ground, blasted and strewn around by fresh explosions, lay shattered gun-carriages crushing the corpses of foes and Russians alike, cast-iron cannons thrown with terrific force into holes and half-buried in the earth and silenced for ever, bombs, cannon-balls and more dead bodies; then holes and splintered beams of what had been bomb-proofs, and again silent corpses in grey or blue uniforms. All

this still shuddered again and again, and was lit up by the lurid
flames of the explosions that continued to shake the air.

The enemy saw that something incomprehensible was happening in awe-inspiring Sevastopol. The explosions and the
deathly stillness on the bastions made them shudder, but under
the influence of the strong and firm resistance of that day they
did not yet dare to believe that their unflinching foe had disappeared, and they awaited the end of the gloomy night
silently, motionless and anxious.

The Sevastopol army, surging and spreading like the sea on
a rough dark night, its whole mass anxiously palpitating,
slowly swayed through the thick darkness by the bridge over
the Roadstead and onto the North Side, away from the place
where it was leaving so many brave comrades, from the place
saturated with its blood, the place it had held for eleven
months against a far stronger foe, but which it was now ordered to abandon without a struggle.

The first effect this command had on every Russian was one
of oppressive bewilderment. The next feeling was a fear of
pursuit. The men felt helpless as soon as they had left the
places where they were accustomed to fight, and crowded
anxiously together in the darkness at the entrance to the
bridge which was rocked by the strong wind. With bayonets
clashing, regiments, vehicles, and militia crowded together and
pressed forward to the bay. While mounted officers pushed
through with orders, the inhabitants wept, orderlies carrying
forbidden luggage entreated, and artillery with rattling wheels
hurried to get away. Notwithstanding the diversion resulting
from their various and bustling occupations, the instinct of
self-preservation and the desire to get away as quickly as possible from this dreadful place of death was present in the soul
of each. It was present in the mortally wounded soldier who
lay among the five hundred other wounded men on the pavement of the Pávlov Quay praying to God for death; in the
militiaman pushing with all his might among the dense crowd
to make way for a general who was riding past; in the general
who conducted the crossing, firmly restraining the impetuosity
of the soldiers; in the sailor who, having got among a moving

battalion, was squeezed by the swaying crowd till he could
scarcely breathe; in the wounded officer whom four soldiers
had been carrying on a stretcher, but stopped by the throng
had put down on the ground near the Nicholas Battery; in the
artilleryman who having served with the same gun for sixteeen
years was now, in obedience to an officer's order quite incomprehensible to him, with the help of his comrades pushing that
gun down the steep bank into the Roadstead, and in the sailors
of the fleet who, having just scuttled their ships, were briskly
rowing away from them in the long-boats. On reaching the
North Side and leaving the bridge almost every man took off
his cap and crossed himself. But behind this feeling of self-
preservation there was another, a deeper feeling, sad and
gnawing, akin to remorse, shame, and anger. Almost every
soldier looking back at the abandoned town from the North
Side, sighed with inexpressible bitterness in his heart and made
a menacing gesture towards the enemy.

# MEETING A
# MOSCOW ACQUAINTANCE
# IN THE DETACHMENT*

We were out with a detachment. The work in hand was almost
done, the cutting through the forest was nearly finished, and
we were expecting every day to receive orders from head-
quarters to retire to the fort.

Our division of the battery guns was placed on the slope
of a steep mountain range which stretched down to the rapid
little mountain river Mechik, and we had to command the
plain in front. Occasionally, especially towards evening, on
this picturesque plain beyond the range of our guns, groups of
peaceable mountaineers on horseback appeared here and
there, curious to see the Russian camp. The evening was clear,
quiet, and fresh, as December evenings usually are in the Caucasus. The sun was setting behind the steep spur of the mountain range to the left, and threw rosy beams on the tents scattered over the mountain side, on the moving groups of soldiers,
and on our two guns, standing as if with outstretched necks,
heavy and motionless, on the earthwork battery close by. The
infantry picket, stationed on a knoll to our left, was sharply
outlined against the clear light of the sunset, with its piles of
arms, the figure of its sentry, its group of soldiers, and the

---

* One of the first stories Tolstoy published after his return to Petersburg from Sevastopol. It is based, however, on his earlier experiences in the Caucasus. The long and awkward title was forced
upon him by the censor as a substitute for his original title, a single
Russian word meaning 'A Man Reduced to the Ranks.'

smoke of its dying campfire. To right and to left, half-way
down the hill, white tents gleamed on the trodden black earth,
and beyond the tents loomed the bare black trunks of the
plane forest, where axes continually rang, fire crackled, and
trees fell crashing down. On all sides the pale bluish smoke
rose in columns towards the frosty blue sky. Beyond the tents,
and on the low ground by the stream, Cossacks, dragoons, and
artillery drivers trailed along, returning from watering their
stamping and snorting horses. It was beginning to freeze; all
sounds were heard with unusual distinctness, and one could
see far into the plain through the clear rarefied air. The groups
of natives, no longer exciting the curiosity of our men, rode
quietly over the light-yellow stubble of the maize-fields. Here
and there through the trees could be seen the tall posts of Tartar cemeteries, and the smoke of their *aouls*.

Our tent was pitched near the guns, on a dry and elevated
spot whence the view was specially extensive. By the tent,
close to the battery, we had cleared a space for the games of
Gorodki[1] or Choushki. Here the attentive soldiers had erected
for us rustic seats and a small table. Because of all these con-
veniences our comrades the artillery officers, and some of the
infantry, liked to assemble at our battery, and called this place
'The Club'.

It was a beautiful evening, the best players had come, and
we were playing Gorodki. I, Ensign D., and Lieutenant O.
lost two games running, and to the general amusement and
laughter of the onlooking officers, and of soldiers and orderlies
who were watching us from their tents, we twice carried the
winners pick-a-back from one end of the ground to the other.
Specially amusing was the position of the enormous, fat Lieutenant-Captain S., who puffing and smiling good-humouredly,
with his feet trailing on the ground, rode on the back of the
small and puny Lieutenant O. But it was growing late. The

---

[1] Gorodki is a game in which short, thick sticks are arranged in certain figures within squares. Each side has its own square, and each
player in turn throws a stick to try to clear out the enemy's square.
The side wins which first accomplishes this with the six figures in
which the sticks are successively arranged.

orderlies brought three tumblers of tea without any saucers for the whole six of us, and having finished our game we came to the rustic seats. Near them stood a short, bandy-legged man whom we did not know, dressed in a sheepskin coat and with a large, white, long-woolled sheepskin cap on his head. As soon as we approached him he hesitatingly took off and put on his cap several times and repeatedly seemed on the point of coming up to us, but then stopped again. But probably having decided that he could no longer remain unnoticed, this stranger again raised his cap, and passing round us approached Lieutenant-Captain S.

'Ah, Guskantini! Well, what is it, old chap?' said S., still continuing to smile good-humouredly after his ride.

Guskantini, as S. called him, put on his cap at once, and made as if to put his hands in the pockets of his sheepskin coat; but on the side turned to me I could see it had no pocket, so that his little red hand remained in an awkward position. I tried to make up my mind what this man could be (a cadet or an officer reduced to the ranks?), and without noticing that my attention (the attention of an unknown officer) confused him, I looked intently at his clothing and general appearance. He seemed to be about thirty. His small round grey eyes seemed to look sleepily and yet anxiously from under the dirty white wool which hung over his face from his shaggy cap. The thick irregular nose between the sunken cheeks accentuated his sickly, unnatural emaciation. His lips, only slightly covered by thin light-coloured moustaches, were continually in motion, as if trying to put on now one, now another expression. But all these expressions seemed unfinished; his face still kept its one predominant expression of mingled fear and hurry. His thin scraggy neck was enveloped in a green woollen scarf, partly hidden under his sheepskin coat. The coat was worn bare and was short; it was trimmed with dog's fur round the collar and at the false pockets. He had greyish check trousers on, and soldier's boots with short unblacked tops.

'Please don't trouble,' said I, when he again raised his cap, looking timidly at me.

He bowed with a grateful look, put on his cap, and taking

from his trouser pocket a dirty calico tobacco-pouch tied with a cord, began to make a cigarette.

It was not long since I myself had been a cadet; an old cadet who could no longer act the good-humoured attentive younger comrade to the officers, and a cadet without means. Understanding, therefore, all the wretchedness of such a position for a proud man no longer young, I felt for all who were in that state, and tried to discern their characters and the degree and direction of their mental capacities, in order to be able to judge the extent of their moral suffering. This cadet, or degraded officer, judging by his restless look and the purposely varying expression of his face, seemed to be far from stupid, but very self-conscious, and therefore very pitiable.

Lieutenant-Captain S. proposed another game of Gorodki, the losers, besides carrying the winners pick-a-back, to stand a couple of bottles of claret, with rum, sugar, cinnamon, and cloves, to make mulled wine, which was very popular in our detachment that winter because of the cold weather. Guskantini, as S. again called him, was also asked to join, but before beginning, evidently wavering between the pleasure this invitation gave him and fear of some kind, he led Lieutenant-Captain S. aside and whispered something into his ear. The good-natured Lieutenant-Captain slapped him on the stomach with the palm of his big fat hand, and answered aloud, 'Never mind, old chap, I'll give you credit!'

When the game was finished, and when, the side of the lower-grade stranger having won, he should have ridden on one of our officers, Ensign D., the latter blushed, turned aside to the seats, and offered the stranger some cigarettes by way of ransom. When the mulled wine had been ordered, and one could hear Nikita's bustling arrangements in the orderlies' tent and how he sent a messenger for cinnamon and cloves, and could then see his back, first here and then there, bulging the dirty sides of the tent,—we, the seven of us, sat down by the little table, drinking tea in turns out of the three tumblers and looking out over the plain, which began to veil itself in evening twilight, while we talked and laughed over the different incidents of the game. The stranger in the sheepskin coat took no part in the conversation, persistently refused the tea I repeatedly offered him, and, sitting on the ground Tartar-fashion, made cigarettes one after the other out of tobacco-dust, and smoked them evidently not so much for his own pleasure as to give himself an appearance of being occupied. When it was mentioned that a retreat was expected next day, and that perhaps we should have a fight, he rose to his knees and, addressing only Lieutenant-Captain S., said that he had just been at home with the Adjutant and had himself written out the order to move next day. We were all silent while he spoke, and, though he was evidently abashed, we made him repeat this communication—highly interesting to us. He repeated what he had said, adding, however, that at the time the order arrived, he was *with,* and *sat with,* the Adjutant, *with whom he lived.*

'Mind, if you are not telling us a lie, old chap, I must be off to my company to give some order for to-morrow,' said Lieutenant-Captain S.

'No. . . . Why should? . . . Is it likely? . . . It is certain . . .' began the stranger, but stopped suddenly, having evidently determined to feel hurt, frowned unnaturally and, muttering something between his teeth, again began making cigarettes. But the dregs of tobacco-dust that he could extract from his pouch being insufficient, he asked S. to *favour him with the loan of a cigarette.* We long continued among ourselves that monotonous military chatter familiar to all who have been on campaign. We complained, ever in the same terms, of the tediousness and duration of the expedition; discussed our commanders in the same old way; and, just as often before, we praised one comrade, pitied another, were astonished that So-and-so won so much, and that So-and-so lost so much at cards, and so on and so on.

'Our Adjutant has got himself into a mess, and no mistake,' said Lieutenant-Captain S. 'He always used to win when he was on the staff—whoever he sat down with he'd pluck clean —but now these last two months he does nothing but lose. He has not hit it off in this detachment! I should think he's lost 1,000 rubles in money, and things for another 500: the carpet

he won of Mukhin, Nikitin's pistols, the gold watch from
Sada's that Vorontsov gave him—have all gone.'

'Serves him right,' said Lieutenant O.; 'he gulled everybody,
it was impossible to play with him.'

'He gulled everybody, and now he himself is gravelled,' and
Lieutenant-Captain S. laughed good-naturedly. 'Guskov, here,
lives with him—the Adjutant nearly lost him one day at cards!
Really! Am I not right, old chap?' he said, turning to Guskov.

Guskov laughed. It was a pitifully sickly laugh which completely changed the expression of his face. This change suggested to me the idea that I had seen and known the man before, besides, Guskov, his real name, was familiar to me. But
how and when I had seen him I was quite unable to remember.

'Yes,' said Guskov, who kept raising his hand to his moustaches and letting it sink again without touching them, 'Paul
Dmitrich has been very unlucky this campaign: such a *veine
de malheur*,' [2] he added, in carefully spoken but good French,
and I again thought I had met, and even often met, him somewhere. 'I know Paul Dmitrich well; he has great confidence in
me,' continued he; 'we are old acquaintances—I mean he is
fond of me,' he added, evidently alarmed at his own too bold
assertion of being an old acquaintance of the Adjutant. 'Paul
Dmitrich plays remarkably well, but now it is incomprehensible what has happened to him; he seems quite lost—*la
chance a tourné*,' [3] he said, addressing himself chiefly to me.

At first we had listened to Guskov with condescending attention, but as soon as he uttered this second French phrase
we all involuntarily turned away from him.

'I have played hundreds of times with him,' said Lieutenant
O., 'and you won't deny that it is *strange*' (he put a special
emphasis on the word 'strange'), 'remarkably strange, that I
never once won even a twenty-kopek piece of him. How is it I
win when playing with others?'

'Paul Dmitrich plays admirably: I have long known him,'

---

[2] Run of ill luck.
[3] The luck has turned.

said I. I had really known the Adjutant for some years; had more than once seen him playing for stakes high in proportion to the officers' means; and had admired his handsome, rather stern, and always imperturbably calm face, his slow Ukrainian pronunciation, his beautiful things, his horses, his leisurely Ukrainian disposition, and especially his ability to play with self-control—systematically and pleasantly. I confess that more than once when looking at his plump white hands with a diamond ring on the first finger as he beat my cards one after the other, I was enraged with this ring, with the white hands, with the whole person of the Adjutant, and evil thoughts concerning him rose in my mind. But on thinking matters over in cool blood I became convinced that he was simply a more sagacious player than all those with whom he happened to play. I was confirmed in this by the fact that when listening to his general reflection on gaming—how, having been lucky starting with a small stake, one should follow up one's luck; how in certain cases one ought to stop playing; that the first rule was to play for *ready-money*, &c., &c.—it was clear that he always won simply because he was cleverer and more self-possessed than the rest of us. And it now appeared that this self-possessed, strong player had, in the detachment, lost completely, not only money, but other belongings as well—which among officers indicates the lowest depth of loss.

'He was always devilish lucky when playing against me,' continued Lieutenant O.; 'I have sworn never to play with him again.'

'What a queer fellow you are, old man!' said S., winking at me so that his whole head moved while he addressed O.; 'you have lost some 300 rubles to him—lost it, haven't you?'

'More!' said the Lieutenant crossly.

'And now you've suddenly come to your senses; but it's too late, old chap! Everyone else has long known him to be the sharper of our regiment,' said S., hardly able to refrain from laughter and highly delighted at his invention.

'Here's Guskov himself—he prepares the cards for him. That is why they are friends, old chap! . . .' And Lieutenant-Captain S. laughed good-humouredly so that he shook all over and spilt some of the mulled wine he held in his hand. A faint tinge of colour seemed to rise on Guskov's thin, yellow face; he opened his mouth repeatedly, lifted his hands to his moustache and let them drop again to the places where his pockets should have been, several times began to rise but sat down again, and at last said in an unnatural voice, turning to S.:

'This is not a joke, Nicholas Ivanich, you are saying *such things*! And in the presence of people who don't know me and who see me in a common sheepskin coat . . . because . . .' His voice failed him, and again the little red hands with their dirty nails moved from his coat to his face, now smoothing his moustaches or hair, now touching his nose, rubbing his eye, or unnecessarily scratching his cheek.

'What's the good of talking; everyone knows it, old chap!' continued S., really enjoying his joke and not in the least noticing Guskov's excitement. Guskov again muttered something, and leaning his right elbow on his left knee in a most unnatural position, looked at S. and tried to smile contemptuously.

'Yes,' thought I, watching that smile, 'I have not only seen him before, but have spoken with him somewhere.'

'We must have met somewhere before,' I said to him when, under the influence of the general silence, S.'s laughter began to subside.

Guskov's mobile face suddenly brightened, and his eyes, taking for the first time a sincerely pleased expression, turned to me.

'Certainly; I knew you at once!' he began in French. 'In '48 I had the pleasure of meeting you rather often in Moscow at my sister's—the Ivashins.'

I apologized for not having recognized him in his present costume. He rose, approached me, and with his moist hand irresolutely and feebly pressed mine. Instead of looking at me, whom he professed to be so glad to see, he looked round in an unpleasantly boastful kind of way at the other officers. Either because he had been recognized by me who had seen him some years before in a drawing-room in a dress-coat, or

because that recollection suddenly raised him in his own es-
teem, his face and even his movements, as it seemed to me,
changed completely. They now expressed a lively intellect,
childish self-satisfaction at the consciousness of that intellect,
and a kind of contemptuous indifference. So that I admit, notwithstanding the pitiful position he was in, my old acquaintance no longer inspired me with sympathy, but with an almost inimical feeling.

I vividly recalled our first meeting. In 1848, during my stay
in Moscow, I often visited Ivashin. We had grown up together and were old friends. His wife was a pleasant hostess
and what is considered an amiable woman, but I never liked
her. The winter I visited them she often spoke with ill-
concealed pride of her brother, who had lately finished his
studies and was, it seemed, among the best-educated and
most popular young men in the best Petersburg society. Knowing by reputation Guskov's father, who was very rich and
held an important position, and knowing his sister's leanings,
I was prejudiced before I met Guskov. One evening, having
come to see Ivashin, I found there a very pleasant-looking
young man, not tall, in a black swallow-tail coat and white
waistcoat and tie; but the host forgot to introduce us to one
another. The young man, evidently prepared to go to a ball,
stood hat in hand in front of Ivashin, hotly but politely arguing about a common acquaintance of ours who had recently
distinguished himself in the Hungarian campaign. He was
maintaining that this acquaintance of ours was not at all a
hero or a man born for war, as was said of him, but merely
a clever and well-educated man. I remember that I took part
against Guskov in the dispute and went to an extreme, even
undertaking to show that intelligence and education were
always in inverse ratio to bravery; and I remember how Guskov pleasantly and cleverly argued that bravery is an inevitable result of intelligence and of a certain degree of development, with which view (considering myself to be intelligent
and well educated) I could not help secretly agreeing. I remember also how, at the end of our conversation, Ivashin's

wife introduced us to one another and how her brother, with a condescending smile, gave me his little hand on which he had not quite finished drawing a kid glove, and pressed mine in the same feeble and irresolute manner as he did now. Though prejudiced against Guskov, I could not then help doing him the justice of agreeing with his sister that he really was an intelligent and pleasant young man who ought to succeed in society. He was exceedingly neat, elegantly dressed, fresh looking, and had self-confidently modest manners and a very youthful, almost childlike, appearance which made one unconsciously forgive the expression of self-satisfaction and of a desire to mitigate the degree of his superiority over you, which his intelligent face, and especially his smile, always showed. It was reported that he had great success among the Moscow ladies that winter. Meeting him at his sister's I could only infer the amount of truth in these reports from the expression of pleasure and satisfaction he always wore, and from the indiscreet stories he sometimes told. We met some half-dozen times and talked a good deal, or rather he talked a good deal and I listened. He usually spoke French, in a very correct, fluent, and ornamental style, and knew how to interrupt others in conversation politely and gently. In general he treated me and everyone rather condescendingly; and as always happens to me with people who are firmly convinced that I ought to be treated with condescension and whom I do not know well, I felt that he was quite right in so doing.

Now, when he sat down beside me and gave me his hand of his own accord, I vividly recalled his former supercilious expression, and thought that he, as one of inferior rank, was making a rather unfair use of the advantage of his position by questioning me, an officer, in an off-hand manner, as to what I had been doing all this time and how I came to be here. Though I answered in Russian every time, he always began again in French, in which it was noticeable that he no longer expressed himself as easily as formerly. About himself he only told me in passing that after that unfortunate and stupid affair of his (I did not know what this affair was, and he did not tell me) he had been three months under arrest, and was afterwards sent to the Caucasus to the N—— Regiment and had now served three years as a private.

'You would not believe,' said he, in French, 'what I have suffered at the hands of the officer sets! It was lucky I formerly knew this Adjutant we have just been talking about: he is really a good fellow,' he remarked condescendingly. 'I am living with him, and it is after all some mitigation. *Oui, mon cher, les jours se suivent, mais ne se ressemblent pas,*[4] he added, but suddenly became confused, blushed, and rose from his seat, having noticed that the Adjutant we had been talking about was approaching us.

'It is such a consolation to meet a man like you,' whispered Guskov as he was leaving my side; 'there is very much I should like to talk over with you.'

I told him I should be very glad, though I confess that in reality Guskov inspired me with an unsympathetic, painful kind of pity.

I foresaw that I should feel uncomfortable when alone with him, but I wanted to hear a good many things from him, especially how it was that, while his father was so wealthy, he was poor, as his clothes and habits showed.

The Adjutant greeted us all except Guskov, and sat down beside me where the latter had been.

Paul Dmitrich, whom I had always known as a calm, deliberate, strong gambler and a moneyed man, was now very different from what he had been in the flourishing days of his card-playing. He seemed to be in a hurry, kept looking round at everybody, and before five minutes were over he, who always used to be reluctant to play, now proposed to Lieutenant O. that the latter should start a 'bank.'

Lieutenant O. declined, under pretext of having duties to attend to; his real reason being that, knowing how little money and how few things Paul Dmitrich still possessed, he considered it unwise to risk his three hundred rubles against the hundred or less he might win.

---

[4] Yes, my dear fellow, the days follow, but do not resemble one another.

'Is it true, Paul Dmitrich,' said the Lieutenant, evidently wishing to avoid a repetition of the request, 'that we are to leave here to-morrow?'

'I don't know,' replied Paul Dmitrich, 'but the orders are, to be ready! But really we'd better have a game: I would stake my Kabardá[5] horse.'

'No, to-day . . .'

'The grey one. Come what may! Or else, if you like, we'll play for money. Well?'

'Oh, but I—I would readily—you must not think—' began Lieutenant O., answering his own doubts, 'but you know, we may have an attack or a march before us to-morrow and I want to have a good sleep.'

The Adjutant rose, and putting his hands in his pockets began pacing up and down. His face assumed the usual cold and somewhat proud expression which I liked in him.

'Won't you have a glass of mulled wine?' I asked.

'I don't mind if I do,' he said, coming towards me.

But Guskov hurriedly took the tumbler out of my hand and carried it to the Adjutant, trying at the same time not to look at him. But he did not notice one of the cords with which the tent was fastened, stumbled over it, and letting the tumbler drop, fell on his hands.

'What a muff!' said the Adjutant, who had already stretched out his hand for the tumbler. Everyone burst out laughing, including Guskov, who was rubbing his bony knee which he could not have hurt in falling.

'That's the way the bear served the hermit,' continued the Adjutant. 'It's the way he serves me every day! He has wrenched out all the tent-pegs stumbling over them.' Guskov, paying no heed to him, apologized, looking at me with a scarcely perceptible, sad smile, which seemed to say that I alone could understand him. He was very pitiable, but the Adjutant, his protector, seemed for some reason to be angry with his lodger and would not let him alone.

---

[5] Kabardá is a district in the Térek Territory of the Caucasus, and Kabardá horses are famous for their powers of endurance.

'Oh yes, he's a sharp boy, turn him which way you will.'

'But who does not stumble over those pegs, Paul Dmitrich?' said Guskov; 'you yourself stumbled the day before yesterday.'

'I, old fellow, am not in the ranks; smartness is not expected of me.'

'He may drag his feet,' added Lieutenant-Captain S., 'but a private must skip. . . .'

'What curious jokes! . . .' said Guskov, almost in a whisper, with eyes cast down. The Adjutant evidently did not feel indifferent to his lodger, he watched keenly every word he uttered.

'He'll have to be sent to the ambuscades again,' he said, addressing S., and winking towards the degraded one.

'Well, then, tears will flow again,' said S., laughing.

Guskov no longer looked at me, but pretended to be getting tobacco from the pouch which had long been empty.

'Get ready to go to the outposts, old chap,' said S., laughing, 'the scouts have reported that the camp will be attacked to-night, so reliable lads will have to be told off.'

Guskov smiled undecidedly, as if preparing to say something, and cast several imploring looks at S.

'Well, you know I have been before, and I shall go again if I am sent,' muttered he.

'Yes, and you will be sent!'

'Well, and I'll go. What of that?'

'Yes, just as you did at Argun—ran away from the ambuscade and threw away your musket,' said the Adjutant, and turning away from him began telling us about the order for the next day.

It was true that the enemy was expected to fire at the camp in the night, and a movement of some sort was to take place next day. After talking for a while on various subjects of general interest, the Adjutant, as if he had suddenly chanced to recollect it, proposed to Lieutenant O. to have a little game. The Lieutenant quite unexpectedly accepted and they went with S. and the Ensign to the Adjutant's tent, where a green folding-table and cards were to be found. The Captain, who was commander of our division, went to his tent to sleep, the other gentlemen also went away and Guskov and I were left alone.

I had not been mistaken; I really felt uncomfortable alone with him, and I could not help rising and pacing up and down the battery. Guskov walked silently by my side, turning round hurriedly and nervously so as neither to lag behind nor pass before me.

'I am not in your way?' he said, in a meek, sad voice. As far as I could judge in the darkness his face seemed deeply thoughtful and melancholy.

'Not at all,' I answered, but as he did not begin to speak, and I did not know what to say to him, we walked a good while in silence.

The twilight was now quite replaced by the darkness of night, but over the black outlines of the mountains the sheet-lightnings so common there in the evening flashed brilliantly. Above our heads tiny stars twinkled in the pale-blue frosty sky, and the red flames of smoking camp-fires glared all around: the tents near us seemed grey, and the embankment of our battery a gloomy black. From the fire nearest to us, round which our orderlies sat warming themselves and talking low, a gleam now and then fell on the brass of our heavy guns and made visible the figure of the sentry, as, with his cloak thrown over his shoulders, he walked with measured steps along the embankment.

'You can't think what a relief it is to me to talk to a man like you!' said Guskov, though he had not yet spoken to me about anything. 'Only a man who has been in my position can understand it.'

I did not know what to answer, and again we were silent, though it was evident that he wished to speak out and I wished to hear him.

'For what were you. . . . What was the cause of your misfortune?' I asked at last, unable to think of any better way to start the conversation.

'Did you not hear about the unfortunate affair with Metenin?'

'Oh yes; a duel, I think. I heard some reference to it,' I answered. 'You see, I have been some time in the Caucasus.'

'No, not a duel, but that stupid and terrible affair! I will tell you all about it if you have not heard it. It was the same year that you and I used to meet at my sister's. I was then living in Petersburg. But first I must tell you that I then had what is called *une position dans le monde*,[6] and a tolerably lucrative if not brilliant one. *Mon père me donnait* 10,000 *par an*.[7] In '49 I was promised a place in the embassy at Turin; an uncle on my mother's side had influence and was always ready to give me a lift. It's now a thing of the past. *J'étais reçu dans la meilleure société de Pétersbourg: je pouvais prétendre*[8] to make a good match. I had learnt—as we all learn at school; so that I possessed no special education. It is true I read a good deal afterwards, *mais j'avais surtout*, you know, *ce jargon du monde*;[9] and, whatever the cause, I was considered one of the leading young men in Petersburg. What raised me most in the general estimation, *c'est cette liaison avec Mme D——*,[10] which was much talked of in Petersburg. But I was awfully young at the time and set little value on these advantages. I was simply young and foolish. What more did I need? At that time in Petersburg that fellow Metenin had a reputation. . . .' And Guskov continued in this manner to tell me the story of his misfortune, which, being quite uninteresting, I will here omit.

'Two months,' continued he, 'I was under arrest and quite alone. I don't know what did not pass through my mind in that time; but, do you know, when it was all over, when it seemed as if every link with the past was severed, it became easier for me. *Mon père, vous en avez entendu parler*[11] surely: he is a man with an iron will and firm convictions; *il*

---

[6] A position in the world.
[7] My father allowed me 10,000 rubles a year.
[8] I was received in the best society of Petersburg; I could aspire . . .
[9] But in particular I spoke the society jargon.
[10] Was that liaison with Mme D——.
[11] My father; you will have heard him spoken of.

*m'a déshérité*[12] and ceased all intercourse with me. According to his convictions it was the proper thing to do, and I do not blame him at all; *il a été conséquent.*[13] And I also did not take a step to induce him to change his mind. My sister was abroad. Mme D—— was the only one who wrote to me when letters were allowed, and she offered me help; but you will understand that I could not accept it, so that I had none of those trifles which somewhat mitigate such a position, you know—no books, no linen, no private food, nothing. Many, very many thoughts passed through my brain at that time and I began to look at everything with other eyes; for instance, all that noise and gossip about me in Petersburg society no longer interested or flattered me in the least; it all seemed ridiculous. I felt I was myself to blame; I had been careless and young and had spoilt my career, and my only thought was how to retrieve it. And I felt I had strength and energy enough to do it. After my arrest was over, I was, as I told you, sent to the Caucasus to the N—— Regiment.

'I thought that here, in the Caucasus,' he continued, growing more and more animated, '*la vie de camp,*[14] the simple, honest men with whom I should be in contact, the war, the dangers—all this would just suit my frame of mind and I thought I should begin life anew. *On me verra au feu*[15]— people would like me, would respect me not for my name only; then I should receive a cross, become a non-commissioned officer and at last be pardoned and should return, *et, vous savez, avec ce prestige du malheur!*[16] But *quel désenchantement!*[17] You can't think how I was mistaken! . . . You know the officer set of our regiment?' He paused for some time, probably expecting me to say that I knew how bad the society of officers here is; but I did not reply to him. I was disgusted that—on account, no doubt, of my knowing French—he

---

[12] He disinherited me.
[13] He has been consistent.
[14] Camp life.
[15] I should be seen under fire.
[16] You know, with the prestige that misfortune gives.
[17] (But) what a disenchantment!

should suppose that I ought to despise the officer set, which
on the contrary I, having lived long in the Caucasus, had
fully learnt to appreciate, and which I esteemed a thousand
times more than the society Mr. Guskov had left. I wished
to tell him so, but his position restrained me.

'In the N—— Regiment the officers set is a thousand times
worse than here,' he continued—'*J'espère que c'est beaucoup
dire*,[18]—so that you can't imagine what it is like! Not to mention the cadets and the soldiers—it was just awful! At first
I was well received, that's perfectly true, but afterwards,
when they saw I couldn't help despising them—when in those
scarcely noticeable everyday relations, you know, they saw
that I was a totally different sort of man standing on a far
higher level than they—they were exasperated with me and
began to retaliate by subjecting me to all kinds of petty indig-
nities. *Ce que j'ai eu à souffrir, vous ne vous faites une idée.*[19]
Then, being obliged to associate with the cadets; and above
all, *avec les petits moyens que j'avais, je manquais de tout*,[20]
I had only what my sister sent me. A proof of what I have
suffered is that I, with my character, *avec ma fierté, j'ai écrit
à mon père*,[21] imploring him to send me something, however
little. . . . I can understand how after five years of such a
life one may become like our cashiered officer Dromov, who
drinks with the soldiers and writes notes to all the officers
begging them to *lend* him three rubles, and signs himself,
"*Tout à vous*, Dromov." One needs a character like mine in
order not to sink quite into the mire of this terrible position.'
He then walked silently by my side for a long time. '*Avez-vous
un papiros?*'[22] he said at last. 'Yes, . . . where had I got to?
Oh yes, I could not stand it. I don't mean physically, for
although it was bad enough and I suffered from cold and
hunger and lived like a soldier, yet the officers still had a
sort of regard for me. I still had a kind of *prestige* in their

---

[18] I hope that is saying a good deal.
[19] You can have no idea of what I had to suffer.
[20] With the small means I had, I lacked everything.
[21] With my pride, I wrote to my father.
[22] Have you a cigarette?

eyes. They did not send me to do sentry duty or drill. I could
not have borne that. But morally I suffered terribly, and above
all I could see no escape from this position. I wrote to my
uncle imploring him to transfer me to this regiment, which
is at least on active duty, and I thought that here Paul Dmitrich, *qui est le fils de l'intendant de mon père*,[23] would be
of use to me. My uncle did this much for me, and I was
transferred. After that other regiment this seemed an assembly of courtiers. And Paul Dmitrich was here; he knew who
I was, and I was capitally received—at my uncle's request.
. . . Guskov, *vous savez*. But I noticed that these people,
without education or culture, cannot respect a man nor show
him respect when he is not surrounded by an aureole of
wealth and rank. I noticed how, little by little, when they
saw that I was poor, their behaviour to me became more
and more careless, and at last almost contemptuous. It is
dreadful, but it is perfectly true.

'Here I have been in action, have fought, *on m'a vu au
feu*,'[24] he continued, 'but when will it end? Never, I think!
And my strength and energy are beginning to fail. And then
I had imagined *la guerre, la vie de camp*,[25] but it turns out
to be quite different from what I expected: dressed in a sheepskin, in soldier's boots, unwashed, you are sent to the outposts and lie all night in a ditch with some Antonov or other
who has been sent into the army for drunkenness, and at any
moment you may be shot from behind a bush—you or Antonov, all the same. . . . That is not courage! It is horrible.
*C'est affreux, ça tue*.'[26]

'Well, but you may be made a non-commissioned officer for
this expedition, and next year may become an ensign,' I said.

'Yes, possibly. I was promised it, but that would be another two years and it is very doubtful. And does any one
realize what two such years mean? Just imagine the life with
this Paul Dmitrich: gambling, rough jokes, dissipation. . . .

[23] Who is the son of my father's steward.
[24] I have been seen under fire.
[25] War, camp-life.
[26] It is dreadful, it is killing.

You want to speak out about something that has risen in your soul, but you are not understood or you are laughed at. They talk to you not to communicate their thoughts, but to make a fool of you if possible. And it's all so vulgar, coarse, horrid; and all the time you feel you are a private—they always make you feel that. That is why you can't imagine what a pleasure it is to talk *à coeur ouvert* [27] to a man like you!'

I could not imagine what sort of a man I was supposed to be and therefore did not know how to reply to him.

'Will you have supper?' at this moment asked Nikita, who had approached unseen in the darkness, and who, I noticed, was not pleased at the presence of my visitor: 'there's nothing but dumplings and a little beef left.'

'And has the captain had his supper?'

'He's asleep long ago,' said Nikita, crossly.

On my telling him to bring us something to eat and some vodka, he muttered discontentedly and went slowly to his tent. However, after grumbling there a bit, he brought us the cellaret, on which he placed a candle (round which he first tied a piece of paper to keep the wind off), a saucepan, a pot of mustard, a tin cup with a handle, and a bottle of vodka bitters. Having arranged all this, Nikita stood some time near us and watched with evident disapproval while Guskov and I drank some of the spirit. By the dim light of the candle shining through the paper the only things one could see amid the surrounding darkness were the sealskin with which the cellaret was covered, the supper standing on it, and Guskov's face, his sheepskin coat, and the little red hands with which he took the dumplings out of the saucepan. All around was black, and only by looking intently could one discern the black battery, the equally black figure of the sentry visible over the breastwork, the camp-fires around, and the reddish stars above. Guskov smiled just perceptibly in a sad and bashful way as if it were awkward for him to look me in the eyes after his confession. He drank another cup of vodka and ate greedily, scraping out the saucepan.

---

[27] Quite frankly.

'Yes, it must at any rate be some relief to you,' I remarked, in order to say something, 'to be acquainted with the Adjutant; I have heard he is a very decent fellow.'

'Yes,' he answered, 'he is a kind-hearted man, but he can't help being what he is; he can't be a man, with his education one can't expect it,' and he suddenly seemed to blush. 'You noticed his coarse jokes to-day about the ambuscades.' And Guskov, in spite of my repeated efforts to turn the conversation, began to justify himself to me and to demonstrate that he did not run away from the ambuscades, and that he was not a coward as the Adjutant and Captain S. wished to imply.

'As I told you,' he said, wiping his hands on his sheepskin, 'people of that kind can't be considerate to a man who is a private and who has but little money: that is beyond them. And these last five months, during which it has somehow happened that I have received nothing from my sister, I have noticed how they have changed towards me. This sheepskin I bought of a soldier, and which is so worn that there is no warmth in it' (here he showed me the bare skirt of the coat), 'does not inspire him with sympathy or respect for my misfortunes, but only contempt which he is unable to conceal. However great my need, as, for instance, at the present time, when I have nothing to eat except the soldiers' buckwheat, and nothing to wear,' he continued, seemingly abashed, and pouring out for himself yet another cup of vodka, 'he does not think of offering to lend me any money, although he knows that I should certainly repay him, but he waits that I, in my position, should ask him for it. You understand what it would mean for me to have to go to him. Now, to you, for instance, I could say quite straight: *Vous êtes au-dessus de cela, mon cher, je n'ai pas le sou.*[28] And do you know,' said he, looking desperately into my eyes, 'I tell you straight, I am now in terrible difficulties; *Pouvez-vous me prêter dix roubles argent?*[29] My sister must send me something by the next mail, *et mon père. . . .'*

---

[28] You are above that [i.e. above despising me for my misfortunes], my dear fellow. I have not a halfpenny.
[29] Can you lend me ten rubles?

'Oh, with pleasure,' said I, though on the contrary it was painful and vexatious, especially because, having lost at cards the day before, I myself had only a little over five rubles and they were in Nikita's possession. 'Directly,' I said, rising, 'I will go and get them from the tent.'

'No, it will do later, *ne vous dérangez pas.*' [30]

But without listening to him I crept into the closed tent where my bed stood and where the captain lay asleep.

'Alexey Ivanich, please lend me ten rubles till our allowances are paid,' said I to the captain, shaking him.

'What! cleared out again? And it's only yesterday you resolved not to play any more!' said the captain, still half-asleep.

'No, I have not been playing! But I want it—please lend it me.'

'Makatyuk!' shouted the captain to his orderly, 'get me the money-box and bring it here.'

'Hush, not so loud,' I said, listening to Guskov's measured footsteps outside the tent.

'What! . . . Why not so loud?'

'Oh, that fellow in the ranks asked me for a loan. He's just outside.'

'If I had known that, I would not have given it you,' remarked the captain. 'I have heard about him, he's the dirtiest young scamp.'

Still the captain let me have the money all the same, ordered the money-box to be put away and the tent properly closed, and again repeating, 'If I had known what it was for I would not have given it you,' he wrapped himself, head and all, in his blanket. 'Remember you owe me thirty-two now!' he shouted after me.

When I came out of the tent Guskov was pacing up and down in front of the little seats, his short bandy-legged figure in the ugly cap with the long white wool disappearing in the darkness and reappearing as he passed in and out of the candle-light. He pretended not to notice me. I gave him

---

[30] Do not trouble yourself.

the paper-money. He said '*Merci*,' and crumpling it up he put it in his trouser-pocket.

'I suppose play is in full swing at Paul Dmitrich's now!' he then began.

'Yes, I suppose so.'

'He plays so queerly, always *à rebours*,[31] and does not hedge. When you have luck it is all right, but when it goes against you you may lose terribly. He is a proof of it. On this expedition he has lost more than fifteen hundred rubles, counting the things he has lost. And with what self-control he used to play formerly! So that that officer of yours seemed even to doubt his honesty.'

'Oh, he did not mean anything. . . . Nikita, have we any Caucasian wine left?' I asked, very much relieved by Guskov's loquacity. Nikita grumbled again, but brought us the wine all the same, and again crossly watched Guskov emptying his cup. In Guskov's manner the former nonchalance again became apparent. I wished him to go away, and thought he stopped only because he did not like to go immediately after receiving the money. I was silent.

'How could you, with means at your disposal and no necessity, *de gaieté de coeur* [32] make up your mind to come and serve in the Caucasus? That is what I don't understand,' he said.

I tried to justify myself for this step that seemed to him so strange.

'I can imagine how uncongenial the society of these officers must be to you: men without an idea of education. It is impossible for you and them to understand one another. Why, you may live here for ten years, and except cards and wine and talk about rewards and campaigns, you will see nothing and hear nothing.'

I did not like his being so certain that I shared his opinion, and I assured him with perfect sincerity that I was very fond

---

[31] Reversing.
[32] From light-heartedness.

of cards and wine, and of talks about campaigns, and that I did not wish for better comrades than those I had. But he would not believe me.

'Oh, you do not really mean it,' he continued; 'and the absence of women—I mean *femmes comme il faut*[33]—is not that a terrible privation? I don't know what I wouldn't give to transport myself into a drawing-room now, and take a peep, though but through a crack, at a charming woman.'

He was silent a moment and drank another cup of wine

'O God, O God! It is still possible we may some day meet again in Petersburg among men, live with human beings, with women.'

He emptied the bottle and said: 'Oh, *pardon*, perhaps you would have taken some more, I am so terribly absent-minded. And I'm afraid I have drunk too much, *et je n'ai pas la tête forte.*[34] There was a time when I lived on the Morskaya[35] *au rez-de-chaussée.*[36] I had a delightful little flat and furniture—you know I had a knack for arranging things elegantly and not too expensively. It is true *mon père* gave me the crockery, and plants, and excellent silver plate. *Le matin je sortais,*[37] then calls, at five o'clock *régulièrement* I went to dine with her, and often found her alone. *Il faut avouer que c'était une femme ravissante!*[38] Did you not know her? Not at all?'

'No.'

'You know, there was so much of that womanliness about her, that tenderness, and then such love! . . . O God! I did not know how to value my happiness then. . . . Or when we returned from the theatre and had supper together. It was never dull in her company, *toujours gaie, toujours animante.*[39]

---

[33] Women of good breeding.
[34] And I have not a strong head.
[35] Morskaya—one of the best streets in Petersburg.
[36] On the ground floor.
[37] In the morning I went out.
[38] It must be admitted that she was a ravishing woman.
[39] Always gay, always loving.

Yes, I did not then foresee how rare a joy it was. *Et j'ai beaucoup à me reprocher*[40] in regard to her. *Je l'ai fait souffrir, et souvent* [41]—I was cruel. Oh, what a delightful time it was! But I am wearying you.'

'No, not at all.'

'Then I will tell you about our evenings. I used to enter— oh, that staircase, I knew every plant-pot on it—the very door-handle—all was so nice, so familiar to me—then the ante-room, and then her room. . . . No, it will never, never, return! She writes to me even now; I can, if you like, even show you her letters. But I am no longer what I was—I am ruined, I am no longer worthy of her. . . . Yes, I am completely ruined! *Je suis cassé.*[42] I have neither energy nor pride; nothing, not even nobility. . . . Yes, I am ruined! and no one will ever understand what I have suffered. Every one is indifferent. I am a lost man! I can never rise again, because I have sunk morally . . . sunk into the mire . . . sunk. . . .' And a real, deep despair sounded in his voice at that moment; he did not look at me, but sat motionless.

'Why give way to such despair?' I said.

'Because I am vile; this life has destroyed me; all that was in me has perished. I no longer suffer proudly, but basely; I have no *dignité dans le malheur.*[43] I am insulted every moment and I bear it all, and go to meet insults half-way. The mud *a déteint sur moi.*[44] I have become coarse myself, have forgotten what I knew, I can't even speak French now, and I feel that I am base and despicable. I can't fight in these surroundings; it is impossible! I might perhaps have been a hero: give me a regiment, gold epaulettes, and trumpeters; but to march side by side with some uncivilized Antonov Bondarenko or other and to think there is no difference between him and me, it is all the same whether I get killed or he does—that is the thought that is killing me. You under-

---

40 And I have much to reproach myself with.
41 I made her suffer, often.
42 I am broken.
43 Dignity in misfortune.
44 Has stained me.

stand how terrible it is that some ragamuffin may kill me—a
man who thinks and feels—and that he might as well kill
Antonov by my side, a creature indistinguishable from a brute;
and it is quite likely to happen that it is I who will be killed
and not Antonov—it is always so, *une fatalité* for all that is
lofty or good. I know they call me a coward. Granted that I
am a coward. It is true I am a coward and cannot help it;
but it is not enough that I am a coward, according to them
I am also a beggar and a contemptible fellow. There, I have
just begged money from you, and you have a right to despise
me. No, take back your money,' and he held out to me the
crumpled note; 'I want you to respect me.' He covered his
face with his hands and began to cry, and I did not in the
least know what to say or do.

'Don't go on like that,' said I; 'you are too sensitive; you
should not take things so much to heart: don't analyse but
look at things simply. You say yourself that you are a man
of character; face your task, you have not much longer to
suffer,' I said to him very incoherently, for I was excited both
by feelings of pity and by a feeling of repentance at having
allowed myself to condemn a man who was truly and deeply
suffering.

'Yes,' he began; 'had I but once since I came into this
hell heard a single word of advice, sympathy, or friendship—
a single human word such as I hear from you—I might have
borne everything calmly, have faced my task, and even behaved like a soldier; but now it is terrible. . . . When I
reason sanely I long for death. Why should I care for a life
of dishonour, or for myself who am dead to all that is good
in life? But at the least sign of danger I can't help craving
for this vile life and guarding it as if it were something very
precious, and I can't, *je ne puis pas*,[45] master myself. . . .
That is, I can,' he continued, after a moment's pause; 'but
it costs me too great an effort, a tremendous effort when I
am alone. When others are present, and in ordinary circumstances when going into action, I am brave enough—*j'ai fait*

---

[45] I cannot.

*mes preuves*,[46]—because I have self-love and am proud—that is my fault—and in the presence of others . . . I say, let me spend the night with you—they'll be playing all night in our tent. I can sleep anywhere—on the ground.'

While Nikita was making up a bed we rose, and again, in the dark, began walking up and down the battery. Guskov must really have had a very weak head, for after only two cups of vodka and two glasses of wine he was unsteady on his feet. When we had walked away from the candle I noticed that he put the ten-ruble note, which he had held in his hand all through the foregoing conversation, back into his pocket, trying not to let me see it. He continued to say that he felt he might yet rise if he had a man like myself to take an interest in him.

We were about to enter the tent to go to bed when suddenly a cannon-ball whistled over us and struck into the ground not far off. It was very strange: the quiet, sleeping camp, our conversation—and suddenly the enemy's ball flying, God knows whence, right in among our tents: so strange that it was some time before I could realise what had happened. But one of our soldiers, Andreev, who was pacing up and down the battery on guard, came towards me.

'He's sneaked within range. There's the place he fired from,' remarked he.

'The captain must be roused,' said I, and glanced at Guskov.

He had crouched nearly to the earth and stammered, trying to say something, 'This . . . this . . . is unple . . . this is . . . most . . . absurd.' He said no more, and I did not see how and where he suddenly vanished.

In the captain's tent a candle was lit and we heard him coughing, as he always did on waking; but he soon appeared, demanding the linstock to light his little pipe with.

'What's the matter, old man?' said he, smiling. 'It seems I am to have no sleep to-night; first you come with your "fellow from the ranks", and now it's Shamyl. What are we going to

---

[46] I have shown it.

do? Shall we reply or not? Nothing was mentioned about it in the orders?'

'Nothing at all. There he is again,' said I; 'and this time with two guns.'

And, in fact, before us, a little to the right, two fires were seen in the darkness like a pair of eyes, and then a ball flew past, as well as an empty shell, probably one of our own returned to us—which gave a loud and shrill whistle. The soldiers crept out of the neighbouring tents and could be heard clearing their throats, stretching themselves, and talking.

'Hear him a-whistling through the fuse-hole just like a nightingale!' remarked an artilleryman.

'Call Nikita!' said the captain, with his usual kindly banter. 'Nikita, don't go hiding yourself; come and listen to the mountain nightingales.'

'Why not, y'r honour?' said Nikita, as he came up and stood by the captain. 'I have seen them nightingales and am not afraid of 'em; but there's that guest who was here a moment ago drinking your wine, he cut his sticks soon enough when he heard 'em; went past our tent like a ball, doubled up like some animal.'

'Well, someone must ride over to the Chief of Artillery,' said the captain to me in a grave and authoritative tone, 'to ask whether we are to reply to the shots or not. We can't hit anything, but we can shoot for all that. Be so good as to go and ask. Order a horse to be saddled, you'll get there quicker; take my Polkan, if you like.'

Five minutes later the horse was brought, and I started to find the Chief of Artillery.

'Mind, the watchword is *pole*,' whispered the careful captain, 'or you won't be allowed to pass the cordon.'

It was barely half a mile to where the Chief of Artillery was stationed. The whole way lay among tents. As soon as I had left the light of our camp-fires behind, it was so dark that I could not even see my horse's ears—only the camp-fires, which seemed now very near, now very far away, flick-

ered before my eyes. Having given the horse the rein and let
him take his own course for a little, I began to distinguish
the white four-cornered tents, and then the black ruts of the
road. Half an hour later, after having asked my way some
three or four times, twice stumbled over tent-pegs and been
sworn at each time from within the tent, and after having
been twice stopped by sentries, I reached the Chief of Artillery at last.

While on my way I heard two more shots fired at our
camp, but they did not reach the place where the staff was
stationed. The Chief of Artillery ordered not to fire, especially
now that the enemy had ceased firing; so I returned, leading
my horse and making my way on foot among the infantry
tents. More than once, while passing a soldier's tent in which
I saw a light, I slackened my pace to listen to a tale told by
some wag, or to a book read out by some 'literate' person, to
whom a whole company listened, tightly packed inside and
crowding outside the tent and now and then interrupting the
reader with their remarks, or I caught merely some scrap of
conversation about an expedition, about home, or about the
officers.

Passing one of the tents of the 3rd Battalion, I heard
Guskov's loud voice speaking very merrily and confidently.
He was answered by young voices, not of privates but of
gentlemen, as merry as his own. This was evidently a cadet's
or sergeant-major's tent. I stopped.

'I have long known him,' Guskov was saying. 'When I was
in Petersburg he often came to see me and I visited him. He
belonged to very good society.'

'Whom are you talking about?' asked a tipsy voice.

'About the prince,' answered Guskov. 'We are related, you
know; more than that, we are old friends. You know, gentlemen, it is a good thing to have such an acquaintance. He is
awfully rich, you see. A hundred rubles is nothing to him; so
I've taken a little of him till my sister sends me some.'

'Well, then send . . .'

'All right! . . . Savelich, old boy!' came Guskov's voice
from the tent as he drew near to the entrance; 'here are

ten rubles, go to the canteen and get two bottles of Kahetin-
sky. . . . What else, gentlemen? Speak up!' and Guskov,
bare-headed and with hair dishevelled, reeled out of the tent.
Throwing open his sheepskin and thrusting his hands into the
pockets of his greyish trousers, he stopped at the entrance.
Though he was in the light and I in the dark, I trembled
with fear lest he should see me, and moved on, trying not
to make a noise.

'Who's there?' shouted Guskov at me in a perfectly tipsy
voice. The cold air evidently had an effect on him. 'What
devil is prowling about there with a horse?'

I did not reply, and silently found my way out on to the
road.

# THE SNOW STORM*

## I

Having drunk tea towards seven o'clock in the evening, I left
a station, the name of which I have forgotten, though I know
it was somewhere in the district of the Don Cossack Army
near Novocherkássk. It was already dark when, having
wrapped myself in my fur coat, I took my seat under the
apron beside Alëshka in the sledge. Near the post-station it
seemed mild and calm. Though no snow was falling, not a
star was visible overhead and the sky looked extremely low
and black, in contrast to the clean snowy plain spread out
before us.

We had hardly passed the dark shapes of the windmills,
one of which clumsily turned its large sails, and left the
settlement behind us, when I noticed that the road had become heavier and deeper in snow, that the wind blew more
fiercely on the left, tossing the horses' tails and manes sideways, and that it kept carrying away the snow stirred up by
the hoofs and sledge-runners. The sound of the bell began
to die down, and through some opening in my sleeve a stream
of cold air forced its way behind my back, and I recalled the
station-master's advice, not to start for fear of going astray
all night and being frozen on the road.

'Shan't we be losing our way?' I said to the driver, and
not receiving an answer I put my question more definitely: 'I
say, driver, do you think we shall reach the next station without losing our way?'

* Tolstoy left the Caucasus, after two and a half years there, in
January 1854. On his way home he encountered a blizzard which
later suggested this short story.

'God only knows,' he answered without turning his head. 'Just see how the snow drifts along the ground! Nothing of the road to be seen. O Lord!'

'Yes, but you'd better tell me whether you expect to get me to the next station or not?' I insisted. 'Shall we get there?'

'We ought to manage it,' said the driver, and went on to add something the wind prevented my hearing.

I did not feel inclined to turn back, but the idea of straying about all night in the frost and snowstorm on the perfectly bare steppe which made up that part of the Don Army district was also far from pleasant. Moreover, though I could not see my driver very well in the dark, I did not much like the look of him and he did not inspire me with confidence. He sat exactly in the middle of his seat with his legs in, instead of to one side; he was too big, he spoke lazily, his cap, not like those usually worn by drivers, was too big and flopped from side to side; besides, he did not urge the horses on properly, but held the reins in both hands, like a footman who had taken the coachman's place on the box. But my chief reason for not believing in him was because he had a kerchief tied over his ears. In a word he did not please me, and that solemn stooping back of his looming in front of me seemed to bode no good.

'In my opinion we'd better turn back,' remarked Alëshka. 'There's no sense in getting lost!'

'O Lord! Just look how the snow is driving, nothing of the road to be seen, and it's closing my eyes right up . . . . O Lord!' muttered the driver.

We had not been going a quarter of an hour before the driver handed the reins to Alëshka, clumsily liberated his legs, and making the snow crunch with his big boots went to look for the track.

'What is it? Where are you going? Are we off the road?' I asked. But the driver did not answer and, turning his face away from the wind which was beating into his eyes, walked away from the sledge.

'Well, is there a road?' I asked when he returned.

'No, there's nothing,' he answered with sudden impatience

and irritation, as if I were to blame that he had strayed off the track, and having slowly thrust his big legs again into the front of the sledge he began arranging the reins with his frozen gloves.

'What are we to do?' I asked when we had started again.

'What are we to do? We'll drive where God sends us.'

And though we were quite evidently not following a road, we went on at the same slow trot, now through dry snow five inches deep, and now over brittle crusts of frozen snow.

Though it was cold, the snow on my fur collar melted very quickly; the drift along the ground grew worse and worse, and a few dry flakes began to fall from above.

It was plain that we were going heaven knows where, for having driven for another quarter of an hour we had not seen a single verst-post.

'Well, what do you think?' I asked the driver again. 'Shall we get to the station?'

'What station? We shall get back, if we give the horses their head they will take us there, but hardly to the next station—we might just perish.'

'Well then, let us go back,' I said. 'And really . . .'

'Then I am to turn back?' said the driver.

'Yes, yes, turn back!'

The driver gave the horses the reins. They began to run faster, and though I did not notice that we were turning, I felt the wind blowing from a different quarter, and we soon saw the windmills appearing through the snow. The driver cheered up and began to talk.

'The other day the return sledges from the other station spent the whole night in a snow storm among haystacks and did not get in till the morning. Lucky that they got among those stacks, else they'd have all been frozen, it was so cold. As it is one of them had his feet frozen, and was at death's door for three weeks with them.'

'But it's not cold now, and it seems calmer,' I said, 'we might perhaps go on?'

'It's warm enough, that's true, but the snow is drifting.

Now that we have it at our back it seems easier, but the snow is driving strongly. I might go if it were on courier-duty or something of the kind, but not of my own free will. It's no joke if a passenger gets frozen. How am I to answer for your honour afterwards?'

## II

Just then we heard behind us the bells of several tróykas[1] which were rapidly overtaking us.

'It's the courier's bell,' said my driver. 'There's no other like it in the district.'

And in fact the bell of the front tróyka, the sound of which was already clearly borne to us by the wind, was exceedingly fine: clear, sonorous, deep, and slightly quivering. As I learnt afterwards it had been chosen by men who made a hobby of tróyka bells. There were three bells—a large one in the middle with what is called a *crimson* tone, and two small ones tuned to a third and a fifth. The ringing of that third and of the quivering fifth echoing in the air was extraordinarily effective and strangely beautiful in that silent and deserted steppe.

'The post is going,' said my driver, when the first of the three tróykas overtook us. 'How is the road? Is it usable?' he called out to the driver of the last sledge, but the man only shouted at his horses and did not reply.

The sound of the bells was quickly lost in the wind as soon as the post sledges had passed us.

I suppose my driver felt ashamed.

'Well, let us try it again, sir!' he said to me. 'Others have made their way through and their tracks will be fresh.'

I agreed, and we turned again, facing the wind and struggling forward through the deep snow. I kept my eyes on the side of the road so as not to lose the track left by the tróykas. For some two versts the track was plainly visible, then only a slight unevenness where the runners had gone, and soon I

---

[1] A tróyka is a three-horse sledge, or, more correctly, a team of three horses.

was quite unable to tell whether it was a track or only a layer of driven snow. My eyes were dimmed by looking at the snow monotonously receding under the runners, and I began to look ahead. We saw the third verst-post, but were quite unable to find a fourth. As before we drove against the wind, and with the wind, and to the right and to the left, and at last we came to such a pass that the driver said we must have turned off to the right, I said we had gone to the left, and Alëshka was sure we had turned right back. Again we stopped several times and the driver disengaged his big feet and climbed out to look for the road, but all in vain. I too once went to see whether something I caught a glimpse of was not the road, but hardly had I taken some six steps with difficulty against the wind before I became convinced that similar layers of snow lay everywhere, and that I had seen the road only in my imagination. When I could no longer see the sledge I cried out: 'Driver! Alëshka!' but I felt how the wind caught my voice straight from my mouth and bore it instantly to a distance. I went to where the sledge had been— but it was not there; I went to the right, it was not there either. I am ashamed to remember in what a loud, piercing, and even rather despairing voice I again shouted 'Driver!' and there he was within two steps of me. His black figure with the little whip and enormous cap pushed to one side, suddenly loomed up before me. He led me to the sledge.

'Thank the Lord, it's still warm,' he said, 'if the frost seized us it would be terrible . . . O Lord!'

'Give the horses their head: let them take us back,' I said, having seated myself in the sledge. 'They will take us back, driver, eh?'

'They ought to.'

He let go of the reins, struck the harness-pad of the middle horse with the whip, and we again moved on somewhere. We had travelled on for about half an hour when suddenly ahead of us we recognized the connoisseur's bell and the other two, but this time they were coming towards us. There were the same three tróykas, which having delivered the mail were now returning to the station with relay horses attached. The courier's tróyka with its big horses and musical bells ran quickly in front, with one driver on the driver's seat shouting vigorously. Two drivers were sitting in the middle of each of the empty sledges that followed, and one could hear their loud and merry voices. One of them was smoking a pipe, and the spark that flared up in the wind showed part of his face.

Looking at them I felt ashamed that I had been afraid to go on, and my driver probably shared the same feeling, for we both said at once: 'Let us follow them!'

## III

My driver, before the third tróyka had passed, began turning so clumsily that his shafts hit the horses attached behind it. They all three shied, broke their strap, and galloped aside.

'You cross-eyed devil! Can't you see when you're turning into someone, you devil?' one of the drivers seated in the last sledge—a short old man, as far as I could judge by his voice and figure—began to curse in hoarse, quivering tones, and quickly jumping out of the sledge he ran after the horses, still continuing his coarse and harsh abuse of my driver.

But the horses did not stop. The driver followed them, and in a moment both he and they were lost in the white mist of driving snow.

'Vasí-i-li! Bring along the dun horse! I can't catch them without,' came his voice.

One of the other drivers, a very tall man, got out of his sledge, silently unfastened his three horses, climbed on one of them by its breeching, and disappeared at a clumsy gallop in the direction of the first driver.

We and the other two tróykas started after the courier's tróyka, which with its bell ringing went along at full trot though there was no road.

'Catch them! Not likely!' said my driver of the one who had run after the horses. 'If a horse won't come to other horses, that shows it's bewitched and will take you somewhere you'll never return from.'

From the time he began following the others my driver seemed more cheerful and talkative, a fact of which I naturally took advantage, as I did not yet feel sleepy. I began asking where he came from, and why, and who he was, and it turned out that like myself he was from Túla province, a serf from Kirpíchnoe village, that they were short of land there and had had bad harvests since the cholera year. He was one of two brothers in the family, the third having gone as a soldier; that they had not enough grain to last till Christmas, and had to live on outside earnings. His youngest brother was head of the house, being married, while he himself was a widower. An *artél*[1] of drivers came from their village to these parts every year. Though he had not driven before, he had taken the job to help his brother, and lived, thank God, quite well, earning a hundred and twenty assignation rubles a year, of which he sent a hundred home to the family; and that life would be quite good 'if only the couriers were not such beasts, and the people hereabouts not so abusive.'

'Now why did that driver scold me so? O Lord! Did I set his horses loose on purpose? Do I mean harm to anybody? And why did he go galloping after them? They'd have come back of themselves, and now he'll only tire out the horses and get lost himself,' said the God-fearing peasant.

'And what is that black thing there?' I asked, noticing several dark objects in front of us.

'Why, a train of carts. That's pleasant driving!' he went on, when we had come abreast of the huge mat-covered wagons on wheels, following one another. 'Look, you can't see a single soul—they're all asleep. Wise horses know of themselves . . . you can't make them miss the way anyhow . . . We've driven that way on contract work ourselves,' he added, 'so we know.'

It really was strange to see those huge wagons covered with snow from their matted tops to their very wheels, and

---

[1] An *artél* was a voluntary association of workers, which had a manager, contracted as a unit, and divided its earnings among its members.

moving along all alone. Only in the front corner of the wagon did the matting, covered two inches thick with snow, lift a bit and a cap appear for a moment from under it as our bells tinkled past. The large piebald horse, stretching its neck and straining its back, went evenly along the completely snow-hidden road, monotonously shaking its shaggy head under the whitened harness-bow, and pricking one snow-covered ear when we overtook it.

When we had gone on for another half-hour the driver again turned to me.

'What d'you think, sir, are we going right?'

'I don't know,' I answered.

'At first the wind came that way, and now we are going right under the wind. No, we are not going where we ought, we are going astray again,' he said quite calmly.

One saw that, though he was inclined to be a coward, yet 'death itself is pleasant in company' as the saying is, and he had become quite tranquil now that there were several of us and he no longer had to lead and be responsible. He made remarks on the blunders of the driver in front with the greatest coolness, as if it were none of his business. And in fact I noticed that we sometimes saw the front tróyka on the left and sometimes on the right; it even seemed to me that we were going round in a very small circle. However, that might be an optical illusion, like the impression that the leading tróyka was sometimes going uphill, and then along a slope, or downhill, whereas I knew that the steppe was perfectly level.

After we had gone on again for some time, I saw a long way off, on the very horizon as it seemed to me, a long, dark, moving stripe; and a moment later it became clear that it was the same train of wagons we had passed before. The snow was still covering their creaking wheels, some of which did not even turn any longer, the men were still asleep as before under the matting, and the piebald horse in front blew out its nostrils as before, sniffed at the road, and pricked its ears.

'There, we've turned and turned and come back to the same wagons!' exclaimed my driver in a dissatisfied voice. 'The courier's horses are good ones, that's why he's driving them so recklessly, but ours will stop altogether if we go on like this all night.'

He cleared his throat.

'Let us turn back, sir, before we get into trouble!'

'No! Why? We shall get somewhere.'

'Where shall we get to? We shall spend the night in the steppe. How it is blowing! . . . O Lord!'

Though I was surprised that the driver of the front tróyka, having evidently lost the road and the direction, went on at a fast trot without looking for the road, and cheerfully shouting, I did not want to lag behind them.

'Follow them!' I said.

My driver obeyed, whipping up his horses more reluctantly than before, and did not turn to talk to me any more.

## IV

The storm grew more and more violent, and the snow fell dry and fine. I thought it was beginning to freeze: my cheeks and nose felt colder than before, and streams of cold air made their way more frequently under my fur coat, so that I had to wrap it closer around me. Sometimes the sledge bumped on the bare ice-glazed ground from which the wind had swept the snow. As I had already travelled more than five hundred versts without stopping anywhere for the night, I involuntarily kept closing my eyes and dozing off, although I was much interested to know how our wandering would end. Once when I opened my eyes I was struck for a moment by what seemed to me a bright light falling on the white plain; the horizon had widened considerably, the lowering black sky had suddenly vanished, and on all sides slanting white streaks of falling snow could be seen. The outlines of the front tróykas were more distinct, and as I looked up it seemed for a minute as though the clouds had dispersed, and that only the falling snow veiled the sky. While I was dozing the moon had risen and was casting its cold bright light through the tenuous clouds and the falling snow. The only things I saw clearly were my sledge, the horses, my driver, and the three tróykas in front of us: the courier's sledge in which a driver still sat, as before, driving at a fast trot; the second, in which two drivers having laid down the reins and made a shelter for themselves out of a coat sat smoking their pipes all the time, as could be seen by the sparks that flew from them; and the third in which no one was visible, as probably the driver was lying asleep in the body of the sledge. The driver of the first tróyka, however, at the time I awoke, occasionally stopped his horses and sought for the road. As soon as we stopped the howling of the wind sounded louder and the vast quantity of snow borne through the air became more apparent. In the snow-shrouded moonlight I could see the driver's short figure probing the snow in front of him with the handle of his whip, moving backwards and forwards in the white dimness, again returning to his sledge and jumping sideways onto his seat, and again amid the monotonous whistling of the wind I heard his dexterous, resonant cries urging on the horses, and the ringing of the bells. Whenever the driver of the front tróyka got out to search for some sign of a road or haystacks, there came from the second tróyka the bold, self-confident voice of one of the drivers shouting to him:

'Hey, Ignáshka, you've borne quite to the left! Bear to the right, facing the wind!' Or: 'What are you twisting about for, quite uselessly? Follow the snow, see how the drifts lie, and we'll come out just right.' Or: 'Take to the right, to the right, mate! See, there's something black—it must be a post.' Or: 'What are you straying about for? Unhitch the piebald and let him run in front, he'll lead you right out onto the road. That would be better.'

But the man who was giving this advice not only did not unhitch one of his own side-horses or get out to look for the road, but did not show his nose from under his sheltering coat, and when Ignáshka, the leader, shouted in reply to one of his counsels that he should take on the lead himself if he knew which way to go, the advice-giver replied that if he were driving the courier's tróyka he would take the lead and take us right onto the road. 'But our horses won't take the lead in a snow storm!' he shouted—'they're not that kind of horses!'

'Then don't bother me!' Ignáshka replied, whistling cheerfully to his horses.

The other driver in the second sledge did not speak to Ignáshka at all, and in general took no part in the matter, though he was not asleep, as I concluded from his pipe being always alight, and because, whenever we stopped, I heard the even and continuous sound of his voice. He was telling a folk tale. Only once, when Ignáshka stopped for the sixth or seventh time, he apparently grew vexed at being interrupted during the pleasure of his drive, and shouted to him:

'Hullo, why have you stopped again? Just look, he wants to find the road! He's been told there's a snow storm! The surveyor himself couldn't find the road now. You should drive on as long as the horses will go, and then maybe we shan't freeze to death . . . Go on, do!'

'I daresay! Didn't a postillion freeze to death last year?' my driver remarked.

The driver of the third sledge did not wake up all the time. Once when we had stopped the advice-giver shouted:

'Philip! Hullo, Philip!' and receiving no reply remarked: 'Hasn't he frozen, perhaps? . . . Go and have a look, Ignáshka.'

Ignáshka, who found time for everything, walked up to the sledge and began to shake the sleeping man.

'Just see what half a bottle of vódka has done! Talk about freezing!' he said, shaking him.

The sleeper grunted something and cursed.

'He's alive, all right,' said Ignáshka, and ran forward again. We drove on, and so fast that the little off-side sorrel of my tróyka, which my driver continually touched with the whip near his tail, now and then broke into an awkward little gallop.

## V

It was I think already near midnight when the little old man and Vasíli, who had gone after the run-away horses, rode up to us. They had managed to catch the horses and to find and overtake us; but how they had managed to do this in the thick blinding snow storm amid the bare steppe will always remain a mystery to me. The old man, swinging his elbows and legs, was riding the shaft-horse at a trot (the two side-horses were attached to its collar: one dare not let horses loose in a snow storm). When he came abreast of us he again began to scold my driver.

'Look at the cross-eyed devil, really . . .'

'Eh, Uncle Mítrich!' the folk-tale teller in the second sledge called out: 'Are you alive? Get in here with us.'

But the old man did not reply and continued his abuse. When he thought he had said enough he rode up to the second sledge.

'Have you caught them all?' someone in it asked.

'What do you think?'

His small figure threw itself forward on the back of the trotting horse, then jumped down on the snow, and without stopping he ran after the sledge and tumbled in, his legs sticking out over its side. The tall Vasíli silently took his old place in the front sledge beside Ignáshka, and the two began to look for the road together.

'How the old man nags . . . Lord God!' muttered my driver.

For a long time after that we drove on without stopping over the white waste, in the cold, pellucid, and quivering light of the snow storm. I would open my eyes and the same clumsy snow-covered cap and back would be jolting before me: the same low shaft-bow, under which, between the taut leather reins and always at the same distance from me, the head of our shaft-horse kept bobbing with its black mane blown to one side by the wind. Looking across its back I could see the same little piebald off-horse on the right, with its tail tied up short, and the swingletree which sometimes knocked against the front of the sledge. I would look down—there was the same scurrying snow through which our runners were cutting, and which the wind resolutely bore away to one side. In front, always at the same distance away, glided the first tróyka, while to right and left everything glimmered white and dim.

Vainly did my eye look for any new object: neither post, nor haystack, nor fence was to be seen. Everywhere all was white and fluctuating: now the horizon seemed immeasurably distant, now it closed in on all sides to within two paces of me; suddenly a high white wall would seem to rise up on the right and run beside the sledge, then it would suddenly vanish and rise again in front, only to glide on farther and farther away and again disappear. When I looked up it would seem lighter for a moment, as if I might see the stars through the haze, but the stars would run away higher and higher from my sight and only the snow would be visible, falling past my eyes onto my face and the collar of my fur cloak. The sky everywhere remained equally light, equally white, monotonous, colourless, and constantly shifting. The wind seemed to be changing: now it blew in my face and the snow plastered my eyes, now it blew from one side and annoyingly tossed the fur-collar of my cloak against my head and mockingly flapped my face with it; now it howled through some opening. I heard the soft incessant crunching of the hoofs and the runners on the snow, and the clang of the bells dying down when we drove through deep drifts. Only now and then, when we drove against the snow and glided over bare frozen ground, did Ignáshka's energetic whistling and the sonorous sound of the bell with its accompanying bare fifth reach me, and give sudden relief to the dismal character of the desert; and then again the bells would sound monotonous, playing always with insufferable precision the same tune, which I involuntarily imagined I was hearing. One of my feet began to feel the frost, and when I turned to wrap myself up better, the snow that had settled on my collar and cap sifted down my neck and made me shiver, but on the whole I still felt warm in my fur cloak, and drowsiness overcame me.

## VI

Recollections and pictures of the distant past superseded one another with increasing rapidity in my imagination.

'That advice-giver who is always calling out from the second sledge—what sort of fellow can he be?' I thought. 'Probably red-haired, thick-set, and with short legs, like Theodore Filípych, our old butler.' And I saw the staircase of our big house and five domestic serfs with heavy steps bringing a piano from the wing on slings made of towels, and Theodore Filípych with the sleeves of his nankeen coat turned up, holding one of the pedals, running forward, lifting a latch, pulling here at the slings, pushing there, crawling between people's legs, getting into everybody's way, and shouting incessantly in an anxious voice:

'Lean it against yourselves, you there in front, you in front! That's the way—the tail end up, up, up! Turn into the door! That's the way.'

'Just let us do it, Theodore Filípych! We can manage it alone,' timidly remarks the gardener, pressed against the bannisters quite red with straining, and with great effort holding up one corner of the grand piano.

But Theodore Filípych will not be quiet.

'What does it mean?' I reflect. 'Does he think he is useful or necessary for the work in hand, or is he simply glad God has given him this self-confident persuasive eloquence, and enjoys dispensing it? That must be it.' And then somehow I see the lake, and tired domestic serfs up to their knees in the water dragging a fishing-net, and again Theodore Filípych with a watering-pot, shouting at everybody as he runs up and down on the bank, now and then approaching the brink to empty out some turbid water and to take up fresh, while holding back the golden carp with his hand. But now it is a July noon. I am going somewhere over the freshly mown grass in the garden, under the burning, vertical rays of the sun; I am still very young, and I feel a lack of something and a desire to fill that lack. I go to my favourite place by the lake, between the briar-rose bed and the birch avenue, and lie down to sleep. I remember the feeling with which, lying down, I looked across between the prickly red stems of the rose trees at the dark, dry, crumbly earth, and at the bright blue mirror of the lake. It is a feeling of naïve self-satisfaction and melancholy. Everything around me is beautiful, and that beauty affects me so

powerfully that it seems to me that I myself am good, and the
one thing that vexes me is that nobody is there to admire me.
It is hot. I try to sleep so as to console myself, but the flies, the
unendurable flies, give me no peace here either: they gather
round me and, with a kind of dull persistence, hard as cherry-
stones, jump from my forehead onto my hands. A bee buzzes
not far from me in the blazing sunlight; yellow-winged butter-
flies fly from one blade of grass to another as if exhausted by
the heat. I look up: it hurts my eyes—the sun glitters too
brightly through the light foliage of the curly birch tree whose
branches sway softly high above me, and it seems hotter than
ever. I cover my face with my handkerchief: it feels stifling,
and the flies seem to stick to my hands which begin to per-
spire. In the very centre of the wild rose bush sparrows begin
to bustle about. One of them hops to the ground about two
feet from me, energetically pretends to peck at the ground a
couple of times, flies back into the bush, rustling the twigs,
and chirping merrily flies away. Another also hops down, jerks
his little tail, looks about him, chirps, and flies off quick as an
arrow after the first one. From the lake comes a sound of
beetles[1] beating the wet linen, and the sound re-echoes and is
borne down along the lake. Sounds of laughter and the voices
and splashing of bathers are heard. A gust of wind rustles the
crowns of the birch trees, still far from me, now it comes
nearer and I hear it stir the grass, and now the leaves of the
wold roses begin to flutter, pressed against their stems, and at
last a fresh stream of air reaches me, lifting a corner of my
handkerchief and tickling my moist face. Through the gap
where the corner of the kerchief was lifted a fly comes in and
flutters with fright close to my moist mouth. A dry twig presses
against my back. No, I can't lie still: I had better go and have
a bathe. But just then, close to the rose bush, I hear hurried
steps and a woman's frightened voice:

'O God! How could such a thing happen! And none of the
men are here!'

---

[1] The women take their clothes to rinse in lakes or streams, where
they beat them with wooden beetles.

'What is it? What is it?' running out into the sunshine I ask a woman serf who hurries past me groaning. She only looks round, waves her arms, and runs on. But here comes seventy-year-old Matrëna hurrying to the lake, holding down with one hand the kerchief which is slipping off her head, and hopping and dragging one of her feet in its worsted stocking. Two little girls come running up hand in hand, and a ten-year-old boy, wearing his father's coat and clutching the homespun skirt of one of the girls, keeps close behind them.

'What has happened?' I asked them.

'A peasant is drowning.'

'Where?'

'In the lake.'

'Who is he? One of ours?'

'No, a stranger.'

Iván the coachman, dragging his heavy boots through the newly-mown grass, and the fat clerk Jacob, all out of breath, run to the pond and I after them.

I remember the feeling which said to me: 'There you are, plunge in and pull out the peasant and save him, and everyone will admire you,' which was exactly what I wanted.

'Where is he? Where?' I ask the throng of domestic serfs gathered on the bank.

'Out there, in the very deepest part near the other bank, almost at the boathouse,' says the washerwoman, hanging the wet linen on her wooden yoke. 'I look, and see him dive; he just comes up and is gone, then comes up again and calls out: "I'm drowning, help!" and goes down again, and nothing but bubbles come up. Then I see that the man is drowning, so I give a yell: "Folk! A peasant's drowning!"'

And lifting the yoke to her shoulder the laundress waddles sideways along the path away from the lake.

'Oh gracious, what a business!' says Jacob Ivánov, the office clerk, in a despairing tone. 'What a bother there'll be with the rural court. We'll never get through with it!'

A peasant carrying a scythe pushes his way through the throng of women, children, and old men who have gathered on the farther shore, and hanging his scythe on the branch of a willow slowly begins to take off his boots.

'Where? Where did he go down?' I keep asking, wishing to rush there and do something extraordinary.

But they point to the smooth surface of the lake which is occasionally rippled by the passing breeze. I do not understand how he came to drown; the water is just as smooth, lovely, and calm above him, shining golden in the midday sun, and it seems that I can do nothing and can astonish no one, especially as I am a very poor swimmer and the peasant is already pulling his shirt over his head and ready to plunge in. Everybody looks at him hopefully and with bated breath, but after going in up to his shoulders he slowly turns back and puts his shirt on again—he cannot swim.

People still come running and the thing grows and grows; the women cling to one another, but nobody does anything to help. Those who have just come give advice, and sigh, and their faces express fear and despair; but of those who have been there awhile, some, tired with standing, sit down on the grass, while some go away. Old Matrëna asks her daughter whether she shut the oven door, and the boy who is wearing his father's coat diligently throws small stones into the water.

But now Theodore Filípych's dog Tresórka, barking and looking back in perplexity, comes running down the hill, and then Theodore himself, running downhill and shouting, appears from behind the briar-rose bushes:

'What are you standing there for?' he cries, taking off his coat as he runs, 'A man drowning, and they stand there! . . . Get me a rope!'

Everybody looks at Theodore Filípych with hope and fear as, leaning his hand on the shoulder of an obliging domestic serf, he prizes off his right boot with the toe of the left.

'Over there, where the people are, a little to the right of the willow, Theodore Filípjych, just there!' someone says to him.

'I know,' he replies, and knitting his brows, in response, no doubt, to the signs of shame among the crowd of women, he pulls off his shirt, removes the cross from his neck and hands it to the gardener's boy who stands obsequiously before him, and then, stepping energetically over the cut grass, approaches the lake.

Tresórka, perplexed by the quickness of his master's movements, has stopped near the crowd and with a smack of his lips eats a few blades of grass near the bank, then looks at his master intently and with a joyful yelp suddenly plunges with him into the water. For a moment nothing can be seen but foam and spray, which even reaches to us; but now Theodore Filípych, gracefully swinging his arms and rhythmically raising and lowering his back, swims briskly with long strokes to the opposite shore. Tresórka, having swallowed some water, returns hurriedly, shakes himself near the throng, and rubs his back on the grass. Just as Theodore Filípych reaches the opposite shore two coachmen come running up to the willow with a fishing-net wrapped round a pole. Theodore Filípych for some unknown reason lifts his arms, dives down once and then a second and a third time, on each occasion squirting a jet of water from his mouth, and gracefully tosses back his hair without answering the questions that are hurled at him from all sides. At last he comes out onto the bank, and as far as I can see only gives instruction as to spreading out the net. The net is drawn in, but there is nothing in it except ooze with a few small carp entangled in it. While the net is being lowered again I go round to that side.

The only sounds to be heard are Theodore Filípych's voice giving orders, the plashing of the wet rope on the water, and sighs of terror. The wet rope attached to the right side of the net, more and more covered by grass, comes farther and farther out of the water.

'Now then, pull together, harder, all together!' shouts Theodore Filípych.

The floats appear dripping with water.

'There is something coming, mates. It pulls heavy!' someone calls out.

Now the net—in which two or three little carp are struggling—is dragged to the bank, wetting and pressing down the grass. And in the extended wings of the net, through a thin swaying layer of turbid water, something white comes in sight. Amid dead silence an impressive, though not loud, gasp of horror passes through the crowd.

'Pull harder, onto the land!' comes Theodore Filípych's resolute voice, and the drowned body is dragged out to the willow over the stubble of burdock and thistle.

And now I see my good old aunt in her silk dress, with her face ready to burst into tears. I see her lilac sunshade with its fringe, which seems somehow incongruous in this scene of death, so terrible in its simplicity. I recall the disappointment her face expressed because arnica could be of no use, and I also recall the painful feeling of annoyance I experienced when, with the naïve egotism of love, she said: 'Come away my dear. Oh, how dreadful it is! And you always go bathing and swimming by yourself.'

I remember how bright and hot the sun was as it baked the powdery earth underfoot; how it sparkled and mirrored in the lake; how the plump carp plashed near the banks and shoals of little fish rippled the water in the middle; how a hawk hovering high in the air circled over the ducklings, which quacking and splashing had come swimming out through the reeds into the middle of the lake; how curling white thunder-clouds gathered on the horizon; how the mud drawn out onto the bank by the net gradually receded; and how as I crossed the dike I again heard the blows of the beetles re-echoing over the lake.

But that beetle sounds as if two beetles were beating together in thirds, and that sound torments and worries me, the more so because I know that this beetle is a bell, and that Theodore Filípych will not make it stop. Then that beetle, like an instrument of torture, presses my foot which is freezing, and I fall asleep.

I am awakened, as it seems to me, by our galloping very fast and by two voices calling out quite close to me:

'I say, Ignát! Eh, Ignát!' my driver is saying. 'You take my passenger. You have to go on anyhow, but what's the use of my goading my horses uselessly? You take him!'

Ignát's voice quite close to me replies:

'Where's the pleasure of making myself responsible for the passenger? . . . Will you stand me a bottle?'

'Oh, come, a bottle . . . say half a bottle.'

'Half a bottle, indeed!' shouts another voice. 'Wear out the horses for half a bottle!'

I open my eyes. Before them still flickers the same intolerable swaying snow, the same drivers and horses, but now we are abreast of another sledge. My driver has overtaken Ignát, and we drive side by side for some time. Though the voice from the other sledge advises him not to accept less than a bottle, Ignát suddenly reins in his tróyka.

'Well, shift over. So be it! It's your luck. You'll stand half a bottle when we return to-morrow. Is there much luggage?'

My driver jumps out into the snow with unusual alacrity for him, bows to me, and begs me to change over into Ignát's sledge. I am quite willing to, but evidently the God-fearing peasant is so pleased that he has to pour out his gratitude and delight to someone. He bows and thanks me, Alëshka, and Ignát.

'There now, the Lord be praised! What was it like . . . O Lord! We have been driving half the night and don't know where we are going. He'll get you there, dear sir, but my horses are quite worn out.'

And he shifts my things with increased zeal.

While my things were being transferred I went with the wind, which almost lifted me off my feet, to the second sledge. That sledge, especially outside the coat which had been arranged over the two men's heads to shelter them from the wind, was more than six inches deep in snow, but behind the coat it was quiet and comfortable. The old man still lay with his legs sticking out, and the story-teller was still going on with his tale:

'Well, when the general comes to Mary in prison, in the King's name, you know, Mary at once says to him: "General, I don't need you and can't love you, and so, you see, you are not my lover, but my lover is the prince himself . . ." '

'And just then . . .' he went on, but seeing me he stopped for a moment and began filling his pipe.

'Well, sir, have you come to listen to the tale?' asked the other whom I called the advice-giver.

'Yes, you're well off here, quite jolly,' I said.

'Why not? It whiles away the time, anyhow it keeps one from thinking.'

'And do you know where we are now?'

This question did not seem to please the drivers.

'Who can make out where we are? Maybe we've driven into the Kulmýk country,' answered the advice-giver.

'Then what are we going to do?' I asked.

'What can we do? We'll go on, and maybe we'll get somewhere,' he said in a dissatisfied tone.

'But suppose we don't get anywhere, and the horses stick in the snow—what then?'

'What then? Why, nothing.'

'But we might freeze.'

'Of course we might, because one can't even see any haystacks: we have got right among the Kulmýks. The chief thing is to watch the snow.'

'And you seem afraid of getting frozen, sir,' remarked the old man in a shaky voice.

Though he seemed to be chaffing me, it was evident that he was chilled to his very bones.

'Yes, it is getting very cold,' I said.

'Eh, sir, you should do as I do, take a run now and then, that will warm you up.'

'Yes, the chief thing is to have a run behind the sledge,' said the advice-giver.

## VII

'We're ready, your honour!' shouted Alëshka from the front sledge.

The storm was so violent that, though I bent almost double and clutched the skirts of my cloak with both hands, I was hardly able to walk the few steps that separated me from the sledge, over the drifting snow which the wind swept from under my feet. My former driver was already kneeling in the middle of his empty sledge, but when he saw me going he took off his big cap (whereupon the wind lifted his hair furiously) and asked for a tip. Evidently he did not expect me to give him one, for my refusal did not grieve him in the least. He thanked me anyway, put his cap on again, and said: 'God keep you, sir . . .' and jerking his reins and clicking his tongue, turned away from us. Then Ignát swayed his whole back and shouted to the horses, and the sound of the snow crunching under their hoofs, the cries, and the bells, replaced the howling of the wind which had been peculiarly noticeable while we stood still.

For a quarter of an hour after my transfer I kept awake and amused myself watching my new driver and his horses. Ignát sat like a mettlesome fellow, continually rising in his seat, flourishing over the horses the arm from which his whip was hung, shouting, beating one foot against the other, and bending forward to adjust the breeching of the shaft-horse, which kept slipping to the right. He was not tall, but seemed to be well built. Over his sheepskin he wore a large, loose cloak without a girdle, the collar of which was turned down so that his neck was bare. He wore not felt but leather boots, and a small cap which he kept taking off and putting straight. His ears were only protected by his hair. In all his movements one was aware not only of energy, but even more, as it seemed to me, of a desire to arouse that energy in himself. And the farther we went the more often he straightened himself out, rose in his seat, beat his feet together, and addressed himself to Alëshka and me. It seemed to me that he was afraid of losing courage. And there was good reason for it: though the horses were good the road grew heavier and heavier at every step, and it was plain that they were running less willingly: it was already necessary to touch them up with the whip, and the shaft-horse, a good, big, shaggy animal, stumbled more than once, though immediately, as if frightened, it jerked forward again and tossed its shaggy head almost as high as the bell hanging from the bow above it. The right off-horse, which I could not help watching, with a long leather tassel to its breeching which shook and jerked on its off side, noticeably let its traces slacken and required the whip, but from habit as a good and even mettlesome horse seemed vexed at its own weakness, and angrily lowered and tossed its head at the reins. It was terrible to realize that the snow storm and the frost were increasing, the horses growing weaker, the road becoming worse, and that we did not at all know where we were, or where we were going—or whether we should reach a station or even a shelter of any sort; it seemed strange and ridiculous to hear the bells ringing so easily and cheerfully, and Ignát shouting as lustily and pleasantly as if we were out for a drive along a village street on a frosty noon during a Twelfth Night holiday—and it was stranger still that we were always driving and driving fast somewhere from where we were. Ignát began to sing some song in a horrid falsetto, but so loud and with such intervals, during which he whistled, that it seemed ridiculous to be afraid while one heard him.

'Hey there, what are you splitting your throat for, Ignát?' came the advice-giver's voice. 'Stop a minute!'

'What?'

'Sto-o-op!'

Ignát stopped. Again all became silent, and the wind howled and whined, and the whirling snow fell still more thickly into the sledge. The advice-giver came up to us.

'Well, what now?'

'What now? Where are we going?'

'Who can tell?'

'Are your feet freezing, that you knock them together so?'

'Quite numb!'

'You should go over there: look, where there's something glimmering. It must be a Kulmýk camp. It would warm your feet too.'

'All right. Hold the reins . . . here you are.'

And Ignát ran in the direction indicated.

'You always have to go about a bit and look, then you find the way, or else what's the good of driving about like a fool?' the advice-giver said to me. 'See how the horses are steaming.'

All the time Ignát was gone—and that lasted so long that

I even began to fear he might have lost his way—the advice-giver kept telling me in a self-confident and calm tone how one should behave in a snow storm, that it was best to un-harness a horse and let it go, and, as God is holy, it would be sure to lead one out, and how it is sometimes possible to find the way by the stars, and that had he been driving in front we should long ago have reached the station.

'Well, is there anything?' he asked Ignát when the latter came back, stepping with difficulty knee-deep through the snow.

'There is, there is a camp of some sort,' replied Ignát, gasp-ing for breath, 'but I can't tell what it is. We must have strayed right into the Prológov estate. We must bear off to the left.'

'What's he jabbering about? It's our camp that's behind the Cossack village,' rejoined the advice-giver.

'I tell you it's not!'

'Well, I've had a look too, and I know: that's what it is, and if it isn't, then it's Tamýshevsk. Anyhow we must bear to the right, and then we'll come right out to the big bridge at the eighth verst.'

'I tell you it's nothing of the sort. Haven't I looked?' said Ignát with annoyance.

'Eh, mate, and you call yourself a driver!'

'Yes, a driver! . . . Go and look for yourself.'

'Why should I go? I know without going.'

Ignát had evidently grown angry: he jumped into the sledge without replying and drove on.

'How numb my legs have got! I can't warm them up,' said he to Alëshka, knocking his feet together oftener and oftener, and scooping up and emptying out the snow that had got into his boot-legs.

I felt dreadfully sleepy.

## VIII

'Can it be that I am freezing to death?' I thought, half asleep. 'They say it always begins with drowsiness. It would be better to drown than to freeze—let them drag me out with a net; but it does not matter much whether I freeze or drown if only that stick, or whatever it is, would not prod me in the back and I could forget myself!'

I did so for a few seconds.

'But how will all this end?' I suddenly asked myself, opening my eyes for a moment and peering into the white expanse before me. 'How will it all end? If we don't find any haystacks and the horses stop, as they seem likely to do soon, we shall all freeze to death.' I confess that, though I was a little afraid, the desire that something extraordinary, something rather tragic, should happen to us, was stronger in me than that fear. It seemed to me that it would not be bad if towards morning the horses brought us of their own accord, half-frozen, to some far-off unknown village, or if some of us were even to perish of the cold. Fancies of this kind presented themselves to me with extraordinary clearness and rapidity. The horses stop, the snow drifts higher and higher, and now nothing is seen of the horses but their ears and the bows above their heads, but suddenly Ignát appears above us with his tróyka, and drives past. We entreat him, we shout that he should take us, but the wind carries our voices away—we have no voices left. Ignát grins, shouts to his horses, whistles, and disappears into some deep, snow-covered ravine. The little old man jumps astride a horse, flourishes his elbows and tries to gallop away, but cannot stir from the spot; my former driver with the big cap rushes at him, drags him to the ground and tramples him into the snow. 'You're a wizard!' he shouts. 'You're a scold! We shall all be lost together!' But the old man breaks through the heap of snow with his head; and now he is not so much an old man as a hare, and leaps away from us. All the dogs bound after him. The advice-giver, who is Theodore Filípych, tells us all to sit round in a circle, that if the snow covers us it will be all right—we shall be warm that way. And really we are warm and cosy, only I want a drink. I fetch out my lunch-basket, and treat everybody to rum and sugar, and enjoy a drink myself. The story-teller spins a tale about the rainbow, and now there is a ceiling of snow and a rainbow above us. 'Now let us each make himself a room in the snow and let us go to sleep!' I say. The snow is soft and warm, like fur. I make myself a room and want to enter it, but Theodore Filípych, who has seen the money in my lunch-basket, says: 'Stop! Give me your money—you have to die anyway!' And he grabs me by the leg. I hand over the money and only ask him to let me go; but they won't believe it is all the money I have, and want to kill me. I seize the old man's hand and begin to kiss it with inexpressible pleasure: his hand is tender and sweet. At first he snatches it from me, but afterwards lets me have it, and even caresses me with his other hand. Then Theodore Filípych comes near and threatens me. I run away into my room: it is, however, no longer a room but a long white corridor, and someone is holding my legs. I wrench myself free. My clothes and part of my skin remain in the hands of the man who was holding me, but I only feel cold and ashamed—all the more ashamed because my aunt with her parasol and homoeopathic medicine-chest under her arm is coming towards me arm-in-arm with the drowned man. They are laughing and do not understand the signs I make to them. I throw myself into the sledge, my feet trail behind me in the snow, but the old man rushes after me flapping his elbows. He is already near, but I hear two church bells ringing in front of me, and know that I shall be saved when I get to them. The church bells sound nearer and nearer; but the little old man has caught up with me and falls with his stomach on my face, so that I can scarcely hear the bells. I again grasp his hand and begin to kiss it, but the little old man is no longer the little old man, he is the man who was drowned . . . and he shouts: 'Ignát, stop! There are the Akhmétkins' stacks, I think! Go and have a look at them!' This is too terrible. No, I had better wake up . . .

I open my eyes. The wind has thrown the flap of Alëshka's cloak over my face, my knee is uncovered, we are going over the bare frozen road, and the bells with their quivering third can be distinctly heard.

I look to see the haystacks, but now that my eyes are open I see no stacks, but a house with a balcony and the crenellated wall of a fortress. I am not interested enough to scrutinize this house and fortress: I am chiefly anxious to see the white corridor along which I ran, to hear the sound of the church bells, and to kiss the little old man's hand. I close my eyes again and fall asleep.

## IX

I slept soundly, but heard the ringing of the bells all the time. They appeared to me in my dream now in the guise of a dog that barked and attacked me, now of an organ in which I was one of the pipes, and now of some French verses I was composing. Sometimes those bells seemed to be an instrument of torture which kept squeezing my right heel. I felt that so strongly that I woke up and opened my eyes, rubbing my foot. It was getting frost-bitten. The night was still light, misty, and white. The same motion was still shaking me and the sledge; the same Ignát sat sideways, knocking his feet together; the same off-horse with outstretched neck ran at a trot over the deep snow without lifting its feet much, while the tassel on the breeching bobbed and flapped against its belly. The head of the shaft-horse with its flying mane stooped and rose rhythmically as it alternately drew the reins tight and loosened them. But all this was covered with snow even more than before. The snow whirled about in front, at the side it covered the horses' legs knee-deep, and the runners of the sledge, while it fell from above on our collars and caps. The wind blew now from the right, now from the left, playing with Ignát's collar, the skirt of his cloak, the mane of the side-horse, and howling between the shafts and above the bow over the shaft-horse's head.

It was growing terribly cold, and hardly had I put my head out of my coat-collar before the frosty, crisp, whirling snow covered my eyelashes, got into my nose and mouth, and penetrated behind my neck. When I looked round, everything was white, light and snowy, there was nothing to be seen but the dull light and the snow. I became seriously frightened. Alëshka was asleep at my feet at the bottom of the sledge, his whole back covered by a thick layer of snow. Ignát did not lose courage: he kept pulling at the reins, shouting, and clapping his feet together. The bell went on ringing just as wonderfully. The horses snorted a little, but ran more slowly and stumbled more and more often. Ignát again leaped up, waved his mitten, and again began singing in his strained falsetto. Before finishing the song he stopped the tróyka, threw down the reins on the front of the sledge, and got out. The wind howled furiously; the snow poured on the skirts of our cloaks as out of a scoop. I turned round: the third tróyka was not to be seen (it had lagged behind somewhere). Near the second sledge, in the snowy mist, I saw the little old man jumping from foot to foot. Ignát went some three steps from the sledge, and sitting down in the snow undid his girdle and pulled off his boots.

'What are you doing?' I asked.

'I must change, or my feet will be quite frozen,' he replied, and went on with what he was doing.

It was too cold to keep my neck out of my collar to watch what he was doing. I sat up straight, looking at the off-horse, which with one leg wearily stretched out, painfully whisked its tail that was tied in a knot and covered with snow. The thump Ignát gave the sledge as he jumped onto his seat roused me.

'Where are we now?' I asked. 'Shall we get anywhere— say by daybreak?'

'Don't worry, we'll get you there,' he replied. 'Now that I have changed, my feet are much warmer.'

And he drove on, the bell began to ring, the sledge swayed again, and the wind whistled under the runners. We again started to swim over the limitless sea of snow.

## X

I fell soundly asleep. When Alëshka woke me up by pushing me with his foot, and I opened my eyes, it was already morning. It seemed even colder than in the night. No more snow was falling from above, but a stiff dry wind continued to sweep the powdery snow across the plain, and especially under the hoofs of the horses and the runners of the sledge. In the east, to our right, the sky was heavy and of a dark bluish colour, but bright orange oblique streaks were growing more and more defined in it. Overhead, through flying white clouds as yet scarcely tinged, gleamed the pale blue of the sky; on the left, bright, light clouds were drifting. Everywhere, as far as eye could see, deep snow lay over the plain in sharply defined layers. Here and there could be seen greyish mounds, over which fine, crisp, powdery snow swept steadily. No track either of sledge, man, or beast could be seen. The outlines and colour of the driver's back and of the horses were clearly and sharply visible even on the white background. The rim of Ignát's dark-blue cap, his collar, his hair, and even his boots were white. The sledge was completely covered with snow. The right side and forelock of the grey shaft-horse were thick with snow, the legs of the off-horse on my side were covered with it up to the knee, and its curly sweating flank was covered and frozen to a rough surface. The tassel still bobbed up and down in tune to any rhythm you liked to imagine, and the off-horse itself kept running in the same way, only the sunken, heaving belly and drooping ears showing how exhausted she was. The one novel object that attracted my attention was a verst-post from which the snow was falling to the ground, and near which to the right the snow was swept into a mound by the wind, which still kept raging and throwing the crisp snow from side to side. I was very much surprised that we had travelled all night, twelve hours, with the same horses, without knowing where, and had arrived after all. Our bell seemed to tinkle yet more cheerfully. Ignát kept wrapping his cloak around him and shouting; the horses behind us snorted, and the bells of the little old man's and the advice-giver's tróyka tinkled, but the driver who had been asleep had certainly strayed from us in the steppe. After going another half-mile we came across the fresh, only partly obliterated, traces of a three-horse sledge, and here and there pink spots of blood, probably from a horse that had overreached itself.

'That's Philip. Fancy his being ahead of us!' said Ignát.

But here by the roadside a lonely little house with a sign-board was seen in the midst of the snow, which covered it almost to the top of the windows and to the roof. Near the inn stood a tróyka of grey horses, their coats curly with sweat, their legs outstretched and their heads drooping wearily. At the door there was a shovel and the snow had been cleared away, but the howling wind continued to sweep and whirl snow off the roof.

At the sound of our bells, a tall, ruddy-faced, red-haired peasant came out with a glass of vodka in his hand, and shouted something. Ignát turned to me and asked permission to stop. Then for the first time I fairly saw his face.

## XI

His face was not swarthy and lean with a straight nose, as I had expected judging by his hair and figure. It was a round, jolly, very snub-nosed face, with a large mouth and bright light-blue eyes. His cheeks and neck were red, as if rubbed with a flannel; his eyebrows, his long eyelashes, and the down that smoothly covered the bottom of his face, were plastered with snow and were quite white. We were only half a mile from our station and we stopped.

'Only be quick about it!' I said.

'Just one moment,' replied Ignát, springing down and walking over to Philip.

'Let's have it, brother,' he said, taking the mitten from his right hand and throwing it down with his whip on the snow, and tossing back his head he emptied at a gulp the glass that was handed to him.

The innkeeper, probably a discharged Cossack, came out with a half-bottle in his hand.

'Who shall I serve?' said he.

Tall Vasíli, a thin, brown-haired peasant, with a goatee beard, and the advice-giver, a stout, light-haired man with a thick beard framing his red face, came forward and also drank a glass each. The little old man too went over to the drinkers, but was not served, and he went back to his horses, which were fastened behind the sledge, and began stroking one of them on the back and croup.

The little old man's appearance was just what I had imagined it to be: small, thin, with a wrinkled livid face, a scanty beard, sharp little nose, and worn yellow teeth. He had a new driver's cap on, but his coat was shabby, worn, smeared with tar, torn on one shoulder, had holes in the skirt, and did not cover his knees and the homespun trousers which were tucked into his huge felt boots. He himself was bent double, puckered up, his face and knees trembled, and he tramped about near the sledge evidently trying to get warm.

'Come, Mítrich, you should have a glass; you'd get fine and warm,' said the advice-giver.

Mítrich's face twitched. He adjusted the harness of one of his horses, straightened the bow above its head, and came over to me.

'Well, sir,' he said, taking the cap off his grey head and bending low, 'we have been wandering about together all night, looking for the road: won't you give me enough for a small glass? Really sir, your honour! I haven't anything to get warm on,' he added with an ingratiating smile.

I gave him a quarter-ruble.[1] The innkeeper brought out a small glass of vodka and handed it to the old man. He took off his mitten, together with the whip that hung on it, and put out his small, dark, rough, and rather livid hand towards the glass; but his thumb refused to obey him, as though it did not belong to him. He was unable to hold the glass and dropped it on the snow, spilling the vodka.

All the drivers burst out laughing.

'See how frozen Mítrich is, he can't even hold the vodka.'

But Mítrich was greatly grieved at having spilt the vodka.

However, they filled another glass for him and poured it into his mouth. He became cheerful in a moment, ran into the inn, lit his pipe, showed his worn yellow teeth, and began to

---

[1] At that time about sixpence.

swear at every word he spoke. Having drained the last glass, the drivers returned to their tróykas and we started again.

The snow kept growing whiter and brighter so that it hurt one's eyes to look at it. The orange-tinted reddish streaks rose higher and higher, and growing brighter and brighter spread upwards over the sky; even the red disk of the sun became visible on the horizon through the blue-grey clouds; the sky grew more brilliant and of a deeper blue. On the road near the settlement the sledge tracks were clear, distinct, and yellowish, and here and there we were jolted by cradle-holes in the road; one could feel a pleasant lightness and freshness in the tense, frosty air.

My tróyka went very fast. The head of the shaft-horse, and its neck with its mane fluttering around the bow, swayed swiftly from side to side almost in one place under the special bell, the tongue of which no longer struck the sides but scraped against them. The good off-horses tugged together at the frozen and twisted traces, and sprang energetically, while the tassel bobbed from right under the horse's belly to the breeching. Now and then an off-horse would stumble from the beaten track into the snowdrift, throwing up the snow into one's eyes as it briskly got out again. Ignát shouted in his merry tenor; the dry frosty snow squeaked under the runners; behind us two little bells were ringing resonantly and festively, and I could hear the tipsy shouting of the drivers. I looked back. The grey shaggy off-horses, with their necks outstretched and breathing evenly, their bits awry, were leaping over the snow. Philip, flourishing his whip, was adjusting his cap; the little old man, with his legs hanging out, lay in the middle of the sledge as before.

Two minutes later my sledge scraped over the boards before the clean-swept entrance of the station house, and Ignát turned to me his snow-covered merry face, smelling of frost.

'We've got you here after all, sir!' he said.

# LUCERNE*

*[From Prince Nekhlyúdov's Memoirs.]*

8th July, 1857.

Last night I arrived at Lucerne, and put up at the Schweizerhof, the best hotel.

Lucerne, an ancient town and the capital of the canton,
situated on the shore of the Lake of Lucerne, says Murray, is
one of the most romantic places in Switzerland: here three important high roads meet, and it is only one hour by steamboat to Mount Rigi, from which one of the most magnificent
views in the world can be seen.

Whether this be right or not, other guide-books say the
same, and so tourists of all nationalities, especially the English, flock there.

The magnificent five-storied Schweizerhof Hotel has been
recently erected on the quay, close to the lake at the very
place where of old there was a roofed and crooked bridge[1]
with chapels at its corners and carvings on its beams. Now,
thanks to the enormous influx of English people, their needs,
their tastes, and their money, the old bridge has been torn
down and a granite quay, as straight as a stick, erected, on
which straight, rectangular, five-storied houses have been
built, in front of which two rows of little lindens with stakes
to them have been planted, between which the usual small

---

* After his discharge from the army, Tolstoy went on his first trip
to Western Europe in 1857. Among the various places he visited
was Lucerne, where he stayed at a fashionable hotel. There occurred the incident which aroused his indignation and is recounted
in considerable detail in this piece.
[1] The Hofbrücke, removed in 1852.

green benches have been placed. This is a promenade, and here Englishwomen wearing Swiss straw hats, and Englishmen in stout and comfortable clothes, walk about enjoying the work they have inspired. Perhaps such quays and houses and lime trees and Englishmen are all very well in some places, but not here amid this strangely majestic and yet inexpressibly genial and harmonious Nature.

When I went up to my room and opened the window facing the lake I was at first literally blinded and shaken by the beauty of that water, those mountains, and the sky. I felt an inward restlessness and a need to find expression for the emotion that filled my soul to overflowing. At that moment I felt a wish to embrace someone, to hug him closely, to tickle and pinch him—in a word to do something extraordinary to myself and to him.

It was past six and had rained all day, but was now beginning to clear up. The lake, light-blue like burning sulphur, and dotted with little boats which left vanishing tracks behind them, spread out before my windows motionless, smooth, and apparently convex between its variegated green shores, then passed into the distance where it narrowed between two enormous promontories, and, darkening, leaned against and disappeared among the pile of mountains, clouds, and glaciers, that towered one above the other. In the foreground where the moist, fresh-green, far-stretching shores with their reeds, meadows, gardens, and chalets; further off were dark-green wooded promontories crowned by ruined castles; in the background was the rugged, purple-white distance with its fantastic, rocky, dull-white, snow-covered mountain crests, the whole bathed in the delicate, transparent azure of the air and lit up by warm sunset rays that pierced the torn clouds. Neither on the lake nor on the mountains, nor in the sky, was there a single precise line, or one precise colour, or one unchanging moment: everywhere was motion, irregularity, fantastic shapes, an endless intermingling and variety of shades and lines, and over it all lay tranquility, softness, unity, and inevitable beauty. And here, before my very window, amid this undefined, confused, unfettered beauty, the straight white

line of the quay stretched stupidly and artificially, with its
lime trees, their supports, and the green benches—miserable,
vulgar human productions which did not blend with the general harmony and beauty as did the distant chalets and ruins,
but on the contrary clashed coarsely with it. My eyes continually encountered that dreadfully straight quay, and I felt a
desire to push it away or demolish it, as one would wipe off a
black smudge that disfigured the nose just under one's eye. But
the embankment with the English people walking about on it
remained where it was, and I instinctively tried to find a point
of view from which it would not be visible. I found a way to
do this, and sat till dinner-time all alone, enjoying the in-
complete, but all the more tormentingly sweet feeling one experiences when one gazes in solitude on the beauty of Nature.

At half-past seven I was called to dinner. In the large,
splendidly decorated room on the ground floor two tables
were laid for at least a hundred persons. For about three
minutes the silent movement of assembling visitors continued
—the rustle of women's dresses, light footsteps, whispered
discussions with the very polite and elegant waiters—but at
last all the seats were occupied by men and women very well
and even richly and generally most immaculately dressed. As
usual in Switzerland the majority of the visitors were English,
and therefore the chief characteristic of the common table
was the strict decorum they regard as an obligation—a reserve not based on pride, but on the absence of any necessity
for social intercourse, and on content with the comfortable and
agreeable satisfaction of their requirements. On all sides
gleamed the whitest of laces, the whitest of collars, the whitest
of teeth—natural or artificial—and the whitest of complexions
and hands. But the faces, many of them very handsome, expressed only a consciousness of their own well-being and a
complete lack of interest in all that surrounded them unless
it directly concerned themselves; and the whitest of hands in
rings and mittens moved only to adjust a collar, to cut up
beef, or to lift a wine glass: no mental emotion was reflected
in their movements. Occasionally families would exchange a
few words among themselves in subdued voices about the

pleasant flavour of this or that dish or wine, or the lovely view
from Mount Rigi. Individual tourists, men and women, sat
beside one another not even exchanging a look. If occasionally some two among these hundred people spoke to one another it was sure to be about the weather and the ascent of
Mount Rigi. Knives and forks moved on the plates with
scarcely any sound, food was taken a little at a time, peas and
other vegetables were invariably eaten with a fork. The waiters, involuntarily subdued by the general silence, asked in a
whisper what wine you would take. At such dinners I always
feel depressed, uncomfortable, and at last melancholy. I always
feel as if I were guilty of something and am being punished, as
I used to be when, as a child, I was put in a chair when I had
been naughty, and ironically told: 'Rest yourself, my dear!'
while my youthful blood surged in my veins and I heard the
merry shouts of my brothers in the next room. Formerly I tried
to rebel against the feeling of oppression I experienced during
such dinners, but in vain: all those inanimate countenances
have an insuperable effect on me and I become similarly inanimate myself. I wish nothing, think nothing, and cease even
to observe what is going on. At first I used to try to talk to
my neighbours; but except for phrases apparently repeated a
hundred thousand times in the same place and by the same
people I got no response. And yet not all these frozen people
are stupid and unfeeling, on the contrary many of them, no
doubt, have an inner life just such as my own, and in many of
them it may be much more complex and interesting. Then
why do they deprive themselves of one of life's greatest pleasures—the enjoyment that comes from the intercourse of man
with man?

How different it was in our Paris *pension,* where some
twenty of us, of various nationalities, professions, and disposi-
tions, under the influence of French sociability used to meet
at the common table as at a game! There, from one end of the
table to the other, conversation, interspersed with jests and
puns, even if in broken language, at once became general.
There everyone, not troubling how it would sound, said anything that came into his head. There we had our philosopher,

our debater, our *bel esprit,* and our butt, all in common. There immediately after dinner we pushed away the table and, in time and out, danced the polka on the dusty carpet till late in the evening. There, even if we were inclined to flirt and were not very clever or respectable, we were human beings. The Spanish countess with her romantic adventures, the Italian abbé who declaimed the *Divine Comedy* after dinner, the American doctor who had the entrée to the Tuileries, the young playwright with long hair, and the pianist who, according to her account, had composed the best polka in the world, the unhappy widow who was a beauty and had three rings on every finger—we all treated one another like human beings, in a friendly if superficial manner, and carried away, some of us light, and others sincere and cordial, memories. But of these English at the *table d'hôte,* I often think as I look at all these silk dresses, laces, ribbons, rings, and pommaded locks, how many live women would be happy and make others happy with these adornments. It is strange to think how many potential friends and lovers—very happy friends and lovers—may be sitting there side by side without knowing it, and, God knows why, will never know it and give one another the happiness they desire so much and which they might so easily give.

I began to feel depressed, as always after such a dinner, and without finishing my dessert went in very low spirits to stroll about the town. The narrow, dirty, unlighted streets, the shops closing, the encounters I had with tipsy workmen and with women going bareheaded to fetch water, or others wearing hats who flitted along the walls of the sidestreets and continually glanced round, not only did not dispel my illhumour but even increased it. It had already grown quite dark in the streets when, without looking around me and without any thought in my head, I turned back to the hotel hoping by sleep to rid myself of my dismal frame of mind. I was feeling terribly chilled at heart, lonely and depressed, as sometimes happens without cause to those who have just arrived at a new place.

Looking at nothing but the ground at my feet I walked along the quay towards the Schweizerhof, when I was suddenly struck by the sound of some strange but exceedingly sweet and agreeable music. These sounds had an immediately vivifying effect on me, as if a bright cheerful light had penetrated my soul. I felt myself happy and cheerful. My dormant attention was again alive to all the objects surrounding me. The beauty of the night and of the lake, to which I had been feeling indifferent, suddenly struck me joyfully like a novelty. In an instant I involuntarily noticed both the heavy grey patches of cloud on the dark blue of the sky lit up by a rising moon, the smooth dark-green lake with the little lights reflected on it, and the mist-covered mountains in the distance; I heard the croaking of the frogs from Freschenburg, and the fresh limpid whistle of quails on the opposite shore. But directly in front of me, on the spot whence the sounds to which my attention was chiefly directed came, I saw amid the semi-darkness a throng of people collected in a half-circle in the middle of the road, and at some short distance from them a tiny man in black clothes. Behind the people and the man the black poplars in the garden were gracefully silhouetted on the dark grey and blue ragged sky, and the severe spires on each side of the ancient cathedral towered majestically.

I drew nearer, the sounds became more distinct, and at some distance I could clearly distinguish the full chords of a guitar which vibrated sweetly in the evening air and several voices, which intercepting one another did not actually sing the melody but indicated it by chiming in at the chief passages. The tune was something in the nature of a charming and graceful mazurka. The voices sometimes seemed nearer and sometimes farther away; now you could hear a tenor, now a bass, and now a guttural falsetto with a warbling Tyrolese yodel. It was not a song, but the light, masterly sketch of a song. I could not make out what it was, but it was beautiful. The passionate soft chords of the guitar, that sweet gentle melody, and the lonely little figure of the man in black against the fantastic background of the dark lake, the gleaming moon, the two tall spires silently stretching upwards, and the black poplars in the garden, were all strangely but inexpressibly beautiful, or so it seemed to me.

All the confused and arbitrary impressions of life suddenly received meaning and charm. It was as if a fresh and fragrant flower had bloomed within me. Instead of the weariness, dullness, and indifference towards everything in the world that I had felt a moment before, I suddenly experienced the need of love, a fulness of hope, and a spontanous joy in life. 'What can I possibly want, what desire?' I involuntarily thought. 'Here it is all around me—beauty, poetry. Inhale full deep draughts of it with all the strength that is in you, enjoying it. What more do you need? It is all yours, and all good . . .'

I went nearer. The little man seemed to be an itinerant singer from the Tyrol. He stood before the windows of the hotel with one foot advanced, his head thrown back, and while thrumming his guitar was singing his graceful song in those different voices. I immediately felt an affection for him, and gratitude for the change he had brought about in me. As far as I could see, he was dressed in an old black coat, had short black hair, and wore a very ordinary old cap on his head. There was nothing artistic about his attire, but his jaunty, childishly merry pose and movements, with his diminutive stature, produced a touching yet amusing effect. On the steps, at the windows, and on the balconies of the brilliantly lighted hotel, stood ladies resplendent in full-skirted dresses, gentlemen with the whitest of collars, a porter and footmen in gold-embroidered liveries; in the street, in the semicircle of the crowd, and farther along the boulevard among the lime-trees, elegantly dressed waiters, cooks in the whitest of caps and blouses, girls with their arms around one another, and passers-by, had gathered and stopped. They all seemed to experience the same sensation that I did, and stood in silence round the singer, listening attentively. All were quiet, only at intervals in the singing, from far away across the water came the rhythmic sound of a hammer, and from the Freschenburg shore the staccato trills of the frogs intermingled with the fresh, monotonous whistle of the quails.

In the darkness of the street the little man warbled like a nightingale, couplet after couplet and song after song. Though I had drawn close to him, his singing continued to give me great pleasure. His small voice was extremely pleasing, and the delicacy, the taste, and the sense of proportion with which he managed that voice were extraordinary, and showed immense natural gifts. He sang the refrain differently after each couplet and it was evident that all these graceful variations came to him freely and instantaneously.

Among the throng, above in the Schweizerhof and below on the boulevard, appreciative whispers could often be heard, and a respectful silence reigned. The balconies and windows kept filling, and by the hotel lights more and more elegantly dressed men and women could be seen leaning out picturesquely. The passers-by stopped and everywhere in the shadows on the embankment groups of men and women stood under the lime-trees. Near me, separated from the rest of the crowd and smoking cigars, stood an aristocratic waiter and the chef. The chef seemed to feel the charm of the music strongly and at every high falsetto note rapturously winked, nodded, and nudged the waiter in ecstatic perplexity, with a look that said: 'How he sings, eh?' The waiter, by whose broad smile I detected the pleasure the singing gave him, replied to the chef's nudging by shrugging his shoulders to show that it was hard to surprise him, and that he had heard much better things than this.

In an interval of the singing, while the singer was clearing his throat, I asked the waiter who the man was and whether he came there often.

'Well, he comes about twice a summer,' replied the waiter. 'He is from Aargau—just a beggar.'

'And are there many like him about?' I asked.

'Oh, yes,' replied the man not having at first understood what I was asking, but having afterwards made it out, he added: 'Oh no, he is the only one I know of. There are no others.'

Just then the little man, having finished his first song, briskly turned his guitar over and said something in his Ger-

man patois, which I could not understand but which caused
the crowd to laugh.

'What did he say?' I asked.

'He says his throat is dry and he would like some wine,'
replied the waiter near me.

'Well, I suppose he is fond of drink.'

'Yes, such people are all like that,' answered the waiter with
a depreciatory gesture of his hand.

The singer raised his cap and with a flourish of the guitar
went up to the hotel. Throwing back his head he addressed
the gentlefolk at the windows and on the balconies: '*Messieurs
et Mesdames,*' he said with a half-Italian and half-German accent and the intonation conjours employ when addressing
their audience: '*Si vous croyez que je gagne quelque chose,
vous vous trompez; je ne suis qu'un pauvre diable.*' [1] He
paused and waited a moment in silence, but as no one gave
him anything, he again jerked his guitar and said: '*A présent,
messieurs et mesdames, je vous chanterais l'air du Righi.*' [2]

The audience up above kept silent, but continued to stand
in expectation of the next song; below, among the throng,
there was laughter, probably because he expressed himself so
queerly and because no one had given him anything. I gave
him a few centimes, which he threw nimbly from one hand
to the other, and put into his waistcoat pocket. Then putting
on his cap again he began to sing a sweet and graceful Tyrolese song which he called '*l'air du Righi*'. This song, which he
had left to the last, was even better than the others, and on all
sides among the now increased crowd one heard sounds of
appreciation. He finished the song. Again he flourished his
guitar, took off his cap, held it out, made two steps towards
the windows, and again repeated his incomprehensible phrase:
'*Messieurs et Mesdames, si vous croyez que je gagne quelque
chose—*' which he evidently considered very smart and witty,
but in his voice and movements I now detected a certain
hesitation and childlike timidity which were the more notice-

---

[1] 'If you think I earn anything you are mistaken. I am only a poor
devil.'

[2] 'Now, gentlemen and ladies, I will sing you the Rigi song.'

able on account of his small figure. The elegant audience
still stood just as picturesquely grouped in the windows and
on the balconies, the lights shining.on their rich attire. A few
of them talked in decorously subdued voices, apparently
about the singer who was standing before them with outstretched hand, others looked with attentive curiosity down
at the little black figure; on one balcony could be heard a
young girl's merry laughter.

In the crowd below the talking and laughter grew louder
and louder. The singer repeated his phrase a third time, in a
still feebler voice, and this time he did not even finish it, but
again held out his cap, and then drew it back immediately.
And for the second time not one of those hundreds of brilliantly dressed people who had come to hear him threw him
a single penny. The crowd laughed unmercifully. The little
singer seemed to me to shrink still more into himself. He took
the guitar in his other hand, lifted his cap above his head, and
said: '*Messieurs et Mesdames, je vous remercie, et je vous
souhaite une bonne nuit.*' [3] Then he replaced his cap. The
crowd roared with merry laughter. The handsome men and
women, quietly conversing, gradually disappeared from the
balconies. The strolls on the boulevard were resumed. The
street that had been quiet during the singing again became
animated, only a few persons looked at the singer from a distance and laughed. I heard the little man mutter something to
himself. He turned and, seeming to grow still smaller, went
quickly towards the town. The merry strollers, still watching
him, followed him at a certain distance, and laughed.

My mind was in a whirl. I was at a loss to understand
what it all meant, and without moving from the spot where
I had been, I senselessly gazed into the darkness after the
tiny retreating figure of the man as he went striding rapidly
towards the town and at the laughing strollers who followed
him. I felt pained, grieved, and above all ashamed for the
little man, for the crowd, and for myself, as if it were I who
had been asking for money and had received nothing, and

---

[3] 'Thank you, ladies and gentlemen. I wish you good-night.'

had been laughed at. I, too, without looking back and with an aching heart, moved off with rapid steps and went to the entrance of the Schweizerhof. I could not yet account for my emotions, but only knew that something heavy and unsolved filled my heart and oppressed me.

At the brilliantly lit entrance I met the hall porter who politely stepped aside, and an English family. A tall, portly, handsome man with black side-whiskers worn in the English fashion, a black hat on his head, a plaid over his arm, and an expensive cane in his hand, was walking with lazy self-confidence arm in arm with a lady in a grey silk gown, and a cap trimmed with bright ribbons and exquisite lace. Beside them walked a pretty, fresh-complexioned girl wearing a graceful Swiss hat trimmed with a feather *à la Mousquetaire,* and with charming long soft flaxen curls that fell over her fair face. In front of them skipped a ten-year-old girl with rosy cheeks, and plump white knees showing from under the finest embroideries.

'A lovely night!' said the lady in a tender, happy voice, just as I passed them.

'Ohe!' lazily muttered the Englishman, for whom life was so comfortable that he did not even feel like talking. To all of them life in this world was so comfortable, convenient, clean, and easy; their movements and faces expressed such indifference to any other kind of life than their own, such assurance that the porter would step aside for them and bow, and that on returning they would find comfortable rooms and beds, that it all must be so and that they had a right to it all, that I involuntarily contrasted them with the vagrant singer who, tired and perhaps hungry, was escaping ashamed from the laughing crowd, and I realized what it was that weighed on my heart like a stone, and I felt indescribable anger against these people. Twice I walked to and fro past the Englishman, and each time with inexpressible pleasure avoided making way for him and pushed him with my elbow; then darting down the steps I hastened through the darkness in the direction of the town, where the little man had disappeared.

Having overtaken three men who were walking together, I asked them where the singer was. They laughed and pointed straight ahead. He was walking quickly, by himself. No one went near him, and he seemed to me to be angrily muttering something to himself. I caught him up and proposed to him to go somewhere and drink a bottle of wine. He went on walking just as fast and looked disconsolately at me, but when he had made out what I wanted, he stopped.

"Well, I won't refuse it, if you are so kind,' he said. 'There is a small café here, we could go in there. It's a plain place,' he added, pointing to a drink shop which was still open.

The word 'plain' involuntarily suggested to me the idea of not going to the plain café but to the Schweizerhof, where the people were who had listened to him. Though in timid agitation he several times declined to go to the Schweizerhof, saying that it was too fine there, I insisted on it and he walked back along the quay with me pretending not to be at all abashed, and gaily swinging his guitar. Several idle strollers drew near as soon as I went up to the singer and listened to what I was saying: and now, after arguing among themselves, they followed us to the hotel entrance, probably expecting some further performance from the Tyrolese.

I met a waiter in the vestibule and asked him for a bottle of wine, but he merely looked at us with a smile and ran past. The head waiter, to whom I addressed the same request, listened to me seriously, and having scanned the tiny figure of the timid singer from head to foot, sternly told the porter to take us to the room on the left. This room was a bar for common people, the whole furniture consisted of bare wooden tables and benches, and a hunchbacked woman was washing up dishes in a corner. The waiter who came to take our order looked at us with a mildly supercilious smile and, thrusting his hands in his pockets, exchanged remarks with the hunchbacked dish-washer. He evidently wished to let us know that, feeling himself immeasurably superior to the singer in social standing as well as on his own merits, he was not at all offended, but even quite amused, to be waiting on us.

'Will you have *vin ordinaire?*' he asked with a knowing look, winking towards my companion and shifting his napkin from one arm to the other.

'Champagne, and your very best!' said I, trying to assume a haughty and imposing air. But neither the champagne nor my endeavour to look haughty and imposing had any effect on the waiter: he grinned, stood awhile gazing at us, looked deliberately at his gold watch, and went leisurely and with soft steps out of the room as if he were out for a stroll. He soon returned with the wine and with two other waiters. The two waiters sat down near the dish-washer and gazed at us with amused attention and bland smiles with which parents watch their dear children when they play nicely. Only the hunchbacked dish-washer seemed to look at us with sympathy rather than irony. Though I felt it very uncomfortable and awkward to talk with the singer and entertain him under the fire of those eyes, I tried to do my part with as little constraint as possible. In the lighted room I could see him better. He was a tiny, well-proportioned, wiry man, almost a midget, with bristly black hair, large tearful black eyes without lashes, and a thoroughly pleasant and attractively shaped little mouth. He had short side-whiskers, rather short hair, and his clothes were simple and poor. He was dingy, tattered, sunburnt, and had in general the look of a labourer. He was more like a poor pedlar than an artist. Only in his humid, shining eyes and puckering mouth was there something original and touching. Judging by his appearance he might have been anything from twenty-five to forty years old; he was really thirty-eight.

This is what he told me, with good-natured readiness and evident sincerity, about his life. He was from Aargau. While still a child he had lost his father and mother and had no other relations. He had never had any means of his own. He had been apprenticed to a joiner, but twenty-two years ago a bone of his finger had begun to decay, which made it impossible for him to work. He had been fond of music from his childhood, and began to go round singing. Foreigners occasionally gave him money. He made a profession of it, bought a guitar, and for eighteen years had wandered through

Switzerland and Italy singing in front of hotels. His whole belongings were the guitar and a purse, in which he now had only a franc and a half, which he would have to spend that night on food and lodging. He had gone every year to all the best and most frequented places in Switzerland: Zurich, Lucerne, Interlaken, Chamonix and so on; and was now going round for the eighteenth time. He passed over the St. Bernard into Italy and returned by St. Gotthard or through Savoy. It was getting hard for him to walk now, because a pain in his feet which he called *Gliederzucht* (rheumatism) got worse every year when he caught cold, and his eyes and his voice were growing weaker. In spite of this he was now on his way to Interlaken, Aix-les-Bains, and over the little St. Bernard to Italy, of which country he was particularly fond; in general he seemed to be very well satisfied with his life. When I asked him why he was going home and whether he had any relations there, or a house and land, his mouth puckered into a merry smile and he replied: '*Oui, le sucre est bon, il est doux pour les enfants!*' [4] and winked at the waiters.

I did not understand what he meant, but the group of waiters burst out laughing.

'I've got nothing, or would I be going about like this?' he explained. 'I go home because, after all, something draws me back to my native land.'

And he again repeated, with a sly self-satisfied smile, the phrase: '*Oui, le sucre est bon!*' and laughed good-naturedly. The waiters were very pleased and laughed heartily. Only the hunchbacked dish-washer looked at the little man seriously with her large kindly eyes and picked up the cap he had dropped from the bench during our conversation. I had noticed that wandering singers, acrobats, and even jugglers, liked to call themselves artists, and so I hinted several times to my companion that he was an artist; but he did not at all acknowledge that quality in himself, and considered his occupation simply as a means of subsistence. When I asked him whether he did not himself compose the songs he sang, he

---

[4] 'Yes, sugar is good: it is sweet for children.'

was surprised at so strange a question, and answered: 'How could I? They are all old Tyrolese songs.'

'But what about the Rigi song—that is not old, is it?' I said.

'No, that was composed about fifteen years ago,' he said. 'There was a German in Basle, a very clever man. He composed it. It's a splendid song! You see, he composed it for the tourists.'

And, translating them into French as he went along, he began repeating to me the words of the Rigi song, which he liked so much:

> *'If you would go up the Rigi*
> *You need no shoes as far as Weggis*
>    *(Because you go that far by steamer)*
> *But in Weggis take a big stick,*
> *And upon your arm a maiden.*
> *Drink a glass of wine at starting,*
>    *Only do not drink too much.*
> *For he who wants to have a drink*
>    *Should first have earned . . .*

'Oh, it's a splendid song!' he said, as he finished.

The waiters, too, probably considered the song very good, for they came nearer to us.

'Yes, but who composed the music?' I asked.

'Oh, nobody! It comes of itself, you know—one must have something new to sing to the foreigners.'

When the ice was brought and I had poured out a glass of champagne for my companion, he seemed to feel ill at ease, and glancing round at the waiters shifted uneasily in his seat. We clinked glasses to the health of artists; he drank half a glass, and then found it necessary to raise his eyebrows in profound thought.

'It's a long time since I drank such wine, *je ne vous dis que ça.*[5] In Italy the d'Asti wine is good, but this is better still. Ah, Italy! It's splendid to be there!' he added.

'Yes, there they know how to appreciate music and artists,'

---

[5] 'I only say that to you.'

I said, wishing to lead him back to the subject of his failure that evening before the Schweizerhof.

'No,' he replied. 'There, as far as music is concerned, I cannot give anyone pleasure. The Italians are themselves musicians like none others in the world: I sing only Tyrolese songs—that at any rate is a novelty for them.'

'And are the gentlefolk more generous there?' I went on, wishing to make him share my resentment against the guests at the Schweizerhof. 'It couldn't happen there, could it, as it did here, that in an immense hotel frequented by rich people, out of a hundred who listen to an artist not one gives him anything?'

My question had quite a different effect on him from what I had expected. It did not enter his head to be indignant with them: on the contrary he detected in my remark a reflection on his talent, which I had failed to elicit any reward, and he tried to justify himself to me.

'One does not get much every time,' he replied. 'Sometimes my voice fails or I am tired. To-day, you know, I have been walking for nine hours and singing almost all the time. That is hard. And the great people, the aristocrats, don't always care to hear Tyrolese songs.'

'But still, how could they give nothing at all?' I insisted.

He did not understand my remark.

'It's not that,' he said, 'the chief thing here is, *on est très serré pour la police*,[6] that's where the trouble is. Here under their republican laws you are not allowed to sing, but in Italy you may go about as much as you please, and no one will say a word to you. Here they allow it only when they please, and if they don't please, they may put you in prison.'

'How is that? Is it possible?'

'Yes, if they caution you once and you sing again they may imprison you. I was there for three months,' he said smiling, as though this were one of his pleasantest recollections.

'Oh, that's dreadful!' I said. 'What for?'

---

[6] 'One is much cramped by the police.'

'That is so under the new republican laws,' he continued, growing animated. 'They don't want to understand that a poor fellow must live somehow. If I were not a cripple, I would work. But does my singing hurt anyone? What does it mean? The rich can live as they please, but _un pauvre diable_ like myself mayn't even live. Are these the laws a republic should have? If so, we don't want a republic—isn't that so, dear sir? We don't want a republic, but we want—we simply want . . . we want'—he hesitated awhile—'we want natural laws.'

I filled up his glass.

'You are not drinking,' I said to him.

He took the glass in his hand and bowed to me.

'I know what you want,' he said, screwing up his eyes and shaking his finger at me. 'You want to make me drunk, so as to see what will happen to me; but no, you won't succeed!'

'Why should I want to make you drunk?' I said. 'I only want to give you pleasure.'

Probably he was sorry to have offended me by interpreting my intention wrongly, for he grew confused, got up, and pressed my elbow.

'No, no, I was only joking!' he said, looking at me with a beseeching expression in his moist eyes.

Then he uttered some fearfully intricate, complicated sentence intended to imply that I was a good fellow after all.

'_Je ne vous dis que ça!_' he concluded.

So we continued drinking and talking and the waiters continued to watch us unceremoniously and, as it seemed, to make fun of us. Despite my interest in our conversation I could not help noticing them and, I confess, I grew more and more angry. One of them got up, came over to the little man, looked down on the crown of his head, and began to smile. I had accumulated a store of anger for the guests at the Schweizerhof which I had not yet been able to vent on anyone, and I own that this audience of waiters irritated me beyond endurance. Then the porter came in and, leaning his elbows on the table without taking off his hat, sat down beside me. This last circumstance stung my self-esteem or vanity, and finally

323 ))                                    *Lucerne*

caused the oppressive rage that had been smouldering in me all the evening to explode. 'Why when I was alone at the entrance did he humbly bow to me, and now that I am sitting with an itinerant singer, sprawls near me so rudely?' I was filled with a boiling rage of indignation which I like in myself and even stimulate when it besets me, because it has a tranquilizing effect, and gives, at least for a short time, an unusual suppleness, energy, and power to all my physical and mental faculties.

I jumped up.

'What are you laughing at?' I shouted at the waiter, feeling that I was growing pale and that my lips were involuntarily twitching.

'I am not laughing; it's nothing!' said the waiter stepping back.

'No, you are laughing at this gentleman. . . . And what right have you to be here and to be sitting down, when there are visitors here? Don't dare to sit here!' I cried turning to the porter.

He got up with a growl and moved towards the door.

'What right have you to laugh at this gentleman and to sit near him, when he is a visitor and you are a lackey? Why didn't you laugh at me or sit beside me at dinner this evening? Is it because he is poorly dressed and sings in the street? Is it? While I wear good clothes? He is poor, but I am convinced that he is a thousand times better than you, for he insults no one, while you are insulting him!'

'But I am not doing anything!' replied my enemy the waiter, timidly. 'Do I prevent his sitting here?'

The waiter did not understand me and my German speech was lost on him. The rude porter tried to take the waiter's part, but I attacked him so vehemently that he pretended that he, too, did not understand me, and waved his arm. The hunchbacked dish-washer, either noticing my heated condition and afraid of a scandal, or because she really shared my views, took my part and, trying to interpose between me and the porter, began to persuade him to be quiet, saying that I was right and asking me to calm myself. '*Der Herr hat recht; Sie haben recht!'* [7] she said firmly. The singer presented a most piteous, frightened appearance, and, evidently without understanding why I was excited or what I was aiming at, begged me to go away quickly. But my angry loquacity burned stronger and stronger in me. I recalled everything: the crowd that had laughed at him, and the audience that had given him nothing—and I would not quiet down on any account. I think that if the waiters and the porter had not been so yielding I should have enjoyed a fight with them, or could have whacked the defenceless young English lady on the head with a stick. Had I been at Sevastopol at that moment I would gladly have rushed into an English trench to hack and slash at them.

'And why did you show me and this gentleman into this room, and not the other, eh?' I asked the porter, seizing his arm to prevent his going away. 'What right had you to decide from his appearance that this gentleman must be in this and not in the other room? Are not all who pay on an equal footing in an hotel—not only in a republic, but all over the world? Yours is a scurvy republic! . . . This is your equality! You dare not show those English people into this room—the very Englishmen who listened to this gentleman without paying him—that is, who each stole from him the few centimes they ought to have given him. How dared you show us in here?'

'The other room is closed,' replied the porter.

'No!' I cried. 'That's not true—it's not closed.'

'You know better then.'

'I know! I know that you are lying.'

The porter turned his shoulder towards me.

'What is the use of talking?' he muttered.

'No, not "what is the use . . ."' I shouted. 'Take us to the other room at once!'

Despite the hunchbacked woman's and the singer's entreaties that we should go away, I had the head waiter called and went into the other room with my companion. When the

---

[7] 'The gentleman is right; you are right.'

head waiter heard my angry voice and saw my excited face he did not argue with me, but told me with contemptuous civility that I might go where I liked. I could not convict the porter of his lie, as he had disappeared before I went into the other room.

The room was really open and lighted up, and at one of the tables the Englishman with the lady was having supper. Though we were shown to another table, I sat down with the dirty singer close to the Englishman, and ordered the unfinished bottle to be brought me.

The Englishman and the lady looked first with surprise and then with anger at the little man who sat beside me more dead than alive. They exchanged some words, and the lady pushed away her plate, and rustled her silk dress as they went away. Through the panes in the door I could see the Englishman speaking angrily to the waiter, pointing in our direction all the time. The waiter thrust his head in at the door and looked towards us. I waited with pleasure for them to come to turn us out, and to be able at last to vent my whole indignation on them—but fortunately, though I then regretted it, they left us in peace.

The singer, who had before refused the wine, now hastened to empty the bottle in order to get away as soon as possible. However, he thanked me, feelingly I thought, for his entertainment. His moist eyes became still more tearful and shining, and he expressed his gratitude in a most curious and confused little speech. But that speech, in which he said that if everyone respected artists as I did he would be well off, and that he wished me all happiness, was very pleasant to me. We went out into the vestibule. The waiters were there and my enemy the porter who seemed to be complaining of me to them. They all looked on me, I think, as insane. I let the little man come up to them all, and then, with all the respect I could show, I took off my hat and pressed his hand with its ossified and withered finger. The waiters made a show of not taking any notice of me, but one of them burst into a sardonic laugh.

After bowing to me, the singer disappeared into the darkness, and I went up to my room, wishing to sleep off all these

impressions and the foolish, childish anger which had so unexpectedly beset me. Feeling too agitated however for sleep, I
went out again into the street to walk about till I should have
calmed down, and also I must admit with a vague hope of
finding an opportunity to come across the porter, the waiter,
or the Englishman, to prove to them how cruel and above all
how unjust they had been. But I met no one except the porter,
who turned his back on seeing me, and I paced up and down
the embankment all alone.

'This is the strange fate of art!' I reflected, having grown
a little calmer. 'All seek it and love it—it is the one thing
everybody wants and tries to find in life, yet nobody ac-
knowledges its power, nobody values this greatest blessing in
the world, nor esteems or is grateful to those who give it to
mankind. Ask anyone you like of all these guests at the
Schweizerhof what is the greatest blessing in the world, and
everyone, or ninety-nine out of a hundred, assuming a sardonic expression, will say that the best thing in the world is
money! "Maybe this idea does not please you and does not
conform to your lofty ideas," he will tell you, "but what is to
be done if human life is so constituted that money alone gives
people happiness? I cannot help letting my reason see the
world as it is," he will add, "that is—see the truth."

'Pitiful is your reason, pitiful the happiness you desire, and
you are a miserable being who does not know what you want.
. . . Why have you all left your country, your relations, your
occupations, and your financial affairs, and congregated here
in this small Swiss town of Lucerne? Why did you all come
out onto the balcony this evening and listen in respectful
silence to the songs of that poor little mendicant? And had he
chosen to go on singing you would still have remained silent
and listened. What money, even millions of it, could have
driven you all from your country and assembled you in this
little corner, Lucerne? Could money have gathered you all
on those balconies and made you stand for half an hour silent
and motionless? No! One thing alone causes you to act, and
will always influence you more strongly than any other motive
power in life, and that is the need for art, which you do not

acknowledge, but which you feel and will always feel as long as there is anything human left in you. The word "art" seems ridiculous to you. You use it as a scornful reproach; you perhaps allow love of the poetic in children and in silly girls, but even then you laugh at them; but for yourselves you require something positive. But children see life healthily, they love and know what men should love, and what gives happiness, but life has so enmeshed and depraved you that you laugh at the one thing you love, and seek only that which you hate and which causes you unhappiness. You are so enmeshed that you do not understand your obligation to this poor Tyrolese who has afforded you a pure enjoyment, yet you feel yourselves bound to humble yourselves gratuitously before a lord, without advantage or pleasure, and for some reason sacrifice for him your comfort and convenience. What nonsense! What incomprehensible senselessness! But it was not this that struck me most this evening. This ignorance of what gives happiness, this unconsciousness of poetic enjoyment, I almost understand, or have become used to, having often met it in my life; nor was the coarse, unconscious cruelty of the crowd new to me. Whatever the advocates of the popular spirit may say, a crowd is a combination possibly of good people, but of people who have come in touch merely on their base, animal sides, and it expresses only the weakness and cruelty of human nature. How could you, children of a free, humane nation, as Christians or simply as human beings, respond with coldness and ridicule to the pleasure afforded you by an unfortunate mendicant? But no, in your country there are institutions for the needy. There are no beggars and must be none, nor must there be any compassion, on which mendicancy is based. But this man had laboured, he gave you pleasure, he implored you to give him something from your superabundance for his pains, of which you availed yourselves. But you, from your lofty, brilliant palace, regarded him with a cold smile and there was not one among you hundred, happy, rich people who threw him anything. He went away humiliated, and the senseless crowd followed him laughing, and insulted not you but him, because you were cold, cruel, and dishonest; because you stole the pleasure he had afforded you, they insulted him.'

'On the seventh of July 1857, in Lucerne, in front of the Hotel Schweizerhof in which the richest people stay, an itinerant beggar singer sang and played the guitar for half an hour. About a hundred people listened to him. The singer asked them all three times to give him something. Not one of them gave him anything, and many people laughed at him.'

This is not fiction, but a positive fact, which can be verified by anyone who likes from the permanent residents at the Hotel Schweizerhof, after ascertaining from the papers who the foreigners were who were staying at the Schweizerhof on the 7th of July.

Here is an occurrence the historians of our time ought to record in indelible letters of fire. This incident is more significant, more serious, and has a profounder meaning, than the facts usually printed in newspapers and histories. That the English have killed another thousand Chinamen because the Chinese buy nothing for money while their country absorbs metal coins, that the French have killed another thousand Arabs because corn grows easily in Africa and constant warfare is useful for training armies; that the Turkish Ambassador in Naples must not be a Jew, and that the Emperor Napoleon walks on foot at Plombières and assures the people in print that he reigns only by the will of the whole nation—all these are words that conceal or reveal what has long been known; but what happened at Lucerne on July the 7th appears to me to be something quite knew and strange, and relates not to the eternally evil side of human nature, but to a certain epoch in social evolution. This is a fact not for the history of human actions, but for the history of progress and civilization.

Why is this inhuman occurrence, which would be impossible in any German, French, or Italian village, possible here where civilization, liberty, and equality have been brought to the highest point, and where the most civilized travellers from the most civilized nations congregate? Why have these developed, humane people, who collectively are capable of any honourable and humane action, no human, cordial inclination to perform a kindly personal action? Why do these people— who in their parliaments, meetings, and societies are warmly concerned about the condition of the celibate Chinese in India, about propagating Christianity and education in Africa, about the establishment of societies for the betterment of the whole human race—not find in their souls the simple elemental feeling of human sympathy? Is it possible that they do not possess that feeling, and that its place has been occupied by the vanity, ambition, and cupidity governing these men in their parliaments, meetings, and societies? Can it be that the spread of the sensible and selfish association of men called civilization, destroys and contradicts the need for instinctive, loving association? And is it possible that this is the equality for which so much innocent blood has been shed and so many crimes committed? Is it possible that nations, like children, can be made happy by the mere sound of the word equality?

'Equality before the law?' But does the whole life of man take place in the sphere of law? Only a thousandth part of it depends on law, the rest takes place outside, in the sphere of social customs and conceptions. In this society the waiter is better dressed than the singer and insults him with impunity. I am better dressed than the waiter and insult him with impunity. The porter regards me as superior, and the singer as inferior, to himself; when I joined the singer he considered himself our equal and became rude. I grew insolent to the porter and he felt himself inferior to me. The waiter was insolent to the singer and the latter felt himself inferior to him. Can this be a free country—'positively free' as people say— in which there is a single citizen who, without having caused harm to anyone, is put in prison for doing the only thing he can do to save himself from starvation?

What an unfortunate, pitiful creature is man, with his desire for positive decisions, thrown into this ever moving, limitless ocean of good and evil, of facts, conceptions, and contradictions! For ages men have struggled and laboured to place good on one side and evil on the other. Centuries pass, and whenever an impartial mind places good and evil on the scales, the balance remains even, and the proportion of good and evil remains unaltered. If only man would learn not to judge, not to think sharply and positively, and not to answer questions presented to him only because they are for ever unanswerable! If only he understood that every thought is both false and true! False by one-sidedness resulting from man's inability to embrace the whole of truth, and true as an expression of one fact of human endeavor.

Men have made subdivisions for themselves in this eternally moving, unending, intermingled chaos of good and evil; they have traced imaginary lines on that ocean, and expect the ocean to divide itself accordingly, as if there were not millions of other subdivisions made from quite other points of view on another plane. It is true that fresh subdivisions are worked out from century to century, but millions of centuries have passed and millions more will pass. 'Civilization is good, barbarianism is bad. Freedom is good, subjection is bad.' This imaginary knowledge destroys the instinctive, beatific, primitive demand for kindliness in human nature. And who will define for me what is freedom, what is despotism, what is civilization, and what barbarianism? Where does the boundary lie between the one and the other? Whose soul possesses so absolute a standard of good and evil that he can measure all the confused and fleeting facts? Whose mind is so great that it can comprehend and measure even the facts of the stationary past? And who has seen a condition in which good and evil did not exist together? And how do I know that it is not my point of view which decides whether I see more of the one than of the other? Who is capable, even for a moment, of severing himself so completely from life as to look down on it with complete detachment? We have one unerring guide, and only one—the universal Spirit which inspiring each and all of us, implants in every individual a craving for what ought to be; that same Spirit which causes the tree to grow towards the sun, the flower to shed its seeds in the autumn, and bids us instinctively draw closer together.

And it is that one blissful and impeccable voice that the

noisy, hasty development of civilization stifles. Who is more a man and less a barbarian: that lord who, seeing the thread-bare clothes of the singer, angrily left the table, and for his efforts did not give him a millionth part of his wealth, and who now sits, well fed, in a bright comfortable room, calmly discussing the affairs in China and finding the massacres committed there quite justified—or the little singer, who risking imprisonment and with a franc in his pocket has for twenty years been going over mountains and valleys doing no one any harm, but bringing consolation to them by his singing, and who was to-day insulted and almost driven out and, tired, hungry, and humiliated, has gone to sleep somewhere on rotting straw?

At that moment, in the dead stillness of the night, I heard somewhere in the far distance the little man's guitar and voice.

'No,' I said to myself involuntarily, 'you have no right to pity him and to be indignant at the lord's well-being. Who has weighed the inner happiness to be found in the soul of each of them? He is now sitting somewhere on a dirty door-step, gazing at the gleaming moonlit sky and gaily singing in the calm of the fragrant night; in his heart there is no reproach, or malice, or regret. And who knows what is now going on in the souls of all the people within these palatial walls? Who can tell whether among them all there is as much carefree benign joy in life and harmony with the world as lives in the soul of that little man? Endless is the mercy and wisdom of Him who has allowed and ordained that all these contradictions should exist. Only to you, insignificant worm, who rashly and wrongly try to penetrate His laws and His intentions—only to you do they seem contradictions. He looked down benignly from His bright immeasurable height and rejoices in the infinite harmony into which all your endless contradictory movements resolve themselves.

'In your pride you thought you could separate yourself from the universal law. But you, too, with your mean and petty indignation at the waiters, have been playing your necessary part in the eternal and infinite harmony.'

# ALBERT*

## I

Five wealthy young men had come, after two in the morning, to amuse themselves at a small Petersburg party.

Much champagne had been drunk, most of the men were very young, the girls were pretty, the piano and violin indefatigably played one polka after another, and dancing and noise went on unceasingly: yet for some reason it was dull and awkward, and, as often happens, everybody felt that it was all unnecessary and was not the thing.

Several times they tried to get things going, but forced merriment was worse even than boredom.

One of the five young men, more dissatisfied than the others with himself, with the others, and with the whole evening, rose with a feeling of disgust, found his hat, and went out quietly, intending to go home.

There was no one in the ante-room, but in the adjoining room he heard two voices disputing. The young man stopped to listen.

'You can't, there are guests there,' said a woman's voice.

'Let me in, please. I'm all right!' a man's weak voice entreated.

'No, I won't let you in without Madame's permission,' said

---

* This story, also written during Tolstoy's stay in Western Europe in 1857, reflects his conviction at that time of the lack of public appreciation of real art. The tale was at first rejected by the editor of *The Contemporary* and Tolstoy reworked it in an effort to eliminate the special pleading, after which it was published by the magazine in 1858.

the woman. 'Where are you going? Ah! What a man you are!'

The door burst open and a strange figure of a man appeared on the threshold. The servant on seeing a visitor no longer protested, and the strange figure, bowing timidly, entered the room, swaying on his bent legs. He was of medium height, with a narrow, stooping back, and long tangled hair. He wore a short overcoat, and narrow torn trousers over a pair of rough uncleaned boots. A necktie, twisted into a cord, was fastened round his long white neck. A dirty shirt showed from under his coat and hung over his thin hands. Yet despite the extreme emaciation of his body, his face was white and delicate, and freshness and colour played on his cheeks above his scanty black beard and whiskers. His unkempt hair, thrown back, revealed a rather low and extremely clear forehead. His dark languid eyes looked softly, imploringly, and yet with dignity, before him. Their expression corresponded alluringly with that of the fresh lips, curved at the corners, which showed from under his thin moustache.

Having advanced a few steps he stopped, turned to the young man, and smiled. He seemed to smile with difficulty, but when the smile lit up his face the young man—without knowing why—smiled too.

'Who is that?' he whispered to the servant, when the strange figure had passed into the room from which came the sounds of a dance.

'A crazy musician from the theatre,' replied the maid. 'He comes sometimes to see the mistress.'

'Where have you been, Delésov?' someone just then called out, and the young man, who was named Delésov, returned to the ball-room.

The musician was standing at the door and, looking at the dancers, showed by his smile, his look, and the tapping of his foot, the satisfaction the spectacle afforded him.

'Come in and dance yourself,' said one of the visitors to him.

The musician bowed and looked inquiringly at the hostess.

'Go, go . . . Why not, when the gentlemen ask you to?' she said.

The thin, weak limbs of the musician suddenly came into active motion, and winking, smiling, and twitching, he began to prance awkwardly and heavily about the room. In the middle of the quadrille a merry officer, who danced very vivaciously and well, accidentally bumped into the musician with his back. The latter's weak and weary legs did not maintain their balance and after a few stumbling steps aside, he fell full length on the floor. Notwithstanding the dull thud produced by his fall, at first nearly everyone burst out laughing.

But the musician did not get up. The visitors grew silent and even the piano ceased. Delésov and the hostess were the first to run up to the fallen man. He was lying on his elbow, staring with dull eyes at the floor. When they lifted him and seated him on a chair, he brushed the hair back from his forehead with a quick movement of his bony hand and began to smile without answering their questions.

'Mr. Albert! Mr. Albert!' said the hostess. 'Have you hurt yourself? Where? There now, I said you ought not to dance. He is so weak,' she continued, addressing her guests, '—he can hardly walk. How could he dance?'

'Who is he?' they asked her.

'A poor man—an artist. A very good fellow, but pitiable, as you see.'

She said this unembarrassed by the presence of the musician. He suddenly came to himself and, as if afraid of something, shrank into a heap and pushed those around him away.

'It's all nothing!' he suddenly said, rising from his chair with an obvious effort.

And to show that he was not at all hurt he went into the middle of the room and tried to jump about, but staggered and would have fallen down again had someone not supported him.

Everyone felt awkward, and looking at him they all became silent.

The musician's eyes again grew dim, and evidently oblivious of everyone he began rubbing his knee with his hand. Suddenly he raised his head, advanced a trembling leg, threw back his hair with the same heedless movement as before, and going up to the violinist took his violin from him.

'It's nothing!' he said once more, flourishing the violin. 'Gentlemen, let's have some music!'

'What a strange person!' the visitors remarked to one another.

'Perhaps a fine talent is perishing in this unfortunate creature,' said one of the guests.

'Yes, he's pitiable, pitiable!' said a third.

'What a beautiful face! . . . There is something extraordinary about him,' said Delésov. 'Let us see . . .'

## II

Albert meanwhile, paying no attention to anyone, pressed the violin to his shoulder and paced slowly up and down by the piano tuning it. His lips took on an impassive expression, his eyes could not be seen, but his narrow bony back, his long white neck, his crooked legs and shaggy black head, presented a queer—but for some reason not at all ridiculous—spectacle. Having tuned the violin he briskly struck a chord, and throwing back his head turned to the pianist who was preparing to accompany him.

'*Mélancolie G-dur!*' he said, addressing the pianist with a gesture of command.

Then, as if begging forgiveness for that gesture, he smiled meekly, and glanced round at the audience with that same smile. Having pushed back his hair with the hand in which he held the bow, he stopped at the corner of the piano, and with a smooth and easy movement drew the bow across the strings. A clear melodious sound was borne through the room and complete silence ensued.

After that first note the theme flowed freely and elegantly, suddenly illumining the inner world of every listener with an unexpectedly clear and tranquillizing light. Not one false or exaggerated sound impaired the acquiescence of the listeners: the notes were all clear, elegant, and significant. Everyone silently followed their development with tremulous expectation. From the state of dullness, noisy distraction and mental torpor in which they had been, these people were suddenly and imperceptibly carried into another quite different world that they had forgotten. Now a calm contemplation of the past arose in their souls, now an impassioned memory of some past happiness, now a boundless desire for power and splendour, now a feeling of resignation, of unsatisfied love and sadness. Sounds now tenderly sad, now vehemently despairing, mingled freely, flowing and flowing one after the other so elegantly, so strongly, and so unconsciously, that the sounds themselves were not noticed, but there flowed of itself into the soul a beautiful torrent of poetry, long familiar but only now expressed. At each note Albert grew taller and taller. He was far from appearing misshapen or strange. Pressing the violin with his chin and listening to his notes with an expression of passionate attention, he convulsively moved his feet. Now he straightened himself to his full height, now he strenuously bent his back. His left arm seemed to have become set in the bent position to which he had strained it and only the bony fingers moved convulsively: the right arm moved smoothly, elegantly, and almost imperceptibly. His face shone with uninterrupted, ecstatic joy; his eyes burnt with a bright, dry brilliance, his nostrils expanded, his red lips opened with delight.

Sometimes his head bent closer to the violin, his eyes closed, and his face, half covered by his hair, lit up with a smile of mild rapture. Sometimes he drew himself up rapidly, advancing one foot, and his clear brow and the beaming look he cast round the room gleamed with pride, dignity, and a consciousness of power. Once the pianist blundered and struck a wrong chord. Physical suffering was apparent in the whole face and figure of the musician. He paused for an instant and stamping his foot with an expression of childish anger, cried: '*Moll, ce moll!*' The pianist recovered himself. Albert closed his eyes, smiled, and again forgetting himself, the others, and the whole world, gave himself up rapturously to his task.

All who were in the room preserved a submissive silence while Albert was playing, and seemed to live and breathe only in his music.

The merry officer sat motionless on a chair by a window, directing a lifeless gaze upon the floor and breathing slowly and heavily. The girls sat in complete silence along the walls, and only occasionally threw approving and bewildered glances at one another. The hostess's fat smiling face expanded with pleasure. The pianist riveted his eyes on Albert's face and, with a fear of blundering which expressed itself in his whole taut figure, tried to keep up with him. One of the visitors who had drunk more than the others lay prone on the sofa, trying not to move for fear of betraying his agitation. Delésov experienced an unaccustomed sensation. It was as if a cold circle, now expanding, now contracting, held his head in a vice. The roots of his hair became sensitive, cold shivers ran up his spine, something rising higher and higher in his throat pricked his nose and palate as if with fine needles, and tears involuntarily wetted his cheeks. He shook himself, tried to restrain them and wipe them unperceived, but others rose and ran down his cheeks. By some strange concatenation of impressions the first sounds of Albert's violin carried Delésov back to his early youth. Now no longer very young, tired of life and exhausted, he suddenly felt himself a self-satisfied, good-looking, blissfully foolish and unconsciously happy lad of seventeen. He remembered his first love—for his cousin in a little pink dress; remembered his first declaration of love made in a linden avenue; remembered the warmth and incomprehensible delight of a spontaneous kiss, and the magic and undivined mystery of the Nature that then surrounded him. In the memories that returned to him *she* shone out amid a mist of vague hopes, uncomprehended desires, and questioning faith in the possibility of impossible happiness. All the unappreciated moments of that time arose before him one after another, not as insignificant moments of a fleeting present, but as arrested, growing, reproachful images of the past. He contemplated them with joy, and wept—wept not because the time was past that he might have spent better (if he had it again he would not have undertaken to employ it better), but merely because it was past and would never return. Memories rose up of themselves, and Albert's violin

repeated again and again: 'For you that time of vigour, love,
and happiness has passed for ever, and will not return. Weep
for it, shed all your tears, die weeping for that time—that is
the best happiness left for you.'

Towards the end of the last variation Albert's face grew
red, his eyes burnt and glowed, and large drops of perspiration ran down his cheeks. The veins of his forehead swelled
up, his whole body came more and more into motion, his pale
lips no longer closed, and his whole figure expressed ecstatic
eagerness for enjoyment.

Passionately swaying his whole body and tossing back his
hair he lowered the violin, and with a smile of proud dignity
and happiness surveyed the audience. Then his back sagged,
his head hung down, his lips closed, his eyes grew dim, and
he timidly glanced round as if ashamed of himself, and made
his way stumblingly into the other room.

## III

Something strange occurred with everyone present and something strange was felt in the dead silence that followed Albert's playing. It was as if each would have liked to express
what all this meant, but was unable to do so. What did it
mean—this bright hot room, brilliant women, the dawn in the
windows, excitement in the blood, and the pure impression
left by sounds that had flowed past? But no one even tried
to say what it all meant: on the contrary everyone, unable to
dwell in those regions which the new impression had revealed
to them, rebelled against it.

'He really plays well, you know!' said the officer.

'Wonderfully!' replied Delésov, stealthily wiping his cheek
with his sleeve.

'However, it's time for us to be going,' said the man who
was lying on the sofa, having somewhat recovered. 'We must
give him something. Let's make a collection.'

Meanwhile Albert sat alone on a sofa in the next room.
Leaning his elbows on his bony knees he stroked his face and

ruffled his hair with his moist and dirty hands, smiling happily to himself.

They made a good collection, which Delésov offered to hand to Albert.

Moreover it had occurred to Delésov, on whom the music had made an unusual and powerful impression, to be of use to this man. It occurred to him to take him home, dress him, get him a place somewhere, and in general rescue him from his sordid condition.

'Well, are you tired?' he asked, coming up to him.

Albert smiled.

'You have real talent. You ought to study music seriously and give public performances.'

'I'd like to have something to drink,' said Albert, as if just awake.

Delésov brought some wine, and the musician eagerly drank two glasses.

'What excellent wine!' he said.

'What a delightful thing that *Mélancolie* is!' said Delésov.

'Oh, yes, yes!' replied Albert with a smile—'but excuse me: I don't know with whom I have the honour of speaking, maybe you are a count, or a prince: could you, perhaps, lend me a little money?' He paused a little. 'I have nothing . . . I am a poor man. I couldn't pay it back.'

Delésov flushed: he felt awkward, and hastily handed the musician the money that had been collected.

'Thank you very much!' said Albert, seizing the money. 'Now let's have some music. I'll play for you as much as you like—only let me have a drink of something, a drink . . .' he added, rising.

Delésov brought him some more wine and asked him to sit beside him.

'Excuse me if I am frank with you,' he said, 'your talent interests me so much. It seems to me you are not in good circumstances.'

Albert looked now at Delésov and now at his hostess who had entered the room.

'Allow me to offer you my services,' continued Delésov. 'If you are in need of anything I should be glad if you would stay with me for a time. I am living alone and could perhaps be of use to you.'

Albert smiled and made no reply.

'Why don't you thank him?' said the hostess. 'Of course it is a godsend for you. Only I should not advise you to,' she continued, turning to Delésov and shaking her head disapprovingly.

'I am very grateful to you!' said Albert, pressing Delésov's hand with his own moist ones—'Only let us have some music now, please.'

But the other visitors were preparing to leave, and despite Albert's endeavours to persuade them to stay they went out into the hall.

Albert took leave of the hostess, put on his shabby broad-brimmed hat and old summer cloak, which was his only winter clothing, and went out into the porch with Delésov.

When Delésov had seated himself with his new acquaintance in his carriage, and became aware of the unpleasant odour of drunkenness and uncleanness which emanated so strongly from the musician, he began to repent of his action and blamed himself for childish soft-heartedness and imprudence. Besides, everything Albert said was so stupid and trivial, and the fresh air suddenly made him so disgustingly drunk that Delésov was repelled. 'What am I to do with him?' he thought.

When they had driven for a quarter of an hour Albert grew silent, his hat fell down at his feet, and he himself tumbled into a corner of the carriage and began to snore. The wheels continued to creak monotonously over the frozen snow; the feeble light of dawn hardly penetrated the frozen windows.

Delésov turned and looked at his companion. The long body covered by the cloak lay lifelessly beside him. The long head with its big black nose seemed to sway on that body, but looking closer Delésov saw that what he had taken for nose and face was hair, and that the real face hung lower. He stooped and was able to distinguish Albert's features. Then the

beauty of the forehead and calmly closed lips struck him
again.

Under the influence of tired nerves, restlessness from lack
of sleep at that hour of the morning, and of the music he had
heard, Delésov, looking at that face, let himself again be carried back to the blissful world into which he had glanced that
night; he again recalled the happy and magnanimous days of
his youth and no longer repented of what he had done. At
that moment he was sincerely and warmly attached to Albert,
and firmly resolved to be of use to him.

IV

Next morning when he was awakened to go to his office,
Delésov with a feeling of unpleasant surprise saw around him
his old screen, his old valet, and his watch lying on the small
side-table. 'But what did I expect to see if not what is always
around me?' he asked himself. Then he remembered the musician's black eyes and happy smile, the motif of *Mélancolie,*
and all the strange experiences of the previous night passed
through his mind.

He had no time however to consider whether he had acted
well or badly by taking the musician into his house. While
dressing he mapped out the day, took his papers, gave the
necessary household orders, and hurriedly put on his overcoat
and overshoes. Passing the dining-room door he looked in.
Albert, after tossing about, had sunk his face in the pillow,
and lay in his dirty ragged shirt, dead asleep on the leather
sofa where he had been deposited unconscious the night before. 'There's something wrong!' thought Delésov involuntarily.

'Please go to Boryuzóvski and ask him to lend me a violin
for a couple of days,' he said to his manservant. 'When he
wakes up, give him coffee and let him have some underclothing and old clothes of mine. In general, make him comfortable—please!'

On returning late in the evening Delésov was surprised not
to find Albert.

'Where is he?' he asked his man.

'He went away immediately after dinner,' replied the servant. 'He took the violin and went away. He promised to be back in an hour, but he's not here yet.'

'Tut, tut! How provoking!' muttered Delésov. 'Why did you let him go, Zakhár?'

Zakhár was a Petersburg valet who had been in Delésov's service for eight years. Delésov, being a lonely bachelor, could not help confiding his intentions to him, and liked to know his opinion about all his undertakings.

'How could I dare not to let him?' Zakhár replied, toying with the fob of his watch. 'If you had told me to keep him in I might have amused him at home. But you only spoke to me about clothes.'

'Pshaw! How provoking! Well, and what was he doing here without me?'

Zakhár smiled.

'One can well call him an "artist",[1] sir. As soon as he woke he asked for Madeira, and then he amused himself with the cook and with the neighbour's manservant. He is so funny. However, he is good-natured. I gave him tea and brought him dinner. He would not eat anything himself, but kept inviting me to do so. But when it comes to playing the violin, even Izler has few artists like him. One may well befriend such a man. When he played *Down the Little Mother Vólga* to us it was as if a man were weeping. It was too beautiful. Even the servants from all the flats came to our back-entrance to hear him.'

'Well, and did you get him dressed?' his master interrupted him.

'Of course. I gave him a night-shirt of yours and put my own paletot on him. A man like that is worth helping—he really is a dear fellow!' Zakhár smiled.

'He kept asking me what your rank is, whether you have influential acquaintances, and how many serfs you own.'

---

[1] In addition to its proper meaning, the word 'artist' was used in Russian to denote a thief, or a man dexterous at anything, good or bad.

'Well, all right, but now he must be found, and in future don't let him have anything to drink, or it'll be worse for him.'

'That's true,' Zakhár interjected. 'He is evidently feeble; our old master had a clerk like that . . .'

But Delésov who had long known the story of the clerk who took hopelessly to drink, did not let Zakhár finish, and telling him to get everything ready for the night, sent him out to find Albert and bring him back.

He then went to bed and put out the light, but could not fall asleep for a long time, thinking about Albert. 'Though it may seem strange to many of my acquaintances,' he thought, 'yet one so seldom does anything for others that one ought to thank God when such an opportunity presents itself, and I will not miss it. I will do anything—positively anything in my power—to help him. He may not be mad at all, but only under the influence of drink. It won't cost me very much. Where there's enough for one there's enough for two. Let him live with me awhile, then we'll find him a place or arrange a concert for him and pull him out of the shallows, and then see what happens.'

He experienced a pleasant feeling of self-satisfaction after this reflection.

'Really I'm not altogether a bad fellow,' he thought. 'Not at all bad even—when I compare myself with others.'

He was already falling asleep when the sound of opening doors and of footsteps in the hall roused him.

'Well, I'll be stricter with him,' he thought, 'that will be best; and I must do it.'

He rang.

'Have you brought him back?' he asked when Zakhár entered.

'A pitiable man, sir,' said Zakhár, shaking his head significantly and closing his eyes.

'Is he drunk?'

'He is very weak.'

'And has he the violin?'

'I've brought it back. The lady gave it me.'

'Well, please don't let him in here now. Put him to bed,

and to-morrow be sure not to let him leave the house on any account.'

But before Zakhár was out of the room Albert entered it.

## V

'Do you want to sleep already?' asked Albert with a smile. 'And I have been at Anna Ivánovna's and had a very pleasant evening. We had music, and laughed, and there was delightful company. Let me have a glass of something,' he added, taking hold of a water-bottle that stood on a little table, '—but not water.'

Albert was just the same as he had been the previous evening: the same beautiful smile in his eyes and on his lips, the same bright inspired forehead, and the same feeble limbs. Zakhár's paletot fitted him well, and the clean wide unstarched collar of the nightshirt encircled his thin white neck picturesquely, giving him a particularly childlike and innocent look. He sat down on Delésov's bed and looked at him silently with a happy and grateful smile. Delésov looked into his eyes, and again suddenly felt himself captivated by that smile. He no longer wanted to sleep, he forgot that it was his duty to be stern: on the contrary he wished to make merry, to hear music, and to chat amicably with Albert till morning. He told Zakhár to bring a bottle of wine, some cigarettes, and the violin.

'There, that's splendid!' said Albert. 'It's still early, and we'll have some music. I'll play for you as much as you like.'

Zakhár, with evident pleasure, brought a bottle of Lafitte, two tumblers, some mild cigarettes such as Albert smoked, and the violin. But instead of going to bed as his master told him to, he himself lit a cigar and sat down in the adjoining room.

'Let us have a talk,' said Delésov to the musician, who was about to take up the violin.

Albert submissively sat down on the bed and again smiled joyfully.

'Oh yes!' said he, suddenly striking his forehead with his hand and assuming an anxiously inquisitive expression. (A change of expression always preceded anything he was about to say.)—'Allow me to ask—' he made a slight pause—'that gentleman who was there with you last night—you called him N—, isn't he the son of the celebrated N—?'

'His own son,' Delésov answered, not at all understanding how that could interest Albert.

'Exactly!' said Albert with a self-satisfied smile. 'I noticed at once something particularly aristocratic in his manner. I love aristocrats: there is something particularly beautiful and elegant in an aristocrat. And that officer who dances so well?' he asked. 'I liked him very much too: he is so merry and so fine. Isn't he Adjutant N. N.?'

'Which one?' asked Delésov.

'The one who bumped against me when we were dancing. He must be an excellent fellow.'

'No, he's a shallow fellow,' Delésov replied.

'Oh, no!' Albert warmly defended him. 'There is something very, very pleasant about him. He is a capital musician,' he added. 'He played something there out of an opera. It's a long time since I took such a liking to anyone.'

'Yes, he plays well, but I don't like his playing,' said Delésov, wishing to get his companion to talk about music. 'He does not understand classical music—Donizetti and Bellini, you know, are not music. You think so too, no doubt?'

'Oh, no, no, excuse me!' began Albert with a gentle, pleading look. 'The old music is music, and the new music is music. There are extraordinary beauties in the new music too. *Sonnambula*,[1] and the finals of *Lucia*,[2] and Chopin, and *Robert!* [3] I often think—' he paused, evidently collecting his thoughts—'that if Beethoven were alive he would weep with joy listening to *Sonnambula*. There is beauty everywhere. I

---

[1] Opera by Bellini, produced in 1831.
[2] *Lucia di Lammermoor*, an opera by Donizetti, produced in 1835.
[3] *Robert the Devil*, an opera by Meyerbeer, produced in 1831, or possibly the allusion may be to *Roberto Devereux* by Donizetti.

heard *Sonnambula* for the first time when Viardot[4] and Rubini[5] were here. It was like this . . .' he said, and his eyes glistened as he made a gesture with both arms as though tearing something out of his breast. 'A little more and it would have been impossible to bear it.'

'And what do you think of the opera at the present time?' asked Delésov.

'Bosio[6] is good, very good,' he said, 'extraordinarily exquisite, but she does not touch one here,'—pointing to his sunken chest. 'A singer needs passion, and she has none. She gives pleasure but does not torment.'

'How about Lablache?' [7]

'I heard him in Paris in the *Barbier de Séville*. He was unique then, but now he is old: he cannot be an artist, he is old.'

'Well, what if he is old? He is still good in *morceaux d'ensemble*,' said Delésov, who was in the habit of saying that of Lablache.

'How "what if he is old?" ' rejoined Albert severely. 'He should not be old. An artist should not be old. Much is needed for art, but above all, fire!' said he with glittering eyes and stretching both arms upwards.

And a terrible inner fire really seemed to burn in his whole body.

'O my God!' he suddenly exclaimed. 'Don't you know Petróv, the artist?'

'No, I don't,' Delésov replied, smiling.

'How I should like you to make his acquaintance! You would enjoy talks with him. How well he understands art, too! I used often to meet him at Anna Ivánovna's, but now she is

---

[4] Pauline Viardot-Garcia. A celebrated operatic singer with whom Turgenev had a close friendship for many years.

[5] Rubini. An Italian tenor who had great success in Russia in the 'forties of the last century.

[6] Angidina Bosio, an Italian singer, who was in Petersburg in 1856-9.

[7] Luigi Lablache. He was regarded as the chief basso of modern times.

angry with him for some reason. I should very much like you to know him. He has great talent, great talent!'

'Does he paint now?' Delésov asked.

'I don't know, I think not, but he was an Academy artist. What ideas he has! It's wonderful when he talks sometimes. Oh, Petróv has great talent, only he leads a very gay life . . . that's a pity,' Albert added with a smile. After that he got off the bed, took the violin, and began tuning it.

'Is it long since you were at the opera?' Delésov asked.

Albert looked round and sighed.

'Ah, I can't go there any more!' he said. 'I will tell you!' And clutching his head he again sat down beside Delésov and muttered almost in a whisper: 'I can't go there. I can't play there—I have nothing—nothing! No clothes, no home, no violin. It is a miserable life! A miserable life!' he repeated several times. And why should I go there? What for? No need!' he said, smiling. 'Ah! *Don Juan* . . .'

He struck his head with his hand.

'Then let us go there together sometime,' said Delésov.

Without answering, Albert jumped up, seized the violin, and began playing the finale of the first act of *Don Juan*, telling the story of the opera in his own words.

Delésov felt the hair stir on his head as Albert played the voice of the dying commandant.

'No!' said Albert, putting down the violin. 'I cannot play to-day. I have had too much to drink.'

But after that he went up to the table, filled a tumbler with wine, drank it at a gulp, and again sat down on Delésov's bed.

Delésov looked at Albert, not taking his eyes off him. Occasionally Albert smiled, and so did Delésov. They were both silent; but their looks and smiles created more and more affectionate relations between them. Delésov felt himself growing fonder of the man, and experienced an incomprehensible joy.

'Have you ever been in love?' he suddenly asked.

Albert thought for a few seconds, and then a sad smile lit up his face. He leaned over to Delésov and looked attentively in his eyes.

'Why have you asked me that?' he whispered. 'I will tell you everything, because I like you,' he continued, after looking at him for a while and then glancing round. 'I won't deceive you, but will tell you everything from the beginning, just as it happened.' He stopped, his eyes wild and strangely fixed. 'You know that my mind is weak,' he suddenly said. 'Yes, yes,' he went on. 'Anna Ivánovna is sure to have told you. She tells everybody that I am mad! That is not true; she says it as a joke, she is a kindly woman, and I have really not been quite well for some time.' He stopped again and gazed with fixed wide-open eyes at the dark doorway. 'You asked whether I have been in love? . . . Yes, I have been in love,' he whispered, lifting his brows. 'It happened long ago, when I still had my job in the theatre. I used to play second violin at the Opera, and she used to have the lower-tier box next the stage, on the left.'

He got up and leaned over to Delésov's ear.

'No, why should I name her?' he said. 'You no doubt know her—everybody knows her. I kept silent and only looked at her; I knew I was a poor artist, and she an aristocratic lady. I knew that very well. I only looked at her and planned nothing . . .'

Albert reflected, trying to remember.

'How it happened I don't remember; but I was once called in to accompany her on the violin. . . . But what was I, a poor artist?' he said, shaking his head and smiling. 'But no, I can't tell it . . .' he added, clutching his head. 'How happy I was!'

'Yes? And did you often go to her house?' Delésov asked.

'Once! Once only . . . but it was my own fault. I was mad! I was a poor artist, and she an aristocratic lady. I ought not to have said anything to her. But I went mad and acted like a fool. Since then all has been over for me. Petróv told the truth, that it would have been better for me to have seen her only at the theatre . . .'

'What was it you did?' asked Delésov.

'Ah, wait! Wait! I can't speak of that!'

With his face hidden in his hands he remained silent for some time.

'I came late to the orchestra. Petróv and I had been drinking that evening, and I was distracted. She was sitting in her box talking to a general. I don't know who that general was. She sat at the very edge of the box, with her arm on the ledge; she had on a white dress and pearls round her neck. She talked to him and looked at me. She looked at me twice. Her hair was done like this. I was not playing, but stood near the basses and looked at her. Then for the first time I felt strange. She smiled at the general and looked at me. I felt she was speaking about me, and I suddenly saw that I was not in the orchestra, but in the box beside her and holding her arm, just there. . . . How was that?' Albert asked after a short silence.

'That was vivid imagination,' said Delésov.

'No, no! . . . but I don't know how to tell it,' Albert replied, frowning. 'Even then I was poor and had no lodging, and when I went to the theatre I sometimes stayed the night there.'

'What, at the theatre? In that dark, empty place?'

'Oh, I am not afraid of such nonsense. Wait a bit. . . . When they had all gone away I would go to the box where she had been sitting and sleep there. That was my one delight. What nights I spent there! But once it began again. Many things appeared to me in the night, but I can't tell you much.' Albert glanced at Delésov with downcast eyes. 'What was it?' he asked.

'It is strange!' said Delésov.

'No, wait, wait!' he continued, whispering in Delésov's ear. 'I kissed her hand, wept there beside her, and talked much with her. I inhaled the scent of her perfume and heard her voice. She told me much in one night. Then I took my violin and played softly; and I played splendidly. But I felt frightened. I am not afraid of those foolish things and don't believe in them, but I was afraid for my head,' he said, touching his forehead with an amiable smile. 'I was frightened for my poor wits. It seemed to me that something had happened to my head. Perhaps it's nothing. What do you think?'

Both were silent for some minutes.

> *'Und wenn die Wolken sie verhüllen*
> *Die Sonne bleibt doch ewig klar.'* [8]

Albert sang with a soft smile. 'Is not that so?' he added.

> *'Ich auch habe gelebt und genossen . . .'* [9]

'Ah, how well old Petróv would have explained it all to you!'

Delésov looked silently and in terror at the pale and agitated face of his companion.

'Do you know the *"Juristen-Waltzer"?'* Albert suddenly exclaimed, and without awaiting an answer he jumped up, seized the violin, and began to play the merry waltz tune, forgetting himself completely, and evidently imagining that a whole orchestra was playing with him. He smiled, swayed, shifted his feet, and played superbly.

'Eh! Enough of merrymaking!' he said when he had finished, and flourished the violin.

'I am going,' he said, after sitting silently for awhile—'won't you come with me?'

'Where to?' Delésov asked in surprise.

'Let's go to Anna Ivánovna's again. It's gay there—noise, people, music!'

At first Delésov almost consented, but bethinking himself he tried to persuade Albert not to go that night.

'Only for a moment.'

'No really, you'd better not!'

Albert sighed and put down the violin.

'So I must stay here?'

---

8        'And even if the clouds do hide it
         The sun remains for ever clear.'
9        'I, too, have lived and enjoyed.'

And looking again at the table (there was no wine left) he said good-night and left the room.

Delésov rang.

'See that you don't let Mr. Albert go anywhere without my permission,' he said to Zakhár.

## VI

The next day was a holiday. Delésov was already awake and sitting in his drawing-room drinking coffee and reading a book. Albert had not yet stirred in the next room.

Zakhár cautiously opened the door and looked into the dining-room.

'Would you believe it, sir? He is asleep on the bare sofa! He wouldn't have anything spread on it, really. Like a little child. Truly, an artist.'

Towards noon groaning and coughing were heard through the door.

Zakhár again went into the dining-room, and Delésov could hear his kindly voice and Albert's weak, entreating one.

'Well?' he asked, when Zakhár returned.

'He's fretting, sir, won't wash, and seems gloomy. He keeps asking for a drink.'

'No. Having taken this matter up I must show character,' said Delésov to himself.

He ordered that no wine should be given to Albert and resumed his book, but involuntarily listened to what was going on in the dining-room. There was no sound of movement there and an occasional deep cough and spitting was all that could be heard. Two hours passed. Having dressed, Delésov decided to look in at his visitor before going out. Albert was sitting motionless at the window, his head resting on his hand. He looked round. His face was yellow, wrinkled, and not merely sad but profoundly miserable. He tried to smile by way of greeting, but his face took on a still more sorrowful expression. He seemed ready to cry. He rose with difficulty and bowed.

'If I might just have a glass of simple vodka!' he said with a look of entreaty. 'I am so weak—please!'

'Coffee will do you more good. Have some of that instead.'

Albert's face suddenly lost its childlike expression; he looked coldly, dim-eyed, out of the window, and sank feebly onto his chair.

'Or would you like some lunch?'

'No thank you, I have no appetite.'

'If you wish to play the violin you will not disturb me,' said Delésov, laying the violin on the table.

Albert looked at the violin with a contemptuous smile.

'No,' he said. 'I am too weak, I can't play,' and he pushed the instrument away from him.

After that, whatever Delésov might say, offering to go for a walk with him, and to the theatre in the evening, he only bowed humbly and remained stubbornly silent. Delésov went out, paid several calls, dined with friends, and before going to the theatre returned home to change and to see what the musician was doing. Albert was sitting in the dark hall, leaning his head in his hands and looking at the heated stove. He was neatly dressed, washed, and his hair was brushed; but his eyes were dim and lifeless, and his whole figure expressed weakness and exhaustion even more than in the morning.

'Have you dined, Mr. Albert?' asked Delésov.

Albert made an affirmative gesture with his head and, after a frightened look at Delésov, lowered his eyes. Delésov felt uncomfortable.

'I spoke to the director of the theatre about you to-day,' he said, also lowering his eyes. 'He will be very glad to receive you if you will let him hear you.'

'Thank you, I cannot play!' muttered Albert under his breath, and went into his room, shutting the door behind him very softly.

A few minutes later the door-knob was turned just as gently, and he came out of the room with the violin. With a rapid and hostile glance at Delésov he placed the violin on a chair and disappeared again.

Delésov shrugged his shoulders and smiled.

'What more am I to do? In what am I to blame?' he thought.

'Well, how is the musician?' was his first question when he returned home late that evening.

'Bad!' said Zakhár, briefly and clearly. 'He has been sighing and coughing and says nothing, except that he started begging for vodka four or five times. At last I gave him one glass—or else we might finish him off, sir. Just like the clerk . . .'

'Has he not played the violin?'

'Didn't even touch it. I took it to him a couple of times, but he just took it up gently and brought it out again,' Zakhár answered with a smile. 'So your orders are not to give him any drink?'

'No, we'll wait another day and see what happens. And what's he doing now?'

'He has locked himself up in the drawing-room.'

Delésov went into his study and chose several French books and a German Bible. 'Put these books in his room to-morrow, and see that you don't let him out,' he said to Zakhár.

Next morning Zakhár informed his master that the musician had not slept all night: he had paced up and down the rooms, and had been into the pantry, trying to open the cupboard and the door, but he (Zakhár) had taken care to lock everything up. He said that while he pretended to be asleep he had heard Albert in the dark muttering something to himself and waving his arms about.

Albert grew gloomier and more taciturn every day. He seemed to be afraid of Delésov, and when their eyes met his face expressed sickly fear. He did not touch the books or the violin, and did not reply to questions put to him.

On the third day of the musician's stay Delésov returned home late, tired and upset. He had been driving about all day attending to a matter that had promised to be very simple and easy but, as often happens, in spite of strenuous efforts he had been quite unable to advance a single step with it. Besides that he had called in at his club and had lost at whist. He was in bad spirits.

'Well, let him go his way!' he said to Zakhár, who told him
of Albert's sad plight. 'To-morrow I'll get a definite answer
out of him, whether he wants to stay here and follow my advice, or not. If not, he needn't! It seems to me that I have
done all I could.'

'There now, try doing good to people!' he thought to himself. 'I put myself out for him, I keep that dirty creature in my
house, so that I can't receive a visitor in the morning. I bustle
and run about, and he looks on me as if I were a villain who
for his own pleasure has locked him up in a cage. And above
all, he won't take a single step to help himself. They are all
like that.' (The 'they' referred to people in general, and especially to those with whom he had had business that day.)
'And what is the matter with him now? What is he thinking
about and pining for? Pining for the debauchery from which I
have dragged him? For the humiliation in which he was? For
the destitution from which I have saved him? Evidently he
has fallen so low that it hurts him to see a decent life . . .'

'No, it was a childish act,' Delésov concluded. 'How can I
improve others, when God knows whether I can manage myself?' He thought of letting Albert go at once, but after a
little reflection put it off till the next day.

During the night he was roused by the sound of a table
falling in the hall, and the sound of voices and footsteps. He
lighted a candle and listened in surprise.

'Wait a bit. I'll tell my master,' Zakhár was saying; Albert's
voice muttered something incoherently and heatedly. Delésov
jumped up and ran into the hall with the candle. Zakhár stood
against the front door in his night attire, and Albert, with his
hat and cloak on, was pushing him aside and shouting in a
tearful voice:

'You can't keep me here! I have a passport,[1] and have taken
nothing of yours. You may search me. I shall go to the chief
of police! . . .'

'Excuse me, sir!' Zakhár said, addressing his master while

---

[1] To be free to go from place to place it was necessary to have a
properly stamped passport from the police.

continuing to guard the door with his back. 'He got up during
the night, found the key in my overcoat pocket, and drank a
whole decanter of liqueur vodka. Is that right? And now he
wants to go away. You ordered me not to let him out, so I
dare not let him go.'

On seeing Delésov Albert made for Zakhár still more
excitedly.

'No one dare hold me! No one has a right to!' he shouted,
raising his voice more and more.

'Step aside, Zakhár!' said Delésov. 'I can't and don't want
to keep you, but I advise you to stay till the morning,' he said
to Albert.

'No one can keep me! I'll go to the chief of police!' Albert
cried louder and louder, addressing himself to Zakhár alone
and not looking at Delésov. 'Help!' he suddenly screamed in a
furious voice.

'What are you screaming like that for? Nobody is keeping
you!' said Zakhár, opening the door.

Albert stopped shouting. 'You didn't succeed, did you?
Wanted to do for me—did you!' he muttered to himself, putting on his galoshes. Without taking leave, and continuing
to mutter incoherently, he went out. Zakhár held a light for
him as far as the gate, and then came back.

'Well, God be thanked, sir!' he said to his master. 'Who
knows what might happen? As it is I must count the silver
plate . . .'

Delésov merely shook his head and did not reply. He vividly recalled the first two evenings he had spent with the musician, and recalled the last sad days which by his fault Albert
had spent there, and above all he recalled that sweet, mixed
feeling of surprise, affection and pity, which that strange man
had aroused in him at first sight, and he felt sorry for him.
'And what will become of him now?' he thought. 'Without
money, without warm clothing, alone in the middle of the
night . . .' He was about to send Zakhár after him, but it was
too late.

'Is it cold outside?' he inquired.

'A hard frost, sir,' replied Zakhár. 'I forgot to inform you, but we shall have to buy more wood for fuel before the spring.'

'How is that? You said that we should have some left over.'

## VII

It was indeed cold outside, but Albert, heated by the liquor he had drunk and by the dispute, did not feel it. On reaching the street he looked round and rubbed his hands joyfully. The street was empty, but the long row of lamps still burned with ruddy light; the sky was clear and starry. 'There now!' he said, addressing the lighted window of Delésov's lodging, thrusting his hands into his trouser pockets under his cape, and stooping forward. He went with heavy, uncertain steps down the street to the right. He felt an unusual weight in his legs and stomach, something made a noise in his head, and some invisible force was throwing him from side to side, but he still went on in the direction of Anna Ivánovna's house. Strange, incoherent thoughts passed through his mind. Now he remembered his last altercation with Zakhár, then for some reason the sea and his first arrival in Russia by steamboat, then a happy night he had passed with a friend in a small shop he was passing, then suddenly a familiar motif began singing itself in his imagination, and he remembered the object of his passion and the dreadful night in the theatre. Despite their incoherence all these memories presented themselves so clearly to his mind that, closing his eyes, he did not know which was the more real: what he was doing, or what he was thinking. He did not realize or feel how his legs were moving, how he swayed and bumped against the wall, how he looked around him, or passed from street to street. He realized and felt only the things that, intermingling and fantastically following one another, rose in his imagination.

Passing along the Little Morskáya Street, Albert stumbled and fell. Coming to his senses for a moment he saw an immense and splendid building before him and went on. In the sky no stars, nor moon, nor dawn, were visible, nor were there any street lamps, but everything was clearly outlined.

In the windows of the building that towered at the end of the street lights were shining, but those lights quivered like reflections. The building stood out nearer and nearer and clearer and clearer before him. But the lights disappeared directly he entered the wide portals. All was dark within. Solitary footsteps resounded under the vaulted ceiling, and some shadows slid rapidly away as he approached. 'Why have I come here?' thought he; but some irresistible force drew him on into the depths of the immense hall. There was some kind of platform, around which some small people stood silently. 'Who is going to speak?' asked Albert. No one replied, except that someone pointed to the platform. A tall thin man with bristly hair and wearing a parti-coloured dressing-gown was already standing there, and Albert immediately recognized his friend Petróv. 'How strange that he should be here!' thought he. 'No brothers!' Petróv was saying, pointing to someone. "You did not understand a man living among you; you have not understood him! He is not a mercenary artist, not a mechanical performer, not a lunatic or a lost man. He is a genius—a great musical genius who has perished among you unnoticed and unappreciated!' Albert at once understood of whom his friend was speaking, but not wishing to embarrass him he modestly lowered his head.

'The holy fire that we all serve has consumed him like a blade of straw!' the voice went on, 'but he has fulfilled all that God implanted in him and should therefore be called a great man. You could despise, torment, humiliate him,' the voice continued, growing louder and louder—'but he was, is, and will be, immeasurably higher than you all. He is happy, he is kind. He loves or despises all alike, but serves only that which was implanted in him from above. He loves but one thing—beauty, the one indubitable blessing in the world. Yes, such is the man! Fall prostrate before him, all of you! On your knees!' he cried aloud.

But another voice came mildly from the opposite corner of the hall: 'I do not wish to bow my knees before him,' said the voice, which Albert immediately recognized as Delésov's. 'Wherein is he great? Why should we bow before him? Did he behave honourably and justly? Has he been of any use to society? Don't we know how he borrowed money and did not return it, and how he carried away his fellow-artist's violin and pawned it? . . .' ('O God, how does he know all that?' thought Albert, hanging his head still lower.) 'Do we not know how he flattered the most insignificant people, flattered them for the sake of money?' Delésov continued—'Don't we know how he was expelled from the theatre? And how Anna Ivánovna wanted to send him to the police?' ('O God! That is all true, but defend me, Thou who alone knowest why I did it!' muttered Albert.)

'Cease, for shame!' Petróv's voice began again. 'What right have you to accuse him? Have you lived his life? Have you experienced his rapture?' ('True, true!' whispered Albert.) 'Art is the highest manifestation of power in man. It is given to a few of the elect, and raises the chosen one to such a height as turns the head and makes it difficult for him to remain sane. In Art, as in every struggle, there are heroes who have devoted themselves entirely to its service and have perished without having reached the goal.' Petróv stopped, and Albert raised his head and cried out: 'True, true!' but his voice died away without a sound.

'It does not concern you,' said the artist Petróv, turning to him severely. 'Yes, humiliate and despise him,' he continued, 'but yet he is the best and happiest of you all.'

Albert, who had listened to these words with rapture in his soul, could not restrain himself, and went up to his friend wishing to kiss him.

'Go away! I do not know you!' Petróv said. 'Go your way, or you won't get there.'

'Just see how the drink's got hold of you! You won't get there,' shouted a policeman at the crossroad.

Albert stopped, collected his strength and, trying not to stagger, turned into the side street.

Only a few more steps were left to Anna Ivánovna's door. From the hall of her house the light fell on the snow in the courtyard, and sledges and carriages stood at the gate.

Holding onto the bannister with his numbed hands, he ran up the steps and rang. The sleepy face of a maid appeared in the opening of the doorway, and she looked angrily at Albert. 'You can't!' she cried. 'The orders are not to let you in,' and she slammed the door to. The sound of music and of women's voices reached the steps. Albert sat down, leaned his head against the wall, and closed his eyes. Immediately a throng of disconnected but kindred visions beset him with renewed force, engulfed him in their waves, and bore him away into the free and beautiful realm of dreams. 'Yes, he was the best and happiest!' ran involuntarily through his imagination. The sounds of a polka came through the door. These sounds also told him that he was the best and happiest. The bells in the nearest church rang out for early service, and these bells also said: 'Yes, he is the best and happiest!' . . . 'I will go back to the hall,' thought Albert. 'Petróv must tell me much more.' But there was no one in the hall now, and instead of the artist Petróv, Albert himself stood on the platform and played on the violin all that the voice had said before. But the violin was of strange construction; it was made of glass and it had to be held in both hands and slowly pressed to the breast to make it produce sounds. The sounds were the most delicate and delightful Albert had ever heard. The closer he pressed the violin to his breast the more joyful and tender he felt. The louder the sounds grew the faster the shadows dispersed and the brighter the walls of the hall were lit up by transparent light. But it was necessary to play the violin very warily so as not to break it. He played the glass instrument very carefully and well. He played such things as he felt no one would ever hear again. He was beginning to grow tired when another distant, muffled sound distracted his attention. It was the sound of a bell, but it spoke words: 'Yes,' said the bell, droning somewhere high up and far away, 'he seems to you pitiful, you despise him, yet he is the best and happiest of men! No one will ever again play that instrument.'

These familiar words suddenly seemed so wise, so new, and so true, to Albert that he stopped playing and, trying not to

move, raised his arms and eyes to heaven. He felt that he was
beautiful and happy. Although there was no one else in the
hall he expanded his chest and stood on the platform with
head proudly erect so that all might see him. Suddenly someone's hand lightly touched his shoulder; he turned and saw a
woman in the faint light. She looked at him sadly and shook
her head deprecatingly. He immediately realized that what
he was doing was bad, and felt ashamed of himself. 'Whither?'
he asked her. She again gave him a long fixed look and sadly
inclined her head. It was she—none other than she whom
he loved, and her garments were the same; on her full white
neck a string of pearls, and her superb arms bare to above the
elbow. She took his hand and led him out of the hall. 'The
exit is on the other side,' said Albert, but without replying she
smiled and led him out. At the threshold of the hall Albert
saw the moon and some water. But the water was not below as
it usually is, nor was the moon a white circle in one place
up above as it usually is. Moon and water were together and
everywhere—above, below, at the sides, and all around them
both. Albert threw himself with her into the moon and the
water, and realized that he could now embrace her, whom
he loved more than anything in the world. He embraced her
and felt unutterable happiness. 'Is this not a dream?' he asked
himself. But no! It was more than reality: it was reality and
recollection combined. Then he felt that the unutterable bliss
he had at that moment enjoyed had passed and would never
return. 'What am I weeping for?' he asked her. She looked at
him silently and sadly. Albert understood what she meant by
that. 'But how can it be, since I am alive?' he muttered. Without replying or moving she looked straight before her. 'This
is terrible! How can I explain to her that I am alive?' he
thought with horror. 'O Lord! I am alive, do understand me!'
he whispered.

'He is the best and happiest!' a voice was saying. But something was pressing more and more heavily on Albert. Whether
it was the moon and the water, her embraces, or his tears, he
did not know, but he felt he would not be able to say all that
was necessary, and that soon all would be over.

Two visitors, leaving Anna Ivánovna's house, stumbled over Albert, who lay stretched out on the threshold. One of them went back and called the hostess.

'Why, this is inhuman!' he said. 'You might let a man freeze like that!'

'Ah, that Albert! I'm sick to death of him!' replied the hostess. 'Ánnushka, lay him down somewhere in a room,' she said to the maid.

'But I am alive—why bury me?' muttered Albert, as they carried him insensible into the room.

# THREE DEATHS*

## I

It was autumn. Two vehicles were going along the highway at a quick trot. In the first sat two women: a lady, thin and pale, and a maidservant, plump and rosy and shining. The maid's short dry hair escaped from under her faded bonnet and her red hand in its torn glove kept pushing it back by fits and starts; her full bosom, covered by a woollen shawl, breathed health, her quick black eyes now watched the fields as they glided past the window, now glanced timidly at her mistress, and now restlessly scanned the corners of the carriage. In front of her nose dangled her mistress's bonnet, pinned to the luggage carrier, on her lap lay a puppy, her feet were raised on the boxes standing on the floor and just audibly tapping against them to the creaking of the coach-springs and the clatter of the window panes.

Having folded her hands on her knees and closed her eyes, the lady swayed feebly against the pillows placed at her back, and, frowning slightly, coughed inwardly. On her head she had a white nightcap, and a blue kerchief was tied round her delicate white throat. A straight line receding under the cap parted her light brown, extremely flat, pomaded hair, and there was something dry and deathly about the whiteness of the skin of that wide parting. Her features were delicate and handsome, but her skin was flabby and rather sallow, though there was a hectic flush on her cheeks. Her lips were dry and

---

* *Three Deaths*, written in 1858, was intended to exemplify the moral truth of pure art by contrasting the demands on life by the dying old lady and the simple acceptance of death by the peasant and the tree.

restless, her scanty eyelashes had no curl in them, and her cloth travelling coat fell in straight folds over a sunken breast. Though her eyes were closed her face bore an expression of weariness, irritation, and habitual suffering.

A footman, leaning on the arms of his seat, was dozing on the box. The mail-coach driver, shouting lustily, urged on his four big sweating horses, occasionally turning to the other driver who called to him from the calèche behind. The broad parallel tracks of the tyres spread themselves evenly and fast on the muddy, chalky surface of the road. The sky was grey and cold and a damp mist was settling on the fields and road. It was stuffy in the coach and there was a smell of Eau-de-Cologne and dust. The invalid drew back her head and slowly opened her beautiful dark eyes, which were large and brilliant.

'Again,' she said, nervously pushing away with her beautiful thin hand an end of her maid's cloak which had lightly touched her foot, and her mouth twitched painfully. Matrësha gathered up her cloak with both hands, rose on her strong legs, and seated herself farther away, while her fresh face grew scarlet. The lady, leaning with both hands on the seat, also tried to raise herself so as to sit up higher, but her strength failed her. Her mouth twisted and her whole face became distorted by a look of impotent malevolence and irony. 'You might at least help me! . . . No, don't bother! I can do it myself, only don't put your bags or anything behind me, for goodness' sake! . . . No, better not touch me since you don't know how to!' The lady closed her eyes and then, again quickly raising her eyelids, glared at the maid. Matrësha, looking at her, bit her red nether lip. A deep sigh rose from the invalid's chest and turned into a cough before it was completed. She turned away, puckered her face, and clutched her chest with both hands. When the coughing fit was over she once more closed her eyes and continued to sit motionless. The carriage and calèche entered a village. Matrësha stretched out her thick hand from under her shawl and crossed herself.

'What is it?' asked her mistress.

'A post-station, madam.'

'I am asking why you crossed yourself.'

'There's a church, madam.'

The invalid turned to the window and began slowly to cross herself, looking with large wide-open eyes at the big village church her carriage was passing.

The carriage and calèche both stopped at the post-station and the invalid's husband and doctor stepped out of the calèche and went up to the coach.

'How are you feeling?' asked the doctor, taking her pulse.

'Well, my dear, how are you—not tired?' asked her husband in French. 'Wouldn't you like to get out?'

Matrësha, gathering up the bundles, squeezed herself into a corner so as not to interfere with their conversation.

'Nothing much, just the same,' replied the invalid. 'I won't get out.'

Her husband after standing there a while went into the station-house, and Matrësha, too, jumped out of the carriage and ran on tiptoe across the mud and in at the gate.

'If I feel ill, it's no reason for you not to have lunch,' said the sick woman with a slight smile to the doctor, who was standing at her window.

'None of them has any thought for me,' she added to herself as soon as the doctor, having slowly walked away from her, ran quickly up the steps to the station-house. 'They are well, so they don't care. Oh, my God!'

'Well, Edward Ivánovich?' said the husband, rubbing his hands as he met the doctor with a merry smile. 'I have ordered the lunch-basket to be brought in. What do you think about it?'

'A capital idea,' replied the doctor.

'Well, how is she?' asked the husband with a sigh, lowering his voice and lifting his eyebrows.

'As I told you: it is impossible for her to reach Italy—God grant that she gets even as far as Moscow, especially in this weather.'

'But what are we to do? Oh, my God, my God!' and the husband hid his eyes with his hand. 'Bring it here!' he said to the man who had brought in the lunch-basket.

'She ought to have stayed at home,' said the doctor, shrugging his shoulders.

'But what could I do?' rejoined the husband. 'You know I used every possible means to get her to stay. I spoke of the expense, of our children whom we had to leave behind, and of my business affairs, but she would not listen to anything. She is making plans for life abroad as if she were in good health. To tell her of her condition would be to kill her.'

'But she is killed already—you must know that, Vasíli Dmítrich. A person can't live without lungs, and new lungs won't grow. It is sad and hard, but what is to be done? My business and yours is to see that her end is made as peaceful as possible. It's a priest who is needed for that.'

'Oh, my God! Think of my condition, having to remind her about her will. Come what may I can't tell her that, you know how good she is . . .'

'Still, try to persuade her to wait till the roads are fit for sledging,' said the doctor, shaking his head significantly, 'or something bad may happen on the journey.'

'Aksyúsha, hello Aksyúsha!' yelled the station-master's daughter, throwing her jacket over her head and stamping her feet on the muddy back porch. 'Come and let's have a look at the Shírkin lady: they say she is being taken abroad for a chest trouble, and I've never seen what consumptive people look like!'

She jumped onto the threshold, and seizing one another by the hand the two girls ran out of the gate. Checking their pace, they passed by the coach and looked in at the open window. The invalid turned her head towards them but, noticing their curiosity, frowned and turned away.

'De-arie me!' said the station-master's daughter, quickly turning her head away. 'What a wonderful beauty she must have been, and see what she's like now! It's dreadful. Did you see, did you, Aksyúsha?'

'Yes, how thin!' Aksyúsha agreed. 'Let's go and look again, as if we were going to the well. See, she has turned away, and I hadn't seen her yet. What a pity, Másha!'

'Yes, and what mud!' said Másha, and they both ran through the gate.

'Evidently I look frightful,' thought the invalid. 'If only I could get abroad quicker, quicker. I should soon recover there.'

'Well, my dear, how are you?' said her husband, approaching her and still chewing.

'Always the same question,' thought the invalid, 'and he himself is eating.'

'So-so,' she murmured through her closed teeth.

'You know, my dear, I'm afraid you'll get worse travelling in this weather, and Edward Ivánovich says so too. Don't you think we'd better turn back?'

She remained angrily silent.

'The weather will perhaps improve and the roads be fit for sledging; you will get better meanwhile, and we will all go together.'

'Excuse me. If I had not listened to you for so long, I should now at least have reached Berlin, and have been quite well.'

'What could be done, my angel? You know it was impossible. But now if you stayed another month you would get nicely better, I should have finished my business, and we could take the children with us.'

'The children are well, but I am not.'

'But do understand, my dear, that if in this weather you should get worse on the road. . . . At least you would be at home.'

'What of being at home? . . . To die at home?' answered the invalid, flaring up. But the word 'die' evidently frightened her, and she looked imploringly and questioningly at her husband. He hung his head and was silent. The invalid's mouth suddenly widened like a child's, and tears rolled down her cheeks. Her husband hid his face in his handkerchief and stepped silently away from the carriage.

'No, I will go on,' said the invalid, and lifting her eyes to the sky, she folded her hands and began whispering incoherent words: 'Oh, my God, what is it for?' she said, and her tears flowed faster. She prayed long and fervently, but her chest ached and felt as tight as before; the sky, the fields, and the road were just as grey and gloomy, and the autumnal mist fell, neither thickening nor lifting, and settled on the muddy road, the roofs, the carriage, and the sheepskin coats of the drivers, who talking in their strong merry voices were greasing the wheels and harnessing the horses.

## II

The carriage was ready but the driver still loitered. He had gone into the driver's room at the station. It was hot, stuffy, and dark there, with an oppressive smell of baking bread, cabbage, sheepskin garments, and humanity. Several drivers were sitting in the room, and a cook was busy at the oven, on the top of which lay a sick man wrapped in sheepskins.

'Uncle Theodore! I say, Uncle Theodore!' said the young driver, entering the room in his sheepskin coat with a whip stuck in his belt, and addressing the sick man.

'What do you want Theodore for, lazybones?' asked one of the drivers. 'There's your carriage waiting for you.'

'I want to ask for his boots; mine are quite worn out,' answered the young fellow, tossing back his hair and straightening the mittens tucked in his belt. 'Is he asleep? I say, Uncle Theodore!' he repeated, walking over to the oven.

'What is it?' answered a weak voice, and a lean face with a red beard looked down from the oven, while a broad, emaciated, pale, and hairy hand pulled up the coat over the dirty shirt covering his angular shoulder.

'Give me a drink, lad. . . . What is it you want?'

The lad handed him up a dipper with water.

'Well, you see, Theodore,' he said, stepping from foot to foot, 'I expect you don't need your new boots now; won't you let me have them? I don't suppose you'll go about any more.'

The sick man, lowering his weary head to the shiny dipper and immersing his sparse drooping moustache in the turbid water, drank feebly but eagerly. His matted beard was dirty, and his sunken clouded eyes had difficulty looking up at the lad's face. Having finished drinking he tried to lift his hand to wipe his wet lips, but he could not do so, and rubbed them on the sleeve of his coat instead. Silently, and breathing heavily through his nose, he looked straight into the lad's eyes, collecting his strength.

'But perhaps you have promised them to someone else?' asked the lad. 'If so, it's all right. The worst of it is, it's wet outside and I have to go about my work, so I said to myself: "Suppose I ask Theodore for his boots; I expect he doesn't need them." If you need them yourself—just say so.'

Something began to rumble and gurgle in the sick man's chest; he doubled up and began to choke with an abortive cough in his throat.

'Need them indeed!' the cook snapped out unexpectedly so as to be heard by the whole room. 'He hasn't come down from the oven for more than a month! Hear how he's choking —it makes me ache inside just to hear him. What does he want with boots? They won't bury him in new boots. And it was time long ago—God forgive me the sin! See how he chokes. He ought to be taken into the other room or somewhere. They say there are hospitals in the town. Is it right that he should take up the whole corner?—there's no more to be said. I've no room at all, and yet they expect cleanliness!'

'Hullo, Sergéy! Come along and take your place, the gentlefolk are waiting!' shouted the drivers' overseer, looking in at the door.

Sergéy was about to go without waiting for a reply, but the sick man, while coughing, let him understand by a look that he wanted to give him an answer.

'Take my boots, Sergéy,' he said when he had mastered the cough and rested a moment. 'But listen. . . . Buy a stone for me when I die,' he added hoarsely.

'Thank you, uncle. Then I'll take them, and I'll buy a stone for sure.'

'There, lads, you heard that?' the sick man managed to utter, and then bent double again and began to choke.

'All right, we heard,' said one of the drivers. 'Go and take your seat, Sergéy, there's the overseer running back. The Shírkin lady is ill, you know.'

Sergéy quickly pulled off his unduly big, dilapidated boots and threw them under a bench. Uncle Theodore's new boots just fitted him, and having put them on he went to the carriage with his eyes fixed on his feet.

'What fine boots! Let me grease them,' said a driver, who held some axle-grease in his hand, as Sergéy climbed onto the box and gathered up the reins. 'Did he give them to you for nothing?'

'Why, are you envious?' Sergéy replied, rising and wrapping the skirts of his coat under his legs. 'Off with you! Gee up, my beauties!' he shouted to the horses, flourishing the whip, and the carriage and calèche with their occupants, portmanteaux, and trunks rolled rapidly along the wet road and disappeared in the grey autumnal mist.

The sick driver was left on the top of the oven in the stuffy room and, unable to relieve himself by coughing, turned with an effort onto his other side and became silent.

Till late in the evening people came in and out of the room and dined there. The sick man made no sound. When night came, the cook climbed up onto the oven and stretched over his legs to get down her sheepskin coat.

'Don't be cross with me, Nastásya,' said the sick man. 'I shall soon leave your corner empty.'

'All right, all right, never mind,' muttered Nastásya. 'But what is it that hurts you? Tell me, uncle.'

'My whole inside has wasted away. God knows what it is!'

'I suppose your throat hurts when you cough?'

'Everything hurts. My death has come—that's how it is. Oh, oh, oh!' moaned the sick man.

'Cover up your feet like this,' said Nastásya, drawing his coat over him as she climbed down from the oven.

A night-light burnt dimly in the room. Nastásya and some ten drivers slept on the floor or on the benches, loudly snoring. The sick man groaned feebly, coughed, and turned about on the oven. Towards morning he grew quite quiet.

'I had a queer dream last night,' said Nastásya next morning, stretching herself in the dim light. 'I dreamt that Uncle Theodore got down from the oven and went out to chop wood. "Come, Nastásya," he says, "I'll help you!" and I say, "How can you chop wood now?", but he just seizes the axe and begins chopping quickly, quickly, so that the chips fly all about. "Why," I say, "haven't you been ill?" "No," he says, "I am well," and he swings the axe so that I was quite frightened. I gave a cry and woke up. I wonder whether he is dead! Uncle Theodore! I say, Uncle Theodore!'

Theodore did not answer.

'True enough he may have died. I'll go and see,' said one of the drivers, waking up.

The lean hand covered with reddish hair that hung down from the oven was pale and cold.

'I'll go and tell the station-master,' said the driver. 'I think he is dead.'

Theodore had no relatives: he was from some distant place. They buried him next day in the new cemetery beyond the wood, and Nastásya went on for days telling everybody of her dream, and of having been the first to discover that Uncle Theodore was dead.

III

Spring had come. Rivulets of water hurried down the wet streets of the city, gurgling between lumps of frozen manure; the colours of the people's clothes as they moved along the streets looked vivid and their voices sounded shrill. Behind the garden-fences the buds on the trees were swelling and their branches were just audibly swaying in the fresh breeze. Everywhere transparent drops were forming and falling. . . . The sparrows chirped, and fluttered awkwardly with their little wings. On the sunny side of the street, on the fences, houses, and trees, everything was in motion and sparkling. There was joy and youth everywhere in the sky, on the earth, and in the hearts of men.

In one of the chief streets fresh straw had been strewn on

the road before a large, important house, where the invalid
who had been in a hurry to go abroad lay dying.

At the closed door of her room stood the invalid's husband
and an elderly woman. On the sofa a priest sat with bowed
head, holding something wrapped in his stole. In a corner of
the room the sick woman's old mother lay on an invalid chair
weeping bitterly: beside her stood one maidservant holding
a clean handkerchief, waiting for her to ask for it; while another was rubbing her temples with something and blowing
under the old lady's cap onto her grey head.

'Well, may Christ aid you, dear friend,' the husband said
to the elderly woman who stood near him at the door. 'She
has such confidence in you and you know so well how to
talk to her, so persuade her as well as you can, my dear—go
to her.' He was about to open the door, but her cousin stopped
him, pressing her handkerchief several times to her eyes and
giving her head a shake.

'Well, I don't think I look as if I had been crying now,'
said she and, opening the door herself, went in.

The husband was in great agitation and seemed quite distracted. He walked towards the old woman, but while still
several steps from her turned back, walked about the room,
and went up to the priest. The priest looked at him, raised
his eyebrows to heaven, and sighed: his thick, greyish beard
also rose as he sighed and then came down again.

'My God, my God!' said the husband.

'What is to be done?' said the priest with a sigh, and again
his eyebrows and beard rose and fell.

'And her mother is here!' said the husband almost in despair. 'She won't be able to bear it. You see, loving her as
she does . . . I don't know! If you would only try to comfort
her, Father, and persuade her to go away.'

The priest got up and went to the old woman.

'It is true, no one can appreciate a mother's heart,' he
said—'but God is merciful.'

The old woman's face suddenly twitched all over, and she
began to hiccup hysterically.

'God is merciful,' the priest continued when she grew a little calmer. 'Let me tell you of a patient in my parish who was much worse than Mary Dmítrievna, and a simple tradesman cured her in a short time with various herbs. That tradesman is even now in Moscow. I told Vasíli Dmítrich—we might try him. . . . It would at any rate comfort the invalid. To God all is possible.'

'No, she will not live,' said the old woman. 'God is taking her instead of me,' and the hysterical hiccuping grew so violent that she fainted.

The sick woman's husband hid his face in his hands and ran out of the room.

In the passage the first person he met was his six-year-old son, who was running full speed after his younger sister.

'Won't you order the children to be taken to their mamma?' asked the nurse.

'No, she doesn't want to see them—it would upset her.'

The boy stopped a moment, looked intently into his father's face, then gave a kick and ran on, shouting merrily.

'She pretends to be the black horse, Papa!' he shouted, pointing to his sister.

Meanwhile in the other room the cousin sat down beside the invalid, and tried by skilful conversation to prepare her for the thought of death. The doctor was mixing a draught at another window.

The patient, in a white dressing gown, sat up in bed supported all round by pillows, and looked at her cousin in silence.

'Ah, my dear friend,' she said, unexpectedly interrupting her, 'don't prepare me! Don't treat me like a child. I am a Christian. I know it all. I know I have not long to live, and know that if my husband had listened to me sooner I should now have been in Italy and perhaps—no, certainly—should have been well. Everybody told him so. But what is to be done? Evidently this is God's wish. We have all sinned heavily. I know that, but I trust in God's mercy everybody will be forgiven, probably all will be forgiven. I try to understand myself. I have many sins to answer for, dear friend, but

then how much I have had to suffer! I try to bear my sufferings patiently . . .'

'Then shall I call the priest, my dear? You will feel still
more comfortable after receiving communion,' said her cousin.

The sick woman bent her head in assent.

'God forgive me, sinner that I am!' she whispered.

The cousin went out and signalled with her eyes to the
priest.

'She is an angel!' she said to the husband, with tears in her
eyes. The husband burst into tears; the priest went into the
next room; the invalid's mother was still unconscious, and all
was silent there. Five minutes later he came out again, and
after taking off his stole, straightened out his hair.

'Thank God she is calmer now,' she said, 'and wishes to see
you.'

The cousin and the husband went into the sickroom. The
invalid was silently weeping, gazing at an icon.

'I congratulate you, my dear,'[1] said her husband.

'Thank you! How well I feel now, what inexpressible sweetness I feel!' said the sick woman, and a soft smile played on
her thin lips. 'How merciful God is! Is He not? Merciful and
all powerful!' and again she looked at the icon with eager
entreaty and her eyes full of tears.

Then suddenly, as if she remembered something, she beck-
oned to her husband to come closer.

'You never want to do what I ask . . .' she said in a feeble
and dissatisfied voice.

The husband, craning his neck, listened to her humbly.

'What is it, my dear?'

'How many times have I not said that these doctors don't
know anything; there are simple women who can heal, and
who do cure. The priest told me . . . there is also a tradesman . . . Send!'

'For whom, my dear?'

'O God, you don't want to understand anything!' . . . And

---

[1] It was customary in Russia to congratulate people who had received communion.

the sick woman's face puckered and she closed her eyes.

The doctor came up and took her hand. Her pulse was beating more feebly. He glanced at the husband. The invalid noticed that gesture and looked round in affright. The cousin turned away and began to cry.

'Don't cry, don't torture yourself and me,' said the patient. 'Don't take from me the last of my tranquillity.'

'You are an angel,' said the cousin, kissing her hand.

'No, kiss me here! Only dead people are kissed on the hand. My God, my God!'

That same evening the patient was a corpse, and the body lay in a coffin in the music room of the large house. A deacon sat alone in that big room reading the psalms of David through his nose in a monotonous voice. A bright light from the wax candles in their tall silver candlesticks fell on the pale brow of the dead woman, on her heavy wax-like hands, on the stiff folds of the pall which brought out in awesome relief the knees and the toes. The deacon without understanding the words read on monotonously, and in the quiet room the words sounded strangely and died away. Now and then from a distant room came the sounds of children's voices and the patter of their feet.

'Thou hidest thy face, they are troubled,' said the psalter. 'Thou takest away their breath, they die and return to dust. Thou sendest forth thy spirit, they are created: and thou renewest the face of the earth. The glory of the Lord shall endure for ever.'

The dead woman's face looked stern and majestic. Neither in the clear cold brow nor in the firmly closed lips was there any movement. She seemed all attention. But had she even now understood those solemn words?

## IV

A month later a stone chapel was being erected over the grave of the deceased woman. Over the driver's tomb there was still no stone, and only the light green grass sprouted on the

mound which served as the only token of the past existence
of a man.

'It will be a sin, Sergéy,' said the cook at the station-house
one day, 'if you don't buy a stone for Theodore. You kept
saying "It's winter, it's winter!" but why don't you keep your
word now? You know I witnessed it. He has already come back
once to ask you to do it; if you don't buy him one, he'll come
again and choke you.'

'But why? I'm not backing out of it,' replied Sergéy. 'I'll buy
a stone as I said I would, and give a ruble and a half for it.
I haven't forgotten it, but it has to be fetched. When I happen to be in town I'll buy one.'

'You might at least put up a cross—you ought to—else it's
really wrong,' interposed an old driver. 'You know you are
wearing his boots.'

'Where can I get a cross? I can't cut one out of a log.'

'What do you mean, can't cut one out of a log? You take
an axe and go into the forest early, and you can cut one there.
Cut down a young ash or something like that, and you can
make a cross of it . . . you may have to treat the forester to
vodka; but you can't afford to treat him for every trifle. There
now, I broke my splinter-bar and went and cut a new one,
and nobody said a word.'

Early in the morning, as soon as it was daybreak, Sergéy
took an axe and went into the wood.

A cold white cover of dew, which was still falling un-
touched by the sun, lay on everything. The east was imperceptibly growing brighter, reflecting its pale light on the vault
of heaven still veiled by a covering of clouds. Not a blade of
grass below, nor a leaf on the topmost branches of the trees,
stirred. Only occasionally a sound of wings amid the brush-
wood, or a rustling on the ground, broke the silence of the
forest. Suddenly a strange sound, foreign to Nature, resounded
and died away at the outskirts of the forest. Again the sound
was heard, and was rhythmically repeated at the foot of the
trunk of one of the motionless trees. A tree-top began to tremble in an unwonted manner, its juicy leaves whispered some-

thing, and the robin who had been sitting in one of its branches fluttered twice from place to place with a whistle, and jerking its tail sat down on another tree.

The axe at the bottom gave off a more and more muffled sound, sappy white chips were scattered on the dewy grass and a slight creaking was heard above the sound of the blows. The tree, shuddering in its whole body, bent down and quickly rose again, vibrating with fear on its roots. For an instant all was still, but the tree bent again, a crashing sound came from its trunk, and with its branches breaking and its boughs hanging down it fell with its crown on the damp earth.

The sounds of the axe and of the footsteps were silenced. The robin whistled and flitted higher. A twig which it brushed with its wings shook a little and then with all its foliage grew still like the rest. The trees flaunted the beauty of their motionless branches still more joyously in the newly cleared space.

The first sunbeams, piercing the translucent cloud, shone out and spread over earth and sky. The mist began to quiver like waves in the hollows, the dew sparkled and played on the verdure, the transparent cloudlets grew whiter, and hurriedly dispersed over the deepening azure vault of the sky. The birds stirred in the thicket and, as though bewildered, twittered joyfully about something; the sappy leaves whispered gladly and peacefully on the treetops, and the branches of those that were living began to rustle slowly and majestically over the dead and prostrate tree.

# STRIDER:

## *The Story of a Horse*[*]

◇◇◇◇◇◇◇

### I

Higher and higher receded the sky, wider and wider spread
the streak of dawn, whiter grew the pallid silver of the dew,
more lifeless the sickle of the moon, and more vocal the forest.
People began to get up, and in the owner's stable-yard the
sounds of snorting, the rustling of litter, and even the shrill
angry neighing of horses crowded together and at variance
about something, grew more and more frequent.

'Hold on! Plenty of time! Hungry?' said the old huntsman,
quickly opening the creaking gate. 'Where are you going?'
he shouted, threateningly raising his arm at a mare that was
pushing through the gate.

The keeper, Nester, wore a short Cossack coat with an
ornamental leather girdle, had a whip slung over his shoulder,
and a hunk of bread wrapped in a cloth stuck in his girdle.
He carried a saddle and bridle in his arms.

The horses were not at all frightened or offended at the

---

[*] For some time Tolstoy had contemplated writing a story about a
horse and in the early months of 1863 he tried his hand at it. The
tale is based on the life of a real horse, Kholstomer. Apparently dissatisfied with the results, Tolstoy put the manuscript aside. Twenty-
two years later, his wife, who was then editing the first collected
edition of her husband's works, asked permission to print this piece.
He agreed, and after he had reworked it, the story appeared in
1886.

horseman's sarcastic tone: they pretended that it was all the same to them and moved leisurely away from the gate; only one old brown mare, with a thick mane, laid back an ear and quickly turned her back on him. A small filly standing behind her was not at all concerned in the matter and took this opportunity to whinny and kick out at a horse that happened to be near.

'Now then!' shouted the keeper still louder and more sternly, and he went to the opposite corner of the yard.

Of all the horses in the enclosure (there were about a hundred of them) a piebald gelding, standing by himself in a corner under the penthouse and licking an oak post with half-closed eyes, displayed least impatience.

It is impossible to say what flavour the piebald gelding found in the post, but his expression was serious and thoughtful while he licked.

'Stop that!' shouted the groom, drawing nearer to him and putting the saddle and a glossy saddle-cloth on the manure heap beside him.

The piebald gelding stopped licking, and without moving gave Nester a long look. The gelding did not laugh, nor grow angry, nor frown, but his whole belly heaved with a profound sigh and he turned away. The horseman put his arm round the gelding's neck and placed the bridle on him.

'What are you sighing for?' said Nester.

The gelding switched his tail as if to say, 'Nothing in particular, Nester!' Nester put the saddle-cloth and saddle on him, and this caused the gelding to lay back his ears, probably to express dissatisfaction, but he was only called a 'good-for-nothing' for it and his saddle-girth was tightened.

At this the gelding blew himself out, but a finger was thrust into his mouth and a knee hit him in the stomach, so that he had to let out his breath. In spite of this, when the saddle-cloth was being buckled on he again laid back his ears and even looked round. Though he knew it would do no good he considered it necessary to show that it was disagreeable to him and that he would always express his dissatisfaction with it. When he was saddled he thrust forward his swollen off

foot and began champing his bit, this too for some reason of
his own, for he ought to have known by that time that a bit
cannot have any flavour at all.

Nester mounted the gelding by the short stirrup, unwound
his long whip, straightened his coat out from under his knee,
seated himself in the manner peculiar to coachmen, huntsmen,
and horsemen, and jerked the reins. The gelding lifted his
head to show his readiness to go where ordered, but did not
move. He knew that before starting there would be much
shouting, and that Nester, from the seat on his back, would
give many orders to Váska, the other groom, and to the horses.
And Nester did shout: 'Váska! Hullo, Váska. Have you let
out the brood mares? Where are you going, you devil? Now
then! Are you asleep . . . Open the gate! Let the brood
mares get out first!'—and so on.

The gate creaked. Váska, cross and sleepy, stood at the
gate-post holding his horse by the bridle and letting the other
horses pass out. The horses followed one another and stepped
carefully over the straw, smelling at it: fillies, yearling colts
with their manes and tails cut, suckling foals, and mares in
foal carrying their burden heedfully, passed one by one
through the gateway. The fillies sometimes crowded together
in twos and threes, throwing their heads across one another's
backs and hitting their hoofs against the gate, for which they
received a rebuke from the grooms every time. The foals
sometimes darted under the legs of the wrong mares and
neighed loudly in response to the short whinny of their own
mothers.

A playful filly, directly she had got out at the gate, bent
her head sideways, kicked up her hind legs, and squealed,
but all the same she did not dare to run ahead of old dap-
pled Zhuldýba who at a slow and heavy pace, swinging her
belly from side to side, marched as usual ahead of all the
other horses.

In a few minutes the enclosure that had been so animated
became deserted, the posts stood gloomily under the empty
penthouse, and only trampled straw mixed with manure was
to be seen. Used as he was to that desolate sight it probably

depressed the piebald gelding. As if making a bow he slowly lowered his head and raised it again, sighed as deeply as the tightly drawn girth would allow, and hobbling along on his stiff and crooked legs shambled after the herd, bearing old Nester on his bony back.

'I know that as soon as we get out on the road he will begin to strike a light and smoke his wooden pipe with its brass mountings and little chain,' thought the gelding. 'I am glad of it because early in the morning when it is dewy I like that smell, it reminds me of much that was pleasant; but it's annoying that when his pipe is between his teeth the old man always begins to swagger and thinks himself somebody and sits sideways, always sideways—and that side hurts. However, it can't be helped! Suffering for the pleasure of others is nothing new to me. I have even begun to find a certain equine pleasure in it. Let him swagger, poor fellow! Of course he can only do that when he is alone and no one sees him—let him sit sideways!' thought the gelding, and stepping carefully on his crooked legs he went along the middle of the road.

## II

Having driven the horses to the riverside where they were to graze, Nester dismounted and unsaddled. Meanwhile the herd had begun gradually to spread over the untrampled meadow, covered with dew and by the mist that rose from it and the encircling river.

When he had taken the bridle off the piebald gelding, Nester scratched him under the neck, in response to which the gelding expressed his gratitude and satisfaction by closing his eyes. 'He likes it, the old dog!' muttered Nester. The gelding however did not really care for the scratching at all, and pretended that it was agreeable merely out of courtesy. He nodded his head in assent to Nester's words; but suddenly Nester quite unexpectedly and without any reason, perhaps imagining that too much familiarity might give the gelding a wrong idea of his importance, pushed the gelding's head away from himself without any warning and, swinging the bridle, struck him painfully with the buckle on his lean leg, and then without saying a word went up the hillock to a tree-stump beside which he generally seated himself.

Though this action grieved the piebald gelding he gave no indication of it, but leisurely switching his scanty tail, sniffed at something and, biting off some wisps of grass merely to divert his mind, walked to the river. He took no notice whatever of the antics of the young mares, colts, and foals around him, who were filled with the joy of the morning; and knowing that, especially at his age, it is healthier to have a good drink on an empty stomach and to eat afterwards, he chose a spot where the bank was widest and least steep, and wetting his hoofs and fetlocks, dipped his muzzle in the water and began to suck it up through his torn lips, to expand his filling sides, and from pleasure to switch his scanty tail with its half bald stump.

An aggressive chestnut filly, who always teased the old fellow and did all kinds of unpleasant things to him, now came up to him in the water as if attending to some business of her own, but in reality merely to foul the water before his nose. But the piebald gelding, who had already had his fill, as though not noticing the filly's intention quietly drew one foot after the other out of the mud in which they had sunk, jerked his head, and stepping aside from the youthful crowd started grazing. Sprawling his feet apart in different ways and not trampling the grass needlessly, he went on eating without unbending himself for exactly three hours. Having eaten till his belly hung down from his steep skinny ribs like a sack, he balanced himself equally on his four sore legs so as to have as little pain as possible, especially in his off foreleg which was the weakest, and fell asleep.

Old age is sometimes majestic, sometimes ugly, and sometimes pathetic. But old age can be both ugly and majestic, and the gelding's old age was just of that kind.

He was tall, rather over fifteen hands high. His spots were black, or rather they had been black, but had now turned a dirty brown. He had three spots, one on his head, starting from a crooked bald patch on the side of his nose and reaching half-way down his neck. His long mane, filled with burrs, was white in some places and brownish in others. Another spot extended down his off side to the middle of his belly, the third, on his croup, touched part of his tail and went half-way down his quarters. The rest of the tail was whitish and speckled. The big bony head, with deep hollows over the eyes and a black hanging lip that had been torn at some time, hung low and heavily on his neck, which was so lean that it looked as though it were carved of wood. The pendant lip revealed a blackish, bitten tongue and the yellow stumps of the worn lower teeth. The ears, one of which was slit, hung low on either side, and only occasionally moved lazily to drive away the pestering flies. Of the forelock, one tuft of which was still long hung back behind an ear; the uncovered forehead was dented and rough, and the skin hung down like bags on his broad jawbones. The veins of his neck had grown knotty, and twitched and shuddered at every touch of a fly. The expression of his face was one of stern patience, thoughtfulness, and suffering.

His forelegs were crooked to a bow at the knees, there were swellings over both hoofs, and on one leg, on which the piebald spot reached half-way down, there was a swelling at the knee as big as a fist. The hind legs were in better condition, but apparently long ago his haunches had been so rubbed that in places the hair would not grow again. The leanness of his body made all four legs look disproportionately long. The ribs, though straight, were so exposed and the skin so tightly drawn over them, that it seemed to have dried fast to the spaces between. His back and withers were covered with marks of old lashings, and there was a fresh sore behind, still swollen and festering; the black dock of his tail, which showed the vertebrae, hung down long and almost bare. On his dark-brown croup—near the tail—was a scar, as though of a bite, the size of a man's hand and covered with white hair. Another scarred sore was visible on one of his shoulders. His tail and hocks were dirty because of chronic bowel troubles. The hair on the whole body, though short, stood out straight. Yet in spite of the hideous old age of this horse one involuntarily paused to reflect when one saw him, and an expert would have said at once that he had been a remarkably fine horse in his day. The expert would even have said that there was only one breed in Russia that could furnish such breadth of bone, such immense knees, such hoofs, such slender cannons, such a well-shaped neck, and above all such a skull, such eyes—large, black, and clear—and such a thoroughbred network of veins on head and neck, and such delicate skin and hair.

There was really something majestic in that horse's figure and in the terrible union in him of repulsive indications of decrepitude, emphasized by the motley colour of his hair, and his manner which expressed the self-confidence and calm assurance that go with beauty and strength. Like a living ruin he stood alone in the midst of the dewy meadow, while not far from him could be heard the tramping, snorting and youthful neighing and whinnying of the scattered herd.

### III

The sun had risen above the forest and now shone brightly on the grass and the winding river. The dew was drying up and condensing into drops, the last of the morning mist was dispersing like tiny smoke-clouds. The cloudlets were becoming curly but there was as yet no wind. Beyond the river the verdant rye stood bristling, its ears curling into little horns, and there was an odour of fresh verdure and blossom. A cuckoo called rather hoarsely from the forest, and Nester, lying on his back in the grass, was counting the calls to ascertain how many years he still had to live. The larks were rising over the rye and the meadow. A belated hare, finding himself among the horses, leaped into the open, sat down by a bush, and pricked his ears to listen. Váska fell asleep with his head in the grass, the fillies, making a still wider circle about him, scattered over the field below. The old mares went about snorting, and made a shining track across the dewy grass, always choosing a place where no one would disturb them. They no longer grazed, but only nibbled at choice tufts of grass. The whole herd was moving imperceptibly in one direction.

And again it was old Zhuldýba who, stepping sedately in front of the others, showed the possibility of going farther. Black Múshka, a young mare who had foaled for the first time, with uplifted tail kept whinnying and snorting at her bluish foal; the young filly Satin, sleek and brilliant, bending her head till her black silky forelock hid her forehead and eyes, played with the grass, nipping off a little and tossing it and stamping her leg with its shaggy fetlock all wet with dew. One of the older foals, probably imagining he was playing some kind of game, with his curly tail raised like a plume, ran for the twenty-sixth time round his mother, who quietly went on grazing, having grown accustomed to her son's ways, and only occasionally glanced askance at him with one of her large black eyes.

One of the very youngest foals, black, with a big head, a tuft sticking up in astonishment between his ears, and a little tail still twisted to one side as it had been in his mother's womb, stood motionless, his ears pricked and his dull eyes fixed, gazing at the frisking and prancing foal—whether admiring or condemning him it is hard to say. Some of the foals were sucking and butting with their noses, some—heaven knows why—despite their mothers' call were running at an awkward little trot in quite the opposite direction as if searching for something, and then, for no apparent reason, stopping and neighing with desperate shrillness. Some lay on their sides in a row, some were learning to eat grass, some again were scratching themselves behind their ears with their hind legs. Two mares still in foal were walking apart from the rest, and while slowly moving their legs continued to graze. The others evidently respected their condition, and none of the young ones ventured to come near to disturb them. If any saucy youngsters thought of approaching them, the mere movement of an ear or tail sufficed to show them all how improper such behaviour was.

The colts and yearling fillies, pretending to be grown up and sedate, rarely jumped or joined the merry company. They

385 )) *Strider: The Story of a Horse*

grazed in a dignified manner, curving their close-cropped swan-like necks, and flourished their little broom-like tails as if they also had long ones. Just like the grown-ups they lay down, rolled over, or rubbed one another. The merriest group was composed of the two- and three-year-old fillies and mares not yet in foal. They almost always walked about together like a separate merry virgin crowd. Among them you could hear sounds of tramping, whinnying, neighing, and snorting. They drew close together, put their heads over one another's necks, sniffed at one another, jumped, and sometimes at a semi-trot semi-amble, with tails lifted like an oriflamme, raced proudly and coquettishly past their companions. The most beautiful and spirited of them was the mischievous chestnut filly. What she devised the others did; wherever she went the whole crowd of beauties followed. That morning the naughty one was in a specially playful mood. She was seized with a joyous fit, just as human beings sometimes are. Already at the riverside she had played a trick on the old gelding, and after that she ran along through the water pretending to be frightened by something, gave a hoarse squeal, and raced full speed into the field so that Váska had to gallop after her and the others who followed her. Then after grazing a little she began rolling, then teasing the old mares by dashing in front of them, then she drove away a small foal from its dam and chased it as if meaning to bite it. Its mother was frightened and stopped grazing, while the little foal cried in a piteous tone, but the mischievous one did not touch him at all, she only wanted to frighten him and give a performance for the benefit of her companions, who watched her escapade approvingly. Then she set out to turn the head of a little roan horse with which a peasant was ploughing in a rye-field far beyond the river. She stopped, proudly lifted her head somewhat to one side, shook herself, and neighed in a sweet, tender, long-drawn voice. Mischief, feeling, and a certain sadness, were expressed in that call. There was in it the desire for and the promise of love, and a pining for it.

'There in the thick reeds is a corn-crake running backwards and forwards and calling passionately to his mate; there is the

cuckoo, and the quails are singing of love, and the flowers are
sending their fragrant dust to each other by the wind. And I
too am young and beautiful and strong,' the mischievous one's
voice said, 'but it has not yet been allowed me to know the
sweetness of that feeling, and not only to experience it, but no
lover—not a single one—has ever seen me!'

And this neighing, sad and youthful and fraught with feeling, was borne over the lowland and the field to the roan
horse far away. He pricked up his ears and stopped. The
peasant kicked him with his bast shoe, but the little horse
was so enchanted by the silvery sound of the distant neighing
that he neighed too. The peasant grew angry, pulled at the
reins, and kicked the little roan so painfully in the stomach
with his bast shoes that he could not finish his neigh and
walked on. But the little roan felt a sense of sweetness and sadness, and for a long time the sounds of unfinished and passionate neighing, and of the peasant's angry voice, were
carried from the distant rye-field over to the herd.

If the sound of her voice alone so overpowered the little
roan that he forgot his duty, what would have happened had
he seen the naughty beauty as she stood pricking her ears,
breathing in the air with dilated nostrils, ready to run, trembling with her whole beautiful body, and calling to him?

But the mischievous one did not brood long over her impressions. When the neighing of the roan died away she gave
another scornful neigh, lowered her head and began pawing
the ground, and then she went to wake and to tease the piebald gelding. The piebald gelding was the constant martyr
and butt of those happy youngsters. He suffered more from
them than at the hands of men. He did no harm to either.
People needed him, but why should these young horses torment him?

## IV

He was old, they were young; he was lean, they were sleek;
he was miserable, they were gay; and so he was quite alien
to them, an outsider, an utterly different creature whom it

was impossible for them to pity. Horses only have pity on themselves, and very occasionally on those in whose skins they can easily imagine themselves to be. But was it the old gelding's fault that he was old, poor and ugly? . . .

One might think not, but in equine ethics it was, and only those were right who were strong, young, and happy—those who had life still before them, whose every muscle quivered with superfluous energy, and whose tails stood erect. Maybe the piebald gelding himself understood this and in his quiet moments was ready to agree that it was his fault that he had already lived his life, and that he had to pay for that life; but after all he was a horse and often could not suppress a sense of resentment, sadness, and indignation, when he looked at those youngsters who tormented him for what would befall them all at the end of their lives. Another cause of the horses' lack of pity was their aristocratic pride. Every one of them traced back its pedigree, through father or mother, to the famous Creamy, while the piebald was of unknown parentage. He was a chance comer, purchased three years before at a fair for eighty assignat rubles.

The chestnut filly, as if taking a stroll, passed close by the piebald gelding's nose and pushed him. He knew at once what it was, and without opening his eyes laid back his ears and showed his teeth. The filly wheeled round as if to kick him. The gelding opened his eyes and stepped aside. He did not want to sleep any more and began to graze. The mischief-maker, followed by her companions, again approached the gelding. A very stupid two-year-old white-spotted filly who always imitated the chestnut in everything, went up with her and, as imitators always do, went to greater lengths than the instigator. The chestnut always went up as if intent on business of her own, and passed by the gelding's nose without looking at him, so that he really did not know whether to be angry or not, and that was really funny.

She did the same now, but the white-spotted one, who followed her and had grown particularly lively, bumped right against the gelding with her chest. He again showed his teeth, whinnied, and with an agility one could not have expected of him, rushed after her and bit her flank. The white-spotted one kicked out with all her strength and dealt the old horse a heavy blow on his thin bare ribs. He snorted heavily and was going to rush at her again, but bethought himself and drawing a deep sigh stepped aside. The whole crowd of young ones must have taken as a personal affront the impertinence the piebald gelding had permitted himself to offer to the white-spotted one, and for the rest of the day did not let him graze in peace for a moment, so that the keeper had to quieten them several times and could not understand what had come over them.

The gelding felt so offended that he went up himself to Nester when the old man was getting ready to drive the horses home, and felt happier and quieter when he was saddled and the old man had mounted him.

God knows what the gelding was thinking as he carried old Nester on his back: whether he thought bitterly of the pertinacious and merciless youngsters, or forgave his tormentors with the contemptuous and silent pride suited to old age. At all events he did not betray his thoughts till he reached home.

That evening, as Nester drove the horses past the huts of the domestic serfs, he noticed a peasant horse and cart tethered to his porch: some friends had come to see him. When driving the horses in he was in such a hurry that he let the gelding in without unsaddling him and, shouting to Váska to do it, shut the gate and went to his friends. Whether because of the affront to the white-spotted filly—Creamy's great-grand-daughter—by that 'mangy trash' bought at the horse fair, who did not know his father or mother, and the consequent outrage to the aristocratic sentiment of the whole herd, or because the gelding with his high saddle and without a rider presented a strangely fantastic spectacle to the horses, at any rate something quite unusual occurred that night in the paddock. All the horses, young and old, ran after the gelding, showing their teeth and driving him all round the yard; one heard the sound of hoofs striking against his bare ribs, and his deep groaning. He could no longer endure this, nor could he avoid the blows. He stopped in the middle of the paddock, his face expressing first the repulsive weak malevolence of helpless old age, and then despair: he dropped his ears, and then something happened that caused all the horses to quiet down. The oldest of the mares, Vyazapúrikha, went up to the gelding, sniffed at him and sighed. The gelding sighed too . . .

v

In the middle of the moonlit paddock stood the tall gaunt figure of the gelding, still wearing the high saddle with its prominent peak at the bow. The horses stood motionless and in deep silence around him as if they were learning something new and unexpected. And they had learnt something new and unexpected.

This is what they learnt from him . . .

## First Night

Yes, I am the son of Affable I and of Bába. My pedigree name is Muzhík, and I was nicknamed Strider by the crowd because of my long and sweeping strides, the like of which was nowhere to be found in all Russia. There is no more thoroughbred horse in the world. I should never have told you this. What good would it have done? You would never have recognized me: even Vyazapúrikha, who was with me in Khrénovo, did not recognize me till now. You would not have believed me if Vyazapúrikha were not here to be my witness, and I should never have told you this. I don't need equine sympathy. But you wished it. Yes, I am that Strider whom connoisseurs are looking for and cannot find—that Strider whom the count himself knew and got rid of from his stud because I outran Swan, his favourite.

When I was born I did not know what *piebald* meant—I thought it was just a horse. I remember that the first remark we heard about my colour struck my mother and me deeply.

I suppose I was born in the night; by the morning, having been licked by my mother, I already stood on my feet. I remember I kept wanting something and that everything seemed very surprising and yet very simple. Our stalls opened into a long warm passage and had latticed doors through which everything could be seen.

My mother offered me her teats but I was still so innocent that I poked my nose now between her forelegs and now under her udder. Suddenly she glanced at the latticed door and lifting her leg over me stepped aside. The groom on duty was looking into our stall through the lattice.

'Why, Bába has foaled!' he said, and began to draw the bolt. He came in over the fresh bedding and put his arms round me. 'Just look, Tarás!' he shouted, 'what a piebald he is—a regular magpie!'

I darted away from him and fell on my knees.

'Look at him—the little devil!'

My mother became disquieted, but did not take my part, she only stepped a little to one side with a very deep sigh. Other grooms came to look at me, and one of them ran to tell the stud groom.

Everybody laughed when they looked at my spots, and they gave me all kinds of strange names, but neither I nor my mother understood those words. Till then there had been no piebalds among all my relatives. We did not think there was anything bad in it. Everybody even then praised my strength and my form.

'See what a frisky fellow!' said the groom. 'There's no holding him.'

Before long the stud groom came and began to express astonishment at my colour; he even seemed aggrieved.

'And who does the little monster take after?' he said. 'The general won't keep him in the stud. Oh, Bába, you have played me a trick!' he addressed my mother. 'You might at least have dropped one with just a star—but this one is all piebald!'

My mother did not reply, but as usual on such occasions drew a sigh.

'And what devil does he take after—he's just like a peasant-horse!' he continued. 'He can't be left in the stud—he'd shame us. But he's well built—very well!' said he, and so did everyone who saw me.

A few days later the general himself came and looked at me, and again everyone seemed horrified at something, and abused me and my mother for the colour of my hair. 'But he's a fine colt—very fine!' said all who saw me.

Until spring we all lived separately in the brood mares' stable, each with our mother, and only occasionally when the snow on the stable roofs began to melt in the sun were we let out with our mothers into the large paddock strewn with fresh straw. There I first came to know all my near and my distant relations. Here I saw all the famous mares of the day coming out from different doors with their little foals. There was the old mare Dutch, Fly (Creamy's daughter), Ruddy the riding-horse, Wellwisher—all celebrities at that time. They all gathered together with their foals, walking about in the sunshine, rolling on the fresh straw and sniffing at one another like ordinary horses. I have never forgotten the sight of that paddock full of the beauties of that day. It seems strange to you to think, and hard to believe, that I was ever young and frisky, but it was so. This same Vyazapúrikha was then a yearling filly whose mane had just been cut; a dear, merry, lively little thing, but—and I do not say it to offend her— although among you she is now considered a remarkable thoroughbred she was then among the poorest horses in the stud. She will herself confirm this.

My mottled appearance, which men so disliked, was very attractive to all the horses; they all came round me, admired me, and frisked about me. I began to forget what men said about my mottled appearance, and felt happy. But I soon experienced the first sorrow of my life and the cause of it was my mother. When the thaw had set in, the sparrows twittered under the eaves, spring was felt more strongly in the air, and my mother's treatment of me changed.

Her whole disposition changed: she would frisk about without any reason and run round the yard, which did not at all accord with her dignified age, then she would consider and begin to neigh, and would bite and kick her sister mares, and then begin to sniff at me and snort discontentedly; then on going out into the sun she would lay her head across the shoulder of her cousin, Lady Merchant, dreamily rub her back, and push me away from her teats.

One day the stud groom came and had a halter put on her and she was led out of the stall. She neighed and I answered and rushed after her, but she did not even look back at me. The strapper, Tarás, seized me in his arms while they were closing the door after my mother had been led out.

I bolted and upset the strapper on the straw, but the door was shut and I could only hear the receding sound of my mother's neighing; and that neigh did not sound like a call to me but had another expression. Her voice was answered from afar by a powerful voice—that of Dóbry I, as I learned later, who was being led by two grooms, one on each side, to meet my mother.

I don't remember how Tarás got out of my stall: I felt too sad, for I knew that I had lost my mother's love for ever. 'And it's all because I am piebald!' I thought, remembering what people said about my colour, and such passionate anger overcame me that I began to beat my head and knees against the walls of the stall and continued till I was sweating all over and quite exhausted.

After a while my mother came back to me. I heard her run up the passage at a trot and with an unusual gait. They opened the door for her and I hardly knew her—she had grown so much younger and more beautiful. She sniffed at me, snorted, and began to whinny. Her whole demeanour showed that she no longer loved me.

She told me of Dóbry's beauty and her love of him. Those meetings continued and the relations between my mother and me grew colder and colder.

Soon after that we were let out to pasture. I now discovered new joys which made up to me for the loss of my mother's

It was in winter at holiday time. I had not been fed or watered all day. As I learnt later this happened because the lad who fed us was drunk. That day the stud groom came in, saw that I had no food, began to use bad language about the missing lad, and then went away.

Next day the lad came into our stable with another groom to give us hay. I noticed that he was particularly pale and sad and that in the expression of his long back especially there was something significant which evoked compassion.

He threw the hay angrily over the grating. I made a move to put my head over his shoulder, but he struck me such a painful blow on the nose with his fist that I started back. Then he kicked me in the belly with his boot.

'If it hadn't been for this scurvy beast,' he said, 'nothing would have happened!'

'How's that?' inquired the other groom.

'You see, he doesn't go to look after the count's horses, but visits his own twice a day.'

'What, have they given him the piebald?' asked the other.

'Given it, or sold it—the devil only knows! The count's horses might all starve—he wouldn't care—but just dare to leave *his* colt without food! "Lie down!" he says, and they begin walloping me! No Christianity in it. He has more pity on a beast than on a man. He must be an infidel—he counted the strokes himself, the barbarian! The general never flogged like that! My whole back is covered with wales. There's no Christian soul in him!'

What they said about flogging and Christianity I understood well enough, but I was quite in the dark as to what they meant by the words '*his* colt', from which I perceived that people considered that there was some connexion between me and the head groom. What that connexion was I could not at all understand then. Only much later when they separated me from the other horses did I learn what it meant. At that time I could not at all understand what they meant by speaking of *me* as being a man's property. The words '*my* horse' applied to me, a live horse, seemed to me as strange as to say 'my land', 'my air', or 'my water'.

love. I had friends and companions. Together we learnt to eat grass, to neigh like the grown-ups, and to gallop round our mothers with lifted tails. That was a happy time. Everything was forgiven me, everybody loved me, admired me, and looked indulgently at anything I did. But that did not last long.

Soon afterwards something dreadful happened to me . . .

The gelding heaved a deep sigh and walked away from the other horses.

The dawn had broken long before. The gates creaked. Nester came in, and the horses separated. The keeper straightened the saddle on the gelding's back and drove the horses out.

## VI

## *Second Night*

As soon as the horses had been driven in they again gathered round the piebald, who continued:

In August they separated me from my mother and I did not feel particularly grieved. I saw that she was again heavy (with my brother, the famous Usán) and that I could no longer be to her what I had been. I was not jealous, but felt that I had become indifferent to her. Besides I knew that having left my mother I should be put in the general division of foals, where we were kept two or three together and were every day let out in a crowd into the open. I was in the same stall with Darling. Darling was a saddle-horse, who was subsequently ridden by the Emperor and portrayed in pictures and sculpture. At that time he was a mere foal, with soft glossy coat, a swanlike neck, and straight slender legs taut as the strings of an instrument. He was always lively, good-tempered and amiable, always ready to gambol, exchange licks, and play tricks on horse or man. Living together as we did we involuntarily made friends, and our friendship lasted the whole of our youth. He was merry and giddy. Even then he began to make love, courted the fillies, and laughed at my guilelessness. To my misfortune vanity led me to imitate him, and I was soon carried away and fell in love. And this early tendency of mine was the cause of the greatest change in my fate. It happened that I was carried away . . . Vyazapúrikha was a year older than I, and we were special friends, but towards the autumn I noticed that she began to be shy with me . . .

But I will not speak of that unfortunate period of my first love; she herself remembers my mad passion, which ended for me in the most important change of my life.

The strappers rushed to drive her away and to beat me. That evening I was shut up in a special stall where I neighed all night as if foreseeing what was to happen next.

In the morning the General, the stud groom, the stablemen and the strappers came into the passage where my stall was, and there was a terrible hubbub. The General shouted at the stud groom, who tried to justify himself by saying that he had not told them to let me out but that the grooms had done it of their own accord. The General said that he would have everybody flogged, and that it would not do to keep young stallions. The stud groom promised that he would have everything attended to. They grew quiet and went away. I did not understand anything, but could see that they were planning something concerning me.

The day after that I ceased neighing for ever. I became what I am now. The whole world was changed in my eyes. Nothing mattered any more; I became self-absorbed and began to brood. At first everything seemed repulsive to me. I even ceased to eat, drink, or walk, and there was no idea of playing. Now and then it occurred to me to give a kick, to gallop, or to start neighing, but immediately came the question: Why? What for? and all my energy died away.

One evening I was being exercised just when the horses were driven back from pasture. I saw in the distance a cloud of dust enveloping the indistinct but familiar outlines of all

our brood mares. I heard their cheerful snorting and the trampling of their feet. I stopped, though the cord of the halter by which the groom was leading me cut the nape of my neck, and I gazed at the approaching drove as one gazes at a happiness that is lost for ever and cannot return. They approached, and I could distinguish one after another all the familiar, beautiful, stately, healthy, sleek figures. Some of them also turned to look at me. I was unconscious of the pain the groom's jerking at my halter inflicted. I forgot myself and from old habit involuntarily neighed and began to trot, but my neighing sounded sad, ridiculous and meaningless. No one in the drove made sport of me, but I noticed that out of decorum many of them turned away from me. They evidently felt it repugnant, pitiable, indelicate, and above all ridiculous, to look at my thin expressionless neck, my large head (I had grown lean in the meantime), my long, awkward legs, and the silly awkward gait with which by force of habit I trotted round the groom. No one answered my neighing—they all looked away. Suddenly I understood it all, understood how far I was for ever removed from them, and I do not remember how I got home with the groom.

Already before that I had shown a tendency towards gravity and thoughtfulness, but now a decided change came over me. My being piebald, which aroused such curious contempt in men, my terrible and unexpected misfortune, and also my peculiar position in the stud farm which I felt but was unable to explain, made me retire into myself. I pondered over the injustice of men, who blamed me for being piebald; I pondered on the inconstancy of mother-love and feminine love in general and on its dependence on physical conditions; and above all I pondered on the characteristics of that strange race of animals with whom we are so closely connected, and whom we call men—those characteristics which were the source of my own peculiar position in the stud farm, which I felt but could not understand.

The meaning of this peculiarity in people and the characteristic on which it is based was shown me by the following occurrence.

But those words had an enormous effect on me. I thought of them constantly and only after long and varied relations with men did I at last understand the meaning they attach to these strange words, which indicate that men are guided in life not by deeds but by words. They like not so much to do or abstain from doing anything, as to be able to apply conventional words to different objects. Such words, considered very important among them, are *my* and *mine,* which they apply to various things, creatures, or objects: even to land, people, and horses. They have agreed that of any given thing only one person may use the word *mine,* and he who in this game of theirs may use that conventional word about the greatest number of things is considered the happiest. Why this is so I do not know, but it is so. For a long time I tried to explain it by some direct advantage they derive from it, but this proved wrong.

For instance many of those who called me their horse did not ride me, quite other people rode me; nor did they feed me—quite other people did that. Again it was not those who called me *their* horse who treated me kindly, but coachmen, veterinaries, and in general quite other people. Later on, having widened my field of observation, I became convinced that not only as applied to us horses, but in regard to other things, the idea of *mine* has no other basis than a low, mercenary instinct in men, which they call the feeling or right of property. A man who never lives in it says 'my house', but only concerns himself with its building and maintenance; and a tradesman talks of 'my cloth business', but has none of his clothes made of the best cloth that is in his shop.

There are people who call land theirs, though they have never seen that land and never walked on it. There are people who call other people theirs, but have never seen those others, and the whole relationship of the owners to the owned is that they do them harm.

There are men who call women their women or their wives; yet these women live with other men. And men strive in life not to do what they think right, but to call as many things as possible *their own.*

I am now convinced that in this lies the essential difference between men and us. Therefore, not to speak of other things in which we are superior to men, on this ground alone we may boldly say that in the scale of living creatures we stand higher than man. The activity of men, at any rate of those I have had to do with, is guided by words, while ours is guided by deeds.

It was this right to speak of me as *my horse* that the stud groom had obtained, and that was why he had the stable lad flogged. This discovery much astonished me and, together with the thoughts and opinions aroused in men by my piebald colour, and the thoughtfulness produced in me by my mother's betrayal, caused me to become the serious and thoughtful gelding that I am.

I was thrice unfortunate: I was piebald, I was a gelding, and people considered that I did not belong to God and to myself, as is natural to all living creatures, but that I belonged to the stud groom.

Their thinking this about me had many consequences. The first was that I was kept apart from the other horses, was better fed, oftener taken out on the line, and was broken in at an earlier age. I was first harnessed in my third year. I remember how the stud groom, who imagined I was his, himself began to harness me with a crowd of other grooms, expecting me to prove unruly or to resist. They put ropes round me to lead me into the shafts; put a cross of broad straps on my back and fastened it to the shafts so that I could not kick, while I was only awaiting an opportunity to show my readiness and love of work.

They were surprised that I started like an old horse. They began to brake me and I began to practise trotting. Every day I made greater and greater progress, so that after three months the general himself and many others approved of my pace. But strange to say, just because they considered me not as their own, but as belonging to the head groom, they regarded my paces quite differently.

The stallions who were my brothers were raced, their records were kept, people went to look at them, drove them in gilt sulkies, and expensive horse-cloths were thrown over them. I was driven in a common sulky to Chesménka and other farms on the head groom's business. All this was the result of my being piebald, and especially of my being in their opinion not the count's, but the head groom's property.

To-morrow, if we are alive, I will tell you the chief consequence for me of this right of property the head groom considered himself to have.

All that day the horses treated Strider respectfully, but Nester's treatment of him was as rough as ever. The peasant's little roan horse neighed again on coming up to the herd, and the chestnut filly again coquettishly replied to him.

## VII

## *Third Night*

The new moon had risen and its narrow crescent lit up Strider's figure as he once again stood in the middle of the stable yard. The other horses crowded round him.

The gelding continued:

For me the most surprising consequence of my not being the count's, nor God's, but the head groom's, was that the very thing that constitutes our chief merit—a fast pace—was the cause of my banishment. They were driving Swan round the track, and the head groom, returning from Chesménka, drove me up and stopped there. Swan went past. He went well, but all the same he was showing off and had not the exactitude I had developed in myself—so that directly one foot touched the ground another instantaneously lifted and not the slightest effort was lost but every atom of exertion carried me forward. Swan went by us. I pulled towards the ring and the head groom did not check me. 'Here, shall I try my piebald?' he shouted, and when next Swan came abreast of us he let me go. Swan was already going fast, and so I was left behind during the first round, but in the second I began to gain on him, drew near to his sulky, drew level—and passed him. They tried us again—it was the same thing. I was the faster. And this dismayed everybody. The general asked that I should be sold at once to some distant place, so that nothing more should be heard of me: 'Or else the count will get to know of it and there will be trouble!' So they sold me to a horse-dealer as a shaft-horse. I did not remain with him long. An hussar who came to buy remounts bought me. All this was so unfair, so cruel, that I was glad when they took me away from Khrénovo and parted me for ever from all that had been familiar and dear to me. It was too painful for me among them. They had love, honour, freedom, before them; I had labour, humiliation; humiliation, labour, to the end of my life. And why? Because I was piebald, and because of that had to become somebody's horse. . . .

Strider could not continue that evening. An event occurred in the enclosure that upset all the horses. Kupchíkha, a mare big with foal, who had stood listening to the story, suddenly turned way and walked slowly into the shed, and there began to groan so that it drew the attention of all the horses. Then she lay down, then got up again, and again lay down. The old mares understood what was happening to her, but the young ones became excited and, leaving the gelding, surrounded the invalid. Towards morning there was a new foal standing unsteadily on its little legs. Nester shouted to the groom, and the mare and foal were taken into a stall and the other horses driven to the pasture without them.

## VIII

### Fourth Night

In the evening when the gate was closed and all had quieted down, the piebald continued:

I have had opportunity to make many observations both of men and horses during the time I passed from hand to hand.

I stayed longest of all with two masters: a prince (an officer of hussars), and later with an old lady who lived near the church of St. Nicholas the Wonder Worker.

The happiest years of my life I spent with the officer of hussars.

Though he was the cause of my ruin, and though he never loved anything or anyone, I loved and still love him for that very reason.

What I liked about him was that he was handsome, happy, rich, and therefore never loved anybody.

You understand that lofty equine feeling of ours. His coldness and my dependence on him gave special strength to my love for him. 'Kill me, drive me till my wind is broken!' I used to think in our good days, 'and I shall be all the happier.'

He bought me from an agent to whom the head groom had sold me for eight hundred rubles, and he did so just because no one else had piebald horses. That was my best time. He had a mistress. I knew this because I took him to her every day and sometimes took them both out.

His mistress was a handsome woman, and he was handsome, and his coachman was handsome, and I loved them all because they were. Life was worth living then. This was how our time was spent: in the morning the groom came to rub me down—not the coachman himself but the groom. The groom was a lad from among the peasants. He would open the door, let out the steam from the horses, throw out the droppings, take off our rugs, and begin to fidget over our bodies with a brush, and lay whitish streaks of dandruff from a curry-comb on the boards of the floor that was dented by our rough horseshoes. I would playfully nip his sleeve and paw the ground. Then we were led out one after another to the trough filled with cold water, and the lad would admire the smoothness of my spotted coat which he had polished, my foot with its broad hoof, my legs straight as an arrow, my glossy quarters, and my back wide enough to sleep on. Hay was piled onto the high racks, and the oak cribs were filled with oats. Then Feofán, the head coachman, would come in.

Master and coachman resembled one another. Neither of

them was afraid of anything or cared for anyone but himself, and for that reason everybody liked them. Feofán wore a red shirt, black velveteen knickerbockers, and a sleeveless coat. I liked it on a holiday when he would come into the stable, his hair pomaded, and wearing his sleeveless coat, and would shout:

'Now then, beastie, have you forgotten?' and push me with the handle of the stable fork, never so as to hurt me but just as a joke. I immediately knew that it was a joke, and laid back an ear, making my teeth click.

We had a black stallion, who drove in a pair. At night they used to put me in harness with him. That Polkán, as he was called, did not understand a joke but was simply vicious as the devil. I was in the stall next to his and sometimes we bit one another seriously. Feofán was not afraid of him. He would come up and give a shout: it looked as if Polkán would kill him, but no, he'd miss, and Feofán would put the harness on him.

Once he and I bolted down Smiths Bridge Street. Neither my master nor the coachman was frightened; they laughed, shouted at the people, checked us, and turned so that no one was run over.

In their service I lost my best qualities and half my life. They ruined me by watering me wrongly, and they foundered me. . . . Still for all that it was the best time of my life. At twelve o'clock they would come to harness me, black my hoofs, moisten my forelock and mane, and put me in the shafts.

The sledge was of plaited cane upholstered with velvet; the reins were of silk, the harness had silver buckles, sometimes there was a cover of silken fly-net, and altogether it was such that when all the traces and straps were fastened it was difficult to say where the harness ended and the horse began. We were harnessed at ease in the stable. Feofán would come, broader at his hips than at the shoulders, his red belt up under his arms: he would examine the harness, take his seat, wrap his coat round him, put his foot into the sledge stirrup, let off some joke, and for appearance sake always hang a whip over his arm though he hardly ever hit me, and would say, 'Let go!', and playfully stepping from foot to foot I would move out of the gate, and the cook who had come out to empty the slops would stop on the threshold and the peasant who had brought wood into the yard would open his eyes wide. We would come out, go a little way, and stop. Footmen would come out and other coachmen, and a chatter would begin. Everybody would wait: sometimes we had to stand for three hours at the entrance, moving a little way, turning back, and standing again.

At last there would be a stir in the hall: old Tíkhon with his paunch would rush out in his dress coat and cry, 'Drive up!' (In those days there was not that stupid way of saying, 'Forward!' as if one did not know that we moved forward and not back.) Feofán would cluck, drive up, and the prince would hurry out carelessly, as though there were nothing remarkable about the sledge, or the horse, or Feofán—who bent his back and stretched out his arms so that it seemed it would be impossible for him to keep them long in that position. The prince would have a shako on his head and wear a fur coat with a grey beaver collar hiding his rosy, black-browed, handsome face, that should never have been concealed. He would come out clattering his sabre, his spurs, and the brass backs of the heels of his overshoes, stepping over the carpet as if in a hurry and taking no notice of me or Feofán whom everybody but he looked at and admired. Feofán would cluck, I would tug at the reins, and respectably, at a foot pace, we would draw up to the entrance and stop. I would turn my eyes on the prince and jerk my thoroughbred head with its delicate forelock. . . . The prince would be in good spirits and would sometimes jest with Feofán. Feofán would reply, half turning his handsome head, and without lowering his arms would make a scarcely perceptible movement with the reins which I understand: and then one, two, three . . . with ever wider and wider strides, every muscle quivering, and sending the muddy snow against the front of the sledge, I would go. In those days, too, there was none of the present-day stupid habit of crying, 'Oh!' as if the coach-

man were in pain, instead of the sensible, 'Be off! Take care!'
Feofán would shout 'Be off! Look out there!' and the people
would step aside and stand craning their necks to see the
handsome gelding, the handsome coachman, and the handsome gentleman . . .

I was particularly fond of passing a trotter. When Feofán
and I saw at a distance a turn-out worthy of the effort, we
would fly like a whirlwind and gradually gain on it. Now,
throwing the dirt right to the back of the sledge, I would
draw level with the occupant of the vehicle and snort above
his head: then I would reach the horse's harness and the arch
of his troýka, and then would no longer see it but only hear
its sounds in the distance behind. And the prince, Feofán,
and I, would all be silent, and pretend to be merely going on
our own business and not even to notice those with slow
horses whom we happened to meet on our way. I liked to
pass another horse, but also liked to meet a good trotter. An
instant, a sound, a glance, and we had passed each other and
were flying in opposite directions.

The gate creaked and the voices of Nester and Váska were
heard.

## Fifth Night

The weather began to break up. It had been dull since
morning and there was no dew, but it was warm and the
mosquitoes were troublesome. As soon as the horses were
driven in they collected round the piebald, and he finished
his story as follows:

The happy period of my life was soon over. I lived in that
way only two years. Towards the end of the second winter
the happiest event of my life occurred, and following it came
my greatest misfortune. It was during carnival week. I took
the prince to the races. Glossy and Bull were running. I don't
know what people were doing in the pavilion, but I know the
prince came out and ordered Feofán to drive onto the track.

I remember how they took me in and placed me beside
Glossy. He was harnessed to a racing sulky and I, just as I
was, to a town sledge. I outstripped him at the turn. Roars
of laughter and howls of delight greeted me.

When I was led in, a crowd followed me and five or six
people offered the prince thousands for me. He only laughed,
showing his white teeth.

'No,' he said, 'this isn't a horse, but a friend. I wouldn't sell
him for mountains of gold. *Au revoir*, gentlemen!'

He unfastened the sledge apron and got in.

'To Ostózhenka Street!'

That was where his mistress lived, and off we flew . . .

That was our last happy day. We reached her home. He
spoke of her as *his*, but she loved someone else and had run
away with him. The prince learnt this at her lodgings. It was
five o'clock, and without unharnessing me he started in pursuit of her. They did what had never been done to me before,
struck me with the whip and made me gallop. For the first
time I fell out of step and felt ashamed and wished to correct
it, but suddenly I heard the prince shout in an unnatural
voice: 'Get on!' The whip whistled through the air and cut me,
and I galloped, striking my foot against the iron front of the
sledge. We overtook her after going sixteen miles. I got him
there, but trembled all night long and could not eat anything.
In the morning they gave me water. I drank it and after that
was never again the horse that I had been. I was ill, and they
tormented me and maimed me—doctoring me, as people call
it. My hoofs came off, I had swellings and my legs grew bent;
my chest sank in and I became altogether limp and weak. I
was sold to a horse-dealer who fed me on carrots and something else and made something of me quite unlike myself,
though good enough to deceive one who did not know. My
strength and my pace were gone.

When purchasers came the dealer also tormented me by
coming into my stall and beating me with a heavy whip to
frighten and madden me. Then he would rub down the stripes
on my coat and lead me out.

An old woman bought me of him. She always drove to the

Church of St. Nicholas the Wonder Worker, and she used to
have her coachman flogged. He used to weep in my stall and
I learnt that tears have a pleasant, salty taste. Then the old
woman died. Her steward took me to the country and sold
me to a hawker. Then I overate myself with wheat and grew
still worse. They sold me to a peasant. There I ploughed, had
hardly anything to eat, my foot got cut by a ploughshare and
I again became ill. Then a gipsy took me in exchange for
something. He tormented me terribly and finally sold me to
the steward here. And here I am.'

All were silent. A sprinkling of rain began to fall.

## IX

## *The Evening After*

As the herd returned home the following evening they encountered their master with a visitor. Zhuldýba when nearing
the house looked askance at the two male figures: one was the
young master in his straw hat, the other a tall, stout, bloated
military man. The old mare gave the man a side-glance and,
swerving, went near him; the others, the young ones, were
flustered and hesitated, especially when the master and his
visitor purposely stepped among them, pointing something
out to one another and talking.

'That one, the dapple grey, I bought of Voékov,' said the
master.

'And where did you get that young black mare with the
white legs? She's a fine one!' said the visitor. They looked over
many of the horses, going forward and stopping them. They
noticed the chestnut filly too.

'That is one I kept of Khrénov's saddle-horse breed,' said the
master.

They could not see all the horses as they walked past, and
the master called to Nester, and the old man, tapping the
sides of the piebald with his heels, trotted forward. The

piebald limped on one leg but moved in a way that showed
that as long as his strength lasted he would not murmur on
any account, even if they wanted him to run in that way to
the end of the world. He was even ready to gallop, and tried
to do so with his right leg.

'There, I can say for certain that there is no better horse
in Russia than this one,' said the master, pointing to one of
the mares. The visitor admired it. The master walked about
excitedly, ran forward, and showed his visitor all the horses,
mentioning the origin and pedigree of each.

The visitor evidently found the master's talk dull, but devised some questions to show interest.

'Yes, yes,' he said absent-mindedly.

'Just look,' said the master, not answering a question. 'Look
at her legs . . . She cost me a lot but has a third foal already
in harness.'

'And trots well?' asked the guest.

So they went past all the horses till there were no more to
show. Then they were silent.

'Well, shall we go now?'

'Yes, let's go.'

They went through the gate. The visitor was glad the ex-
hibition was over and that he could now go to the house where
they could eat and drink and smoke, and he grew perceptibly
brighter. As he went past Nester, who sat on the piebald waiting for orders, the visitor slapped the piebald's crupper with
his big fat hand.

'What an ornamented one!' he said. 'I once had a piebald
like him; do you remember my telling you of him?'

The master, finding that it was not his horse that was being
spoken about, paid no attention but kept looking round at his
own herd.

Suddenly above his ear he heard a dull, weak, senile neigh.
It was the piebald that had begun to neigh and had broken
off as if ashamed.

Neither the visitor nor the master paid any attention to this
neighing, but went into the house.

In the flabby old man Strider had recognized his beloved master, the once brilliant, handsome, and wealthy Serpukhovskóy.

## X

It kept on drizzling. In the stable yard it was gloomy, but in the master's house it was very different. The table was laid in a luxurious drawing-room for a luxurious evening tea, and at it sat the host, the hostess, and their guest.

The hostess, her pregnancy made very noticeable by her figure, her strained convex pose, her plumpness, and especially by her large eyes with their mild inward look, sat by the samovar.

The host held in his hand a box of special, ten-year-old cigars, such as he said no one else had, and he was preparing to boast about them to his guest. The host was a handsome man of about twenty-five, fresh-looking, well cared for, and well groomed. In the house he was wearing a new loose thick suit made in London. Large expensive pendants hung from his watch-chain. His gold-mounted turquoise shirt studs were also large and massive. He had a beard à la Napoléon III, and the tips of his moustache stuck out in a way that could only have been learned in Paris.

The hostess wore a dress of silk gauze with a large floral pattern of many colours, and large gold hairpins of a peculiar pattern held up her thick, light-brown hair—beautiful though not all her own. On her arms and hands she wore many bracelets and rings, all of them expensive.

The tea-service was of delicate china and the samovar of silver. A footman, resplendent in dress-coat, white waistcoat and necktie, stood like a statue by the door awaiting orders. The furniture was elegantly carved, and upholstered in bright colours, the wall-paper dark with a large flowered pattern. Beside the table, tinkling the silver bells on its collar, was a particularily fine whippet, whose difficult English name its owners, who neither of them knew English, pronounced badly.

In the corner, surrounded by plants, stood an inlaid piano.

Everything gave an impression of newness, luxury, and rarity. Everything was good, but it all bore an imprint of superfluity, wealth, and the absence of intellectual interests.

The host, a lover of trotting races, was sturdy and full-blooded—one of that never-dying race which drives about in sable coats, throws expensive bouquets to actresses, drinks the most expensive wines with the most fashionable labels at the most expensive restaurants, offers prizes engraved with the donor's name, and keeps the most expensive mistresses.

Nikíta Serpukhovskóy, their guest, was a man of over forty, tall, stout, bald-headed, with heavy moustaches and whiskers. He must once have been very handsome, but had now evidently sunk physically, morally, and financially.

He had such debts that he had been obliged to enter the government service to avoid imprisonment for debt, and was now on his way to a provincial town to become the head of a stud farm, a post some important relatives had obtained for him.

He wore a military coat and blue trousers of a kind only a rich man would have had made for himself. His shirt was of similar quality and so was his English watch. His boots had wonderful soles as thick as a man's finger.

Nikíta Serpukhovskóy had during his life run through a fortune of two million rubles, and was now a hundred and twenty thousand in debt. In cases of that kind there always remains a certain momentum of life enabling a man to obtain credit and continue living almost luxuriously for another ten years.

These ten years were however coming to an end, the momentum was exhausted, and life was growing hard for Nikíta. He was already beginning to drink, that is, to get fuddled with wine, a thing that used not to happen, though strictly speaking he had never begun or left off drinking. His decline was most noticeable in the restlessness of his glance (his eyes had grown shifty) and in the uncertainty of his voice and movements. This restlessness struck one the more as it had evidently got hold of him only recently, for one could see that he had all his life been accustomed not to be afraid of anything or anybody, and had only recently, through heavy suffering, reached this state of fear so unnatural to him.

His host and hostess noticed this, and exchanged glances which showed that they understood one another and were only postponing till bedtime a detailed discussion of the subject, putting up meanwhile with poor Nikíta and even showing him attentions.

The sight of his young host's good fortune humiliated Serpukhovskóy, awakening a painful envy in him as he recalled his own irrecoverable past.

'Do you mind my smoking a cigar, Marie?' he asked, addressing the lady in that peculiar tone acquired only by experience—the tone, polite and friendly but not quite respectful, in which men who know the world speak to kept women in contradistinction to wives. Not that he wished to offend her: on the contrary he now wished rather to curry favour with her and with her keeper, though he would on no account have acknowledged the fact to himself. But he was accustomed to speak in that way to such women. He knew she would herself be surprised and even offended were he to treat her as a lady. Besides he had to retain a certain shade of a respectful tone for his friend's real wife. He always treated his friends' mistresses with respect, not because he shared the so-called convictions promulgated in periodicals (he never read trash of that kind) about the respect due to the personality of every man, about the meaninglessness of marriage, and so forth, but because all decent men do so and he was a decent, though fallen, man.

He took a cigar. But his host awkwardly picked up a whole handful and offered them to him.

'Just see how good these are. Take them!'

Serpukhovskóy pushed aside the hand with the cigars, and a gleam of offence and shame showed itself in his eyes.

'Thank you!' he took out his cigar-case. 'Try mine!'

The hostess was sensitive. She noticed his embarrassment and hastened to talk to him.

'I am very fond of cigars. I should smoke myself if everyone about me did not smoke.'

And she smiled her pretty, kindly smile. He smiled in return, but irresolutely. Two of his teeth were missing.

'No, take this!' the tactless host continued. 'The others are weaker. Fritz, *bringen Sie noch einen Kasten*,' he said, '*dort zwey*.' [1]

The German footman brought another box.

'Do you prefer big ones? Strong ones? These are very good. Take them all!' he continued, forcing them on his guest.

He was evidently glad to have someone to boast to of the rare things he possessed, and he noticed nothing amiss. Serpukhovskóy lit his cigar and hastened to resume the conversation they had begun.

'So, how much did you pay for Atlásny?' he asked.

'He cost me a great deal, not less than five thousand, but at any rate I am already safe on him. What colts he gets, I tell you!'

'Do they trot?' asked Serpukhovskóy.

'They trot well! His colt took three prizes this year: in Túla, in Moscow, and in Petersburg; he raced Voékov's Raven. That rascal, the driver, let him make four false steps or he'd have left the other behind the flag.'

'He's a bit green. Too much Dutch blood in him, that's what I say,' remarked Serpukhovskóy.

'Well, but what about the mares? I'll show Goody to you to-morrow. I gave three thousand for her. For Amiable I gave two thousand.'

And the host again began to enumerate his possessions. The hostess saw that this hurt Serpukhovskóy and that he was only pretending to listen.

'Will you have some more tea?' she asked.

'I won't,' replied the host and went on talking. She rose, the host stopped her, embraced her, and kissed her.

As he looked at them Serpukhovskóy for their sakes tried to force a smile, but after the host had got up, embraced her, and led her to the portière, Serpukhovskóy's face suddenly changed. He sighed heavily, and a look of despair showed

---

[1] 'Bring another box. There are two there.'

itself on his flabby face. Even malevolence appeared on it.

The host returned and smilingly sat down opposite him. They were silent awhile.

## XI

'Yes, you were saying you bought him of Voékov,' remarked Serpukhovskóy with assumed carelessness.

'Oh yes, that was of Atlásny, you know. I always meant to buy some mares of Dubovítzki, but he had nothing but rubbish left.'

'He has failed . . .' said Serpukhovskóy, and suddenly stopped and glanced round. He remembered that he owed that bankrupt twenty thousand rubles, and if it came to talking of being bankrupt it was certainly said that he was one. He laughed.

Both again sat silent for a long time. The host considered what he could brag about to his guest. Serpukhovskóy was thinking what he could say to show that he did not consider himself bankrupt. But the minds of both worked with difficulty, in spite of efforts to brace themselves up with cigars. 'When are we going to have a drink?' thought Serpukhovskóy. 'I must certainly have a drink or I shall die of ennui with this fellow,' thought the host.

'Will you be remaining here long?' Serpukhovskóy asked.

'Another month. Well, shall we have supper, eh? Fritz, is it ready?'

They went into the dining-room. There under a hanging lamp stood a table on which were candles and all sorts of extraordinary things: syphons, and little dolls fastened to corks, rare wine in decanters, unusual hors-d'œuvres and vodka. They had a drink, ate a little, drank again, ate again, and their conversation got into swing. Serpukhovskóy was flushed and began to speak without timidity.

They spoke of women and of who kept this one or that, a gipsy, a ballet-girl, or a Frenchwoman.

'And have you given up Mathieu?' asked the host. (That was the woman who had ruined Serpukhovskóy.)

'No, she left me. Ah, my dear fellow, when I recall what I have got through in my life! Now I am really glad when I have a thousand rubles, and am glad to get away from everybody. I can't stand it in Moscow. But what's the good of talking!'

The host found it tiresome to listen to Serpukhovskóy. He wanted to speak about himself—to brag. But Serpukhovskóy also wished to talk about himself, about his brilliant past. His host filled his glass for him and waited for him to stop, so that he might tell him about himself and how his stud was now arranged as no one had ever had a stud arranged before. And that his Marie loved him with her heart and not merely for his wealth.

'I wanted to tell you that in my stud . . .' he began, but Serpukhovskóy interrupted him.

'I may say that there was a time,' Serpukhovskóy began, 'when I liked to live well and knew how to do it. Now you talk about trotting—tell me which is your fastest horse.'

The host, glad of an opportunity to tell more about his stud, was beginning, when Serpukhovskóy again interrupted him.

'Yes, yes,' he said, 'but you breeders do it just out of vanity and not for pleasure, not for the joy of life. It was different with me. You know I told you I had a driving-horse, a piebald with just the same kind of spots as the one your keeper was riding. Oh, what a horse that was! You can't possibly know: it was in 1842, when I had just come to Moscow; I went to a horse-dealer and there I saw a well-bred piebald gelding. I liked him. The price? One thousand rubles. I liked him, so I took him and began to drive with him. I never had, and you have not and never will have, such a horse. I never knew one like him for speed and for strength. You were a boy then and couldn't have known, but you may have heard of him. All Moscow was talking about him.'

'Yes, I heard of him,' the host unwillingly replied. 'But what I wished to say about mine . . .'

'Ah, then you did hear! I bought him just as he was, without his pedigree and without a certificate; it was only after-

wards that I got to know Voékov and found out. He was a
colt by Affable I. Strider—because of his long strides. On
account of his piebald spots he was removed from the Khrénov
stud and given to head keeper, who had him castrated and
sold him to a horse-dealer. There are no such horses now, my
dear chap. Ah, those were days! Ah, vanished youth!'—and
he sang the words of the gipsy song. He was getting tipsy.
—'Ah, those were good times. I was twenty-five and had
eighty thousand rubles a year, not a single grey hair, and all
my teeth like pearls. . . . Whatever I touched succeeded,
and now it is all ended . . .'

'But there was not the same mettlesomeness then,' said the
host, availing himself of the pause. 'Let me tell you that my
first horses began to trot without . . .'

'Your horses! But they used to be more mettlesome . . .'

'How—more mettlesome?'

'Yes, more mettlesome! I remember as if it were to-day how
I drove him once to the trotting races in Moscow. No horse
of mine was running. I did not care for trotters, mine were
thoroughbreds: General Chaulet, Mahomet. I drove up with
my piebald. My driver was a fine fellow, I was fond of him,
but he also took to drink. . . . Well, so I got there.

' "Serpukhovskóy," I was asked, "When are you going to
keep trotters?" "The devil take your lubbers!" I replied. "I
have a piebald hack that can outpace all your trotters!" "Oh
no, he won't!" "I'll bet a thousand rubles!" Agreed, and they
started. He came in five seconds ahead and I won the thousand rubles. But what of it? I did a hundred versts[1] in three
hours with a troýka of thoroughbreds. All Moscow knows it.'

And Serpukhovskóy began to brag so glibly and continuously that his host could not get a single word in and sat
opposite him with a dejected countenance, filling up his own
and his guest's glass every now and then by way of distraction.

The dawn was breaking and still they sat there. It became
intolerably dull for the host. He got up.

[1] A little over sixty-six miles.

'If we are to go to bed, let's go!' said Serpukhovskóy rising, and reeling and puffing he went to the room prepared for him.

The host was lying beside his mistress.

'No, he is unendurable,' he said. 'He gets drunk and swaggers incessantly.'

'And makes up to me.'

'I'm afraid he'll be asking for money.'

Serpukhovskóy was lying on the bed in his clothes, breathing heavily.

'I must have been lying a lot,' he thought. 'Well, no matter! The wine was good, but he is an awful swine. There's something cheap about him. And I'm an awful swine,' he said to himself and laughed aloud. 'First I used to keep women, and now I'm kept. Yes, the Winkler girl will support me. I take money of her. Serves him right. Still, I must undress. Can't get my boots off. Hullo! Hullo!' he called out, but the man who had been told off to wait on him had long since gone to bed.

He sat down, took off his coat and waistcoat and somehow managed to kick off his trousers, but for a long time could not get his boots off—his soft stomach being in the way. He got one off at last, and struggled for a long time with the other, panting and becoming exhausted. And so with his foot in the boot-top he rolled over and began to snore, filling the room with a smell of tobacco, wine, and disagreeable old age.

## XII

If Strider recalled anything that night, he was distracted by Váska, who threw a rug over him, galloped off on him, and kept him standing till morning at the door of a tavern, near a peasant horse. They licked one another. In the morning when Strider returned to the herd he kept rubbing himself.

'Something itches dreadfully,' he thought.

Five days passed. They called in a veterinary, who said cheerfully:

'It's the itch, let me sell him to the gipsies.'

'What's the use? Cut his throat, and get it done to-day.'

The morning was calm and clear. The herd went to pasture, but Strider was left behind. A strange man came—thin, dark, and dirty, in a coat splashed with something black. It was the knacker. Without looking at Strider he took him by the halter they had put on him and led him away. Strider went quietly without looking round, dragging along as usual and catching his hind feet in the straw.

When they were out of the gate he strained towards the well, but the knacker jerked his halter, saying: 'Not worth while.'

The knacker and Váska, who followed behind, went to a hollow behind the brick barn and stopped as if there were something peculiar about this very ordinary place. The knacker, handing the halter to Váska, took off his coat, rolled up his sleeves, and produced a knife and a whetstone from his bootleg. The gelding stretched towards the halter meaning to chew it a little from dullness, but he could not reach it. He sighed and closed his eyes. His nether lip hung down, disclosing his worn yellow teeth, and he began to drowse to the sound of the sharpening of the knife. Only his swollen, aching, outstretched leg kept jerking. Suddenly he felt himself being taken by the lower jaw and his head lifted. He opened his eyes. There were two dogs in front of him; one was sniffing at the knacker, the other was sitting and watching the gelding as if expecting something from him. The gelding looked at them and began to rub his jaw against the arm that was holding him.

'Want to doctor me probably—well, let them!' he thought. And in fact he felt that something had been done to his throat. It hurt, and he shuddered and gave a kick with one foot, but restrained himself and waited for what would follow. . . . Then he felt something liquid streaming down his neck and chest. He heaved a profound sigh and felt much better.

The whole burden of his life was eased.

He closed his eyes and began to droop his head. No one was holding it. Then his legs quivered and his whole body swayed. He was not so much frightened as surprised.

Everything was so new to him. He was surprised, and

started forward and upward, but instead of this, in moving from the spot his legs got entangled, he began to fall sideways, and trying to take a step fell forward and down on his left side.

The knacker waited till the convulsions had ceased; drove away the dogs that had crept nearer, took the gelding by the legs, turned him on his back, told Váska to hold a leg, and began to skin the horse.

'It was a horse, too,' remarked Váska.

'If he had been better fed the skin would have been fine,' said the knacker.

The herd returned downhill in the evening, and those on the left saw down below something red, round which dogs were busy and above which hawks and crows were flying. One of the dogs, pressing its paws against the carcass and swinging his head, with a crackling sound tore off what it had seized hold of. The chestnut filly stopped, stretched out her head and neck, and sniffed the air for a long time. They could hardly drive her away.

At dawn, in a ravine of the old forest, down in an overgrown glade, big-headed wolf cubs were howling joyfully. There were five of them: four almost alike and one little one with a head bigger than his body. A lean old wolf who was shedding her coat, dragging her full belly with its hanging dugs along the ground, came out of the bushes and sat down in front of the cubs. The cubs came and stood round her in a semi-circle. She went up to the smallest, and bending her knee and holding her muzzle down, made some convulsive movements, and opening her large sharp-toothed jaws disgorged a large piece of horseflesh. The bigger cubs rushed towards her, but she moved threateningly at them and let the little one have it all. The little one, growling as if in anger, pulled the horseflesh under him and began to gorge. In the same way the mother wolf coughed up a piece for the second, the third, and all five of them, and then lay down in front of them to rest.

A week later only a large skull and two shoulder-blades lay behind the barn, the rest had all been taken away. In summer a peasant, collecting bones, carried away these shoulder-blades and skull and put them to use.

The dead body of Serpukhovskóy, which had walked about the earth eating and drinking, was put under ground much later. Neither his skin, nor his flesh, nor his bones, were of any use.

Just as for the last twenty years his body that had walked the earth had been a great burden to everybody, so the putting away of that body was again an additional trouble to people. He had not been wanted by anybody for a long time and had only been a burden, yet the dead who bury their dead found it necessary to clothe that swollen body, which at once began to decompose, in a good uniform and good boots and put it into a new and expensive coffin with new tassels at its four corners, and then to place that coffin in another coffin of lead, to take it to Moscow and there dig up some long buried human bones, and to hide in that particular spot this decomposing maggotty body in its new uniform and polished boots, and cover it all up with earth.

# THE PORCELAIN DOLL*

A letter written six months after his marriage by Leo Tolstóy to his wife's younger sister, the Natásha of *War and Peace*. The first few lines are in his wife's handwriting, the rest in his own.

21st March 1863.

Why, Tánya, have you dried up? . . . You don't write to me at all and I so love receiving letters from you, and you have not yet replied to Lëvochka's [Tolstóy's] crazy epistle, of which I did not understand a word.

23rd March.

There, she began to write and suddenly stopped, because she could not continue. And do you know why, Tánya dear? A strange thing has befallen her and a still stranger thing has befallen me. As you know, like the rest of us she has always been made of flesh and blood, with all the advantages and disadvantages of that condition: she breathed, was warm and sometimes hot, blew her nose (and how loud!) and so on, and above all she had control of her limbs, which—both arms and legs—could assume different positions: in a word she was corporeal like all of us. Suddenly on March 21st 1863, at ten o'clock in the evening, this extraordinary thing befell her and me. Tánya! I know you always loved her (I do not know

---

* This curious piece is to be found in a letter which Tolstoy and his wife wrote jointly to her younger sister, Tatiána Bers, on March 21, 1863. The story about the porcelain doll is in Tolstoy's part of the letter and is intimately associated with his wife's first pregnancy at this time.

what feeling she will arouse in you now); I know you felt a sympathetic interest in me, and I know your reasonableness, your sane view of the important affairs of life, and your love of your parents (please prepare them and inform them of this event), and so I write to tell you just how it happened.

I got up early that day and walked and rode a great deal. We lunched and dined together and had been reading (she was still able to read) and I felt tranquil and happy. At ten o'clock I said goodnight to Auntie[1] (Sónya was then still as usual and said she would follow me) and I went off to bed. Through my sleep I heard her open the door and heard her breathe as she undressed. . . . I heard how she came out from behind the screen and approached the bed. I opened my eyes . . . and saw—not the Sónya you and I have known —but a porcelain Sónya! Made of that very porcelain about which your parents had a dispute. You know those porcelain dolls with bare cold shoulders, and necks and arms bent forward, but made of the same lump of porcelain as the body. They have black painted hair arranged in large waves, the paint of which gets rubbed off at the top, and protruding porcelain eyes that are too wide and are also painted black at the corners, and the stiff porcelain folds of their skirts are made of the same one piece of porcelain as the rest. And Sónya was like that! I touched her arm—she was smooth, pleasant to feel, and cold porcelain. I thought I was asleep and gave myself a shake, but she remained like that and stood before me immovable. I said: Are you porcelain? And without opening her mouth (which remained as it was, with curved lips painted bright red) she replied: Yes, I am porcelain. A shiver ran down my back. I looked at her legs: they also were porcelain and (you can imagine my horror) fixed on a porcelain stand, made of one piece with herself, representing the ground and painted green to depict grass. By her left leg, a little above and at the back of the knee, there was a porce-lain column, coloured brown and probably representing the

---

[1] 'Auntie Tatiána'—Tatiána Alexándrovna Érgolski (1795-1874), who brought Tolstoy up.

stump of a tree. This too was in one piece with her. I understood that without this stump she could not remain erect, and
I became very sad, as you who loved her can imagine. I still
did not believe my senses and began to call her. She could
not move without that stump and its base, and only rocked
a little—together with the base—to fall in my direction. I
heard how the porcelain base knocked against the floor and
cold porcelain. I tried to lift her hand, but could not. I
touched her again, and she was all smooth, pleasant. I tried
to pass a finger, or even a nail, between her elbow and her
side—but it was impossible. The obstacle was the same
porcelain mass, such as is made at Auerbach's, and of which
sauce-boats are made. She was planned for external appearance only. I began to examine her chemise, it was all of one
piece with the body, above and below. I looked more closely,
and noticed that at the bottom a bit of the fold of her chemise
was broken off and it showed brown. At the top of her head
it showed white where the paint had come off a little. The
paint had also come off a lip in one place, and a bit was
chipped off one shoulder. But it was all so well made and so
natural that it was still our same Sónya. And the chemise
was one I knew, with lace, and there was a knot of black hair
behind, but of porcelain, and the fine slender hands, and large
eyes, and the lips—all were the same, but of porcelain. And
the dimple in her chin and the small bones in front of her
shoulders, were there too, but of porcelain. I was in a terrible
state and did not know what to say or do or think. She would
have been glad to help me, but what could a porcelain creature do? The half-closed eyes, the eyelashes and eyebrows,
were all like her living self when looked at from a distance.
She did not look at me, but past me at her bed. She evidently
wanted to lie down, and rocked on her pedestal all the time.
I quite lost control of myself, seized her, and tried to take her
to her bed. My fingers made no impression on her cold porcelain body, and what surprised me yet more was that she had
become as light as an empty flask. And suddenly she seemed
to shrink, and became quite small, smaller than the palm of
my hand, although she still looked just the same. I seized a

pillow, put her in a corner of it, pressed down another corner with my fist, and placed her there, then I took her nightcap, folded it in four, and covered her up to the head with it. She lay there still just the same. Then I extinguished the candle and placed her under my beard. Suddenly I heard her voice from the corner of the pillow: 'Lëva, why have I become porcelain?' I did not know what to reply. She said again: 'Does it make any difference that I am porcelain?' I did not want to grieve her, and said that it did not matter. I felt her again in the dark—she was still as before, cold and porcelain. And her stomach was the same as when she was alive, protruding upwards—rather unnatural for a porcelain doll. Then I experienced a strange feeling. I suddenly felt it pleasant that she should be as she was, and ceased to feel surprised—it all seemed natural. I took her out, passed her from one hand to the other, and tucked her under my head. She liked it all. We fell asleep. In the morning I got up and went out without looking at her. All that had happened the day before seemed so terrible. When I returned for lunch she had again become such as she always was. I did not remind her of what had happened the day before, fearing to grieve her and Auntie. I have not yet told anyone but you about it. I thought it had all passed off, but all these days, every time we are alone together, the same thing happens. She suddenly becomes small and porcelain. In the presence of others she is just as she used to be. She is not oppressed by this, nor am I. Strange as it may seem, I frankly confess that I am glad of it, and though she is porcelain we are very happy.

I write to you of all this, dear Tánya, only that you should prepare her parents for the news, and through papa should find out from the doctors what this occurrence means, and whether it will not be bad for our expected child. Now we are alone, and she is sitting under my necktie and I feel how her sharp little nose cuts into my neck. Yesterday she had been left in a room by herself. I went in and saw that Dora (our little dog) had dragged her into a corner, was playing with her, and nearly broke her. I whipped Dora, put Sónya in my waistcoat pocket and took her to my study. To-day however I am expecting from Túla a small wooden box I have ordered, covered outside with morocco and lined inside with raspberry-coloured velvet, with a place arranged in it for her so that she can be laid in it with her elbows, head, and back all supported evenly so that she cannot break. I shall also cover it completely with chamois leather.

I had written this letter when suddenly a terrible misfortune occurred. She was standing on the table, when N.P.[2] pushed against her in passing, and she fell and broke off a leg above the knee with the stump. Alexéy[3] says that it can be mended with a cement made of the white of eggs. If such a recipe is known in Moscow please send it me.

---

[2] Natálya Petróvna Okhótnitskaya, an old woman who was living at Yásnaya Polyána.

[3] Alexéy Stepánovich Orékhov (who died in 1882), a servant of Tolstóy's who had accompanied him to the Caucasus and to Sevastopol during the Crimean War. He was employed as steward at Yásnaya Polyána.

# MODERN LIBRARY GIANTS

*A series of sturdily bound and handsomely printed, full-sized library editions of books formerly available only in expensive sets. These volumes contain from 600 to 1,400 pages each.*

THE MODERN LIBRARY GIANTS REPRESENT A
SELECTION OF THE WORLD'S GREATEST BOOKS